Bat Blood

Part Two

Unshackled Demons

by

Richard
Myerscough

<u>**Other Works by Richard Myerscough**</u>

Bat Blood - The Devil's Claw

The Gilded Harvest

Copyright © 2018 by Richard Myerscough
First Edition copyrighted — 2014

Distributed to the trade by The Ingram Book Company

Dedicated to my devoted and understanding partner
Laurie
my inspiring daughter
Claraicy,
and my inquisitive son
Marquis

Prelude

Amidst the dark, storm clouds looming over Northern Ontario, icy shivers ran up and down Mother Nature's back. In a cold sweat, she looked down and saw the smoke belching out of Doctor Scott's research facility. She felt as if she was being stabbed by thousands of barbed, serrated-edge knives over and over, tearing apart the very fabric of the delicate and balanced world she had created. The first time the doctor lost control over his research, a colony of bats was contaminated. But at least the gargoyle-like creatures he created were just flesh and blood.

She paid no attention to an unfortunate pair of mutated creatures as their flaming bodies hurdled through the air and into a lake. To her, they were freaks, mere misfits in the grand order of things. The outcome of the humans' experiments on them were childish compared to the horrific potential of what the doctor was about to unintentionally release into the wild.

The Grand Lady's entire body began to quiver as she felt the DNA of an ancient uncontrollable demon flowing through the veins of some of her innocent creatures. It was the unnatural rebirth of an unyielding mistake of nature that she thought had been subdued and eradicated forever. "Again, these humans have crossed the line. Why do they pretend to be gods?"

In a cruel, violent and thundering rage, she shouted, "Not this time."

She slowly raised her shaking arms. Her long white hair spread wildly throughout the sky and expanded into plump, dark blue clouds that almost instantly turned day into night. With her fingers spread far apart, she slowly lifted up her hands. Bright, destructive lightning bolts shot out of the ground around the doctor's research facility to illuminate the tips of her long curled nails.

A small section of vast woodlands over Northern Ontario was about to feel the fury of Mother Nature's wrath. The blackened skies, red flares and rain added to the manmade chaos below. Clouds of harsh, toxic smoke formed next to the ground for the survivors to choke on.

From a gap in the asphalt, next to the large fortified structure, a powerful bolt of lightning rose up and cracked the building's thick foundation. As she pulled all the energy she could find out of every crack, part of a wall started to crumble. The ominous lady grinned as a thick multi-coloured cloud of toxic gases blossomed out of the structure and mixed with the black smoke from burning sections of the surrounding asphalt.

The violent rage inside her eased long enough for her to look around and see what she had accomplished. A cold, thick, hazy fog had crept over the lake. The structure beneath her was surrounded by a scattered mess of fallen trees and multitudes of large muddy pools full of manmade debris.

As a handful of resilient, soot-covered people scrambled out of the burning structure, she flew into another thunderous rage. It wasn't good enough. She quickly released another wild series of thunderous lightning bolts upon them. Two bolts hit a section of the back wall of the flaming building and turned it into a large pile of rubble.

With all the men trapped within the huge chain-link fence and the asphalt under their feet afire, she looked again and questioned, *Had she succeeded? Was it enough?*

She wasn't sure if the rumbling in her gut was because the threat to her delicate ecosystem was still alive, or because of the anger she felt towards the human creators had caused her. In the thick, choking smoke, she had no way of knowing that several of the large bats that carried the seed of her nightmare had already escaped.

The dark, rumbling, rampaging storm that Mother Nature had cruelly released slowly crept eastward. Although weakened, it continued its reign of havoc over the vast sprawling boreal forest of Wabakimi Provincial Park, deep in the heart of Northern Ontario's unbridled wilderness.

Within an hour, the distant storm was only a mass of dark purple clouds that nervously tossed around its red and yellow flares in a quivering lightshow over the centre of the massive park. An uneasy sense of peaceful and calming tranquillity lingered over the lake in front of the burning structure. The aura of the pursuing silence was mystically broken by an echoing heart-wrenching cry that could only emerge from the throat of a lonely, love-torn loon searching for its lost mate.

Her second solemn, heartbroken cry was cruelly interrupted as an abrupt earth-quaking explosion heaved the placid lake into a white crested watery hell. A giant, dark billowing plume rose above the engulfed remains of the large structure on the shoreline. The violent explosion had lifted a massive array of twisted metal, bricks, glass, wood and other debris high into the air like a giant fountain. As fumes were released from the building more explosions were ignited filling the sky with more debris.

The falling shrapnel shot away from the building like a hand grenade. Instinctively, the loon dove deep under the water, narrowly dodging unscathed through the sinking missiles.

As she peered upwards through the weeds at the falling menace, a large marauding northern pike seized the opportunity. Its long, wide, powerful jaws snapped, crushing the loon's abdomen. The hungry creature's razor-edged teeth easily sliced their way through the feathers and into the flesh, turning the surrounding water into a giant pink cloud.

With the claws on her feet, the loon sliced the side of the creature's face and the skin under its jaw. At the same time, she beat her wings against the sides of its head in a desperate attempt to escape. Even as her lungs filled with water, she continued to thrash away until her heart rang out its last defiant beat.

Two bloodstained feathers surfaced as her mate returned and landed on the rough, deadly lake. He gently nudged one of the feathers with his beak and took in the sweet scent of his lost mate.

Another battery of explosions erupted from the burning building and shot more debris into the air. Still longing for his mate, the fearless loon looked around amidst the deadly hail. His heartbroken cry could barely be heard. His second cry was cut short. A piece of flying glass sliced through half his neck. His limp head flopped into the water attached by only a small piece of skin. As his lifeless body slowly relaxed, his wings fanned out over the water's surface.

Chapter One

Claraicy

With her hands tied behind a young tree in the middle of the forest, a chubby, round-faced girl watched as her overweight, pompous father slowly paddled down the wide creek. Along its banks, the odd cluster of snow lingered in the shadows.

Despite the fur trim on the hood of her light brown parka partially blocking her view, Claraicy Mitchell watched her father closely for any sign of remorse. With his face hidden inside the hood of his bright red parka, she couldn't tell if he had any or not. As he rounded a bend and vanished from sight, it deeply bothered her that he never once looked back.

Using the tip of her tongue, Claraicy wiggled and forced the rolled-up sock that her father had shoved into her mouth around the bright green tie he used to gag her with. As the sock fell to the ground, the tie loosened to the point that she could yell out, "Don't leave me. I'll do anything you want from now on, but don't leave me like this."

Through the trees, Claraicy heard a faint voice, "The fun and games are over. You've become a liability and are no longer worth the effort."

Claraicy screamed back, "But I'm your daughter."

"Now you are just another young prankster about to find herself lost in the woods on Devil's night." After half a chuckle, he jokingly added, "Have a frightful Halloween, and may the ghosts and ghouls spirit you away to where you belong."

Despite the thick cuffs of her mitts, the tight ropes still cut into her wrists. She could feel the tips of her fingers turning cold as the blood circulation in her hands started to dwindle. Her emotions raced from terror to relief, not knowing if this was just another one of her father's cruel games to teach her yet another lesson in blind obedience, or a way to finally escape his clutches.

After surviving the night, a distant explosion woke her out of the dreamy, imaginary world that she had escaped into. Her dry mouth slowly opened as a plume of smoke lingered above the trees in the distance.

Images of being burnt alive in a forest fire ran through her head. Looking at the tree tops, she felt some relief. The wind was behind her blowing any fires that might erupt in the opposite direction. A few hours later, she could both see and hear a half-dozen helicopters circling the area around the smoke.

While watching the helicopters through the branches, she wondered if any of them could even spot her. With the forest floor covered in fall leaves, she was almost invisible in her drab coloured clothing. She watched the search lights beaming down from the helicopters for almost half that night. None of them came close enough to illuminate her. "They are not looking for me. Why would they? He doesn't want me found. At least not alive."

Helping her father paddle, it took them three days to get into the park. Without it would take her father a lot longer to paddle out. Staring at the babbling creek a few metres away, her mind started to wander. Even if someone noticed that she didn't return and reported her missing, after three days without water all they would find would be her corpse.

As the sun was starting to peek over the horizon the following day, Claraicy woke to the clicking of two giant, long-nosed bats dangling from a branch above her. Almost a metre long, they were the largest bats she had ever seen. "You guys are definitely not from around here."

She watched as one fell to the ground and crawled toward her making a strange clicking noise with its mouth. The second one crept along the branch and started to climb down the tree trunk above her. While screaming as loud as she could, she violently flailed about, shaking the small tree. As pieces of birchbark crumbled in the bat's claws, it slipped down the tree trunk and landed on her back.

Trapped between Claraicy's puffy winter parka and the tree trunk, the frightened animal frantically tried to claw its way out. With her arms blocking both sides, the creature's claws shredded the back of her coat and sweater, and sliced into her flesh.

Claraicy thrashed about furiously as the creature bit into her exposed shoulder blade. Clenching her teeth, she shut her eyes and put all of her weight into a flurry of backward thrusts. As the bat's rib cage snapped, its squealing abruptly stopped.

Claraicy froze. A sharp pain ran through her entire body. Several of the creature's shattered ribs had pierced and hooked themselves into the muscles in her back. With their two bodies fused together, blood poured out of the bat's chest and into the deep gouges on Claraicy's sliced back.

As the bat's tainted blood flowed into the gouges, her heart sucked it through her severed blood vessels and slowly pumped it throughout her badly dehydrated body. As she opened her eyes, she saw the second large bat slowly crawl along the ground toward her.

With most of her energy spent, it took a few seconds for her to muster up the strength to yell, "Go away!"

All the thrashing had jostled the ropes off the cuffs of Claraicy's thick winter mitts and onto her withered wrists. After flexing her fingers, she wiggled her hands to removed one of the mitts. The ropes simply fell off her wrist as she shook off the second mitten.

Out of breath and no longer able to scream, she reached around to her back and grabbed a hold of the crushed bat. After clenching her teeth, she pulled it off along with pieces of her own flesh. Rolling onto her side, she began to crawl toward the creek.

Cautiously, the second bat worked its way toward its dead companion. As it turned its head to hiss at her, Claraicy picked up a large stone and threw it as hard as she could. The stone glanced off the side of the bat and toppled it over. The creature immediately got back up and scampered into the bush, only to reappear behind the tree stained with its companion's blood.

Claraicy watched as the bat slowly worked its way toward its dead companion and pulled its battered body toward the brush. A beam of sunlight broke through the dark clouds and highlighted the creatures. A glaring reflection bounced off them. For the first time, Claraicy noticed the nylon collars fastened around their necks and the round stainless steel pendants dangling from them. "You're not pets. Where did you guys come from?"

After the creatures had vanished from sight, Claraicy turned to the babbling creek. Dying from thirst in front of a large stream of running water had been torturous. She crawled over to its bank and stuck her face through the skim of ice that had formed along its edge.

Glancing back, she confirmed that the bats were still gone. As her stomach started to grumble, she wrapped one arm around her belly. "Too bad, I'm hungry enough that I could've eaten whatever that creature was."

A cold breeze dulled the numbing pain from the wounds on her back. Claraicy took off her parka and tried to twist her sweater and undershirt around her portly torso. She couldn't. Pieces from the bat's rib-cage were still stuck in her back and got caught in the material.

Reaching back, she prepared herself for the pain and pulled out all the pieces she could reach. After she was finished, she turned her sweater and undershirt back to front to help cover up the open wounds. It didn't take long before her undershirt was soaked in blood. It acted like an adhesive and stuck it to her back. It covered her wounds and somewhat protected them.

As a cold breeze blew down the open trough cut into the forest by the wide creek, she put her parka and mitts back on. While she drank some more water, the outside of Claraicy's exposed, blood-drenched sweater started to freeze. The frozen blood helped dull the pain as the young, bewildered and demoralized girl began to shiver.

Claraicy tied the hood of her coat tightly around her face. It had been three days since she had last eaten. With the back of her coat shredded and her back feeling as stiff as meat out of a freezer, any movement she made was agonizing.

With green resin covered needles sticking to the loose strains of her hair, she sat under the protection of a dense spruce tree. In her mind, she went over everything that occurred during the previous month. She had been sick and couldn't keep anything in her stomach. Nothing her mother did for her had helped. After her mother informed her father about her condition, he had turned pale and bitter. His thirteen-year-old daughter was pregnant.

They confined her to the house. She was forbidden to talk or communicate with anyone. All phone and internet access was stripped away from her. Her condition was to remain a secret.

A few days later, a smartly dressed woman appeared at the door with a folder full of paperwork waiting for her parents signatures. After the lady had left, Claraicy remembered her father sitting at the kitchen table and smiling as he told her, "All of our troubles will soon be over. Soon you won't have anything to worry about."

After that meeting, the mere sight of her had put a smile on his face. His grimacing smile had brought shivers down the back of her neck and took her breath away.

She had known a few older girls who had children. Their parents helped raise them. Unfortunately for her, those parents weren't anything like hers and neither were the circumstances.

She remembered the colourful business card that the life insurance agent had left on the kitchen table. She also remember seeing two hundred and fifty thousand dollars written in pen on the back of it.

What better way to get over the loss of an unwanted child than to have all your bills paid off and money left over to spend? It's much more lucrative than an abortion, or even selling an unwanted newborn on the black market. It is especially so when you insure both the mother and unborn child with added clauses that multiply the payout.

Despite the pain that radiated from her back, the sharp stabbing pain from her gut reminded her why she was left in the woods to die. In the distance she noticed puffs of black smoke still lingered over the burnt medical facility. Gazing at them Claraicy decided, "Where there is fire, there are firefighters. There must be someone still there who can help me."

Using the branches of the tree that she was under like the rungs of a ladder, she pulled her rigid body upwards and got to her feet. After snapping off a couple of dead branches to use as walking sticks, Claraicy took one slow, agonizing step at a time and began the long journey across the creek and through the woods toward the lingering black smoke.

The sun was setting over the lake as Claraicy walked up to the fence surrounding what was left of the fortified medical facility. Except for the odd short lived small flame, the fire was mostly out. Through the blown out windows and cracks in the walls, she could see them twinkle as they flared up and died back down. They were limited to the inside of the building and prevented from spreading by the thick walls. The firefighters must have thought that it was safely contained because no one was there.

Disappointed and feeling helpless, she used two sturdy sticks to help her walk around the fence. Her spirit was slightly lifted when she found a small section of fence that had been sliced open by a piece of flying metal. Dropping the sticks next to it, she pulled away the twisted debris from one of the helicopters and examined the size of the opening. After wiggling through the fence, she retrieved the sticks and looked around the property for anything that she could use. Charred rags, bricks and chunks of metal were strewn everywhere.

Along the side of the building was an open door leading to the stairwell. Inside, all Claraicy could see was the twisted metal staircase going up to a floor that no longer existed. Peering through the rungs of the metal stairs she could see the odd flame. She also saw smoke meandering its way out of large piles of the debris covering what was once the basement of the gutted building.

Circling the ruins, she noticed a large breach in the back wall. As she approached the breach, she could feel the warm air escaping the ruins. She stood outside of it and closed her eyes. "At least I will get to warm up for a while."

After crawling inside, she climbed down the mound of concrete that the breach had created. She found herself surrounded by piles of rubble and twisted debris. The outsides of most of the piles were kept warm by the smouldering embers buring inside of them. After checking the temperature of the rubble, she found two large piles that were not hot enough to burn, but still warm enough to curl up against. "Maybe someone will come back to make sure the fire is out." Tired and sore, Claraicy curled up between the two warm piles and quickly fell asleep.

Through the night, a soft snow fell over the northern forest. As it blew over the building, the warm air melted the snow and turned it into a light drizzle. In the mini microclimate inside the structure, the moisture seeped into the rubble and extinguished most of the burning embers. By the time the moisture soaked through her coat, it was morning. Shivering, she quickly discovered that the inside of the burnt out building had cooled considerably. It was only a few degrees warmer than the outside.

After finding a warm smouldering pile of debris, she sat down and contemplated her options. As she wiped her tears away, the pine resin, needles and debris that clung to her sleeve created a wide stripe across her soot covered face.

With nowhere to go, Claraicy hung her coat over a smouldering pile of debris to dry. As the sun rose above the walls and melted the snow that had accumulated, Claraicy rummaged through the charred piles of debris for anything she could use. In the corner of the building she found a pile that had not been completely burned. A scorched, heavily matted, bulletproof vest had been tossed on top of it. She could see pieces of burnt flesh clinging to its inner lining. "I guess the firefighters must have stripped it off a corpse."

Slipping on the vest provided her back with the added protection it badly needed. Under where the vest had been, she spotted a pile of singed fur. Getting down on her knees, she grabbed the warm fur with both hands and gave it a tug. The meat beneath it had been roasted to various degrees. Undaunted and not caring what it was, she ripped off some of the flesh and shoved it into her mouth. After not eating for days, the strange metallic tasting meat was a welcome treat.

******

Claraicy looked up at the snow swirling in the air above her as the wind blew across the top of the walls. Inside the burnt medical facility, large flakes of snow floated back and forth as they slowly made their way to the bottom. With its collapsed ceiling, the structure protected her from the frigid wind but little else. She needed a shelter that she could cuddle up in and keep warm.

Grunting, crying and at times even screaming from pain, Claraicy shifted around large pieces of debris and leaned them against the wall at a forty-five-degree angle. Every muscle in Claraicy's body ached and the open wounds on her back made every move extremely painful. With all the fireproof material used in constructing the building, there was no shortage of debris to choose from.

Using collapsed sections of walls made from fire retardant panels, metal counter tops, metal doors and anything big that she could manoeuver in place, she made a small, rudimentary lean-to. Seeing long, narrow gaps where the pieces overlapped, she began searching through the mounds of debris and collected anything she could use as stuffing and insulation. After separating it by size and texture, she pushed and squeezed the smaller more pliable pieces into the cracks.

Looking around, she found a flat stainless steel bar cut at forty-five degrees at each end. The oblong bolt holes at each end revealed signs of wear. It was probably used to stabilize something heavy. Gripping the end of it she made her way back to her shelter.

Using the bar a machete, she hacked a small, square hole through a piece of wall panelling and made a small entrance. After examining the interior of the shelter she dragged the larger pieces of insulation that she had previously collected inside to use as a mattress. Next to the entrance she placed a large, flat piece of metal that she could lean against it and use as a door.

If it wasn't for the cold numbing her pain, she would not have been able to continue. She could only think of one more thing to do. Snow meant a source of water, but she had nothing to eat. Working on pure adrenaline, she fought off the pain and hobbled over to the corner of the structure where the metallic tasting creature was buried. After lifting a large chunk of thick fire retardant panelling off of the creature, a large section of one of its wings was revealed.

Claraicy took a step back and bit her bottom lip before questioning loudly, "What is it?"

Puzzled but undaunted, Claraicy continued to roll, lift and pull the debris off of the dead creature. "I guess it doesn't matter, as long as it's edible."

After she dragged the creature out of the pile of debris by its hind legs, she stopped to examine it. The large lifeless eyes of the creature's hideous, cat-like face, glared at her. "You may look worse than those giant bats, but you tasted alright to me."

The time that it had taken her to construct the lean-to was enough to freeze the exposed outer layer of the creature's body. Claraicy placed the body over a jagged piece of crumbled wall. Using the steel bar she hammered the creature's bones and joints until its body was easier to move. Dragging it behind her, she crawled into the lean-to and pulled the creature's corpse inside.

Despite the cold, the blackened wall that the lean-to was built against absorbed enough heat from the sun to melt some of the snow that landed on it. Finding a metre long piece of the building's round air ducts, she layed it on the ground and used her foot to cave it in, turning it into a trough. After bending one end over, she used the steel bar to hammer it into an almost water-tight seal. Taking it inside, she leaned it next to the wall with the open end slightly elevated. Afterwards she flattened the edge next to the wall to redirect as much of the water into the tough as she could possibly get.

Exhausted, she curled up on the insulation, reached over and grabbed one of the wings of the strange creature and used it as a blanket. When she woke, the sun was starting to go down.

Grabbing the hind leg of the creature, she used the edge of the flat bar to hammer small strands of meat into soft peelable mouthfuls. With a full stomach and enough black water to at least quench her thirst, Claraicy snuggled next to the back of the corpse. After wiggling one of the creature's fur covered wings under her, she folded the other overtop. It was cold inside the lean-to, but Claraicy was still exhausted. Before she could barely bat her eyes, she had fallen back into a deep sleep.

A gust of wind whistled through the ruins and woke Claraicy. Above the high pitched sound she could faintly hear the whooshing of a helicopter as it circled the burnt facility. Crawling over to the metal plate that she used as a door, she tried to push it open. It wouldn't budge. As she slept, the wind had changed and a large snowdrift had accumulated along the wall where she had constructed her lean-to. Beneath it the metal plate was solidly frozen in place.

Sitting back and looking at the wall she had constructed, she noticed that the entire lean-to was bowed inward. Using her fist, she pounded on the steel plate that she was using as a door and various sections of the wall. A solid 'thud' was all she got back. As the sound of the helicopter's propellers slowly went away, her heart sank along with any hope of being rescued.

Believing that her survival depended on her own will to live, Claraicy reached for the flat steel bar. Using one of its angled ends, she jabbed a hole through the roof at the top corner of the lean-to. Even after widening the hole, all she could see was snow.

As she reached into the hole, she found that her mittens were useless. Taking them off, she used her bare hands to remove all the snow she could reach. With her shoulder pressed against the roof, her finger tips could still feel more snow. After pulling out her arm, she gazed into the hole and saw the glow of the noon sun radiating through the icy blue snow. "How long had I been asleep?"

Without warning, the section of wall next to the hole gave out. As snow piled into the lean-to, Claraicy stumbled backwards. Landing on her injured back, she gave out a shrill, "AAAAAhh." Terrified, she wiggled her feet free from under the snow and crawled to the far end of the lean-to.

As the sound of the pair of helicopters got louder, Claraicy was too scared to move. She could tell that they were directly overhead. With every rotation of the propellers, she could feel the snow vibrate and the outside wall of the lean-to bend inward under the increased pressure. Trapped at the end of the shelter, tears ran down her face. She wrapped the creature's wings around her and curled into a ball. "Daddy, how could you do this to me? I tried to please you. I tried to do everything you asked of me."

Chapter Two

Winter

Buried under the snow drift, Claraicy had nowhere to go and barely any room to move. Huddled in a ball, she stared at the metal bar sticking out of the newly-formed snowbank that filled half of her shelter. Somehow a faint ray of light had filtered through the snow and gave its shiny surface a strange colourful glow. She sat there with her hands tucked under her armpits and her knees folded up to her chest trying to preserve any warmth she could. While her mind mulled over her short, brutal life, she had nothing to do but sit in her snow covered tomb and wait for death.

Even with the creature's wings wrapped around her and her hood tightly tied around her face, she could feel the temperature in her body drop. Unable to think of anything else, her mind focussed on the glowing metal bar. As she stared at it, her shattered mind twisted and turned the glowing image into an elongated surreal effigy of her father's satanically grinning face. With his haunting face embedded in her mind, Claraicy's breathing decreased to the point that her chest became almost motionless. If it wasn't for her eyes occasionally blinking, she could have been easily mistaken for dead.

Claraicy woke from her trance and looked at the once upright bar as it slowly tilted away from the melting snow. It had lost its intoxicating glow. In her zen state, she had lost all sense of time. Had it been hours, days, weeks or maybe only a few minutes? She had no idea.

Looking down at her arms, she found that her once tight fitting parka had become loose and baggy. A thought occurred to her, *Maybe it had been months*. With a large section of the roof of her shelter missing, enough light filtered through the snowdrift that she could see. While looking around she took off one of her mitts and tore a handful of raw flesh off the creature's ribs.

Leaning forward, she looked up through the hole in the roof of the lean-to and all she could see was snow. After pulling out all the loose snow she could, she reached into the hole and discovered that there was a gap along the wall that the lean-to was resting against. The sun had penetrated the drift and warmed up the dark soot covered inner wall enough to melt away a narrow gap.

Grabbing a hold of the metal bar, Claraicy widened the hole and rammed the pointed end into the sheet of ice. After fifteen minutes of muscle-numbing chopping, she had created barely enough room to squeeze her head into. Peering inside, she saw that there was a solid sheet of thick ice running almost parallel to the inner wall.

Overwhelmed, Claraicy wasn't able to think clearly and had to sit down. Along with her confused mental state, her drastically weakened body was in no shape for prolonged physical work. As she sat there, she told herself, "Even if I get out of here, where can I go? The helicopters are long gone and I can't survive in the woods alone, not in the middle of winter."

Crawling to the far end of the lean-to, Claraicy stuck the stainless steel bar on the snow in front of her on a slight angle. After adjusting it slightly to catch the light, she stared at it like she had done before. While chewing on a handful of meat, she muttered, "In here, out there or back home, it doesn't matter where I am. I'm still going to die."

******

A loud exploding crack shook Claraicy out of her stupor. Like a hibernating bear, she woke up hungry. While cracking open the creature's femur and picking at the marrow, she gazed at the hole. She could see that a wide gap that had formed between the wall of the facility and the iced-over snow drift. Tossing off the creature's wings and remaining skin, Claraicy tried to crawl through the hole. It still wasn't big enough.

Grabbing the metal bar, she chipped away at the edges of the hole. It didn't take much to break apart the crumbling panels and twist the metal studs to give her more room to work. Within a few minutes, she had made a hole big enough to get through. With the cold metal bar held tightly in her hand, she lifted herself out of the lean-to and wiggled her body into the gap next to the wall. Squeezing and chipping her way along the wall, she got to large gap in the ice covered drift. She had room to hack and chisel out hand and footholds. With her back resting against the wall, she carefully climbed out of her icy prison.

Crawling out of the rubble, she shaded her eyes and tried to look beyond the fence into the surrounding forest. The bright world outside her shelter appeared foreign to her. Standing outside the ruins with her eyes shut, she stood and smiled as the sun warmed her face. The bright light burned her eyes even through her eyelids and she had to cover them with her hand. She listened to the creaking trees as wet snow broke off their brittle dead branches.

Her mouth started to water as a gentle breeze fanned the aroma of a dead caribou past her twitching nose. She had been trapped inside her self-made prison for too long. Basking in the warm sunlight, it took over fifteen minutes before she finally risked opening her eyes. Even then they had to be shaded with her hand.

As the pain in her belly forced her to unzip her coat, she could see something inside her move. With her face bouncing between a smile and a scowl and back again, she gazed at her stomach as something inside of it was pushing outward. The large bulge reminded her why and how she got there.

While remembering her father abandoning her, she suddenly thought of the giant bats and her injured back. After pushing her shoulders back and rotating them, she could feel a large, itchy growth attached to her back. Judging solely by the size of her gut, she knew she had been entombed in a semi-hibernative state for months. "It should have been healed by now."

With her nose in the air, the faint smell of rotting meat made Claraicy's mouth water. Guided by the intoxicating smell, she ran through the woods searching for its source. When she got to what was left of the dead caribou, she scared away the scavenging birds and knelt next to the scattered bones.

The remnants the scavengers had left behind of the frozen winter wolf kill wasn't very much. After gnawing all the meat she could find off the bones, she used the metal bar to crack open the ribs to get to the marrow. By the time she was finished with the carcass, every bone had been crushed and every piece of its skin had been chewed to the point that it could have been used as shoe leather.

A short few steps away from the kill was a frozen stream. Claraicy smashed the metal bar through the ice and cupped her hands to retrieve some water to drink. After pushing the ice towards the edges, she looked down at the water. She barely recognized herself. Her face was gaunt. In fact, despite her unborn offspring, she had lost almost half her weight.

She didn't know if it was just the angle of her reflection, but even her eyes looked different. They were much larger and rounder than before, plus her nose had grown wider.

With a swift kick, the fetus inside her belly made Claraicy clench her teeth. While rubbing her belly she yelled out, "I can't do this." Looking down at her extended belly, she softly added, "Father, if I get rid of it, will you take me back? I promise I will be good. There will be no more mistakes."

Wanting to end all her suffering, Claraicy stripped off all her clothes and sat next to the small stream as the wind started to pick up. Her entire body quickly turned from blotchy red to a pasty white. Claraicy's long, straggly dirty blonde hair draped in front of her face. Behind it, icicles formed on her nose and the sides of her mouth. She felt nothing; no pain, no cold, no regret, nothing at all.

Another painful kick from inside her belly shook her out of her trance. Looking down at her belly, she could see it move. "What did you do to deserve this?" With both hands, she raised the metal bar high into the air. With tears in her eyes she suspended it above her head, she tried to muster up the strength to stab the fetus growing inside of her. She couldn't. Lowering her arms, she started to weep.

******

As the snow melted and the bodies of the animals killed over the winter started to appear in the snowdrifts, Claraicy gnawed away at their remains. Wolves, cougars, crows and other predators had eaten almost everything. The scraps they left behind barely added up to a single meal. With the hungry fetus preventing her from sleeping, Claraicy aimlessly wandered around the forest, searching for anything that would help stop the stabbing pains in her belly.

Covered in frozen animal skins, the gaunt-faced Claraicy walked out of the brush and stepped on the bank of a large lake. After following its shore line, she saw a giant fence. For weeks, she had been walking in a huge circle. Collapsing to her knees, she looked down at her belly. "Why won't you let me die? Living is not what you think it is. At least in death, nothing can hurt you; not hunger, not the weather and not even your own family."

Hearing something in the woods behind her, Claraicy turned around and saw a pack of wolves. They were loosely spread out at the edge of the forest. Noticing a few partially hidden from sight, she wasn't sure how many there were.

Leaping to her feet, she spread out her arms and released a deep, echoing growl. With the frozen skins almost doubling the length of her arms, the confused, skittish animals turned around and trotted away. As the occasional one turned back to look at her, Claraicy growled and flapped her arms. Barely above a whisper, she cried out, "Abandon me, just like everyone else has."

Dropping her hands, Claraicy rubbed her belly. "You are all I have."

Chapter Three

Unshackled demons

Two long, mind deteriorating months later...

If a man screams in the middle of a forest, will he be heard? If so, by whom and for how long? Life is too short to be that stupid because every action you make has a reaction, and sometimes it can be deadly. That is what Patrick Leer was thinking as he lay on the ground with his head pounding.

He knew that he had to think before he did anything at all. It had been dusk when he was struck and rendered unconscious. The hot burning sensation on the side of his face informed him it was morning. Opening his eyes, he found that he could only make out fuzzy pulsating shapes from the various objects that surrounded him.

The strong lingering smell of ripe decaying flesh filled the air. He knew he was not alone. The strange young unkempt woman that he met in the woods was still there. The rotting furs that she wore gave her away. He could feel his limp limbs being shifted about. After a few minutes, he tried to snap out of his dazed state and resist, but discovered that he couldn't move.

It took a couple more minutes before the fuzzy shape hovering over him slowly manifested itself into the hazy outline of the woman he had found. As his sight cleared, he could see maggots crawling around the decaying animal skins that draped over her body.

A couple of wiggling creatures dropped off and landed on his face. One maggot rolled off his forehead and got tangled in his scruffy, dirty blonde hair. As the other maggot started to squirm its way through the thick stubble on Patrick's unshaven cheeks toward his left eye, he asked, "Who are you?"

The disquieting woman didn't respond. He attempted to shake the maggot away from his eye, but found out that he couldn't move his head. He could feel the small creature twist and turn as it got entangled in his scruffy beard.

As more feeling came back to his limbs, he started to feel the bindings cut into his skin. In desperation, he tried to move his head, arms, legs, and torso. Nothing moved. A few minutes went by and his eyesight started to clear up some more. Out of the corner of his eye, he discovered that his head was wedged between stakes pounded into the ground, and his body and limbs were lashed to a dozen more large stakes. Even with the violent thrashing of his thick, massive muscles, he failed to loosen any of them.

Patrick's mind wandered back to when he first spotted the wild, hunchbacked girl draped in hides. The sun was setting behind her as she washed her face on the shore of the wide, fast flowing creek. His view was obscured by the blinding sunlight as he glided his canoe towards her.

As he pulled his canoe ashore, she had quickly stood up. With the sun radiating still behind her, her dark, obscure figure was the centre of a glowing ball of pure light. While she walked towards him, she had blurted out, "Mr. Leer, I remember you and I remember what you did. Do your wife's thorns still bother you?" Then a blur flashed in front of him and everything went dark.

Patrick's stubborn, sharp-tongued wife had been dead for almost three years. *Thorns?* Patrick licked his dry lips before inquiring, "Claraicy, is that you?" Before the words left his mouth, disbelief confused his thoughts. "No, that can't be? You're dead."

Claraicy looked at him, "So you do remember me after all."

Something inside him snapped as he bellowed, "Untie me right now, you little brat."

With a wide grin, she replied, "Why, so you can treat me like you did your wife?"

Her defiance shook Patrick. As his rage turned into fear, his tone quieted. "You've completely changed. What happened to you? You use to be such a obedient child. Have you forgotten everything your father taught you? What turned a nice girl like you into someone that could do this to your own neighbour?"

Standing over him, Claraicy calmly answered, "As you said, I am supposed to be dead. Being left to die and forced to live like a wild animal can change a person. It gives them a different perspective on life and death. Especially a naive, 'obedient' child."

Patrick finally managed to blink the maggot away from his eye. He couldn't see much. On a large boulder near his head he could make out his unravelled first aid kit. Some of its contents were pulled out of their pouches. Working as a guide for urban shootists (or so called hunters out of Toronto and the United States) his first aid kit was equipped for almost any type of accident or mishap.

Patrick's foggy brain tried to comprehend what was happening. Claraicy didn't appear injured. The side of his face felt like it had been hit by a baseball bat, but he had shaken off worse after bar room brawls. He wiggled his toes and fingers; outside of the restraints all of his limbs were fine.

As fear began to make him sweat, he desperately tried to move his limbs in vain. They still wouldn't budge. Claraicy had effectively bound him solidly to the ground.

His arms were tied to stakes next to his sides and under his armpits, with more rope lashed across his chest. His legs were straddled around the trunk of a large birch tree, crossed and tied in both directions around his ankles. The rope was than tightly stretched and tied off around another tree.

He was unable to move them at all without squeezing the knots even tighter. Even if he got his hands free, he wouldn't be able to reach around the tree to untie his ankles.

In a low subdued voice he asked, "Why? What have I done to you?"

While continuing to search though the pockets of the large first aid kit, she simply replied, "Nothing yet, and I intend to keep it that way."

Looking at her wide, glowing smile, the hairs on the back of his neck straightened. Droplets of sweat rolled off his forehead as he studied her face. Behind her matted clumps of hair she showed no outward signs of sanity. Her twisted, dirty face seemed to radiate the same sinister glow he had once seen on some of his fellow prison inmates as they graphically described what they would do to those who ratted on them.

For the first time in his life, Patrick was not the one giving the orders. Even during the different times he was in jail, he wasn't afraid of anyone. Fear was something that he had always dished out to others, not received. Despite being in his late thirties, fear had been a faint childhood memory. Lying there, he suddenly realized that he had absolutely no control over what was about to happen. He couldn't use his size, strength or any ominous threat to intimidate her. All he could do was lie there and accept his fate.

Throughout his youth, students, teachers and almost all authority figures had feared him. Despite all the local police knowing his cruel and vicious nature, Patrick continued to manipulate everyone around him. The courts didn't take threats from a child seriously. After time, no one dared to press charges against him. He had everyone terrified of his violent temper and sadistic reprisals on those who did. The only exception was his own mother after she finally realized her only child didn't care if she lived or died.

Patrick was only ten when he grabbed a steak knife and stabbed his mother several times in her arms and legs as she tried to defend herself. She had forgotten her place. If she had let him drink his father's beer, nothing would have happened.

In court, Patrick's entire childhood was opened to the public. Even without his name being printed, everyone reading the local newspaper knew who it was. The prosecutor had told the court, "Given the chance, a child raised without any moral guidance can be more ruthless than any adult."

The words the judge said before sentencing him rambled through Patrick's head: *"Young children have no natural fear of mortality, theirs or anyone else's. Unless they are taught proper social morals, they are not even bothered by a guilty conscience. The child that stands before me has clearly demonstrated a total lack of any parental guidance. This is why I am forced to lay down the stiff sentence and conditions I feel that this violent case compels me to."* That was the last time Patrick saw either of his parents.

Shortly after the trial, his mother found the strength to run away, and his abusive father got drunk and did the world a favour by slicing his wrists.

Patrick looked at Claraicy as she stood over him, holding his life in her hands. For the first time, he saw her not as a scared, twisted girl, but as a mirror image of himself after he had finally stood up to his drunken, abusive father and struck back for the first time. It was his seventh birthday. After tying a piece of fishing line across the top of the stairs, he watched his father fall and break an arm, leg and shatter his lower back. That was the best present he could have wished for.

Taunting his wheelchair-bound father taught him the glorifying joy of power. The spiteful acts of terror and vengeance he administered to his parents, classmates, teachers and anyone else that was stupid enough to cross him was more gratifying than a truck load of candy.

Now, helplessly tied and at Claraicy's mercy in the middle of the forest, he knew that the tide had turned. His very life dangled at her whim. He knew if he screamed his life could be instantly over.

Claraicy's big, wild, bulging eyes pulsated as she breathed deeply, in and out, in and out, over and over. Long strands of excited drool dripped from the corners of her mouth through her clenched teeth and curled-up, quivering lips. This once mere child had transformed into a deformed and emotionally deprived woman in a little over half a year. Despite her strange elongated facial features, enlarged hands and the large hump on her back, he could see that she was no longer a child. The patchwork pieces of loose hide that she wore couldn't hide her lean, strong, muscular body and enlarged breasts that occasionally slipped out from under the stiff hides as she turned from side to side. Her appearance was far from the chubby, blonde child he had remembered seeing in the fall. The winter had somehow killed her and replaced her with this evil hag.

Standing over Patrick, Claraicy smiled. "You used to terrify me. Every time you came over for a visit, I was scared to open my mouth. You have no idea what I dreamt of doing to you. I often thought of poisoning you and my dad, but that was too easy. I wanted you to suffer, so I used to dream of other things that I would like to do to you."

His last chance to scream for help disappeared as Claraicy stuffed and duct-taped the hollow, aluminum battery casing from his dismantled flashlight into his mouth. Producing pig-like grunts, he tried in vain to push the tube out with his tongue. Claraicy's long, frizzled, dark hair hung wildly over most of her face as she worked. Patrick could see only a few stubborn strands of blonde showing through. Those few strands were all that was left of the child he had known. Patrick shook his body again to test his bindings.

Contemptuous of his struggling, Claraicy pounded four more stakes into the ground, firmly positioning them around his head, one on both sides of his forehead, and the other two placed tightly against his cheeks. The sticky pine gum on the green wooden stakes ripped out some of his whiskers as they scraped against them. Wrapping tape back and forth across his forehead to the adjacent stakes, they were squeezed together.

"You are a piece of shit. Shit is all you deserve and it's all you will get," rang in his ears as Claraicy tore open his shirt. "Let's see how you like this?"

Patrick watched her twisted smile grow on the right side of her face, wiggling her nose as she flicked her wrist and cut a small opening in his stomach with a scalpel. The sudden shock numbed all Patrick's nerve endings. Claraicy's glimmering eyes sparkled as her smile changed the shape of her face with every gesture she made. As she slowly, methodically deepened the small slit, pure fright had replaced most of Patrick's pain.

Inserting her forefinger into the small incision, Claraicy wiggled it about until she wrapped it around a section of Patrick's small intestines. Slowly and very carefully, she started to pull it out. Patrick was fixated on Claraicy's face as she closely examined his intestines, making sure they weren't twisted or nicked. Then after three arm lengths were withdrawn, she sliced it. Patrick's eyes bulged out as she placed his intestines over a low hanging branch above him. Its putrid contents splashed over his face as the cut end dangled above his head.

"Now let's see if you like to swallow. I hope you like the taste of your own shit, 'cause you're not the only one who can dish it out."

Grabbing the end of the intestine, Claraicy cut off a small piece to correct its length and flung it into the bushes. Slowly she slipped the outer wall of the intestine snugly over the flashlight casing attached to his mouth like a condom. "That fits just right, perfect in fact." With a piece of the remaining duct tape from Patrick's back pack, Claraicy taped his intestines to the tube in his mouth.

On the boulder next to Patrick, Claraicy had already laid out a needle, thread and two small tubes of super glue. With a wide smile on her face, she began to hum. Like a caring nurse, Claraicy told him step by step everything she was doing as she sewed the protruding intestines to the skin around the opening in his stomach with a series of tight stitches.

A seam of super glue secured everything in place and completely stopped the bleeding. "Don't worry Mr. Leer, I've had lots of practice stitching up my mom. She taught me well. You know my dad, he never liked going to doctors. Surely you remember what happened to her after she took me to the hospital with a shattered arm from a flying beer bottle? She couldn't get out of bed for almost two weeks. I had to look after both of them with only one arm."

Patrick knew her father. *He was nothing but a big-mouthed, blowhard. She broke her arm falling out of a tree. I'm sure that's what happened.*

Claraicy's father was a church elder and played Santa Claus for as long as I can remember. Shit, he had bounced every kid in the district on his lap. Claraicy was always more than a little touched! She was never like the other kids in the neighbourhood. Then Patrick remembered why he ventured into the woods.

In modern society, being the king and absolute master of your castle was something that was frowned upon. However, inside the walls of their castles, both Patrick and Claraicy's father's ruled with iron fists. That was part of the reason they had become friends. Looking at Claraicy, Patrick compared his early childhood to hers. He then wondered *What kind of monster did Kerry create.*

After all traces of any bleeding had stopped, Claraicy stood up and smiled like a child after tying up her own shoes for the very first time. While brushing her hair back with her fingers, she revealed to him the leftover fragments of her once sweet innocent face. Patrick watched her smile as she placed his unzipped sleeping bag over the low branch above his torso, forming a small tent.

In a sugary voice, she talked to him like he was a doll or stuffed teddy bear. "Now, are you nice and cozy? Well, I hope so, 'cause I want you to die nice and slow." Then she added with a chuckle, "Besides, bleeding or freezing to death would be too good for the likes of you."

It took a few hours before Patrick's intestines puffed out like a long, poorly stuffed sausage and his own waste started flowing into his month. Within the dark shadows at the very edge of his limited sight he could see the top of Claraicy's head.

As she finally disappeared from view, his thoughts wandered. *How could a young, frightened child survive a winter alone in these northern woods? How did Claraicy manage to grow so quickly into a crazy, demented creature and get the physical strength to overtake me?* He shut his eyes. *What did I do to her to deserve this?*

A chill came over him as he heard Claraicy's voice echo in the forest, "Say hello to your nice wife for me. Oh, sorry, you won't be seeing her. You will be going to Hell instead."

Chapter Four

Jesse

Claraicy sat next to the edge of a small, calm lake and gazed into a still pool of water that was trapped behind a small dam of roots and silt. The reflection that she saw was barely recognizable as being human. *Who am I?*

The strange creature that looked back at her was a misshaped, ugly monster. Was her name still Claraicy? A name issued to her in a previous life. *That girl never truly existed, or did she?*

What she did caught up to her. *Was it real? Was everything that happened just a fantasy, merely another dream? Did it really happen?* Claraicy shook her head and screamed, "Who are you?"

As the echoes resonating over the lake died down, a clump of her hair dropped into the water and the ripples distorted her reflection. In her head she saw a little blonde girl with freshly combed hair and the pretty red bow that she always wore to church. Her face supported a well-rehearsed smile along with the heavy makeup her mother put on her to mask the battered and abused child inside.

As the ripples died out, the strange beast returned. There was no smile, no bow and no makeup concealing the bruises. A dark twisted mat replaced her once shiny hair. Her round face had become a long, lean piece of leather, hardened by neglect and weather. A wide, elongated and slightly turned-up nose had replaced the small, cute round one that was often the target of the back of her father's hand. Claraicy swiped the hideous image in the water with her fist. The ripples made her look even more grotesque. Jumping up, she yelled, "Who am I? What am I?"

She looked at her body. It was covered in blood and filth. What she was forced to do to survive had deeply callused all of her fragile human emotions. Her constantly grumbling stomach had forced her to gnaw away on scavenged leftovers from rotting, abandoned animal kills. Sometimes she was lucky enough to snatch the odd frog or fish, or spear them with a stick. Without being able to make fire, she was forced to eat everything raw. Over time, even worms, maggots and bugs were eagerly consumed to relieve her constantly grumbling stomach.

She survived day to day and sometimes hour to hour, or even moment to moment. Malnutrition along with the past long cold winter had taken its toll on both her body and her mind.

Between her constantly changing body and the harsh environment, her clothes turned into rags. Even the vest she had found no longer fit over the large hump protruding out of her back. She resorted to peeling pieces of hide off of decaying animal carcasses, loosely tying them together in a haphazard manner and either draping them over her shoulders or tying them to her waist, legs or feet. As the rotting hides fell apart, on several occasions she had been left naked.

To her, warmth was a luxury. She instinctively knew that the bitter cold wouldn't kill her. At times she had wanted to die, but something inside her kept her defiant heart beating. It didn't matter what Mother Nature threw at her, her body refused to surrender, even after she had given up.

Claraicy's mind wandered back to a time when she had stripped off the last remnants of her clothes and tried to kill the fetus growing inside of her. After she found out she couldn't, she just sat there and cried. The freezing rain had formed icicles over her cold body. The cold had slowly lulled her into a deep sleep. She dreamt that her ordeal was finally over. She wanted to escape all of the suffering she was going through and simply die.

To her surprise, the bright morning sun woke her and she was forced to break out of her icy shell and face another cold winter day. Memories of her standing up and screaming out, "Why am I still being punished?" while ice crystals fell from her body, haunted her. She should have been frozen solid. She should have died.

Claraicy looked around. Up to the time that Patrick found her, her only possession was the stainless steel bar. After pounding and grinding the edge of it for weeks over course stones, she had transformed it into a crude tool that she used to cut, hack and dig with. To her delight, it had been replaced by a sharp hunting knife, a camp shovel and hatchet. Patrick wasn't a man to be trusted, but he always had the best equipment he could afford.

Having waxed, waterproof matches meant enjoying her first fire since she had been abandoned. Within half an hour after it was lit, she was eating hot food that her taste buds could barely recognize. Eating a can of hot spaghetti next to a warm fire overwhelmed her fragile mind.

Everything was surreal. Claraicy looked around and stabbed the end of the spoon she was using into her leg. As the shocking pain made her leg twitch, she knew she wasn't dreaming. The small fragile world that she created in her mind became hazy and confused. She looked around, trying to focus on what was really real, and hoping that her life was actually only an elaborate nightmare.

A big bulge on her hip gradually crept upwards under her hides. As it worked its way onto her shoulder, a strange, furry, almost cat-like head popped out. Claraicy twisted her head back and forth, rubbing the creature's face with her matted hair. "Jesse, I may not know who I really am any more, but I know you. You're probably the only one that can stand me."

Claraicy reached up and cuddled the creature next to her cheek. She sat there rocking back and forth until Jesse started to lick her ear. "I think you're hungry?"

Claraicy put her finger into the spaghetti and brought it up to Jesse's mouth. The creature shook its head in disgust and scurried back to the comfort of her hip. Claraicy giggled for the first time that she could remember. She felt like she was in a drunken stupor. As she smiled, her hard weathered face felt like it had cracked open. She no longer cared who or what she was. Her stomach was full, she was warm, and at that moment, ecstatically happy.

Claraicy built the fire higher and higher until its reflection made the edge of the small lake in front of her glow. Full of delight, she screeched into the air in a half howl, half growl that couldn't be replicated by any human throat. She ate, danced and ate some more.

Resembling a young, hairy newborn ape with a cat-like head and retractable claws, Jesse creeped into the forest and hid. Staying away from the fire, the young creature scrounged for insects and frogs at the fringes of the clearing. The light of the fire drew in the insects, which in turn drew in the frogs that Jesse quickly turned into tasty treats.

Claraicy laughed as Jesse ran into the water, splashing around in the dark after a large moth. She ended up falling into a peaceful sleep with the constantly hungry Jesse curled up against her warm stomach, munching on some maggots that were embedded in her hides.

As the sun rose, the odd flame still appeared between the bright embers of the dying fire. To escape from the bright sun that shone into her eyes, Claraicy rolled onto her front, then to her other side. Caught by surprise, Jesse leaped off of her and ran into the forest.

Feeling thirsty, Claraicy got up for a drink of water. Instead of scooping it up with her hands, she simply filled up an empty can and drank out of it. With the label burnt off, she didn't know what had been in it, but mixed with water she could taste the tomato and spices in its sauce. After refilling the can, she placed it on the embers to warm up and put some small pieces of wood next to it.

The warmth of the glowing embers drew her face closer to the fire pit. As she leaned over the ashes, a piece of hide slipped off her shoulder and some of its hairs caught fire. Patting the flames out with her hands, she started to shake her head. The stinging in her hands finally woke her from the surreal state she was in.

She looked around and saw all the stuff she had salvaged. Backpacks, blankets, food, empty cans and camping equipment littered the area. It was real, it wasn't a dream. She had actually lived out some of her wild, vindictive fantasies. She was the demented wild creature in her dreams. It wasn't about survival. If she didn't slash holes into Patrick's canoe, she could've used it to paddle out of woods and find help. "What made me do it? Do I really want to stay here?"

Claraicy dropped to her knees and curled up into a ball with her arms wrapped around her knees. Seeing her mother in distress, Jesse scooted to her hip.

Despite the warm sun and all the heat still radiating from the embers and burning kindling, Claraicy began shivering. With tears flowing down her face, she repeated over and over. "I'm a good girl. I'm a good girl. Daddy, please forgive me. I didn't mean to do what I did. It wasn't me. I wasn't thinking straight. I'll behave now. I'll be your good girl again."

After a half hour of wallowing in self-pity and regret, Claraicy crawled over to the water and splashed some on her face. She knew that it was too late. She could never take back what she had done to him.

Chapter Five

Ryan

Sporting a week-old beard and his half-unbuttoned park ranger uniform, Ryan LeChasseur paddled around the bend of a wide creek. As the waterway narrowed into a long stretch of fast running rapids, he shook off his bulletproof vest and wrapped his self-inflating life vest around his neck.

With long deep strokes, he gracefully manoeuvred his agile canoe around every shimmering bend, sunken tree branch and jagged rock in a flawless ballet through one of Wabakimi Provincial Park's many unnamed, constantly changing, uncharted waterways. The vast wilderness park that Ryan had taken an oath to protect was larger than the province of Prince Edward Island, and some eastern US states.

It was only by his uncanny luck that the glossy finish on his three-month-old cedar strip canoe hadn't been marred. It had taken all of his spare time during the past winter and half the spring to hand mould the various wooden pieces from trees he had hauled out of the bush the year before. He would never have used it for a search and rescue mission if he had been notified back at his cabin. Instead they called him while he was on a solo fishing trip. His regular canoe was made from rugged Kevlar and was much better suited for this job.

A distracting bright splash of red on the shore almost ended his luck. With his eyes glued to the shore, the fast-flowing water had grabbed a hold of his bow and redirected the tip of his canoe. A fallen green cedar tree lying on an angle three quarters of the way across the creek acted like both a dam and a funnel. It intensified the current and forced the water through a rocky, narrow passage.

Beneath the passage was the ghastly, slightly submerged head of a woodland caribou. Its giant antlers were secured in place by bent branches and rocks anchoring the skin around the creature's neck in position. Pieces of red fibreglass were clinging to the tips of a few antlers. The trap was carefully designed to catch the canoe in the caribou's wide rack, rock its arc-shaped antlers backwards, scraping holes into the sides of its hull while driving its sharp front tips into the canoe's bottom and ripping it apart.

With the tips of the antlers pointing straight at him, Ryan gave out an, "Ohhhhhhhh!"

Within half a heartbeat, he dug his paddle into the water. With a single strong back stroke of his paddle, he managed to point his canoe away from the trap and towards the shore. He dug his paddle into the water for several fast strokes and forced the canoe between the trap and the rocky shoreline. He had escaped the trap with only a couple minor scrapes to the veneer on both sides of its hull. Glancing back, he could see the dark lifeless eyes of the slain beast as its head rocked slightly back and forth in the swift current.

He turned the canoe around and paddled towards the calm water behind the fallen tree. He grabbed one of its branches and looked up. He was mesmerized by the remains of the large, overturned red canoe that was mounted on top of a mound of boulders. A pair of paddles were embedded in the gouges of its hull forming an 'X'. Even from a distance Ryan could easily see the long gashes the antlers had ripped along the bottom and sides. Its prominent placement along with his near accident made him wonder if it was put there as a distraction, a signal for help, or as a warning.

Ryan could feel the hairs on the back of his neck stand on end. He regretted responding to the search and rescue call alone. By the texture of the branch he was holding he could tell that the tree had been only recently fallen. While holding his canoe against the soft springy branches of the dense tree, he put on his bulletproof vest.

His superiors knew his partner was laid up when they called him. Chris Henderson had been disabled by a poacher's bullet in his thigh and a pair of busted ribs after two high-powered slugs almost pierced his bullet-proof vest. He was lucky the bullets had struck him on an angle. If they had hit his vest straight on, they would have killed him.

A simple request to help locate two campers that were reported late and missing by an upset mother sounded safe and routine. To his superiors, having a trained officer spending some time off in the area was a blessing.

However, as more information trickled in about the campers, the more nervous Ryan and his superiors became. If it wasn't for the possibility that time might be imperative, Ryan would have returned to his cabin and waited to be paired up with at least a semi-trained volunteer. His selfless heroics were always getting him in trouble. Glancing over at the submerged head, he grimaced while biting on his bottom lip. Under his breath, he mumbled, "Chris, I wish you were here."

After laying his paddle alongside his backpack, Ryan grabbed the branches of the tree and pulled his canoe closer to shore. With one hand gripping a sturdy branch, he ruffled through its side pocket for his compact binoculars with his other hand.

The destroyed red canoe had waves in the fibreglass, and its rough uneven ridges showed all the signs of a poorly constructed, homemade job. Speaking softly, he whispered to himself, "Cheapskates! Throw together a cheap glass boat, a few antiquated supplies and look what happens. The fact that there was no route schedule or record of you entering the park meant that you probably snuck in without paying. No wonder nobody knew where to look for you."

The lighter coloured undersides of the plants that were crushed under the busted canoe told him that it had been there for a few days. Despite the bush being bent over, most of their leaves had already twisted themselves around to face the sun. He wanted to go ashore to investigate, but his ears and his eyes held him back. The woods were too quiet. There were no songs ringing from the birds or even chatter from a squirrel. The only thing he could hear was the wind blowing through the trees and a steady splashing of water over the rocks.

As he began methodically surveying the area, the wind shifted direction. The unmistakable ripe odour of decaying flesh kicked Ryan's other senses into overdrive. Scavengers normally disposed of any flesh long before it could be advertised by such a pungent odour, unless something was stopping them. *"Patrick, is this your handy-work?"*

Aside from the babbling creek and wind rustling through the trees, Ryan thought he heard some muffled, whimpering cries accompanied by a few shallow moans. Was it the wind rubbing green sticky branches together, or could it be human? Maybe it could be even a bear cub or an injured animal? Not wanting to confront a mother bear, he cautiously looked around the forest for any movement.

As the moaning turned into a relentless painful cry and the muffled whimpers ceased, Ryan could tell that the sounds were definitely human. Glued to his binoculars, his eyes methodically danced along the tree branches until he saw a camper's food cache. It was suspended by ropes between two birch trees, safely out of a bear's reach. The fallen tree and dense bushes along the shore made it impossible for him to see what was on the ground. After refocusing his binoculars, he could make out the droplets forming on the bottom of the sack from something leaking inside.

He tried hard to convince himself that the smell was from the sack. He couldn't. No one takes fresh meat into the forest. It only attracts predators and scavengers. Even if it was packed in a heavy, bulky cooler with plenty of ice, it would be spoiled and discarded before getting this far into the park.

Instinctively his eyes continued to float through the trees until resting on another large object suspended high on the far side of a maple tree. After shifting positions to get a better look, Ryan also noticed a cluster of three more objects further in the woods. They were all nestled near the top of a tall hardwood tree. The largest object rested on top of a thick branch, while a small one hung a little further down on the same branch, and the third hung from a branch almost directly above them. With the wind constantly waving the foliage around, even with his binoculars he couldn't make out what they were. Reaching back, he rubbed the back of his neck and quietly told himself, "This is getting weird."

The last time he was in this area was when his partner was shot. Their escape was blocked by three well-trained dogs. Ryan looked down at the jagged scars on his forearm that he had received when he pulled one of the dogs off Chris. By the time he got him to safety and returned, the dogs' bodies were gone.

Unfortunately, shots from a shadow and mysterious dogs with no definitive proof of who owned them wasn't enough for a judge to convict Patrick. Afterwards, a rumour of a forty thousand dollar reward for Ryan's head spread quickly around the region. In an area where money was scarce, a rumour like that was taken seriously. In a forest with lots of swamps, a body can easily disappear.

Ryan put down his binoculars and shook his head trying to clear it. He had to focus entirely of what was going on around him. While using one hand to quietly pull the canoe onshore, he opened the watertight compartment he had built into the bow with the other and retrieved his service revolver. Alone and with a bounty on his head, he didn't want to take any chances. Feeling that this entire venture could be nothing more than an elaborate trap, he tied his canoe to a thick branch and got out.

By the time he planted both feet on solid ground, the strange clump of objects in the far tree had vanished. Were they lingering predators protecting their kill? They were too big to be raccoons. Maybe he misjudged their size. As paranoia started to fill Ryan's thoughts, he wondered if they vanished because they had spotted him. After gaining his composure, he crept behind some bushes and slowly used the barrel of his revolver to push aside some of their dense branches.

In the middle of the clearing beyond the brush, he saw a tall, naked, obese man gagged and tied to thick stakes pounded in the ground. His legs were spread so wide apart that Ryan could feel his own groin hurt. Despite the man's entire crotch being caked with dirt, blood, and crawling insects, Ryan could make out the gash where his penis and testicles should've hung.

The man's badly sunburnt gut drooped away from his body, along with his other rolls of flab. The description Ryan was given of Kerry Mitchell was off by the way an over protective mother saw her 'little baby boy'. Add a bushy beard instead of a scruffy patch, subtract a hundred plus pounds and make believe he had a face that a mother could love, it was him, right down to the tattoo of a heart with 'MOM' scrolled through it on the left side of his chest.

Ryan shifted some branches around to survey more of the clearing. His skin crawled as he saw chunks of rotting caribou meat littering the campsite. Ryan could make out the hooves and various other body parts of the hacked-up beast. He thought to himself, *God, someone wanted to draw in every scavenger in the area.*

Even with his body armour secured, Ryan found a new level of fear as he searched for any clue that they were being watched. Knowing that Patrick had baited and ambushed him before made him check and recheck every tree, branch, bush, rock and fallen piece of deadwood. Thinking of Kerry's ordeal, he even wondered if a quick death may be better than facing what happened to him.

Moving another branch, Ryan got a better look at the large object in the tree. It was Carol Mitchell tied upside down in a sleeping bag. Guide ropes were strung to her, forcing her to watch her husband suffer.

Ryan watched Kerry shake and toss his head back. He could see his throat moved up and down as he chewed and began to swallow pieces of whatever was lodged in his mouth. With each swallow, the clump beneath the tightly tied cloth around his mouth slowly disappeared. As his gag got looser, Kerry vigorously shook his head back and forth until it slipped onto his neck. Turning his head to the side, Kerry spit out the remaining pieces of whatever was left in his mouth.

While studying the forest for any sign of a reaction to Kerry's progress, Ryan could hear him whimper, "God, I didn't deserve this. No one deserves this."

Ryan fought back his urge to leap out to the Mitchell's aid. Every muscle in his body was tense and ready to pounce into action. He had to force himself to wait until he knew it was safe. The change in Kerry's situation and whining didn't seem to cause any activity in the surrounding forest. Finally content, Ryan stood up and placed his revolver back into its holster.

Drawing his hunting knife with one hand, he used his radio to report back to the Wabakimi Park Station. "I've found the couple from Souix Lookout. ... They are both alive but Mr. Mitchell badly needs an emergency medical airlift. ... Do you have a fix on my position? ... Is there anyone close by that can assist me? ... How long before a chopper can get here? ... Too long. ... What about Marquis Richardson's floatplane? ... Not the small one. The big one that he just fixed up. ... Fine, tell Marq that I'll meet him on the lake where we went fishing and met those two wild Cape Breton girls. He'll know the place. ... Mr. Mitchell's been castrated, mutilated and has lost a lot of blood. ... His entire crotch has been removed. .. . He looks like a fighter. He'll still be alive. ... Tell him to bring extra help, he's huge. ... I should be able to make it to the lake in about three hours. ... OK, I'll see you in four."

Searching through the trees for any activity or sign that he was being watched, he slowly walked over to Kerry. Kneeling over him, he studied the battered mess on the left side of his face while cutting his ropes. At first, he couldn't force himself to even glimpse at Kerry's mutilated crotch. When he did, all he saw were hundreds of crawling and flying insects. "Who did this? Do you have any idea how long ago they left?"

Pointing to his wife dangling in the tree, Kerry forced out in a dry voice, "That stupid, ugly witch did it. Who did you think?" The blisters on his lips and tongue slurred his words, but they were still clear enough to understand.

"What?" Ryan looked up at Carol Mitchell and added, "How?"

Without the strength to raise his head, he simply rolled it towards his wife before answering, "I don't know how she managed to get up there. Maybe she flew up on her broom or whipped up a spell. All I know is that I was walking back to camp with my arms full of firewood, and got whacked on the side of my head. When I woke up, I was tied naked to the ground and that bitch was shaving off my beard and mustache with my fishing knife. The way her hands were shaking, I thought that she was going to slice my throat." Rolling his head back to face Ryan, he added, "Now, how can I grow another beard before Christmas?"

As Ryan dribbled water out of his canteen and into Kerry's mouth, he studied his face and neck. There were over a dozen small nicks and several shallow cuts on his chin, jowls and neck. *This man had been mutilated and his main concern was his beard?* Ryan rubbed his head in disbelief. "I need to know what happened here for my report."

Kerry closed his eyes and talked barely above a whisper. "I've been tied up for two, maybe three days. Yesterday, I never saw the hag at all. I thought she had abandoned me. This morning I woke up screaming and saw her burning off my dick with a red hot coat hanger. She tried to hide under a half-rotten caribou hide, but I knew it was her. I must have passed out for a while. When I came to, she was sitting by the fire, cooking my privates on a forked stick right in front of me. They looked like a hunk of sausage and a couple of withered up meatballs. I ordered her to untie me and she screamed back at me, 'This will shut you up.' Then she took my privates straight out of the fire, stuffed them into my mouth and gagged me."

"Are you sure that it was her voice?"

"It was muffled a bit, but it couldn't have been anyone else.

There was only the two of us out here." Kerry's mumbled whispers deteriorated into whimpers. "How would you like to be left starving for three days and then have your own balls and pecker cooked and fed to you?

While Ryan was examining the campsite, he answered, "I wouldn't." The campsite was in shambles.

Almost crying, Kerry continued to babble. "Look at her staring at me. Can't you hear her laughing at me? I'll kill her for this." Then he rolled his head to one side and passed out.

Ryan could only hear the odd moan coming from Kerry's wife. As he started to stand up, he felt something dripping on him. Looking up, he spread out his hand and caught a drop coming from the food cache before it could land on Kerry. It was honey. Something that was sure to lure ants, insects and bears. He glanced at Carol. Even wrapped in a sleeping bag, he could tell that she was in no shape to do what her husband accused her of.

After rolling Kerry on his side and pulling up his knee to rest him into the recovery position, Ryan looked around for something to cover him with. All of Kerry's clothes were torn apart.

After retrieving a foil survival blanket from his canoe, he wrapped him in it, then redirected his attention towards Carol. Besides the indecency of being hung upside down, whoever placed her in the tree made sure that she was protected from the weather and out of the reach of most wildlife.

How she got into the tree baffled him. The guide ropes used to secure her in place were tied to two adjacent trees with barely any excess rope left over. The trees' smooth trunks, girth and lack of climbable branches left him stumped. *Whoever hauled her up there either had arms like an orangutan or had done it by climbing and leaping from tree to tree.*

Ryan ran to his canoe and retrieved some rope. On his way back he grabbed a hefty chunk of unburnt wood from their old campfire and tied it to the end of the rope for some weight. Despite Ryan's strong pitching arm, it took him three tries to get the rope over the branch from which Carol was hanging. The weight of the charred wood fed the rope over the branch and back into his waiting hands. After flicking the rope until it wiggled its way along the branch and next to the tree trunk, he tied it off. Grabbing the rope with both hands, he semi-walked up the tree trunk, pulling himself up as he went.

While straddling the branch, he lashed the end of his rope to the one suspending Carol's sleeping bag. Then he cut the two guide ropes that were attached to the sides of the bag that had forced her to watch her husband suffer. With the rope wrapped around his left arm, Ryan cut the last rope and carefully lowered her gently to the ground. As her head touched the surface, he shimmied along the branch and gently eased her body lengthwise to the ground. Feeling the tension off her body, Carol immediately curled up into a fetal ball.

Breathing a little easier, Ryan straddled the branch and surveyed the forest and campsite. The Mitchell's gear had been ripped apart and strewn everywhere. It wasn't until he started to wiggle his way off the branch that he noticed the strange claw marks above where Carol had been hanging.

Confused but driven by his immediate duty, Ryan tied off his rope and repelled down it. Before getting to the ground, he pushed himself away from the trunk of the tree and vaulted over Carol.

Landing on his feet, he went over to Carol and rolled her into a sitting position against the trunk of the tree. With his knife, he cut the sleeping bag's draw string that was tied around her neck. The sleeping bag dropped to her waist revealing the upper portion of her naked body. Like her husband, she too was stripped before being tied up.

Covering her body were scores of scars and bruises of various ages and colour. Almost all of them were in areas that would normally be concealed by pants and a long sleeved shirt. On her back were long thin strips that revealed that she had been repetitively whipped over a long period of time. Long sharp claw marks were etched into both of her shoulders, and three more red, puffed stripes adorned the side of her face. Wrapped in duct tape, her hands rested on her lap.

Despite never being gagged, she remained almost silent. Vibrating her head about with her mouth slightly cracked open, Ryan could barely hear her moans. Her long, brown, unkempt hair tried hard to conceal her sunken, blackened eyes. Her ribs stuck out through her wide flattened breasts that nearly draped down to her stomach. Instead of being in her early thirties, she could have passed for someone in their late sixties.

Despite a cool breeze, Carol made no attempt to cover herself. Ryan got his jacket from the canoe and carefully put it on her, one arm at a time. Glancing at Kerry, he felt that he only knew a small part of the story. As he zipped it up, he asked, "What happened here? Who did this?"

Staring into his eyes she repeated, "Bat, blood, bat, blood, bat, blood," over and over.

"What do you mean? Someone with a baseball bat, cause bats can't do this."

In a more frantic tone, she repeated even louder, "Bat blood bat blood."

Confused, Ryan stepped away and assessed the situation. He had to get the Mitchells to the lake. Kerry's massive size meant that Ryan had to leave behind his backpack and almost all his gear. After finding a rotting, hollow tree trunk a short distance from the camp, he stuffed his rifle, food, equipment and supplies into it. To hide it, he piled bushes over it and covered all his footprints leading up to it with pine needles.

He shoved his radio, night-vision monocular and sidearm into a water-tight compartment built into his canoe. Besides the hunting knife strapped to his side, all he had left were the supplies he could stuff into his pockets and the small pouches on his belt.

As he carried his canoe around the trap and placed it along-side the water, he glanced towards the Mitchells and told them, "We have to leave as soon as possible." He might as well been talking to himself. Kerry was still unconscious and Carol was nothing more than a zombie.

Ryan grabbed Kerry under his armpits and dragged him to the shoreline. Leaning the canoe slightly onto its side next to Kerry, he rolled his comatose body into it. The momentum of his gluttonous body flipped the canoe upright and slid it further into the water. Kerry's weight bottomed out the canoe and held it steady. Ryan then pulled and jerked Kerry under the yoke in the centre of the canoe in an attempt to even out the weight before wrapping the survival blanket back around him.

Even with most of the rocks covered in a thick layer of slippery algae, Ryan had to use all his strength to pull the canoe into deep enough water for it to float. His eyes and shoulders twitched as the canoe scraped against the rocks. "It's no wonder that your canoe was so huge. You needed a cargo canoe just to keep you afloat." Gazing at Carol, he added, "How did your husband ever expect to paddle his way through this, it gets even worse downstream?"

Trying to gently coax Carol into the cold water didn't work. After glancing at Kerry, he decided to change tactics. At the top of his voice, he yelled, "What are you waiting for? Get out here right now."

He didn't want to yell at her so sternly, but speaking softly didn't get any reaction from her at all. Straining to hold the canoe still in the fast water gushing out of the trap, he watched her stand up and walk straight towards him while clinging to the unzipped sleeping bag he had wrapped around her. As she tripped over a rock, he grabbed her with his right hand and guided her into the front of the canoe.

After getting into the back, he steered the canoe while the current propelled them down the creek. As Carol turned and looked down at her husband, Ryan blurted out, "You two are lucky I found you. By nighttime that meat would have drawn in every bear, cat, coon, skunk, wolf, and anything else around. I don't know why it hadn't drawn them here before now. You're awful lucky."

Ryan looked at the marks on Carol's face as she gazed through the tree branches as they passed by them. "Was it a large cat that attacked you?"

She slowly shook her head and said, "Bat, blood," in a shaky, frightened voice.

After an hour of hard paddling with the current, he had to stop the canoe. In calm open water, it could safely hold close to a half a tonne. However, in the fast, shallow water the bottom of the canoe was starting to scrape against the rocky waterbed. Ryan stopped the canoe and jumped out. It only rose a few centimetres, but that was enough to get it off the creek bottom. As the creek widened and got shallower, the canoe began to rub some more.

Looking back at Carol, there was no response. Ryan let go of the front of the canoe and forcefully took the sleeping bag away from her before lifting her gently out. Even the weight of her slight frame was enough to lighten the load and keep the canoe off most of the rocks.

Ryan pulled and guided the canoe around the bigger rocks, cringing every time he heard the smaller stones rubbing against the hull's finish like course sandpaper. As he rounded the bend, the creek got narrower and the water deeper. As the current pushed the canoe to his side, he gave out a sigh of relief, "Finally." Panting, he grabbed the canoe with one hand and splashed water over his face to wash off the sweat with the other.

Standing there, he looked back at Carol as she slowly rounded a bend. Watching her fumble and at times crawl along the slippery creek bed, Ryan decided to tie the canoe to a branch and help her. Unable to carry her over the slippery rocks without increasing the risk of both of them falling, Ryan put his arm around her and helped her walk towards the canoe.

On his own it would have taken him an hour to get to the small lake. It ended up taking them well over four. Despite them being late, the plane was nowhere in sight. With sweat pouring off him, Ryan decided to steer the canoe under the shade of an overhanging tree. As he wiped his forehead, he looked at Carol. She was shivering. Her teeth were chattering even with his coat on and the sleeping bag wrapped around her. She appeared so frail.

She must have been in terrible physical condition well before they had entered the park. A person doesn't get that anorexic unless they had been sick or starved for an extended period. Even though the strange scratches were fresh, the majority of the dark bruises covering her body were much older.

Realizing that both his map and waterproof notepad were still in his backpack along with the equipment he had left behind, Ryan reached ashore and cut off a hunk of birch bark from the tree they were resting under. Using his pen, he sketched out a map to where he found the Mitchells. Satisfied the map was accurate and easy to follow, he splashed water on his face and neck to cool himself off. Then all that was left to do was swat a few black flies while monitoring Carol and Kerry's condition and waiting for the plane to arrival.

A bright red, twin engine plane with a pair of wide yellow stripes along its wings and down the length of its body caught Ryan's eye. By the time Marq circled around and landed, Ryan had paddled over half way out to meet him. He had known Marq's long before he got his pilot's licence. By the time Marq had taken over his uncle's business, the two of them had become best friends. At least, as close as Ryan had to one.

As the canoe approached the plane, a paramedic standing on the pontoon grabbed the bow of the canoe and secured it to the plane. The wind blowing across the lake caused both the plane and canoe to bounce around in the waves.

Before the rear of the canoe was secured, Ryan began to bellow, "Get Mrs. Mitchell in first. She's in extreme shock and somewhat delirious. Mr. Mitchell's entire body is severely sunburnt. He's also been castrated and has started to show signs of hyperthermia. Lying unconscious in cold water for over four hours has drastically dropped his core temperature. He has also suffered both facial and mouth injuries."

Looking down at Kerry, he added, "Believe it or not, he's even heavier than he looks. We are not going to be able to manhandle him onto the plane. You are going to need to winch him aboard."

Marq helped steady the canoe while the paramedic assisted Carol into the plane. It was hard for Marq to miss seeing the water seeping through the cracks in the canoe. "We can strap your canoe to the plane and take you back with us."

Ryan smiled at him. "I'll be fine."

Marq gave out a chuckle while telling him, "Are you sure? I can come back and get you if you want me to."

Ryan grinned as he passed Marq the map that he had drawn. "Why?"

"Because as soon as we move this guy, I think you're going to discover that you have a major leak."

"Nah, it's nothing to worry about. You know me, I'll have this chunk of wood patched up and still have time to paddle home and put the kettle on before you can get back."

Marq shook his head. "You had put a lot of time into that canoe. If I knew that you were just going to take it out and wreck it, I would've bought it off you for a few bucks."

"Believe me, it was never my intention to use it to haul a lard ass down a shallow creek."

Continuing to shake his head, Marq could only smile. Neither one of them would ask for help, unless they were left with no other choice. "By the way, Mrs. Mitchell is clinging to your jacket, you ain't going to get it back for a while. It's a good thing it's wasn't your nice one."

"What can I say? I was out fishing and wanted something a little more flexible for casting."

"Anyway, you need a coat. It's getting late and we're going to have a good downpour tonight. Take mine 'til I see you next. You'll need to keep warm."

Marq tossed his coat at Ryan's head, forcing him to catch it. After exchanging a brief chuckle, Marq looked at the map and put it into his pants pocket without any questions.

Ryan rolled up Marq's coat and stuffed it under his seat. "Your coat will be waiting for you at my cabin next time you come by."

"If not, I'll take yours."

After wrapping a sling around Kerry's chest, the paramedic grabbed his arms. Ryan helped push and manoeuver Kerry from under the canoe's yoke. As Kerry's torso was lifted into the air, his legs splashed in the water almost capsizing the canoe. Marq carefully controlled the custom-made winch. The extendable aluminum boom was designed for loading generators and heavy equipment in and out of the plane. With Kerry's limbs flopping about, he was much more awkward to get aboard and required everyone to pitch in and help.

As Ryan untied the canoe, he heard Marq yell, "I hope this doesn't become a habit. See you later and keep it safe, or as safe as you can possibly keep it."

Ryan yelled back, "You keep it safe too." As the side door was being shut, he could hear someone screaming inside the plane, "God, he's been butchered worse than a pig!"

"He's your problem now." Ryan looked down at the steady flow of water that was gushing out of the long gouges in the bottom of the canoe. "A good batch of hot pitch should patch that right up." Raising his head and looking around, he added, "If it makes it ashore."

Chapter Six

Messages

Without Kerry's gelatinous body plugging up the cracks, a steady stream of water rushed into Ryan's canoe. Spotting a mixed grove of spruce and birch trees along the shore, he paddled as fast as he could towards them. The fuller the canoe got, the harder it was to paddle it through the choppy water. By the time he got to the large rocks that protected the shoreline, the waves were starting to come over the gunwales. The only thing that kept the canoe afloat was the wood it was made from and the air trapped inside the water tight storage compartments that Ryan had built into both ends of it.

Submerged in the cold water, Ryan's legs started to go numb. As soon as he got within throwing distance to shore, he tossed his paddles and Marq's rolled up coat as hard as he could. A gust of air caught the coat, unravelling it in the air and draping it over the side of a bush.

After breathing in a couple deep breaths, Ryan filled his lungs and squeezed his mouth and nose shut. In one fast rocking motion he ducked his head into the canoe and flipped it upside-down in the water. Slipping the canoe's yoke across on his broad shoulders, Ryan slowly lifted the canoe out of the waist high water.

With the water removed, he flipped it upright and began to drag it towards the shore. Between the greasy, algae covered rocks that lined the bottom of the lake and his cold, shaky legs, it was hard for him to keep his footing. As a wave lunged the bow of the canoe forward into his back, his foot slipped off the side of a slippery rock and he fell under the water. While popping back to the surface, another wave smashed the side of the canoe against his head. Wasting no time to shake it off, he inched his way closer to shore.

With the cold water dulling his senses, his left foot slipped between some algae covered tree roots and became snared. The harder he tried to force his foot out of the cris-crossed web of tangled roots, the tighter it was wedged in place. Grabbing the side of the canoe with both hands, he released a strong push and drove the bow of the canoe onto shore. After a couple deep breaths to prepare himself, he dunked his face under the water. Using both hands, he slid them down his leg spreading the roots apart. He worked his fingers around his heel and extracted his foot.

Once ashore, Ryan retrieved Marq's coat and quickly wrapped it around himself. The caribou hide coat that he had sewn together for Marq was a warm blessing. While it was hanging on the bush, most of the water had drained out of the thick, water-repellent fur on the inside of the coat. Despite being submerged, the tanning oils combined with the fuel, grease and engine oil that

Marq was constantly spilling on it made the exterior of the coat waterproof.

Using the coat like a protective blanket, Ryan stripped off his soaked clothes and tossed them on top of a small cluster of bushes. Out of the cold wind, he sat on a fallen tree and rubbed his legs and feet. After some of the colour returned to them, he stood up and looked around as the cold evening air started to creep in. Not used to the smell of the oil and fuel embedded into the coat, his stomach tightened and his head felt a little dizzy. Back at the plane, he had considered tossing the coat back at Marq, but he knew he needed something to keep warm, even if it smelled horrible.

Three years earlier, Ryan and Marq had enjoyed a very successful fall hunt. Marq usually donated his kills to a local native charity, but that year Ryan talked him out of it. With Marq's help, Ryan tanned the hides and over the winter, he cut and sewed the various pieces of the two almost identical coats together.

Looking closer at Marq's coat, he smiled as he spotted a nick he made in the arm while cutting it out. He had tried to covered it up by overlapping part of the adjoining piece. Each caribou hide was barely enough for a coat, but Ryan had taken his time to salvage what they needed.

As he breathed in some fuel fumes, he thought of the hours it took to sew all the pieces together. He smiled and shook his head as he muttered, "Too bad mine is still hanging in my cabin."

With his core temperature getting closer to normal, Ryan slipped on his boots and started to gather some firewood. Above him he could see the faint outline of a half-moon between the cracks of the approaching dark, rain clouds. With the little sun that remained, he knew that he had to hustle.

With a pile of tinder and dead branches beside him, Ryan got on his knees and opened the survival pack on his belt containing; a 15 piece multi-tool, a compass, whistle, small flashlight, reflective metal mirror, a magnesium firelighter and a foil blanket. Ryan pulled out the firelighter. After making a small tinder nest from the paper-like bark of a birch tree and old pine needles, he shaved a tiny cluster of magnesium flakes along its edge. Then he struck the firelighter's striking bar with the back of his knife until the sparks made the magnesium flakes sizzled and burst into tiny flames.

With a little blowing and coaxing, it blossomed into a small inferno that demanded larger and larger twigs and dead-wood to quench its growing appetite. With the fire covered with a mound of larger wood, Ryan stood up and thought of what he had to do next. Chewing on a hunk of soaked venison jerky that Marq had left in his coat pocket, Ryan scanned his surroundings for anything he could use.

Next to the fire, Ryan suspended a long stick between the branches of two trees and hung his wet clothes on it. Wearing Marq's coat and his wet shoes, he began to work on his shelter for the night.

It took him only fifteen minutes to find a large, fallen birch tree that was suitable. Its pliable bark would provide most of the material he would need. After using his hands to clean out the wet, doughy wood from the centre, the tough bark was left intact. Next, he cut the bark into two large V-shaped sections that were longer than his canoe. Using his knife and the saw on his multi-tool, he cut down a couple of medium sized fir trees. Twisting several of their branches together, he formed a crude travois to help carry the bark back to his camp.

Unlike his socks and underwear, his pants and shirt were made from quick-dry material and were almost completely dry. After refuelling the fire, he quickly put them back on.

Ryan cut off the entwined branches of the two small fir trees and spread them neatly into a long, soft pile that would keep him off the ground while he slept. Above the pile, he propped the two long poles into a notch in a tree. After spreading the base of the poles slightly apart, he leaned the first sheet of bark on one side with its slightly curled upper edge wrapped around the first pole. Inside he placed some firewood on the bark's curled bottom to keep it dry overnight and help stretch the bark and hold it in place. He repeated the process on the side closest to the fire using a shorter piece of bark, leaving a gap next to the tree to use for an entrance. After resting the bow of the canoe into the same notch as the poles, he had completed a small, crude shelter the length of the canoe and slightly wider.

For the first time, he stopped and examined the extent of the damage to the canoe's scraped and gouged hull. His heart dropped as he thought of how quickly all of his hard work was destroyed. Even the bow's watertight compartment had a small crack in it. Some scrapes ran down almost the entire length of the canoe, while others were short and penetrated deeper into the hull. The worst gash was almost half a metre long. Considering all the damage, he was just lucky that the canoe had held together.

After stuffing the base of his shelter with brush to help prevent insects and small animals from freely entering it, he took a heavy-duty nylon bag out of one of the canoe's water tight compartments and walked into the woods. The only natural light he had to work with was from the few stars and moonlight that made it through the dark clouds and thick forest canopy. Ryan took out his small flashlight and shoved it in his mouth, between his cheek and teeth. With a corner of the bag tied to his belt, he had both hands free to pry blobs of resin off the sides of pine trees, and pulled out long strands of spruce roots that were buried barely beneath the surface of the thin soil.

After finding two suitable rocks with slightly concaved tops, Ryan positioned them next to the fire. Sitting next to warmth and added light, Ryan split the spruce roots lengthwise into thin, strong, pliable strands. With limited emergency rations and not knowing how long it would take him to get back to his cabin, he used some of the strands to make several quick rabbit snares along the paths that he had spotted while collecting firewood.

With the Mitchell's ordeal at the forefront of his mind, he used half of the split roots that he had left to rig crude alarms around the camp. He also knew that a campfire could draw in unwanted visitors and he wanted to be prepared. By fastening strands between bushes and low hanging dead branches, he created a criss-crossed web around the camp. The lines were loose enough to absorb the natural sway of the trees in the wind, plus bounce around to help snare the leg of any would-be intruder that tried to step over them. After pounding stakes into the ground with a rock, he fastened both the bark and canoe in place. Luckily for him, spruce roots were plentiful. Tying several strands together to achieve the length he needed, he lashed his makeshift shelter to the ground.

As Ryan sat down to put a couple more pieces of wood on the fire, he spat on the concave rock. His spit began to sizzle and evaporate away. The rock was finally hot enough to melt the pine resin without burning it. After placing some resin on it, he got some of his emergency rations out of the bow compartment of the canoe. It didn't matter if his homemade pemican got wet, it was mostly made of fat and that was what Ryan was really after.

Knowing that it wouldn't take an excessive amount of heat to melt it, he place a small chunk of pemican on a piece of birch bark and laid it on the second rock next to the fire. After mixing pieces of crushed charcoal into the resin to strengthen it, he picked up the bark and carefully poured a little fat into the mixture to make it less brittle. Before putting the melted pemican back down, he used a stick to separate the leftover pieces of dried fish from it. He then gathered up the small pile with his fingers and ate them.

Laying the blade of his hunting knife across the edge of a cedar stump, he tapped the tip of the blade with a rock until a flat piece of wood broke off of it. After a few cuts and slices with his knife, he had a wide spatula that he could use to work the resin mixture into the cracks of the canoe. He used a smaller piece of cedar to help load the mixture onto the spatula and over to the canoe without any excess spillage. He had to work fast. The cool night air hardening the mixture within a couple minutes.

Where the roots ran across the cracks in the canoe, he simply wedged twigs under them and lifted them away from the hull so they wouldn't adhere to the resin. In the deeper gouges, he had to embed pre-cut, resin-coated pieces of wood to help plug them and stop the hot mixture from pouring out through the cracks. Coated strips of birch bark were laid across the hull in areas where added rigidity was needs. As the last of the fat from the pemican was mixed into some bubbling resin, he looked over at the canoe with mixed emotions. All the holes had been sealed, but it would never be the beautifully crafted work of art it once was. The long black lines and patches of resin covered bark had permanently scarred both the exterior and interior of it.

It started to drizzle as Ryan finally crawled inside his shelter. He took solace in the fact that it was lined with all the dry fire-wood he would need for the next morning. The soft fir boughs kept him off the ground and he was happy to have a dry place to sleep.

It was about one in the morning when the drizzle had turned to rain and extinguished the fire. The forecasted hard downpour had finally arrived. Ryan briefly woke up and without opening his eyes, smiled at the comforting sound. He knew that normally, both predators and prey avoid leaving their shelters during a heavy downpour.

The sounds of breaking branches were almost lost over the pounding rain beating on the canoe's hull, but it was enough to open Ryan's eyes. Even with no food to attract any wildlife, Ryan knew he couldn't take any chances. Especially after what he had seen happen to the Mitchells. Two legged predators don't go by the same rules as animals.

Ryan twisted around and pulled out a couple small rubber bags from the canoe's rear compartment. One contained his revolver, the other his night-vision monocular. With the canoe's overhanging bow protecting him from the rain, he looked out of his shelter with his revolver in hand. He couldn't hear anything out of the ordinary. Resting on his elbow to steady his view, he looked through the forest with his night vision monocular. He couldn't see anything except a small bird huddled in a crack in a tree.

Alone, in the wild, a person's senses are what keeps him alive, and Ryan's were well-tuned. Despite the heavy rain, Ryan could detect the faint smell of decaying flesh. *The rain could have unearthed the remains of a predator's kill.* The rain started to pour down even harder. With the canoe above him echoing every raindrop, he felt that he was inside a drum. Not able to see or hear anything outside, Ryan retreated into his shelter and huddled under Marq's coat with his hands over his ears. The drumming continued to escalate into a deafening roar.

After fifteen minutes, the pounding rain slowed down and at the same time, the hideous smell started to slowly fade away. Ryan could feel his shelter shake as the wind picked up and rocked the large tree that the poles and canoe were attached to. He could hear the echoing of more cracking branches through the trees. Every gust of wind felled more chunks of heavy, water soaked deadwood. After another ten minutes of analysing every sound, he curled up and went back into an uneasy sleep, haunted by the pungent odour that he had smelt.

After a restless night, a bright, sunny morning came out to meet him as he lit a fire. He was still shivering from the cold, damp night air and welcomed the warmth radiating from both the sun and fire. Flaring his nostrils, Ryan was confident that the odour of rotting flesh was gone. *Maybe a scavenger had dragged it away.* Even as he thought it, he knew that he would have easily heard an animal dragging a carcass through the forest.

Feeling hungry and knowing that he had a long journey ahead of him, he checked his traps. It was worse than nothing. All of his traps were torn apart. Even the tunnels that he had carefully constructed out of brush to guide the rabbits into his snares were destroyed. On one of the roots he had used, he noticed hairs clinging to the sticky sap. "Damn it!"

After studying the area, he knew it wasn't an animal that had stolen the rabbit; there was almost no blood, and it was removed too neatly. Scavengers don't care what kind of mess they leave behind.

More scared than hungry, Ryan went back to examine the repairs he had made on his canoe. Tapped into a large patch of resin covered bark were almost two hundred small dots making up the words 'GO HOME', in bold letters. Just above the canoe was a low branch with two small sections of scraped bark. He immediately recalled the markings that he saw on the branch that Carol was tied to. They were identical.

It wasn't only rain I heard last night. Animals can't write. Someone sat on that branch and patiently waited for the rain to start pouring before they tapped out that message. Ryan looked down at his revolver. *They had to know that I was armed.*

Ryan suddenly thought of what could have happened if it hadn't been pouring rain. "If I had gone out to investigate last night, as soon as I stood up they would have been right on top of me. Armed or not, I would not have stood a chance."

On the ground next to his shelter, he noticed a few squirming maggots and a sharp tipped stone with resin covering its point. A shiver ran up and down his entire body. *Last night I was smelling the monster that terrorized the Mitchells.*

After regaining his composure, he walked around his campsite and examined his alarms. Most were still intact. Under a tree behind his shelter he found that the roots had snapped off several branches and pointed them all in the same direction. Despite knowing where to look, he also knew that the heavy rainfall would have washed away any footprints that were left behind.

Running back to the canoe, he double-checked it to make sure that it would hold together. With almost nothing to pack, it took him only a few minutes to douse the fire with wet muck, cut the roots strapped to his canoe and paddle out of sight of the camp. All he could think about was retrieving his equipment and supplies, and getting back to his cabin.

Without any excess weight, his canoe rode high out of the water and made it harder for Ryan to steer upstream through the rushing current. All the runoff from the overnight downpour had swelled the creek into a small river. The wake behind every obstacle in the creek caused the bow of the canoe to bounce from side to side. Even with all the adrenaline that was pumping through his body, it took him a few gruelling hours of hard paddling to get back to the Mitchell's campsite.

The wind, wet weather and wildlife had changed almost everything there. All of the meat that was scattered about the site had vanished. Only a few gnawed bones remained. The rope suspending the duffle bag above where Kerry had been staked was chewed away and the bag ripped apart. Several stakes that Kerry was lashed to still had rope lashed to them. Looking around the campsite, he saw some of the Mitchell's clothing hanging in a couple thorn bushes and a section of their tent wrapped around a large rock in the middle of the stream. The fast current had pushed away the cedar tree that had dammed the creek against the bank and washed the caribou head downstream. There was hardly any evidence left for the police.

Slowly walking to where he had stashed his supplies, Ryan paid close attention to the trees. Animals don't write, people do, and whoever or whatever it was that was terrorizing the area liked to climb. The bush that he had used to cover his cache was pushed to the side and everything had been taken, including his food, rifle and extra ammunition. Left in its place was a dead rabbit with a piece of birch bark attached to it. Written in charcoal on the bark was, 'GO HOME OR THIS MAY BE YOUR LAST MEAL'.

The sap on the hairs around the rabbit's neck told him that it was the same one that was stolen from his trap the night before. Most people use snare wire, rope or even fish line. But how could anyone beat him here? Outraged, Ryan sharpened both ends of a long stick. In the middle of the clearing he stuck the stick into the ground and impaled the rabbit on the other end of it. "If you are watching, you just threatened the wrong man."

It would take time for the local police to prepare and dispatch a team. He knew he had at least a few hours before they would get there. He also knew that a person threatens someone when they are either afraid, or afraid of being forced to do something that they don't want to do. Otherwise they react the way their instinct tell them to. Flee, attack, hide or stand perfectly still are all primeval instincts. A scared cornered creature threatens.

Anyone capable of doing what they did to the Mitchells could have attacked him in his sleep. He would've been almost helpless. Why would they be scared? After thinking for a moment, Ryan whispered to himself, "The fact that I was not attacked means that I have some kind of trump card that I might be able to use. I wonder what it is."

Looking around the campsite, Ryan could only think of one thing: whoever did this liked climbing trees, and was really good at it. They could creep above his shelter without him even knowing, and were strong enough to haul Mrs. Mitchell into the trees.

For some reason Ryan's mind thought about the three figures he had spotted in a large tree further in the woods when he first approached the Mitchells' campsite. *Whoever did it was probably sitting in that tree watching the campsite. The other two hanging objects were most likely a couple of sacks of stuff stolen from the Mitchells. Maybe it was an intelligent ape.* Recalling the words Carol had repeated over and over, he rethought that idea. *Bat blood. I wonder what she meant. Maybe she was trying to describe who or what did it.*

After pulling his canoe completely out of the water, he looked around for a piece of birch bark to write on. With his pen, he wrote a quick note in bold letters in case the police found the campsite before he got back.

GONE TO GET MY STUFF BACK
BE BACK SOON
RYAN LC
PS DON'T TOUCH THE RABBIT

Ryan hated paperwork and had found that writing out LeChasseur took too long. As a result, he almost always shortened his last name to LC. Walking back to the staked rabbit, he selected a hefty, crescent-shaped rock with a flat bottom. Next to the stake he tucked the note under the rock in such a fashion that most of the words were still visible. As he stepped away, he thought about all the scavengers that the strewn meat had summoned. Moving his note and the rock next to his canoe, he told himself, "They can't steal my canoe if I'm chasing them."

Chapter Seven

Jane

Sioux Lookout's hospital cafeteria was crowded with doctors, technicians and staff that were either too tired to make breakfast or were in need of a pick-me-up before driving home. Doctor Scott got in the line in front of the counter. Trying to salvage his research meant working all hours of the day and night, and sleeping on a fold up cot in his office. With a constant array of experiments underway, the brief periods he spent outside his small basement lab were kept short by the alarm on his watch. In the hospital's parking lot, the layers of filth on his truck showed the length of time he had been inside.

As rumours about two patients that were extracted from the woods reached him, he decided to leave his lab and investigate. If the rumours are correct, the couple were picked up in the vicinity of his destroyed medical facility. With talk about blood and bats, he wanted more details than hospital gossip could provide him. He needed to know if it was linked in any way to his research or not.

It was six in the morning and there were no patients or visitors in the cafeteria. Tired and cranky, some of the more vocal members of the hospital staff felt free to vent their frustrations while catching up on hospital gossip.

Near the front of the line were three chatty nurses. As the trio picked up their trays, Doctor Scott heard one of the nurses say the word 'Bat'. For a split second, the doctor froze. Despite only getting a couple hours sleep, he stood up straight and took in a few deep breaths. He was not comfortable chitchatting with people and he needed to muster up as much composure and charm as he could. One of the nurses stopped to check her wallet and several people in the line scooted around the trio towards the coffee urns. Only three people remained between him and the three nurses.

Despite the doctor being so close, amongst the multitude vying to be heard, the nurses voices were nothing more than garbled words. As the three nurses hesitated at the long selection of coffee urns, the three people that were between them and the doctor poured their coffee and left. Standing next to the nurses, he quickly poured coffee from the first urn that he came to.

Despite trying to be discreet, the doctor could still make out what Jane Arnold said to her co-workers, "The woman is driving me nuts. She keeps crying out, 'bat blood, bat blood', over and over. She even cries it out in her sleep."

Feeling a bit uneasy talking about one of her patients, Jane quickly looked around to see if anyone was listening. Disregarding Dr. Scott as he poured milk into his coffee, she whispered, "When I tried to talk to her, you know, just to see if she was feeling all right, she screamed it out again at the top of her lungs. The woman can't say anything else! It's not right but we just had to put her under. This frail, eighty pound pile of bones has all the patients in the ward terrified. I'm at wits end. I'm going to be glad when she is moved to the batty ward with the rest of the dingbats. It may be cruel of me for saying it, but getting her away from my other patients will make my job a lot easier."

As they were about to pick their seats, Dr. Scott seized the moment. "Excuse me, miss, could I have a word with you?"

The strong assertive voice made Jane think that she was in trouble. Without looking away from her tray, she gave a sigh. "What is it?"

With Jane's body partially turned, the doctor looked down at the name tag sticking out from her chest. She was a striking, svelte woman in her early thirties with black, shoulder length hair surrounding her large hazel eyes and attractive face. "Jane, I couldn't help but hear you talking about the woman that was air-lifted to the hospital with her castrated husband. Do you think she could have done it?"

Jane initially felt relief, then got annoyed. She was used to hospital chatter to break the ice that normally led into a lame pickup line. Feeling exhausted, she was about to dish out a 'buzz off', but decided to look up first and see who it was.

Doctor Scott was far from being ugly. In fact, he was quite the opposite. He had been a common topic of idle chatter amongst the nurses, including Jane. His tall, slim build along with his handsomely chiselled face greatly outweighed the fact he was in his mid-forties. Since he arrived at the hospital, he was like a mysterious ghost that walked through the halls without talking to anyone.

Before the doctor's arrival there was a tremendous upheaval. It was as if the hospital's needs were brushed aside to make way for his research. To empty an entire lab for his specialized equipment, they had to squeeze theirs into the other already cramped labs. Despite causing all the turmoil, his medical reputation along with his mysterious background kept everyone there in awe. It was abnormal for a small, remote hospital to have such a skilled and distinguished medical scientist on staff, even if he spent most of his time cooped up in his own private lab.

It took only a few seconds for Jane to shake off the shock of him speaking to anyone outside his lab, let alone her. "No. No, absolutely not." She tried to regain her composure before conceding, "You must think that I'm some kind of blubbering idiot."

Trying to be as charming as he could, Dr. Scott smiled. "Not at all."

Jane's face turned slightly red. She couldn't look at the doctor as she continued to answer his question. "As you've probably overheard along with the rest of the cafeteria, I think the woman is a basket case. She couldn't tie her shoes without help."

With a small chuckle in his voice, the doctor replied, "So you think she has the mental capacity of a preschooler. Have you ever been to a schoolyard? Kids can be very vindictive. A diminished mental capacity doesn't automatically make a person innocent."

Dr. Scott's flippant remark made Jane bite her lip and take a deep breath before forcefully answering, "You didn't see her bruises. That woman was abused to the point that she had regressed back into a child. Right now, she is nothing more than a walking zombie."

The doctor's face turned sober. "You must know your patient pretty well." Seeing people staring at them, he extending his hand and added, "I think we got off to a bad start, maybe I should have introduced myself. I'm Doctor Michael Scott, the researcher that took over the corner lab in the basement." With a smile, he added, "I take it that you are the dingbat's assigned nurse?"

With her head tilted to the side, she looked up at him half smiling and answered, "Yeah, she's been under my care since she arrived."

With both hands holding his tray, he used his elbow to point to an empty table. "Would you like to sit with me? I have found your troublesome patient's case very interesting."

Jane looked over at her two friends. "Do you mind?"

One of her friends looked the doctor over like he was an elegant diamond necklace. Her other friend was more discreet and only bounced her eyebrows a couple times before replying, "Go head, we'll be fine."

Turning back to Dr. Scott, she told him, "Sure, why not?" Jane walked behind Dr. Scott to the table. Glancing back at her jealous comrades, her raised eyebrows, enlarged eyes and wide grin signalled her delight. Knowing that they would be still watching them walk away, she wiggled her hips just enough to make sure they got the message.

As they sat down, the doctor told her, "I remember seeing you before. You were working in the lab when I first came to the hospital. So, what is your medical background?"

Dr. Scott was not accustomed to small talk, but he wanted Jane to feel at ease. If you want good reliable information from someone, they need to trust you, even if they shouldn't. He saw the way she blushed and the way her friends rushed her off. In the past, several women had tried to get between him and his research. Most of the times they distracted him from his work and were nothing more than a nuisance, but sometimes they were useful tools. At that moment, he needed to pump all the information he could from the attractive, awe-struck female sitting in front of him.

"I was a lab tech for almost eight years. With all the jobs being shuffled during the restructuring, I transferred to the floor. They still call on me now and then when the lab techs gets swamped."

"So indirectly it's my fault that you are not in a lab?"

"No, it was my choice."

The doctor smiled as he asked, "Didn't you like it?"

Feeling like she was in a job interview, she politely replied, "Sure, but I just needed a break from it. It was getting pretty mundane."

"Would you go back?"

"Someday, depending on what I would be doing there. Doing the same tests over and over again made me feel like a robot. It's not like doing research."

Seeing Jane getting tense, the doctor shrugged his shoulders and smiled. "Research is not much different. You do the same thing over and over, change the test slightly and repeat the entire process. The only thing different about it is that you have some control over what changes you make."

Jane rocked her head back and forth while she chewed. "I guess you are mostly right. There is a lot of repetition in research too, unless you get lucky."

After a few bites, Dr. Scott looked at her. "I almost forgot why I asked you to sit with me." He never really forgot but wanted Jane to think that her charm was getting to him. "I know we are not supposed to discuss cases, but I was interested in some of your patient's background. Do you know where they found her?"

"I guess that isn't against the rules. That has nothing to do with her medical condition. I know they picked her up in the park somewhere east of Savant Lake."

The doctor smiled and took some time to think. After nodding a few times he looked into her eyes as he asked, "You wouldn't happen to know which pilot picked them up?"

Jane was mystified by the doctor's strange question and was slow to answer. "No, but I guess I could find that out easily enough."

The doctor wrote his personal cell phone number on the bottom of his card and passed it to her. "This is my private number. I would appreciate learning anything you know about her. Any information about her background and medical history could help in some of the research that I'm presently doing."

The fact that he gave her his personal number caused her face to glow and turn her cheeks pink. Her colour quickly returned after she realized what he was asking. Looking down at her plate, she asked him, "How could it help?"

After he finished chewing his food, he swallowed and replied without any change in his voice, "Part of my research has to do with various kinds of mental and physical trauma. Your patient has obviously encountered both."

Knowing that the doctor was extremely secretive about his work, Jane didn't want to question him any further. Looking down at his private number, she smiled. "That she has."

Dr. Scott filled the rest of the meal with small talk about the lab equipment that Jane had operated and her other hospital duties. Jane's background and intellect began to stir the doctor's interest.

Engulfed in hospital chatter, neither of them had finished eating as one of Jane's friends came over to the table. Paying more attention to Doctor Scott than Jane, she smiled as she bent over and told her, "You are going to be late for your shift."

Jane looked as her friend's cleavage jiggled in front of the doctor's face. As her face turned a bit sour, she glanced at her watch. Three quarters of an hour had flown by. "I'm sorry, I gotta go." After taking a large gulp of coffee, she got up and started to pick up her tray.

"Don't worry about your tray, I'll get it for you." As the words left his mouth, the self-reliant doctor was shocked that a simple nurse could manipulate him so easily.

"Thanks, but I can drop it off on my way out."

As she left the table, he smiled at her and asked, "Will I see you around sometime?"

"Maybe."

Walking away, she butted her hip against her friend's. "Keep your girls in your shirt, it's me he's interested in." Flashing his card for her friend to see, she added, "He even gave me his personal number."

Seeing the playful grin on Jane's face was all the answer Dr. Scott needed. Within an hour, Jane had dropped an envelope into the slot outside his door containing much more than the doctor asked for.

Jane had given him Carol Mitchell's entire medical history along with copies of all the recent tests her doctor had ordered. Within two hours, the doctor had either wrapped up or abruptly terminated all the work he had on the go and left the hospital.

Chapter Eight

Willy

With no clear tracks to begin his hunt for the true culprit, Ryan had decided to work his way through a solid wall of thorn bushes towards the tree where he first saw the three mysterious objects. It had taken him a half an hour to hack and wiggle his way through the twenty-plus metres of long, sharp needles before he finally reached it. After tossing the sticks he had used to the ground he looked back at the bushes. Shaking his head, he said, "I'll never do that again."

He found the remains of two rain flattened mounds of faeces under the limbs that the objects had been resting on. Standing beside the largest pile, he looked up and saw the limb were the biggest object had been. The other deposit was much smaller and a little further away. *They must've spent a long time up there. Maybe the wind shifted and blew some of its scat a little further away?*

With a stick, Ryan poked apart and examined the excrement. The colour, texture and consistency of the two mounds were completely different. Unlike most wild animals, neither had any bones or hair in it and their scat showed they had very similar diets. Puzzled, he looked up into the tree. The answer wasn't there, just more questions.

He walked back and forth through the woods trying to find any sign of a clear trail. The rain along with the other wild creatures had destroyed any chance he had of finding one. Not wanting to go back through the wall of thorns, he tried to circle around them. About a hundred and seventy-five metres downstream he came to a small clearing. Beyond a hedge of thorn bushes that was nestled beside the trunk of a fallen tree, he could hear rushing water.

Partially hid behind a large boulder, on the northern edge of the clearing he noticed a sleeping bag draped over a branch and secured in place with rocks. With his gun in hand, he stepped into the clearing and circled around the boulder. Despite all the bindings and tape that covered a quarter of Patrick's face, Ryan had no problem recognizing his lifeless head sticking out of flimsy shelter.

Ryan smiled as he knelt beside his unconscious adversary. "Patrick, what ever happened to you?"

When Patrick failed to respond, Ryan checked him for any signs of life. With his fingers pressed against the veins in Patrick's neck, he felt a faint pulse. His breathing was very shallow. After holstering his weapon, he looked under the sleeping bag and saw his chest slowly moving up and down. Looking at

Patrick's stomach, he cried out in horror, "Who could have done this to another human being?" A moment later, he felt uncomfortably delighted that the victim was Patrick. "Boy, I hope someone recorded it. I would have paid to see it. For what you put me and my partner through, I would've been there front and centre."

Standing up, Ryan gazed into the forest and saw the branch of the same tall tree. "Whoever committed this was keeping a watch over both Patrick and the Mitchells" Getting out his radio, Ryan called the station. Before he could get a response he heard a splash in the water. Dropping to the ground, he went for his gun.

It was barely out of its holster when he looked up and saw the broad brim of an Ontario Provincial Police hat above the brush. Corporal William Stuart stood up in his canoe and peeked over the brush. "Hello, Ryan. It seems that you are a trouble magnet. Is this the Mitchells' campsite?"

With only half of the officer's face visible, Ryan shook his head. The ugly scars on the left side of the officer's forehead instantly gave him away. "Willy! What are you doing in the park? Ain't you out of your element here? There is laws against harassing wildlife like you do people."

Ryan had gone to school with Willy. People sometimes mistook them as kin; both Willy and Ryan had the same dirty blonde hair, same size, muscular build and wide cheek bones. However, that was where the likeness ended. Willy was a bully and liked playing cruel games. In the dark they looked so much alike that Ryan was blamed for a lot of Willy's pranks. At times Willy would deliberately wear the same cloths as Ryan in an attempt to deflect his misadventures.

Squinting his eyes, Willy yelled out, "Just answer the bloody question!"

Feeling in no mood to bicker, Ryan sharply told him, "No, this isn't the Mitchell's campsite, I'll take you there later. Right now I need help here. I found another victim and he's barely alive."

Willy's face turned red. "I'm wearing the badge. I give the orders, not you."

"This isn't the time to renew old grudges."

Hanging onto some branches with both hands to steady the canoe, Willy's partner stood up. As it rocked back and forth from the water hitting against it, he asked, "What's the problem?"

Ryan told him, "I got Patrick Leer here and he needs medical help."

Before he stopped talking, Willy had clawed his way through the prickly brush. As he got to his feet, he asked, "Are you sure he's alive?"

Willy's concern caught Ryan off guard. "Yes, I checked his vital signs as soon as I got here. He's still alive."

Willy pushed him aside saying, "You just stay put. Don't go near him, I'm taking over."

As Willy removed the sleeping bag, he had to swallow the lump in his throat. Except for a short section next to Patrick's stomach, most of the extracted intestines had dried out and looked like a piece of grape vine. Body fluids were leaking out of the holes in the dead skin created by hungry maggots.

Willy bent over and worked the stakes around Patrick's head back and forth before the damp ground allowed him to pull them out. After removing the duct tape, he touched the flashlight casing in Patrick's mouth. To his surprise, Patrick opened his eyes.

Slowly removing the casing, Willy was relieved to see Patrick take a breath. He glanced at Ryan, then back at Patrick. "Who did this?"

Patrick had heard everything. Rolling his head to the side, he saw Ryan wearing Marq's coat. Their two coats were both unique and he hated both of their owners, Ryan for doggedly pursuing him and the high-flying Marq for acting as his snitch. Closing his eyes, Patrick rested a moment before muttering. "Ryan, did you think you would get away with everything that you have done to me? Pay back is going to be a bitch."

Willy turned to Ryan with a gleam in his eyes and a smile that covered half his face. "It's not hard to figure out what happened here. You never did like Patrick, did ya?"

Ryan had no doubt about how Willy would handle the situation. Willy hated him even more than Patrick did. Before their senior prom it was just dislike, but afterwards every time he looked into a mirror it festered and grown into pure hatred.

******

Despite Willy asking Natalie Hutchison to the prom a number of times, she had accepted Ryan's invitation instead. To get even, Willy and two of his buddies had decided to bushwhack Ryan after the prom was over. If they had been sober, Ryan wouldn't have stood a chance.

Natalie was on the prom committee and had asked Ryan if he would stay to help clean up the gym. His untimely delay drove the trio to drink harder and harder. As the lights in the gym started to go out, they started to believe that he had slipped by them. By the time Ryan and Natalie finally left the dark school, the trio were drunk and could barely walk.

As Natalie unlocked the door of her father's car, Willy and his two comrades tried to rush Ryan. Even with Willy busting the bottom of a beer bottle and using it like a knife, it wasn't much of a fight. In a flurry of punches and a few well placed kicks and punches, Ryan knocked the three drunk teenagers back into the ditch they had crawled out of.

With a torn shoulder and sleeve on his rented suit, Ryan turned towards his car. Behind him, Willy had crawled back out of the ditch. Ryan heard the metallic click of Willy's knife as his thumb locked the blade into position.

Quickly turning around, Ryan rotated his right leg and smashed his foot against the left side of Willy's face. A few sharp shards of the broken beer bottle had gotten embedded into the sole of his shoe and tore apart Willy's cheek.

The force of the kick rolled Willy down the side of the ditch. He never let go of his knife. As he tumbled down he accidentally stuck it into his thigh.

Looking over the side of the ditch, Ryan saw him trying to get to his feet. With blood smeared over half of his face, Willy pulled his knife out of his leg and pointed it at Ryan. With blood pouring out of his leg and face, he yelled out, "You can't hide from me. You'll pay for this."

Willy was in the hospital for over a week for what was reported as a bear attack during a camping trip. He had no opportunity to retaliate. Parks and Recreation had already accepted Ryan's job application and had sent him to a wilderness training camp. By the time his training was over, Willy and his friends had found jobs in Thunder Bay.

******

Despite all of the years that had gone by, Ryan's gut started to tighten as he saw Willy rub the scars on the side of his forehead. Ryan had no idea what the other officer was like, but the stripes on Willy's arm told him how things would play out. As Constable Andrew Brown was finishing his way through the tangled brush, Ryan saw Willy unfasten his holster and extract his pistol as he turned around.

To Ryan, those few seconds felt like minutes. Everything was in slow motion. Knowing what was coming, Ryan flipped backwards onto the thorn bush only an arm's length away from the young native constable.

Marq's tough leather coat shielded him from the sharp thorns as a shot rang out over his head. He could almost see the second bullet make its way between his legs as he rolled over the bush and into the water. Willy's third shot went wild.

Aided by the swift current, Ryan quickly swam, pushed and pulled himself downstream. Behind him Willy's voice echoed through the woods. "Ryan, you are not going to get away from me this time."

Ryan yelled back, "Find someone else to railroad, or even better, do your job and find out what really happened."

The constable glanced at Willy's enraged face but was afraid to say anything out loud. Turning to wards Patrick, he stepped backward.

Half swimming and half crawling with his hands and legs, Ryan scurried downstream. The fast flowing current aided his speedy escape. Instead of running into the thick bushes and putting distance between them, he decided to wait them out. He knew that with Patrick to look after they would not have much spare time to chase after him.

Ryan slipped under the water and crawled behind a log that was half submerged underneath the dark shadow of an overhanging pine tree. Draped with weeds, only Ryan's face appeared above the water. As Willy splashed around looking for any trace of him, he walked within an arm's length of Ryan.

Out of frustration, Willy Smacked his pistol against the surface of the water and bellowed out, "Damn-it-all, he got away! The water probably carried the creep half way to the lake by now."

Glancing at his partner, he added, "Andy, call dispatch and inform them what is going on. Make sure you tell them that Ryan LeChasseur is our chief suspect and he is still at large."

Ryan could hear both of the officers talking as he sneaked through the forest on the opposite bank of the creek. Constable Brown was concentrating all of his attention on Patrick, while Willy rambled on endlessly about Ryan, almost completely flip-flopping their childhood misadventures. His account of the prom night was also twisted. In his version, he was the one leaving the prom and got injured while protecting Natalie from a jealous Ryan and a bunch of his drunken friends.

Ryan shook his head. *That's right. Point the first finger to make your story gain credibility and make them question the truth, just like you always have. It has always been the other person's fault. That uniform hasn't changed you at all.*

Ryan knew that the only witness was Natalie. Her father owned the clothing store that had rented him his suit. After examining the torn jacket smeared with blood and pants reeking of alcoholic vomit, she was forbidden to see him. Even after he paid for the suit, he was considered a trouble-maker by her close-knit family. The heartbreak of losing Natalie had made him seek the solitude of the wilderness park. After time, he grew to love the freedom of living on his own.

Using the rustling of every breeze that flowed through the trees to conceal his slow, methodical movements, Ryan made his way back to his canoe. With the yoke of the canoe resting on his shoulders, he carried it across the fast-flowing creek. The noisy rushing water acted like both a sound buffer and a physical barrier between him and the officers as he methodically carried the canoe past them.

While patiently sitting under the canoe, he waited for the wind to pick up to help mask any noise he made during his portage. He could hear the rushing water and the subtle sounds of wildlife. Their presence comforted him. There was nothing roaming the forest scaring them away.

After completing a wide circle around the officers, he got into his canoe and paddled downstream towards the lake. With Willy involved in the case, he knew that he could not rely on the police. Willy would try to pin anything and everything he could on him. Ryan also knew that he needed to find whoever or whatever tortured these people in order to clear himself.

With Willy pacing back and forth scrutinising everything he did, the constable started to prepare Patrick for transport. Willy was much better at using his mouth instead of his hands when it came to any emergency. While watching and criticizing the constable's work, his overbearing attitude slowed down their progress. Disappointed, he studied the surrounding forest as he told his partner, "Now this is what I want you to put in your report."

As the frustrated constable gazed up at him, he spewed out, "So now you are telling me what I saw and heard?"

With a wide grin on his face, Willy told him, "That is exactly what I'm saying, and if you want to keep that uniform, you better do what I tell you. If our stories differ, who do you think that they are going to believe, a rookie or a seasoned veteran? I'll cremate you."

Chapter Nine

The Lake

With the current pushing Ryan's canoe down the creek, all he had to do was steer and paddle around the obstacles in the way. Believing that he might have overlooked some clues, he wanted to return to his makeshift campsite and look around. From working with the police on different occasions, he knew that he may have only three, maybe four hours before they could get to the lake, so he had to hurry.

A few minutes after Ryan got to the lake, he looked up and noticed a small plane in the far distance. Taken by surprise, he paddled to the lake's eastern bank and jumped into the water. Placing rocks in his canoe, he lowered it just below the water line. The air sealed in its water-tight compartments kept the canoe slightly buoyant and off of the rocky bottom, while the waves distorted the outline of the canoe.

Decades of pounding waves had undermined the soil on that side of the lake. It left behind an overhanging canopy of tree roots and other vegetation along the shore. The rain had risen the water level in the lake. It was high enough that Ryan could drag his canoe behind him beneath the protection of the canopy. In some places along the bank, the waves had hollowed out caverns that were completely dry under low water conditions. Ryan knew of a large cut-out, midway along the lake that was big enough to conceal both him and his canoe.

As Ryan worked his way along the bank, he thought about the sanity, or insanity of whoever had mutilated Kerry Mitchell and surgically gutted Patrick. *What would a person like that be capable of if they were cornered?* Ryan knew he had to find that out for himself if he wanted to prove his innocence.

Making his way along the bank, Ryan crawled, walked and even swam using a gentle sidestroke, while towing his canoe behind him. He never allowed more than his head to show above the water at any time. In areas where Ryan had to venture away from the shore, he found that the overhanging tree branches protected both him and his submerged canoe from being sighted from the air. Even then, he only breathed in the valley of the waves as they cascaded over his head. He was virtually invisible to anyone in the air. As he approached a huge rock that gently sloped into the lake, he was forced to stop. He had run out of cover.

Ryan piled more rocks into his canoe and forced it to the bottom of the lake. After tying the tow rope to some thick tree roots, he crawled ashore. Hiding behind some thick brush under a big maple tree, he watched the plane circle the lake.

The water wasn't unusually cold for that time of year, but cold enough to drop Ryan's core body temperature. He had to fight the urge of chattering his teeth as he shivered. After wringing out as much water as he possible could from his clothes, he huddled under Marq's heavy coat to retain all the warmth he could. At the same time it helped protect him from the hordes of mosquitoes.

The markings on Marq's plane were unmistakable as it landed in the choppy water less than a hundred metres of Ryan. Wondering if Marq may have come back for him, he stood up behind the heavy foliage as the plane's side door opened. Seeing that it definitely wasn't Marq standing in the doorway, Ryan dropped to his knees and retrieved his compact binoculars from one of a pockets in his belt.

Wearing military combat fatigues, a large muscular man with his face smeared with camo paint filled the wide opening. As the man untied the two camo coloured canoes strapped to the plane's pontoons, Ryan could tell that it was Duncan Stuart. The smeared paint covering his skin had smoothed over the scars he had accumulated since their last meeting and made it easier for Ryan to recognize him.

Duncan was a local war hero. Along with many of the locals, Ryan read all about his military career in the newspaper, including his lengthy obituary. He was supposed to have been tragically burnt to death in Afghanistan during a rescue mission.

Duncan may have been born Willy's older brother, but he wasn't anything like him. He was always a serious, steadfast rock that acted more like a machine than human. After he had joined the Canadian Special Operations Regiment, no one heard from him, not even his parents. Rumours of his death slowly trickled throughout Sioux Lookout. Most deaths in his outfit normally never made it to the newspapers. After his family was discreetly notified, even with no body to mourn, they held a small wake for him at the local legion. Because of Willy, Ryan felt that he should not attend.

As Duncan held the first canoe steady. Two soldiers with backpacks, pistols on their belts, assault rifles slung over their shoulders and carrying long duffle bags full of gear, climbed out of the plane and got into it. Through his binoculars, Ryan noticed the absence of both the Canadian flag on their shoulders and any sign of rank. After a brief chat with Duncan, the pair pushed away from the plane and paddled to the far shore.

As soon as a deflated pontoon boat was slid out of the plane, Duncan pulled a red line to self inflate it. Another soldier jumped out and helped Duncan position the inflating boat into the water. When it was fully inflated, the soldier hopped into the raft and attached an electric motor. Duncan passed him a large battery. After it was connected, a soldier in the plane handed Duncan several bags and boxes, and he then passed them to the soldier in the boat.

When the gear was secure, the soldier in the plane helped a woman dressed in blue jeans and a puffy red coat onto the pontoon and into the boat. Her curly, long brunette hair whipped across Duncan's face as she squeezed by him.

By the way he looked away, it was clear to Ryan that Duncan was not impressed with her. As the two soldiers fussed over getting the young woman situated, Duncan helped a wiry elderly man into the boat. Dressed in the kind of hunting fatigues that most sporting goods stores sold, he looked out of place.

After the three departed in the pontoon boat, the last soldier unstrapped the second canoe that had been attacked to the plane's undercarriage. Through his binoculars, Ryan saw Duncan go to the doorway of the plane. After a heated conversation he clamped his hands on the sides of Marq's face. Ryan watched him try to break free. *So why did you bring them here?*

As Duncan and the last soldier pushed off in their almost overloaded canoe, Marq quickly collected all the loose ropes and straps before getting in.

In total disbelief, Ryan watched as the three craft made their way towards the makeshift campsite where he had stayed the night before. *Marq probably had seen where I was heading and knew where I would set up camp.* Ryan knew that Marq would not tell anyone if he felt it would get him into trouble. They were too close for that. *Maybe the soldiers got lucky and spotted it from the air.*

While waiting for the plane to leave, Ryan thought, *Why would they be looking for me? Maybe they know who's really responsible for what happened to both the Mitchells and Patrick?*

He was even more confused after he saw that as soon as the first canoe got close to the shore, it tossed off over half of its cargo and headed towards the mouth of the same stream that he had came down. Protected in the shadows of the overhanging trees, even with binoculars they were hard to spot. *They couldn't be helping the police dressed like that, could they?*

Ryan suddenly realized that Duncan once fished in the lake and was probably aware of the cavern he was trying to reach. With that ruled out as a refuge, he tried to think of where else he could go. On land, a person is fairly easy to track. Duncan had always been a good hunter and an exceptional tracker.

With his body still trying to warm up, Ryan knew that he could not afford to spend an extended period of time in the water. On the far side of the sloped rock was a large newly toppled cedar tree. The tip of the tree was submerged in the water and its dense branches covered the entire trunk. The back half of its twisted, semi-unearthed roots stuck out of the top of the bank while its sides and front section stubbornly clung firmly to the ground. A person could not even get a good look at the tree without getting into the water.

After taking his pen out of his pocket, Ryan pulled out the ink cartridge and placed it back into his pocket. With the pen's hollow shaft in his mouth, he made his way back to the water. After untying the canoe, he removed a few rocks from it and placed them into his pockets.

With the canoe lifted slightly off the bottom and the rocks forcing his body under the water, he used the hollow tube from the pen to breathe through as he crawled on his back around the rock. Between every other wave he methodically spit the water out of the tube and breathed in until he got to the toppled tree.

The tree's wide, dense branches completely concealed the bank. Beneath its protective cover, Ryan removed the rocks from his pockets and then the canoe. As it rose out of the water, he twisted the branches to its sides and used the saw of his multi-tool to cut off the larger ones that refused to bend.

After creating enough space for his canoe, he took off one of his boots and used it as a bailer. Before it got entangled in the tree, he climbed through the branches and wiggled into the canoe. As Ryan finished bailing it out, he adjusted its position and trimmed off some more branches.

With the canoe securely lodged in the tree, he stripped off one piece of clothing at a time, wrung it out and hung it on the branches to dry. His green uniform blended nicely into the tree's branches. With the saw of his multi-tool, he cut off some of the small dense branches from the underside of the tree and laid them inside the canoe. That gave him a place to sit plus insulated the bottom of the canoe from the cold water. After twisting a long limb parallel to both the tree trunk and the canoe, he looped its end around a couple other branches and trimmed it bare.

Over the bare limb he laid Marq's coat inside out to help drain off the saturated interior fur. The edges of the coat slightly draped over the sides of the canoe, allowing the water to drip into the lake. The coat also provided him the added protection he needed from the cool breeze that filtered its way through the dense branches.

The past two days had shaken Ryan worse than he thought. He had gone from enjoying a pleasant fishing trip to running for his life.

Needing to get his mind focussed, he started to clean his revolver. Slime, mud, small floating debris and water had penetrated every part of it. Using twigs and chunks of cloth cut off the tops of his socks, he cleaned and inspected it thoroughly. He needed it to be in good working order. Ryan took his bullets out of the plastic watertight bag that he had put them in before getting into the water. The metallic clicking sound of the first bullet being injected into its cylinder was like a shot of smooth whiskey to his nerves.

Ryan's mind wandered. *Why did they want to scare me away from his campsite and how did they beat me back to his supplies? ... There could be more than one involved, but how many? It doesn't matter. ... Someone out there was brazen enough to tap a message on my canoe knowing that I was sitting under it with a loaded gun. That's the one I need to go after.*

Ryan was used to being the hunter, not the prey. How can he hunt for the person or people responsible for what happened to Patrick and the Mitchells when he's the one being hunted?

Despite insulating the bottom of the canoe with more dense cedar boughs, Ryan knew that he couldn't afford to slip into hyperthermia. He needed to regain some of his body heat. Even though the material in his uniform did not retain water, it still collected in its seams and Ryan could feel the moisture as he put it back on. His boots, underwear and socks were still damp, so he left them hanging.

With deep breaths, he huddled with his arms around his legs. His head started to spin from the loss of body heat. After vigorously rubbing himself all over, some warmth began to return to his body. With all his reserves used up fighting the cold, hunger pangs began to growl inside of him.

Fish love to hide beneath fallen trees. Ryan, like most fisher-men, searched for places just like this. Looking over the side of the canoe, he saw the odd fish swim by.

Ryan wasted no time in fashioning a short fishing spear out of a trimmed branch. At the thickest end he worked his knife length-wise twice to created four spines. After weaving a strain of bark in and out of the splines to spread them apart, he wrapped it around the outside to help prevent them from breaking off. Sharpening and notching the ends of the splines were his finishing touches before the spear was ready to use.

Two of the spear's splines had broken off before Ryan finally stabbed a fish on his ninth try. It wasn't huge, but a nice sized perch would be enough to stop his stomach from growling. He kept it pinned against the lake bottom until all of its fight was gone. It came out of the water without any unwanted commotion.

It only took him a half a minute to gut it. After preaching to tourists about the dangers of drinking water that beavers could have been swimming in, eating something raw from it made him quiver. After twisting his body around to face the bank, he wiggled as close as he could and began digging into the damp soil. It didn't take him long to create a shelf big enough to make a small fire on.

With a dry abandoned bird nest and a pile of dead twigs he made a tiny fire about the size of a small ashtray. Except for the few feathers from the nest, the fire gave off almost no smoke. What little smoke that it did give off was easily dispersed by the dense branches above it.

Ryan placed a large rock on both sides of the fire along with a few smaller ones in front of it to hold in the heat. The skewed fish rested above the fire between the two large rocks. Almost no heat was wasted. By slowly feeding the flames with small dry twigs the size of matches, he kept the tiny, almost smokeless fire going. It was barely hot enough to cook the fish, but it did the job.

Using his fingers, Ryan ate while watching the group across the lake as they quickly finished setting up their camp. After they draped camouflage netting with brush sticking in it over two large tents and three smaller ones the campsite almost disappeared. If it wasn't for the fact that Ryan knew exactly where they were, he would not know it was even there. "These guys are definitely not here to help the police."

As the sun was going down, Ryan watched the canoe return to the camp. No fires, lights, music or anything that would attract attention could be seen or heard. After the canoe was covered with camouflage netting stuffed with weeds and branches, it too vanished from sight.

Ryan looked at his watch. Time had flown by quicker than he had thought. *Where are they?* It was almost eight thirty. It was getting too late to safely land a plane on a small, relatively unknown lake. *Either they had problems transporting Patrick, or Willy needed more time to plant evidence against me.*

Ryan took out his night vision monocular from the canoe's front compartment and opened the sealed rubber pouch he kept it in. Trying to save his batteries, he only periodically turned it on to scan the camp and surrounding area until he eventually fell asleep. He woke to a faint clicking sound on the huge rock that sloped into the lake. The windless sky made the water calm and branches still. In the eerie silence, every sound echoed around the lake.

Trying hard not to create any sound, Ryan peaked through the branches. What looked like a bear was dunking its face into the water at the edge of the rock. He saw the creature lean back and roll its outer coat off its shoulders. Its thick furry coat fell to the ground behind it and revealed a strange, hairless, deformed body unlike anything he had ever seen.

The moonlight lit up the clear sky and bounced off of the creature's pale naked skin. After dipping the long hair on its head into the water, the creature flung it back over its head, spraying water over the huge, ugly, pinkish-red growth that stuck out of its back. With its head tilted all the way back, Ryan could see the creature's large human-like breasts sticking out of its chest.

After wetting down its back a dozen or more times, the cold, soothing water drew some of the redness out of the growth and turned it pink. The ghastly growth was shaped like three entwined teardrops. Two started past the tail bone and formed large circles at the shoulders. The third looped opposite the others. It started at the neck and went between the others and formed a round flat bumpy loop that reattached itself to the base of the creature's tail bone. As the growth cooled, it began to move as if large snakes were slowly crawling around beneath its surface.

As the creature stood up, the fur that it was wearing rolled off the bottom half of its hind legs. With the creature's long hind legs revealed, Ryan knew that what he thought was a bear-shaped creature was actually a deformed human. The creature threw its arms and head up into the air and shrieked out an echoing painful howl unlike anything he had ever heard. Ryan spread apart a couple branches to get a better look.

In a battered, tearful voice, the creature whimpered, "What's happening to me?"

The shock of the soft female voice coming from the creature made Ryan flinch and cause the branch that he was holding to snap. She turned and Ryan got a good look at the face and naked body of the deformed young woman.

Claraicy growled in a low course voice, "Did you enjoy the show, pervert?"

After a flurry of growls and screams, another wild echoing howl rang over the lake.

Chapter Ten

Reconnaissance

The first eerie howl made the hairs on the back of Constable Brown's neck stand on end. On a clear night he used to enjoy hearing the sounds of howling wolves. But that wasn't a wolf. Propping himself up, he looked around.

Willy was sound asleep with a wide smile on his face. On the far side of him, the constable could see Patrick staring into the sky. Hanging from a stick stuck in the dirt beside him was an intravenous drip restoring his depleted fluid levels. A large bandage covered what was left of his extracted shrivelled intestines.

Not knowing he was being watched, Patrick cast aside the pain he was in. With a devilish grin on his face, he started to tap his fingers on the top of his chest. As a series of snarling growls ended and a strange howl reverberated over the lake, he could hear Patrick softly whisper into the night, "Howl while you can. It's not over yet."

******

The wild howl had also caught Kurt DeGroot's attention. In the still night air, he heard the snapping branches, grunts, growls and muffled screams echoing across the lake. The violent ruckus only lasted for about a minute. That gave the alert sentry plenty of time to aim and focus his infrared binoculars on the huge, sloping rock on the far shore. Even from that distance, he managed to catch a glimpse of the creature releasing its final howl and disappear into the woods.

Before the echoes had stopped ringing, Duncan was kneeling beside DeGroot. "DeGroot, what was it? Did you see anything?"

Duncan's sudden appearance didn't distract DeGroot away from the far shore. Replying in the similar low voice, DeGroot calmly replied, "Yes, it came from across the lake. If you look to the right a ways you can see a large rock formation sloping into the lake. That's where I spotted it. At first, I thought it was a bear but it stood up and ran upright with what looked like a blanket or something on its back. It looked too human to be one the creatures we are after. It could have been a drunk camper. From this distance, I can't be sure."

"Could it have been Sarah?"

The last time he had seen Sarah, she was a furry, half human hybrid with a cat-like face. DeGroot slowly replied, "I don't know, maybe."

"When we circled the lake, we never saw any evidence of campers. Keep both eyes open and stay alert. That sound wasn't from the throat of any animal or human I've ever heard before. Sarah may have survived the blast. We'll need to check it out at first light."

DeGroot quietly replied, "Yes, Sir."

Duncan crawled back into his tent and closed his eyes. Through an ear jack he listened to the police chatter over his radio. With most of the transmittance being unrecognizable static, he started to doze off.

About four-thirty in the morning, he caught the ending of a clear transmission. 'Corporal Stuart and I can have Patrick Leer ready for transport by nine a.m.. Our camp is at the north end of the lake in the sheltered inlet behind a rocky peninsula. Have the pilot contact us to let us know when we should start paddling out to meet him. In Patrick's condition, he can not be stuck in a canoe for any length of time.'

"Willy!" Duncan shook his head and got out of his sleeping bag. Running over to another small tent, he unzipped its door and shook Andrew Drake's feet. "Drake, describe the two police officers you spotted up stream."

Drake sat up in his sleeping bag. After blinking a couple times to clear his eyes, he answered in a calm, monotone voice, "One was a clean shaven, young, native kid that looked like he lived in a gym. He was around twenty-two or three, just under six foot. The other officer was taller, about six-four, big white guy with brown curly hair, a real mouth piece, you know, lots of attitude. He had an ugly scar on the left side of his face. That guy has a real mean streak in him. Using my scanner to eavesdrop on them, I overheard him ordering the kid to back up his story. When the kid tried to refuse, he grabbed him by the neck and almost lifting him off the ground. I don't know what happened in the bush, but that poor kid pissed his pants."

"Did the tall mean one look anything like me?"

After gazing at Duncan's face for a while, Drake responded, "Yes sir, but with a lot less scars."

Duncan grinned. "That's my brother Willy for yah. That badge hasn't changed him at all." He stood up and paced back and forth a couple times before adding, "What about the injured man with them?"

"He looks stable enough to travel. It was odd though, he and your brother seemed like old pals. They were really chatting it up when the young kid wasn't around. If I had a little more time to properly set up my equipment, I could've overheard what they were talking about."

Duncan put his hands behind his head and looked up into the night sky. "Brother, brother, what are you up to now? If you weren't a cop, you probably would be running from them."

"From what I could make out, they want to frame someone they referred to as LC for everything. I don't know who he is, but they both hate this guy's guts."

The police officers' campsite was hidden from view by a long, narrow peninsula jutting out in a semi-circle in front of the mouth of the stream. The time the officers needed to paddle around the peninsula would be enough for the soldiers to stop what they were doing and hide. In the dark, Duncan and Drake quietly paddled to the peninsula and hauled several bags of gear to the top of a rocky mound.

Looking across the inlet at the sandy beach next to the mouth of the creek, they saw the police campsite. The young constable was sitting next to the fire, nervously sipping on a cup of coffee while the others appeared to be sleeping. In the still morning air, any sound they made would echo across the still water. With a few hand gestures, Duncan signed out his final instructions to Drake and left. Before he took his second step, Drake had already started setting up his equipment.

As soon as Duncan got back to camp, he asked, "DeGroot, any more chatter over the radio?"

"Yes sir, they are flying in some more officers."

"Shit! This mission is quickly getting a lot more complicated."

Duncan sat down and poured himself a coffee. "Go and wake up the queen, and try not to disturb the doc, the old guy needs his rest. I'll keep an ear out for the cops."

Wrapped in a red, silk housecoat Doctor Ann Kukan stormed out of one of the bigger tents in a huff. In a low gravelly voice, she blurted out, "What do you bloody want this time of the night?"

As her voice echoed around the lake, Duncan turned and faced her. "Tone it down. Your voice is echoing all over the lake. Do you want everything scrubbed?"

Standing behind Duncan as he sat on a log holding his coffee, she replied in a quiet defiant voice. "Fine."

"Okay then." After taking a sip of coffee, he told her, "It's almost morning and we're going to have a bunch of unwelcome visitors. I want you to be awake and alert in case the camp is spotted. I can't have you wasting time putting on your makeup if we have to evacuate."

Duncan turned away from his coffee cup and saw her shapely, bare legs for the first time in the three months he had known her. They were normally hidden under loose fitting scrubs and a lab coat. His eyes floated upwards. With her hands planted on her hips, they pulled her housecoat into her narrow waist and popped out her well developed curves. Even her curly long hair was far from the tight bun she normally wore in the lab.

Duncan's cold eyes stared into hers as he added, "I'm taking Ratlin and MacNeil with me to investigate an incident that happened last night. We may have gotten lucky. We have to act now or maybe lose an opportunity to catch the phantom creature. A clean trail is easier to follow than the tales of ghosts and made up rumours that we have been blindly investigating since the facility was destroyed. I already posted Drake as a spotter to give us some advance warning of any police movement. DeGroot's staying behind with you and the doc to oversee everything here. So please, don't do anything stupid to give us away, and put on something less conspicuous. This isn't a bullring."

Without giving Ann any time to answer, Duncan took her left wrist and started to squeeze it. "If we are spotted, make sure that everything that can identify the project is wired to all go up at once. Our company is due around nine. To be safe, have everything ready by eight."

Ann stared into Duncan's icy eyes as he released his grip. Duncan had always frightened Ann with his unyielding, mechanical manner. As she rubbed her wrist she replied, "That's over two hours away. All the pieces of equipment have incinerating devices hardwired in them. It is just a matter of connecting the wires to a timer and flipping a few switches. That'll take only about fifteen minutes, so what's your problem?"

"You! You and that red flag you're wearing shouldn't be here."

Duncan watched her walk back to her tent. Back in the lab, it was mainly her smooth, pretty young face that was distracting. Without her baggy clothes and lab coat to hide behind, her well proportioned body seemed to invite men to dream about running their hands all over it. The few extra pounds she carried only smoothed out her curves in all the right places.

Duncan looked over at DeGroot. His head rocked back and forth to the rhythm of Ann's hips as she walked away. *She shouldn't be here. She's either going to get us caught or someone badly hurt.*

Before dawn, all three men piled into one canoe with Duncan sitting in the middle. As the others paddled, his binoculars were glued to his eyes as he looked for any signs of their elusive prey. As the sun started to peer over the tree tops, Ratlin and MacNeil drove the canoe onto shore.

Duncan stepped out into the water and walked ashore with a finger resting against the trigger guard of his rifle. After experiencing what had happened at the Devil's Claw, he didn't want to be caught off guard. Besides their weapons, all three of them were carrying backpacks, full belts and stuffed pockets. Knowing how volatile things could get, they carried everything they could possibly need. As Duncan and MacNeil scouted ahead, Ratlin rammed the blotched, camo painted canoe under some bushes and cut some tree branches to cover the protruding end of it.

Over his headset, Duncan updated Drake. "We're ashore. Let everyone know if you hear or see anything... Good... Keep out of sight."

Duncan and MacNeil swiftly proceeded along the bank towards the sloping rock. It offered no protection or cover. Feeling exposed, they quickly went to work looking for any signs and tracks that they could find. The gentle undulating waves bounced around the fallen cedar tree lying in the water at the far edge of the rock. The tree's strange and awkward movement had caught Duncan's attention.

As he started to walk towards it, a trail of dark red droplets running across the rock distracted him. In a shallow depression midway across the rock, he saw a large, dark pool of blood the size of a small dessert plate. As he stood over the pool, he noticed a clear blood trail leading into the woods.

After swiping his finger in the blood, he held it up in the air. As he turned his finger towards the sunlight, he could see the faint twinkle of a minute golden speck. With a wide grin on his face, he turned to MacNeil and whispered, "It's her. It has to be her."

The pair followed the blood trail to the edge of the woods, where Duncan stopped to study a broken branch. The coarse break had pulled out strands from the middle of the branch and twisted them clockwise. "It's as if someone had tried to pull themselves up with it. Whatever she fought last night was capable of defending itself and gave us a decent trail to follow."

MacNeil queried, "I wonder what it was?"

With his eyes combing the forest, Duncan answered, "Does it really matter?" Turning to face MacNeil, he blurted out, "Cover up the blood with some dirt and pine needles. We don't want the cops to spot it."

Duncan returned to the blood on the rock. Kneeling down, he scraped as much as he could out of the small dark pool into a vial. As he capped the vial, he glanced at MacNeil. "Some modern detectors can identify blood from the air. Pile rocks over the larger puddles."

Duncan ran and met Ratlin as he approached the rock. Handing him the sample, he said, "Take this to the queen and have her test it ASAP. We're going inland to look around. As soon as she knows anything at all, radio me immediately. If the sample is clean, I don't want us to be wasting time searching for anymore ghosts." With a smile on his face, he added, "But this time, I don't think we will be."

******

In the quiet morning air, Claraicy's keen hearing picked up Patrick's screams as the two officers picked him up and carried him over to the canoe. From under the protection of the forest canopy, Claraicy grinned and whispered, "Sucky baby. Next time I won't be so nice."

******

Ratlin was three quarters across the lake when he heard Drake broadcast, "They just put their canoe into the water. You got about ten minutes before they can get around the bend."

Ratlin quickened his pace. With a wide wake forming behind him, the canoe's bow rose out of the water. As he was about to ram into the shore, he quickly leaned back and bounced the bow of the canoe over the bank. DeGroot was right there to grab the bow of the canoe and help him get out. As he raced towards Ann's tent, DeGroot draped a camouflage netting stuffed with branches, grass and leaves over the canoe. He then he kicked pine needles over the canoe's skid mark.

Doctor Stern stood in front of Ann's tent as Ratlin approached. The tall, thin, elderly man spoke up. "What's going on?"

As he scooted around him, Ratlin put his forefinger against his lips. DeGroot ran to the dumbfounded doctor and escorted him into the big heavily concealed tent. Wearing a hospital gown and her hair tucked under a surgical cap, Ratlin found Ann eagerly waiting in front of a table full of equipment. "I overheard some of the communications. Tell Duncan it will take a while before I can give him any results, but I will work as fast as I can."

******

Duncan saw the outline of his brother's large frame as the canoe entered the main body of the lake. It had been years since he last saw him. As the plane began to circle the lake, looking for the best way to land, MacNeil patiently sat beside Duncan beneath the grove of young birch trees. The foliage overhead combined with their dress made them virtually invisible to anyone on the plane as it circled and landed.

Inside his carefully concealed hiding spot, Drake watched the plane taxi closer to the inlet. He quickly readjusting the settings on his gunstock mounted, eavesdropping microphone and pointed it at the planes side cargo door. With most of the engine sounds muted out, he heard the men inside getting ready to depart.

******

Patrick's complaining and rants got louder as the canoe transporting him got closer to the plane. "I'm coming back to get you. This isn't over yet."

Curled up under a dense cedar tree, Claraicy could hear every word Patrick uttered. Every syllable tore dark festering gouges into her heart and fragile mind. All of her efforts were spoiled. She wasn't able to kill either of them. She saw herself as the same weak, stupid kid she always was. Nothing had changed but her appearance. It would be just a matter of time before the two men renewed their hunt. Neither of them could afford for her to leave the forest alive and reveal what she knew about them.

As rage built up inside her, she told herself, "Next time, I won't be so timid. Next time, I'll stay 'til the very end and make sure it's over."

******

Through his binoculars, Duncan watched as four officers loaded their equipment and supplies into their canoes to make room in the plane for Patrick. As they hauled him aboard, DeGroot relayed everything Drake overheard. Comments were made about Patrick's surgical nightmare, their plans to hunt for Ryan, and about the investigation of both the Mitchell's and Patrick's crime sites. Duncan gave out a small chuckle when he heard that Willy was volunteering to lead the hunt for Ryan. "Run, Ryan, run. Willy has finally got you right where he always wanted you—at the other end of his pistol."

After studying the paper that came off the printer, Ann tapped on the doctor's shoulder. Seconds passed before he looked away from the microscope and accepted the paper. Pointing to two spikes on the graph on the top of the page, Ann questioned, "I've never seen these in a blood sample before."

"Not to worry. I've seen similar spikes before."

"Well I haven't."

Doctor Stern looked at her blank face and coldly told her, "As things progress, I'll fill you in some more. For now, you know what you need to know."

Ann looked up at the roof and forcibly replied, "How can I do my job if I don't know what is going on?"

Dr. Stern smiled and shook his head. "Dr. Scott hired you for your DNA expertise, and I brought you out here because you know how to setup and run these machines. That's all." The doctor turned serious. "Now, did any of the DNA match the samples Dr. Scott gave you?"

Ann was a bit shaken. Wanting to hide her true emotions from the doctor, she replied in a cold professional manner. "Not exactly. I found three different strains of DNA in the sample, so it was obviously contaminated. None of them fully matched Dr. Scott's sample, but one came awfully close"

"Which one of the doctor's samples?"

"The shortest strain. It was an exact duplicate except for a few extra chromosomes."

With a puzzled face, Dr. Stern inquired, "How close were the others?"

"The DNA from the human cells didn't match, but one of the samples did have some of the same strange abnormalities as the humanoid target sample had. The third one looked like it came from an unevolved species. My guess is, it was from some kind of fish. When Duncan collected the sample, he could have scraped off some residual DNA from the rock." With a bit of sarcasm in her voice, Ann added, "With a few more tests I could probably identify the species for you."

Doctor Stern snapped back, "Don't worry about the fish. Concentrate on the other two specimens."

"No problem." With a little smirk, she added, "You keep on preparing the samples, and I'll run them through the machines, but I still think it would be much easier if I could prepare my own samples."

"In time." Dr. Stern thought for a moment before adding in a subdued voice, "Believe it or not, we have a good reason to keep you in the dark. For now, we need you to be completely unbiased. Hopefully soon, after a few more tests, all the mystery and intrigue will be over."

Ann stormed out of the tent, took the headset from DeGroot and put it on. "Duncan, there were some irregularities in the test results." Ann hesitated a couple seconds before adding, "Can you please get me another sample? But this time get it from a different site. The last one was contaminated by three different types of DNA."

Duncan snapped back, "How close were the DNA strains?"

A bit shocked that Duncan would question her results, she toned down her voice. "One was fairly close, why did you ask?"

"I needed to know what my men are up against."

With the doctors keeping her in the dark and Duncan knowing much more than any soldier should, Ann realized that they were not just searching for a missing patient. After going back to her tent, she closely scrutinized the test results along with the samples Doctor Scott gave her until she came to a conclusion. *Maybe it is best that I don't know what they are searching for.*

After a couple hours of low level flights around the lake and up and down the creek, the plane finally disappeared. To Duncan's delight, it flew over without paying any additional attention to either their camp or Drake's hiding spot. With the sky clear, Duncan stood up and stretched. "Drake, the plane has probably just gone back for more fuel. What's going on from your vantage point?"

A gentle breeze ruffled the leaves on the branches fastened to the mesh above Drake, like it would any normal bush. "They are setting up their base camp by the mouth of the stream, the same site as before. Two of the new officers are still with your brother. The native kid has already gone up stream with the other two officers to investigate the crime sites. I overheard your brother and one of the officers going over all the logistics required for a massive search for Ryan. Your brother wants them to bring in the dogs, while the other officer is a lot more laid back. Your brother uses 'sir' a lot, so I think that the other officer might be the detective taking charge of the case."

"What do they have in surveillance gear?"

"I haven't seen any high-tech gear, so we should be okay using our present equipment."

"In case you didn't overhear the queen, we have to collect more samples before we begin our hunt. If any activity is coming our way, give us as much notice as possible, we may need it. The sample they analysed sounds promising. Our search may be coming to an end."

MacNeil scouted the wooded area at the edge of the rock while Duncan returned to the fallen cedar tree that had caught his attention before. A few metres from it he saw a splattering of blood on the rock next to the tree. "That's where the blood trail begins."

With all the droplets leading away from the tree, Duncan's curiosity took over. The way the fallen tree bounced around in the water seemed wrong. It wasn't until he was leaning directly over it that he saw the bow of Ryan's canoe rubbing against a branch.

Crawling down the bank, he stuck his head under the dense branches. He recognized the grease stains on the sleeve of the coat hanging over the side. "Marq ain't going to like what you did to his coat."

After breaking off a couple branches to look inside the canoe, Duncan bit his lower lip. The branches Ryan had used to insulate the bottom of the canoe were covered in blood, along with several sets of claw marks on the gunwales. Duncan could only speculate what had transpired. "Bad luck seems to follow you around every corner."

Turning towards the blood on the sloping rock, he added, "He may have got the last shot in, but I wonder who got the worst of it?"

Duncan picked up Marq's coat and examined it for clues. The only blood on it was on the arm that was lying on the bottom of the canoe. At the back of the coat, there was a small, round hole near the bottom. He instantly knew what had caused it. Ryan had a good reason to run away from Willy. His next shot may not have missed.

Duncan was studying the claw marks on the gunwales when Ratlin pulled his canoe next to him. The blood smears on the sides and bottom weren't the same colour as the sample he had taken from the rock. It was much darker and had nothing in it that reflected the light as he shone his flashlight over it.

Ratlin finally spoke. "What did you find?"

"The canoe belonging to the man the police are after. It's lodged under this tree. After we get it out, I want you to tow it as far away from here as possible. We can't search this area if it's swarming with cops. Wear gloves, the police will probably fingerprint it." Duncan thought for a moment. "Hide it in the marsh just this side of the peninsula. That way Drake can oversee everything. You can coordinate your movements through him. Make sure that you lay down a good false trail to keep the police busy for a while. That should give us a little more time."

"What if they take DNA samples from it?"

Duncan shrugged it off. "They can take all the samples they want. The creature's blood trail starts at the rock and leads directly into the woods. None of its blood was in the canoe. Any saliva they get will be contaminated as soon as you roll the canoe over a couple times to wash it out. There is tons of DNA floating around in that swamp. How are they going to separate it all?"

"What if I bump into Ryan?"

"You won't. In fact, I don't think he's going to bother us at all."

Ratlin looked the canoe over as they both put on neoprene gloves. Nodding, he replied, "Yah, I see your point."

Duncan helped him extract the canoe. Ratlin pulled while Duncan pushed it through the side of the tree. Other than a few scrapes from the tree branches, they got it out without leaving any of their own DNA behind. With the claw marks being the only visible evidence of the creature, Duncan took his knife and shaved them off the canoe. As he reached in to pick out a piece of shavings, he spotted a small wad of fabric. After closely examining it, he inquired, "He had a gun. Why didn't he use it?"

"Maybe he didn't have time to get it out of his holster."

Duncan was watching Ratlin tow the canoe away when MacNeil announced over his headset, "Duncan, I found something."

Directed by MacNeil's personal locator, he darted through the trees. The blood trail was easy to follow without the need of any special equipment. After putting his locator into his pocket, he practically ran a half of a kilometre into the dense brush before finding MacNeil kneeling next to a small red pool of blood. "Here, this is what I think caused it."

MacNeil handed Duncan the barbed fishing spear that Ryan had made. A small hunk of blood soaked skin and tissue was still trapped within the barbs along with a strange yellow excretion. "The creature must have rested here a bit and yanked it out."

Duncan pulled out a plastic sample bag and put it over the splines. After trimming the end of the spear with his knife, he sealed the bag and turned to MacNeil. "Good work. This trail may be six hours old by now, a bit longer shouldn't matter. Let's treat this creature like any other wounded animal. Let's give it some time to find a place to lick its wounds. After its muscles have had a chance to stiffen up and its reflexes are slower, we'll have a better chance of capturing it."

MacNeil wasn't happy, but knew what was best. "I'll stay here and make sure it doesn't decide to do any backtracking on us."

Duncan patted his shoulder before replying, "Stay vigilant, keep your wits and don't engage it without backup. I'll be right back."

Duncan walked back to the rock and took off his backpack. Over his headset, he announced, "DeGroot, We can't risk paddling another sample across. I'm going to shoot it over instead." Out of his backpack, Duncan pulled out a narrow tube and pointed it across the lake. "Drake, is everything clear?"

With a "You're clear" coming back, Duncan fired the almost silent, compressed air powered missile over a kilometre across the lake with a twisted stream of braided fishing line trailing behind it. "DeGroot, can you nab the line?"

"Give me a minute, it's hung up in a tree." DeGroot tied a stick to the end of a rope and tossed it around the branch that the line was snag on. With a quick tug on the rope, the branch snapped and smacked him in the face. Shaking his head, he picked up the line and announced, "Got it."

Duncan placed the sample inside a rubber container attached to the end of the line and blew it up with a few puffs of air. As its sides formed a protective football shaped shell around the sample, Duncan called out, "Ready."

DeGroot had his end of the line already fixed to a battery powered reel and hauled it in. The sample bounced over the waves and into Ann's waiting hands at the water's edge. With her pant legs soaking wet, she ran back to her tent. She couldn't wait to properly deflate it and simply sliced the side of the shell open with a scalpel. Taking out the sample, she smiled. "Tell Duncan that the sample looks terrific. Whatever it was from, it's fresh. We definitely have something we can work with this time."

Dr. Stern followed Ann into her tent. After a long forty minutes, the doctor left Ann's tent smiling and briskly walked over to DeGroot, "Tell Duncan that he has a green light. Also tell him that the DNA sample wasn't an exact match, it may have mutated. I honestly don't know what he'll be up against."

Chapter Eleven

Cat and Mouse

Claraicy crawled to the edge of a small pool of water beside a swampy area next to the lake. After scooping up and drinking a few mouthfuls with her hands, she waited for the water to settle. As the dark, debris filled puddle reflected back a hazy image of her, she ran her fingers over her face to verify what she was seeing. The strange face that stared back at her appeared too old and battered for a thirteen-year-old. Her eyes and ears were growing larger every day, and her nose was getting wider and starting to turn upwards.

Of all of her deformities, the burning lump on her back and her protruding jaw caused her more pain than Ryan's spear had. She tried to keep the burning sensation on her back under control by dousing it with cold water.

Her constantly growing jaw made chewing painfully awkward. Every time she tried to mesh her teeth, it seemed that they were sticking out further and a bit wider. Day by day, as her body changed, she felt that all traces of her humanity were being slowly replaced by this new, frightening stranger.

Every time she was about to fall asleep, she was afraid of what new changes she would wake up to. Once she got to sleep she didn't know if her nightmares were real or not. At dawn, reality sank in and the creature that she was slowly turning into would take over. A constantly hungry deformed creature that would eat anything it could find no matter how disgusting. In the forest, she had no enemies. For some reason that she didn't understand, even the predators feared her. Wolf packs, cougars and even bears would keep their distance and back away. The only reason she could come up with was that their senses were confused by her appearance and the variety of rotting animal hides that she wore.

Away from the restraints of the laws of man, she could reign havoc over those she feared the most. Despite both her neighbour and father surviving their ordeals, all traces of the power they held over her had vanished. The old Claraicy would have cowed under a few sharply spoken words. As the reality of what she had done sunk in, she knew that the old Claraicy had died over the bitter winter. Only her vivid, painful memories remained behind to haunt her.

The overwhelming, burning pain radiating from her back got worse. Claraicy could barely feel the large, open gash in her side that Ryan's spear had created. As the searing pain brought tears to her eyes, she gazed into the still dark water again. She could see the sharp tips of her ears sticking through her matted hair and extending upwards to the top of her head. "What am I turning into? Why is this happening to me?"

Jesse slowly crawled around the outskirts of the small clearing. Even she was slowly evolving into whatever her genetically altered DNA was forcing to turn her into. Claraicy extended her arms and smiled. Her face and body was turning more cat-like every day. Overlooking Jesse's deformities, Claraicy picked her up and held her against her bare chest. "What are we turning into?"

Watching Jesse suckle on one of her breasts, she added, "How are we going to survive? We are just two abominations against the rest of the world. The men out there would probably kill us without giving it a second thought. But don't you worry. I won't let them hurt us."

Claraicy stripped off all her furs and crawled into the muddy swamp, Claraicy rolled over to cool off the growth on her back. She had found that cold mud baths were the next best way for her to escape the searing pain. As she stretched out, Jesse leaped off a fallen tree trunk and onto her bare legs. Covered in mud, Claraicy floated on her back while carefully clinging to her offspring. With a full stomach, Jesse nestled her head between Claraicy's bare breasts and fell asleep.

As she floated amongst the cat-tails, her thoughts wandered to the young man who refused to run away. *Why did he spear me? Am I that hideous? It wasn't my fault that he was still there. I warned him. I never wanted to hurt him, but he wouldn't go away.*

Lying in the swamp both cooled off her back and robbed her extremities of body heat. It wasn't until her feet were so cold that she could barely feel her toes that Claraicy decided it was time to crawl out. After gathering her skins, she crawled under a pine tree and wrapped them tightly over her. Despite being cold, she felt unusually tired and weak. Luckily, with her skin caked in mud, even the insects left her alone.

The only buzzing she heard came from the flies drawn to the rotting skins. A warm smile filled Claraicy's face as Jesse crawled up next to her. "I'm glad I have you. Life would be unbearable without you."

High in a tree, a large metre long bat hung upside down, watching her. It shadowed Claraicy wherever she went. Each morning, it would always be there. Even if she could elude it during the day, it would always find her during the night. The shiny piece of metal around its neck reminded her of what happened to its mate. Even with her increased vision, the wary giant bat would never get close enough for her to read the etching on the medallion.

All she knew was that the hump on her back, along with her other physical changes had happened after she had killed its mate and its crushed bones had pierced her back. Now, its mate had become the source of her nightmares, be it bats hunting her down to drink her blood, vampires wanting to turn her into one of them or the unknown mutated creature she was turning into.

A commotion in the water woke Claraicy. Trying to get up, she discovered that her back had gotten hard and stiff. She couldn't move. She reached around and found the growth on her back had hardened into a giant scab-like shell. Grabbing the trunk of the tree, she pulled herself further under its dense branches. Curling her body into a tight ball, she hid beneath the rotting skins.

Ratlin pulled the canoe on shore only metres away from Claraicy. As soon as he stepped out of his canoe, the smell of the rotting hides forced him to peer under the tree. With his nose pressed against the inside of his elbow, he gasped, "God, what is it?" Judging from the size and shape, he came to the conclusion, "A dead, half rotten, stinking bear. That'll make the cops happy." With a grin, he added, "They are not going to be overly fussy with that odour lingering about. All they will want to do is get the hell away from here."

Ratlin had no time to waste and got down to business. With a gradual twist of her hand, Claraicy lifted the edge of one of the hides and created a narrow opening to observe him. She watched him methodically erase all evidence of him being there. Concentrating on what he was doing, he was too busy to pay any attention to the shadow gliding away from the tree above him. Within a short two minutes, Ratlin had ditched the canoe and was gone.

After getting down wind from the pungent odour, Ratlin took a breather under the shade of an overhanging tree next to the shore before calling in. "Duncan, the bait is set."

"Good, return to the rock and stash your canoe deep into the brush. Then use your locator to catch up with us. Over."

Claraicy heard every word Ratlin said. Her mind raced. *If they are using the canoe as bait for the cops, I have to get out of here before they spot it.*

Crawling on all fours like a turtle, she made it to the edge of the water. After dipping her long hair into the water, she flipped it over her head and soaked the hump on her back. It took over a dozen flips before the rigid shell loosened to the point that she could even straighten her back. Using tree branches like the rungs of a ladder, she pulled herself upright. Checking her wound, she discovered that it was already covered by a crusty scab. The dark brown scab was almost twice the size of the actual wound.

She used a stick to pick up her skins. After soaking them in the water she draped them over her back. They helped keep her hump moist along with reducing the burning pain radiating from it. With small pieces of skins tied to her feet, she started to walk through the dense forest with Jesse in her arms.

Something inside of her made her stop and look back at the canoe. Under her breath, she cursed, "Leave me alone. It was your own fault. You should've left when I told you to. You shouldn't have been there."

******

Ratlin got to the rock, picked up the canoe and carried it into the woods. After pulling out his GPS locator, he was shocked to find out that Duncan had changed directions and was heading north. Over his radio he blurted out a warning. "Duncan, you are heading straight towards the swamp where I ditched the canoe."

Duncan looked away from one of Claraicy's muddy footprints and stood up. "How easily can the canoe be spotted?"

"I didn't want to make it too obvious but from the air it wouldn't be that hard for a trained spotter to find. If they did a waterside inspection, a good pair of eyes could see it from maybe ten to fifteen metres away."

"Drake, is there any new activity that we should know about?"

Drake took his time before answering. After a quick, methodical search, he put down his binoculars and replied, "Nothing at the moment. Your brother is still at the camp with another officer. There is definitely a heated power struggle going on between him and whoever is on the other end of the walkie-talky. No sign of the two canoes that went down the creek. There has been no word about any planes returning and there is nothing going on along the shoreline. I think you are clear for now."

Duncan turned to MacNeil. "DeGroot, what kind of chatter are you picking up?"

"What we expected. The pencil pushers don't want to waste any fuel. They're waiting 'til the area around the sites is searched and fully assessed before sending out another plane. They want to know what kind of manpower and supplies are needed before they are willing to commit to anything. The new officers are also concerned about the possibility of finding more victims and what they may be up against." DeGroot looked at the sky above the lake. "The sky above you is clear, not even a vapour trail from a jetliner."

At a brisk pace, Duncan continued along Claraicy's trail. "MacNeil, we need to step up the pace."

Claraicy's trail was easy to follow. Droplets of blood and yellow puss had leaked out of from her wound at regular intervals. The colourful blotches were always on the same side of the trail. If the drops didn't make it to the ground, they were deposited on leaves or branches. If Duncan didn't see any trace of them, all he had to do was go back to the previous splatter and look a little harder. After Duncan identified them, MacNeil collected the stained twigs and leaves and shoved them into a canvas bag.

MacNeil flipped over the stained rocks and scattering mud, small stones and pine needles over all the blotches on the ground along with their footprints. He did everything he could to eliminate the trail. It was very slow and tedious work. For smudges on trees and boulders, he sprayed the stain with an oily pine solvent and dusted its sticky residue with dirt and debris. Claraicy's footprints were the least of his worry. They were so obscure they needed almost no hiding at all.

Ratlin cut through the forest trying to catch up to them. He found Duncan leaning over the spot where Claraicy had rested.

Using tweezers, Duncan picked up a few small, roundish, dark brown objects and strands of hair, and put them into individual plastic bags. Without showing any sign of acknowledging his presence, he quietly asked, "Ratlin, where is the canoe?"

"I ditched it in the bushes over..." Ratlin stopped mid-sentence.

"Three scenarios. One, our prey took it. Two, Ryan is still out there and he took it. Three, one of them sank it to prevent the cops from finding it." Standing up, Duncan continued. "If the cops had found it, Drake would have noticed."

Inquisitively, Ratlin spoke out. "What happened to the dead bear that was under the tree?"

Duncan turned to Rankin. "There were a few hairs, some dead skin and maggots lying around, but no dead bear."

"Shit. It must have been our quarry and I let her slip away."

Duncan shut his eyes and clenched his teeth before responding, "Shit happens. This was a bad location for a capture anyway. If there was any kind of resistance, the cops would be on top of us."

MacNeil piped up. "So where's she now?"

Pointing into the marsh Duncan sighed. "It stopped bleeding so it will be harder to follow, plus it has company. From the footprints in the mud, I would say that it is a small creature that is capable of walking on both two and four legs. They are not like any animal tracks that I know of. By the way they suddenly disappeared, I believe she's probably carrying it. Our job just got tougher. We now have at least two creatures to capture."

Without another word, the three worked their way through the dense brush that skirted around the marsh. Duncan spotted a chunk of damp hair clinging to some brush. He picked it off and smelled it. After handing it to Ratlin, he asked, "Is this what you smelled?"

Ratlin took the clump of hair and closely examined it. "Yah. That's what was tucked under the tree, same smell and colour."

Duncan smiled. "In that case, this may be easier than I thought. For some reason, the creature must have soaked the hides, in doing so, loosened some of the fur."

They had only gone a few hundred metres before Claraicy's footprints disappeared. A long, bare ridge of solid rock lay in front of them. With Duncan and Ratlin walking along the edges of the ridge, MacNeil navigated his way through the rocks and boulders along the top. They communicated only by hand signals. MacNeil clenched his fist in the air and froze.

A moment later, Ratlin caught a whiff of the pungent odour. Puzzled,

Duncan quietly climbed the ridge. Seeing MacNeil tapping a finger against his nose, Duncan flared his nostrils. After licking his palm, he held it in the air and tried to detect the wind direction. As the tall trees along the sides of the ridge deflected the faint breeze, he tried to carefully narrow down where the smell was actually coming from.

Duncan had just got his binoculars out of their case when DeGroot's voice announced, "Duncan, we got more company coming. No time frame was given, but they will be here as soon as they can be loaded up and flown in. They also announced that a Detective Arnold is being put in charge of the investigation. I guess he was the officer that your brother was arguing with. He has returned from the crime scene and has called for an urgent pick up. The helicopter picking him up is already airborne. An all-out search is going to be under way as soon as he comes back. Your brother isn't very happy."

DeGroot's warning blew away any chance of a quick apprehension. "Ratlin, stay here in case we missed her. She can't be far away. Remember that they will probably be using both infrared heat sensors, professional trackers, dogs and everything else in their arsenal, so act accordingly. MacNeil, you come with me. No matter what, we can't let the police find out about any of this. If any of it goes public, it could be all over."

******

Sitting in the dark, Claraicy cringed as she listened to the soldiers talk. Holding Jesse in her arms, she held her breath and tried hard not to make a sound. Her ears could pick up the soldiers' almost silent footsteps echoing through the rocks above her as the pair walked away. The next thing she heard was the sound of a few stones rolling down the side of the narrow crevice outside the entrance of the cave that hid the small cavern that she was hiding in. As Ratlin tossed stones into the cave to both check its size and stir a reaction of anything inside, Claraicy froze. As the echoes came back, Ratlin was convinced that nothing was inside the cave. He then crawled inside.

Claraicy was trapped. Every sound he made was amplified by the rocks. There was only a few metres separating them. The only obstacle that kept them apart was a flat stone. It was braced against the hole separating the cave from the small dome shaped cavern where she sought refuge.

The cavern was where she had given birth to Jesse. The highest point was barely a metre and a half high. Stuffed against the walls was everything that she had taken from Patrick, Ryan and her parents.

Fear of being trapped brought beads of sweat to Claraicy's forehead. What made matters worse was that the furs had dried out and the growth on her back had started to solidify. The longer she stayed motionless, the stiffer it got. As something inside of her hump began to rub against the outer crust, sharp creases developed and the level of pain that she was under increased. She desperately wanted to scream, but knew she couldn't. Curled in a ball, she shoved some rancid raw hide into her mouth and bit down on it.

As the pain made Claraicy tighten her grip, Jesse wiggled free. She was scared but still needed to be near her mother. She slowly curled up next to Claraicy's head. With the tips of their noses touching each other, Jesse could smell the air exiting Claraicy's lungs and felt her pain. At the same time, Claraicy smelled Jesse's youthful aroma and that gave her the strength to endure the pain.

The walls of the cavern magnified every sound. Lying motionless in the dark, Claraicy could hear everything going on around her. She made out the various sounds that Ratlin made as he adjusted his position to get better view of what was going on outside. She could even hear their heartbeats as they faintly echoed off the walls of the cavern.

Unfortunately, Claraicy could also hear the cavern's ghost. A faint moaning sound echoed from the tunnels deep beneath her. She had heard it several times before. The wind has a way of playing tricks and mind games as it whistles through rocks. This time it was different. The moans were louder and sounded more tortured, more agonizing, more human.

Chapter Twelve

Questions

A young nurse woke Kerry from his drug induced sleep. "Do you think you are able to talk to the police now?"

His eyes opened and stared at the nurse's pretty face. "Sure, I'll talk to witless Willy. I'd do anything for you." Looking around, Kerry's face turned cold when he saw Detective Jack Arnold standing next to the doctor. "Where's Willy? I thought he was in charge of after this case."

Detective Arnold spoke up. "I took it over."

The doctor put his hand on the nurse's shoulder. "Leave us and close the door behind you. I believe the patient in the next room needs his ostomy checked. Can you look after it?"

The nurse smiled at the doctor. "No problem."

The doctor waited until the door clicked shut before telling the detective, "The pain killers will make the patient groggy, however, he may be able to give you something to go on."

The doctor stepped back as the detective approached the bed. "Mr. Mitchell, I just got back from what is left of your campsite. Between the animals and the storm the other night, there wasn't much left for us to go on. Can you enlighten me as to what exactly happened to you and your wife?"

Looking into the face of the old unshaven police officer, Kerry blinked his eyes and tried to think. "I don't know you. Where is Willy? I mean Officer Stuart. I want to talk to him."

"He is still working the case, but I'm in charge of the investigation." Confused by Kerry's strangely combative response, the detective started to wonder about Kerry's relationship with Willy. After regaining his thoughts, he continued, "So what happened?"

"The damn bitch turned on me, that's what. All women are she-devils. They should be all chained up." Kerry's head slumped to the side. With a slur in his voice he muttered, "Fucking and house work is all women are good for", before slipping into unconsciousness.

The doctor stood beside the detective. "That could be the drugs talking. He has gone through a lot of physical and emotional trauma. As his body recovers, I'll be lowering his meds. In a couple days he should be more helpful."

The detective smiled and shook his head. "Under medication, be it drugs or alcohol, I've found that people tell more inner truth than they do when they are sober and have time to think about it." Detective Arnold turned to the doctor and asked him, "Doctor, I haven't seen Mrs. Mitchell yet. In your opinion, could she have done it?"

"Not a chance. She's barely a shell." Shaking his head, he added, "I've seen a lot of battered wives, but Mrs. Mitchell's case is one of the worst I've ever seen. She is neither physically nor mentally capable of standing up to anyone at all, especially her husband."

The detective opened the door for the doctor. Neither one of them saw Kerry crack open one eye and watch them leave the room. Under his breath, he mumbled, "That's your opinion."

Leaning against the wall outside the door, Willy waited for the detective. Hospital doors were designed for physical privacy, not muffling people's voices. He had no problem catching every word that was said. As the detective exited, Willy walked quietly beside him down the corridor and into the elevator.

Alone together, the detective broke the silence. "Don't say a word. I know you heard everything. If it wasn't for the fact that you were the first officer on the scene, I'd have you taken off the case. It seems like you know everyone involved in it on a personal level."

Before leaving the elevator, the detective added in a low voice, "I've made some inquiries. I know that Ryan and Mr. Leer have locked horns before. Ryan had been the key crown witness in a number of court cases against him. Up to this point, he has always done everything legally. I also know that Mr. Mitchell, and Mr. Leer are more then just neighbours. Mr. Leer was once married to Kerry's sister. I feel that there has to be something else. Something that could tie this all together?"

"I know them all because I grew up in the same neighbourhood as they did. I can help."

"That's the problem. You know everyone involved." The detective stopped and turned to Willy. "And I know that you would love nothing more than to nail Ryan for all of it. I've heard rumours about you two, and I will not allow a witch hunt. Do you understand me?"

Willy looked straight into the detective's eyes and answered, "Crystal clear."

"Good, because I have arranged for both men to be put into the same ward as one of our chaps. He will be able to record everything they say. I'll find out what happened out there, one way or another."

******

Patrick woke up in a small hospital ward without recalling being moved. In the bed next to him was a large man with bandages around his face and two younger men across from him that he didn't recognize. With tourism being such a huge industry, it was normal for the hospital to care for more strangers than locals. The large man in the next bed had his head turned away from him.

The light from the window glared off his earring. It was gold with a Santa's head dangling from it. Patrick knew of only one person that it could be. "Kerry, is that you?"

A nurse walked backwards into the room carrying a small basket of flowers. Before another word could be said, she turned around and told Patrick, "Mr. Leer, these are for you."

Putting the flowers down next to Patrick's bed, she glanced around the room, then left. Puzzled, Patrick picked up the card on the flowers. 'A friend', was the only thing written on the envelope. He pulled out the letter. Before he finished unfolding it, he heard a low, raspy voice from the bed beside him, "Pat, what are you doing in here?"

"Claraicy,..." Patrick suddenly stopped talking as if the typed words in letter jumped out at him and slapped him in the face. Stammering a bit, Patrick slowly continued, "Ohhhhh, Kerry, I, I got into some trouble with that crazy warden again."

"What? What are you talking about? What about Claraicy?"

"Nothing. For some reason I thought of your daughter when I heard your voice. First she disappeared and then you go back into the park for some closure. Now this? That area of the woods must be cursed."

The strange quivering in Patrick's voice alerted Kerry. It wasn't like Patrick to hold back his words for anyone, or any reason. Kerry looked around the room. The young native man lying in the bed next to the door seemed too restless to be under any medication nor in need of hospitalization. Even with his leg in a case and some discolouration around his neck, it didn't make sense for him to be tying up a hospital bed. Kerry carefully choose his words before they left his lips. "Strange isn't it?"

"Willy told me what happened to you. Did Ryan do it?"

Kerry thought for a moment. "Only if my wife was in cahoots with him. He could have provided her with an alibi by helping her into the tree. For all I know, he could have even been fucking her behind my back trying to get information on you. He'll do anything to put you in jail."

With various pumps and equipment running, it was easy for Andrew to change the SD cards in his recorder. Slipping the used card under his dinner plate, minutes after the tray was collected Detective Arnold was reviewing it. On his way back to the park he looked over at Willy and told him, "Something sounds fishy. Corporal, I need to know everything we have on the Claraicy Mitchell disappearance."

Sitting next to him in the helicopter Willy replied, "Yes sir. I am very familiar with the case. Kerry's mother got worried and alerted the police before he got out of the woods. In his statement he said that the battery in his phone was dead. He had spent a few days searching for his daughter before deciding to paddle out to get help. The search covered a large stretch of woods, about ten kilometres east of where that big building went up in flames last Halloween. I remember checking out the ruins in the helicopter. We had a heavy snow and the search was called off early. Both Kerry and Patrick were in the search party."

"What about Ryan?"

"Ryan was working for the park at the time, but he was nowhere in sight. That, I would have remembered."

"That works in Ryan's favour. Most criminals would want to help in the search in order to deflect attention away from them and keep abreast on what is found." The detective twisted his body towards Willy before adding, "Now, that aside, I need to know everything I can about everyone involved, including everyone associated with the Mitchell family, Patrick and Ryan."

After taking a deep breath, Willy tried to hid his frustration. "I will get Angie in records to dig it all up for you."

******

Patrick waited until a nurse helped the young officer into the washroom before passing Kerry a note. 'Claraicy is alive. She is the one that gutted me, but I told the cops it was LC. If we play our cards right, we can pin everything on him. After we are released, while they are chasing him, we can silence her for good.'

Kerry rolled the note in a ball and pushed it into a half filled can of cola. After lowering his hand to the side of the bed for no one else to see, he clinched his fingers and lifted his thumb. Seeing Patrick smile, he knew that they were both in agreement.

******

Ratlin heard the copters weaving across the sky in a typical grid pattern. After placing a small camera on the end of his rifle, he poked it out of the crevice to look around. Through a small monitor he saw a black bear with a young cub picking through some berries. Despite being only metres away and their keen sense of smell, they acted as if they didn't know he was there.

Questioning why, he held out his arm and lit his lighter. The tip of the flame curled towards him. That meant the air was travelling into the cave. There had to be at least one other opening.

After re-evaluating the cave's dimensions, he thought, *A bear could be living in here, or maybe even our quarry.* After convincing himself that if that was the case, his presence would have invoked a response.

His mind thought of other possibilities. *What if this Ryan that everyone is looking for had managed to drag himself in here? With his injuries, his trail could lead the cops right to it. If not, it might be big enough to be used as a secondary base camp.* Ratlin felt that he had no choice but to search it.

Taking out his flashlight, he looked into the cave as far as he could. After twisting the end of the flashlight to concentrate its beam, he noticed a mound of loose rocks that looked out of place at the far end. There was barely any sand, gravel or even dust on them. It was clear to Ratlin that someone had recently piled them there. Curious, he stooped over to avoid hitting his head on the low ceiling and approached the pile. As he rolled the second rock off the pile, he thought he heard someone moaning.

He stayed perfectly still and listened. Thinking that it could be Ryan and knowing that they never saw any signs of his trail, he came to the conclusion, "He might've found another entrance, but still, who piled these rocks?"

It took ten minutes for him to discover what the pile was hiding. Behind it was the entrance to a small tunnel that led inward a couple metres and then almost straight down. The echoing moans got louder as he crawled into the tunnel and stuck his head over the drop. Then he made out two muffled words: "Help me."

The two laboured words had come from someone that was in dire need. Ratlin reminded himself what his mission was, and then looked into the hole. If it was Ryan, helping him could compromise it. If it was either their quarry or a stranger in need of medical help, it was his duty to assist them. He could tell if the words came from a male of female. After weighing out his options, he yelled into the hole, "I'm coming, just give me a couple minutes."

Outside of the tunnel, Ratlin took some rope out of his backpack and tied it to the barrel of his rifle. Bracing it across the small opening, he placed heavy rocks next to its ends to prevent it from shifting and slipping into the hole. With all the air traffic overhead, Ratlin weighed breaking radio silence and letting Duncan know what was going on, verses taking his chances and dealing with whatever he comes against on his own.

"Duncan would do the same thing. He would understand." After making sure the rope was secure, he wrapped his first aid kit around his neck and crawled into the hole.

Claraicy heard everything and knew that he had discovered the tunnel. With the stiff hump on her back, she crawled on all fours to the large slab of rock and rolled it to the side. Peering out of the cavern, she saw the rope tied to Ratlin's rifle jiggle as he worked his way down. With Patrick's hunting knife clenched between her teeth, she wiggled through the opening. As she grabbed the rope, she realized that there was no weight on the other end of it. Not wanting the soldier to get out, she cut it. The rope slid down the hole. Screams echoed out of the pit followed by five gunshots, then nothing.

Claraicy smiled, "At least you are not being tortured. You got off lucky."

After shoving Ratlin's rifle and backpack to the side, Claraicy stacked the rocks back in front of the tunnel as fast as she could. Pushing Ratlin's backpack and rifle in front of her, she crawled back into her cavern and rolled the slab over the opening.

Even though her strong muscular body could withstand whatever she asked of it, the pain radiating from her back was overwhelming. It had crusted over like a giant scab. With only pin holes of light penetrating through cracks in the rocks above her, she could barely see. When night comes, she knew that she would be left in total darkness. After pushing Ryan's fishing pole and tackle box away from the pile, she gathered everything she needed and placed it all within arm's reach. Instinctively, Jesse tried to help by nudging some of the smaller things closer to her.

Claraicy could feel her neck tighten up. At first, she thought she had pulled some muscles moving the heavy rocks. As her upper back, shoulders and neck fused together into a solid mass, she knew it was something else. Working her way onto her parents' large self-inflating air mattress, she pulled an unzipped sleeping bag over her like a blanket.

As her torso slowly solidified, she began to panic. Barely able to move, she looked into Jesse's inquisitive face and started to cry. "I'm sorry. Because of me, we are both trapped in here."

Chapter Thirteen

Confusion

Ann walked into Doctor Stern's tent. "I have finally completed the rest of the tests you wanted. The yellow, slimy ooze on the barbs was fundamentally the same as egg yolk. It was full of immature developing stem cells, ripe for rapid growth." Twisting her head to the side, she sarcastically added, "It was also totally saturated with the strange cells that you have yet to explain. I'm not stupid. I know when I am being taken for a ride."

Doctor Stern looked up at her from his desk. "Give it time. What about the second sample?"

Rolling her head, Ann took a deep breath before answering him. "Under the creature's outer layer of human skin is an inner layer of skin that has the consistency of a newly hatched reptile."

Frustrated from being kept in the dark, Ann slammed her clipboard on the doctor's desk. "From what I have seen, I believe that those modified cells that you and Dr. Scott had developed have embedded themselves amongst every group of cells in its body. Factoring in the high amount of enzymes in the sample, if this had come from an insect, I would say that it was getting ready to morph. The fact that it obviously came from a humanoid mammal has me stumped."

Seeing a child-like grin engulf the doctor's face, Ann turned away as she continued her rant. "Despite retaining human DNA, some of its cells have outward characteristics from a variety of other species, some of which have been extinct for thousands of years. How can that happen?"

Doctor Stern picked up the clipboard. "Sarah, what is happening to you?"

Ann shook her head and turned to the doctor. "Who is Sarah?"

The doctor couldn't look at her as he replied. "A confused young girl, who happened to be in the wrong place at the right time." The doctor smacked the clipboard against his thigh as he continued. "It was after a saboteur had burned down Doctor Scott's first research facility. At the time, he was trying to salvage what he could of his research. When he found out that Sarah had gotten accidentally infected by the cells he had made, he decided to use her as a guinea pig."

Turning to Ann, he looked into her questioning eyes. "Right now she has almost a billion dollars' worth of research floating around in her body. That is why we are here. To find her and retrieve our research."

Ann shook her head. "I'm sorry but I don't think the sample Duncan gave me was from this Sarah. None of its DNA matches the human DNA that Dr. Scott gave me."

Dr. Stern turned serious. "Are you positive?"

Ann crossed her arms and blasted out, "You hire me because of my DNA expertise. When I tell you they are not a match, it's because they are not a match. They had different parents."

Stunned, Dr. Stern flipped through the papers on the clipboard. "This can't be. We carefully designed the second generation of modified cells in such a way that they could not survive in a foreign body."

"And I'm telling you, they obviously can."

The doctor shook his head. "But how?"

"Maybe they got cross-contaminated or somehow changed in order to accept a new host. Take AIDS for an example. It mutated and found a way to spread from monkey to man. Maybe the doctor's cells did the same."

"AIDS is a virus, not a complex living organism that quickly dies if it's not nourished by a living host. The cells we developed cannot survive outside of its designated host."

Ann leaned against the folding table the doctor was using as a desk. "I want to know what is really going on. Tell me, what are these cells designed to do?"

The doctor placed his hands over his face. After shaking his head a bit, he answered her. "Total cellular rejuvenation."

Ann stepped back. "What?"

"They are designed to identify and replace damaged cells by stimulating the production of rapid maturing stem cells. As an added bonus, they kill off and consume anything that they believe poses a threat to the host."

Ann took another step back and thought for a moment. "So they can kill off bacteria and viruses."

"Plus cancerous and old genetically deteriorated cells." The doctor turned so he could study Ann's response. "Sarah was given less then three months to live when she got infected. Amazingly, the cells had not only destroyed all the cancerous cells in her body, but also drastically shortened her recovery time. Unfortunately, she ran away before we could extract them."

Ann walked around in a circle before grabbing a chair and sitting down. "If it can cure cancer, it could be worth trillions."

With all the colour drained from her face, Ann turned to the doctor. "You also mentioned old cells. People would pay anything to be young again. If the doctor can harness the cells' full potential, they could change the entire medical industry." Feeling light headed, she sat on the floor. "So now what?"

"We wrap up the samples and ship them to Doctor Scott. He will want to test them himself. If the cells have contaminated another human, this has the potential of becoming a bigger mess then anyone could have thought of. If the process can't be retrieved and stabilised, it's worthless."

******

Looking out the side window of a helicopter, a police spotter reported, "Detective Arnold, we found something."

The spotter waited for a reply before continuing. "I'm looking at a naked man lying face down on a pile of rocks. There is blood everywhere. The victim is missing an arm and most of the flesh off one of his legs." As the pilot tried to maintain his craft's position, she focussed its cameras on the body.

After the images were sent to the detective's phone, he shook his head. "Animals concentrate on the gut first, not muscle. They want to get quick nourishment that is easy to digest before they go after the bulky meat." Talking to the spotter, he asked her, "Is his belly intact?"

"Can't see, he's lying on it. I'll send you all the video and stills I can."

Willy and the detective sat beside each other in the cargo area of the helicopter and watched the incoming video. They carefully examined every frame of it. "Corporal, this man appears to be too thin to be Ryan. Can you ID the victim?"

Willy zoomed in on the man's bare back. "That's definitely not Ryan. The man is way too thin, plus Ryan had a large scar on his left shoulder."

"Are you sure?"

"Positive. I'm the one that put it there."

The detective saw the disappointment on Willy's face as he squeezed his eyebrows together. "So, how did it happen?"

With a giant grin on his face, Willy looked at the detective. "I guess you could say that we were year-round rivals. We never played for the same team. He broke my arm playing lacrosse, and two years later I screwed up his shoulder at a hockey game." With the tips of his fingers rubbing the scar on his forehead, he added, "We both have our scars. As you pointed out, our paths had crossed a time or two."

Willy neglected to tell the detective that they weren't playing when Ryan was injured. Willy had smashed a beer bottle on the back of Ryan's head in the parking lot after losing a game. With Ryan lying unconscious on the ground, Willy twisted the stem of the broken bottle into Ryan's right shoulder and dug the glass shards deep into his muscles. With Ryan out for the rest of the season, Willy's team made it to the playoffs that year.

As they approached the site, the detective looked out the window at the dense forest canopy. "Feelings aside, we have to get to the body as fast as possible. He could still be alive."

Willy spoke up. "Ryan could have planted the body. He could be setting us up. He has a hunting rifle and he's an excellent shot."

"I am still not sure Ryan is guilty of anything yet. After all, he was accused by a guy that has a serious grudge against him." As soon as he had finished the sentence, the detective turned away from the window and looked into Willy's eyes. "And a cop that apparently has unsettled issues with him. Keep your emotions under check or I'll take you off this case. We may have a serious maniac on our hands. We don't want some whacko running around free while we are wasting our time hunting down an innocent man. Right?"

Willy nodded his head and peered out the window. The pair looked over the surrounding terrain as the copter circled around for a place to land. The rock was stained with long streaks of blood. Each time they passed over the man's body, more and more of it was hidden under a bush. The detective unbuckled his seatbelt and leaned into the cockpit. "He must still be alive. Either that or somebody or something is pulling him into the bushes. Either way, we have to get down there as soon as possible."

Feeling pressured the pilot finally made his decision. "The ridge is too jagged to land on. Plus, if he isn't already dead, the flying debris could cause him further injury. I'm going to have to let you down on the bank of the lake."

By the time they jumped out of the helicopter, walked through the bush and up the side of the ridge, the body had vanished. They followed the victim's trail using the special blue light setting on their flashlights designed to highlight blood splatter. They only managed to track him two hundred metres before his trail disappeared.

"Where did he go?" The detective stared at Willy. "There must be some sort of trail that we could follow. A body in that condition can't just vanish without a trace."

Chapter Fourteen

The Search

DeGroot turned away from his scanner and looked at Duncan. "I've thoroughly checked the airways. They're clean. I couldn't detect any interference that would indicate the use of radio scanning devices. However, the police could be still using a park radio and monitoring Ryan's unit. As long as we stay away from that pre-set frequency, we should be fine."

"The park's radios have a built-in GPS transmitter. They could use it to find him. Ryan isn't stupid. He would have ditched the radio by now."

Crouched under a thick, dense cedar tree, Duncan heard the planes and helicopters criss-crossing the sky. "Have you heard anything from Ratlin?"

"No, and I can't even get any signal from his locator."

Worried, Duncan inquired, "Did his locator move at all from the time we left him?"

"Judging from his location history, I would say that he had only travelled a half dozen metres." On his laptop, DeGroot superimposed a topographical map over Ratlin's location history. "Judging from the strength of his signal, I would say he went deeper into the rocks. They could contain minerals that could block his locator's signals. The location where the police spotted the body is just a few dozen metres south of there." DeGroot looked up at Duncan. "It can't be Ratlin. I don't care what the creature did to those civilians. It's injured and he is too well trained."

While he placed a reassuring hand on DeGroot's shoulder, Duncan stated, "I know you are right, but we need to find him and get him out of there."

DeGroot took a few seconds to respond. "What about the police?"

In a cold voice, Duncan told him, "Pray they don't get in our way. You know what's at stake." Standing up, he turned around and added, "I can't and won't allow anyone to be either captured or left behind."

Even with Drake's guidance, it took Duncan and MacNeil several hours to navigate their way around the lake. With no trail to follow and the police combing the area, all they could do was hide as close as they could to the rock where the mutilated man was last seen. With their radios set to the same frequency as the police, they were able to hear them directing both their land and aerial searches.

Overhead, a pair of helicopters were systematically zig-zigging back and forth. One travelling in a north to south pattern and the other east to west. On the ground below them, over two dozen seasoned search and rescue volunteers had joined the police in combing the forest, one section at a time. In a long crude line, they tried to keep a couple metres apart as they slowly clawed and worked their way through the boggy forest.

Treating the location like a crime scene, every time the hundred metre wide column travelled a kilometre, they needed to take a break. From his perch on top of the rocky ridge, detective Arnold monitored their every move. As the search party moved further and further away from the ridge, Duncan and MacNeil stealthily began their own search.

When the search party stopped for supper, the pair started combing the opposite side of the ridge. Afterwards, the search party began combing through the woods on the lake side of the ridge. The detective and his sub-ordinate's attention was solely on them. Duncan noticed that everyone on the ridge was facing away from the crevice that Ratlin had hidden in.

With Duncan in the bushes acting as a lookout and telling MacNeil when it was safe to move, he quietly snuck up to and slid into the deep crevice in front of the cave. Despite the footprints littering the area in front of the small cave, he knew that the police didn't find anything. If they had, DeGroot would've heard something over the radio. Crawling inside the cave, he got a faint signal off Ratlin's locator.

"Duncan, he's here. His signal is faint but I'm able to pick it up. I think you were right. There may be something in the rocks interfering with it."

As MacNeil crawled to the back of the cave and sat next to the pile of rocks that Claraicy had restacked, the signal from Ratlin's locator got stronger. He quietly rolled the rocks aside and discovered the tunnel. The signal from Ratlin's locator grew even stronger. "He is in a tunnel. Maybe he was trapped inside of it. I had to remove a bunch of rocks just to find it."

Hiding amongst some bushes, Duncan whispered back, "Be careful."

Putting his head inside the hole, MacNeil gently whispered, "Ratlin, are you in there?" The words got louder as they vibrated down the tunnel.

There was no reply. MacNeil repeated himself three more times. Still no response.

On top of the ridge, a constable was cutting down brush and preparing an area for helicopters to land. While squatting down to pick up some branches he thought he heard something. Away from Duncan's view, he rested his head against the rock to listen. "Detective you may want to come over here."

Seeing the constable get up and walk toward the crevice, Duncan gave a warning, "MacNeil, your position has been compromised. Get out of there."

MacNeil ran on all fours back to the opening. He quickly pulled out a pack of putty from his belt and wedged it into a large crack just inside of the cave's entrance. Seeing the lower half of the constable's legs approach the crevice, MacNeil quickly inserted a detonator into the putty.

With most of the constable's torso in his sight, MacNeil tossed a smoke bomb in front of him as he exited the cavern. The eye burning smog forced the constable to stumble backwards in pain. Holding a mask against his face, MacNeil ran through the red smoke and scaled the far side of the crevice.

The specially made lenses in his mask eliminated the red and enabled him to see Detective Arnold running towards him. In a crouched position, MacNeil kept within the drifting red cloud and ran towards the brush. Glancing back, he could see the constable staggering away from the crevice.

With the push of a button, a giant cloud of dust shot out of the imploded crevice and rolled over the top of the ridge. Protected within the cloud, Duncan got up and patted MacNeil's back as they ran away. "Great execution." Then, like a well-rehearsed magic act, the pair vanished into the dense marsh that surrounded most of the rocky ridge.

******

Jesse was snuggled in front of Claraicy when the blast shook the cavern. As dust swirled through the cracks around the slab, she sprang up and ran behind her mother. With only Claraicy's shallow breathing and faint heart beat to comfort her, Jesse curled up next to the large, shell-like hump that encased her mother's back and along her sides.

******

The detective reached the constable as he curled up on the ground. "Are you all right?"

Covered in dust and gravel, the young officer got to his feet and hacked out, "I can barely see. Man that stuff stings."

Trying to help him get out of the cloud of dust, the detective asked, "What happened? All I could see was red smoke."

The constable had to stop coughing before he could reply. "I thought I heard something beneath the rocks I was standing on. I wasn't sure if it was animal, human or just the wind, so I wanted to investigate it."

With his arm wrapped around the detective's shoulder for support, he continued, "Shortly after I called you, I started to climb down the side of the small ravine and as I reached the bottom, a loud red flash exploded in front of me. Then another more powerful explosion knocked me off my feet."

Amidst the cloud of fine falling debris, the detective turned the constable to see his face. "Did you see who it was?"

The constable coughed a couple more times before answering him. "I didn't have time to see anything."

As they walked out of the dust cloud, the detective told him, "Wash your eyes out and pack up. We need to get you to a hospital."

Out of breath, Willy and two volunteers ran to Detective Arnold. "What happened?"

As other members of the search party approached, he blasted out, "Someone armed with explosives just waltzed out of here, that's what."

"What direction did he go?"

"Forget it. Right now, none of us are equipped to mess with him." Detective Arnold cocked his head and looked at Willy. "He used just enough flash to shock and blind the constable. Just enough chemical smoke to escape without being seen and just enough explosives to scare the crap out of us without anyone getting hurt. Factor in the time it took him to set them off and get away, I am guessing he was trained by either SWAT or Special Forces."

After sitting the constable down and handing him a bottle of water to wash out his eyes, he further inquired, "To your knowledge, has Ryan ever received any such training?"

In a timid voice, Willy replied, "No sir. Not to my knowledge."

Detective Arnold steered Willy away from the rest and quietly told him, "Whoever it was had waltzed out of here easier than you could draw your gun. Go back and dig up everything you can about Ryan's past, because if it wasn't him, things could turn real bloody."

Willy looked away. He didn't know why, but he began thinking of all the training his brother would had undergone with the Canadian Special Operations Regiment. *He's dead, it couldn't be him.*

As Willy ran to the radio, the detective walked away from the crowd. He had once volunteered for policing duties overseas. His position required him to work very closely with both Canadian and foreign troops. His brief experience had taught him the difference between regular and elite soldiers. While regular troops were quick to obey orders. Guided by their motto 'We will find a way', the elite members of the Special Forces were conditioned to complete the mission at any cost. Thinking about how easily the shadowy figure slipped away, Detective Arnold mumbled to himself, "I would like to know what is really going on out here."

With the volunteers sent home, armed officers continued the search on the ground while helicopters criss-crossed the air above them. Their infrared heat sensors had picked up a few caribou, a couple of raccoons and the a family of black bears. Even though the two soldiers wore uniforms treated with special chemicals to avoid detection, they didn't want to take any chances. Submerged up to their necks in the cold water, most of their body heat was dispersed, leaving nothing solid for the police to zoom in on. They knew all the tricks and were well-versed in avoiding all the latest methods of detection. Giving off an indistinguishable signature no bigger than a frog or maybe a squirrel, in a forest full of animals, they were virtually invisible.

After two days, the police found nothing. Using rubber rafts to search the deeper marshes, the police poked and felt their way through the quagmire of rotting branches and sunken trees with long poles and gaffs. Their predicable and methodical approach made it easy for Duncan and MacNeil to evade and outguess them. With the cold water constantly draining their core body heat, they took turns fighting off hypothermia on shore. While one was warming up, the other watched over the police investigation. During the day, the pair stayed close enough to react to anything the police might discover. At night, they freely orchestrated their own search.

Echoing through the trees, "Detective, we found something", caught Duncan's attention. Breathing through a snorkel fashioned out of reeds, he poked half his face out of the water. With his eyes barely above the muddy water, he peered through the vegetation draped over his head. As he slowly turned towards the commotion, he saw an officer bend over the side of a raft. He was pulling the bow of Ryan's canoe out of the water.

While officers in wet suits and scuba gear removed some of the heavy rocks holding it under, several others swam over to assist them. It took three of them to roll the biggest rock out of the canoe. With six men lifting the canoe to the surface of the muddy, waist high water, the two officers in the raft extracted the rest while carefully examining the canoe for evidence.

Despite the canoe being under the water for a few days, small traces of blood and clumps of hair were still clinging to its sides, bottom and under some of its ribs. The senior officer in the raft noticed some strange markings on the gunwales, rear seat and yoke and began taking photos. "Someone had deliberately sliced off portions of the woodwork and I can guarantee it wasn't the owner. No one would callously deface something that took them months to build."

As the camera continued to flash, Duncan became more concerned about what the police had uncovered. With almost a dozen people surrounding Ryan's canoe, he felt helpless.

By the time the canoe was floating on its own, Detective Arnold had arrived at the site. Despite everything it had gone through, the canoe was still intact and its hull had remained watertight. After looking the canoe over, the detective announced, "It's getting late. The lake is calm and it seems seaworthy. Let's haul it back to camp and process it there."

With the canoe tied behind the raft, the entire search party packed up and returned to their base camp all under Drake's watchful eye. Standing up, Duncan began to walk out of the swamp looking like a large clump of lily pads. The large mat of vegetation not only prevented him from being found by the police, but also helped insulate him from the cold water as he huddled under the surface. The police had poked him with their sticks and had even stepped on him a few times without knowing it.

MacNeil walked over to Duncan and helped him climb over the bank and peeled off his disguise. Wearing only a wet suit that he had stolen from the police while they were eating lunch, he told MacNeil, "Neither Sarah nor Ryan could've sunk that canoe."

MacNeil shook his head in disbelief. "Did you see the size of some of those rocks they removed? From up in the tree I had a bird's eye view. Whoever put them into the canoe must've been as strong as an ox."

Duncan looked at him. "The creature may be strong, but I'm worried about what other capabilities it has."

At the campsite, the police immediately carried the canoe ashore and wrapped a large tarp around it. Drake sent out the alarm, "Duncan, they are not examining the canoe, they are preparing it to be airlifted out of here."

Curled up under a spruce tree trying to warm up, Duncan replied, "Then we'll have to act fast. It's almost nightfall. We have until morning. From what we have seen, it was our prey that sunk it. With the amount of work involved, plus its injury, it may have left some traceable evidence behind. The canoe has to be destroyed. You're the closest. I will leave it up to your discretion how you want to do it."

Drake waited til after dark. With snake-like grace, he slithered down the ridge and into the water with only a knife on his belt and a small pack over his shoulder. As he waded to shore, he watched the guard on duty go into the bushes to relieve himself. When the officer returned, he casually set up his folding chair next to the fire in the middle of the camp.

Drake smiled as the naive sentry made his job a lot easier. While quietly working his way behind him, he pulled a damp cloth out of a plastic bag. As the tired officer started to nod his head, Drake snuck through the rows of tents, got behind him and smothered his mouth and nose with the cloth. The officer was too scared to breath.

After placing the blade of his knife tightly against the officer's neck, Drake softly whispered in his ear, "Breath in or die. If you give me any resistance at all, I've no qualms about slitting your throat and letting you bleed out like a pig. It's your choice. What will it be?"

The officer's made the right choice and Drake gently laid his limp body down with barely a sound. After cutting the fuel line in the police raft, he used their own cache of gasoline to thoroughly soak Ryan's canoe, along with the other vessels lined up along the shoreline. To give himself some time to get away, he stuck a lit fuse into the ground at the end of a long rope that he had poured gasoline over. It led next to the edge of the woods.

Drake left a brief trail into the woods before getting into the water. He swam half way back to the nearby peninsula before the fuse burnt down far enough to ignite the rope. In a series of small puff-like explosions, flames and clouds of black smoke quickly engulfed the vessels. As he crawled ashore, he could hear a chorus of obscenities being yelled out in French, English and native dialects.

Glancing back at the campsite, all he could see was a wall of flames beneath a long, rolling, black cloud. Taking a breather behind a boulder, he called in, "It's done. With all that light and heat from the fire, their equipment is useless. They have no way of knowing where I came from or where I went. My position is still secure."

DeGroot watched the red glow light up the northern end of the lake as he listened to the police chatter over the radio. With a wide grin, he announced, "Duncan, great news. They have officially requested military assistance. It may finally be time for us to bring in the goat and clear everyone out of our way."

Chapter Fifteen

Trapped

Claraicy woke up coughing and reached for a canteen. As she drank, every move she made created small twirling clouds of dust. Still in a sleeping fog, it took her a while to reorient herself. The explosion that she thought was a dream had really happened. As she regained her faculties, the fact that she could freely move her arm shocked her. The torturous restrictions that her constantly stiffening body had forced upon her had disappeared. Then she realized that the pain was also gone.

Flinging her arm behind her, she felt her back. The large hump had been replaced by a loose mass of tissue. After pulling some of the tissue to the front of her, she examined the thin, damp, mud covered membrane with her hands.

Overwhelmed, Claraicy stood on her knees and put her hands on her hips. Slowly rotating them in a wide circle, she tested every joint in her body for any sign of pain. There was none. She wanted to yell out her delight. The shouting voices filtering down from above her quickly brought her back to reality. She had keep quiet.

As she walked on all fours towards the entrance, the loose mass clinging to her back unravelled over her sides like a set of rumpled up roman drapes. Rubbing her hands across her forehead she mumbled, "What's next?"

Despite feeling awkward, she found it easier to move around. With her ear pressed against the wall, she heard obscure voices and heavy boots clambering around outside. Deciding it was safe, she attempted to move the slab of rock she used as a door. She didn't have the strength to budge it.

Feeling exhausted, she sat down. Tiny beams of light made their way through the rocks above her and shone on the pile of backpacks. Not knowing how long it had been since she last ate, she rummaged through them for something to eat.

In one of the side pockets of Patrick's pack, she found a can of jellied cooking fuel and a pack of matches. She used her fingernails to pry off the lid. After lighting the jelly, the soft, smokeless flame warmed her mind more than her body. It also gave her some more light to see with as she searched through the packs for food. Under a jagged rock she noticed a cache of food wrappers and smashed open cans.

Looking over at Jessie, Claraicy watched her turn away as if she had done something terribly wrong. "It's all right. You needed to eat too."

Jerky, trail-mix, and dry food packs were the mainstay of both Ryan and Ratlin's food supplies. She had already been into Patrick's stash of cans, jerky and meals that you are suppose to boil in a pot of water. Needing to know what supplies she had left, she walked over to her parent's pack. She didn't know why, but her fingers fumbled about as she searched for the zipper.

With the pack's contents spilled over the ground, drool dripped from the side of her mouth. Before her lay a child's fantasy. Even in the dim light, the shape and feel of cans of pop, bags of crushed chips and mushed chocolate bars made her mouth water. At that moment, it was better than any Christmas dinner she could imagine.

She wondered what had stopped her from searching the pack before. Did they still hold some kind of power over her? Thinking of her father, Claraicy smiled. "He doesn't even have anything to play with anymore. Why should I be afraid of that fat, castrated steer?"

The influx of sugar flowing through her veins brought back her strength and energy. Kneeling at the blocked entrance, she took a deep breath and began to shovel all the loose gravel and rocks from around the bottom of the large flat slab. After she rolled it away, she found out that another large, heavy boulder had lodged itself into the opening. Hoping to split it into smaller pieces, she used Patrick's steel shanked hatchet to twist, turn and pry at every crack in the rock she could wiggle it into. With only a few flakes of stone breaking off, she knew that she would have to chisel grooves into the natural seams of the rock to split it.

Grabbing a second hatchet, she held the blade of one against a fault line in the rock while hammering the back of it with the other. Every time the helicopters flew overhead, she would chip away at the rock. In between the helicopters, all the yelling and commotion going on outside was enough to mask the scraping and digging she needed to do.

Chipping a deep groove along the diagonal fault line in the rock was hard work. After a couple hours plus several water breaks, she heard the boulder crack. The weight of the debris leaning against it forced the large upper section of the boulder to twist inward and fall on top of her bent knees. Cascading behind it was a landslide of smaller rocks and gravel.

Pinned to the ground and buried to her waist in rocks, Claraicy bit down on the tough piece of jerky that she was chewing. In desperation, she pushed, rolled and tossed the rocks to the side. Every rock she removed freed-up a gap for another one to take its place. After ten minute of frantically dispersing the smaller rocks, the landslide finally ceased. Pumped full of adrenaline, she took a deep breath and twisted, slid and pushed the split boulder off her legs.

By the time she was finally free, half her knees were pushed into the gravel. She quickly felt up and down her legs and checked for any injuries but discovered nothing more than a few surface scrapes. Her skin was rough, almost scale-like, and lacked the smooth softness that it once had.

The can of cooking jelly was almost burnt out, but it didn't matter. Her eyes were getting adjusted to the dim light. She looked at the back of her hands as they rested on her knee caps. Her skin was no longer white. It was now a reddish brown.

Looking back to where she had been sleeping, she saw hundreds of curled up rolls of molted, dry skin littering the area. She had shed most of her skin while she slept. More of it had either rubbed and scraped off as she worked at removing the slab. Reaching up, she felt her face. Without any effort, she peeled off a large flake of skin from her forehead. All she could do was stare speechless at it as the dry skin curled up in her hand.

With no daylight coming though the opening, Claraicy knew that the main entrance must be completely sealed. Although debris filled most of the cave, there was a small gap on top of it. Lying on her side, Claraicy placed a flashlight between her teeth and her cheek and wiggled her head through the gap to examine it. The opening was blocked by giant boulders and tightly filled in with rocks, sand and gravel.

Twisting her head in the opposite direction, she knew that there was only other one way out. The hole was only a little more than the length of her body away. The explosion had placed two boulders in her path. With all the activity going on above her, she couldn't hammer through the rocks blocking the main entrance without being discovered. The eerie pit was her only other exit.

Inside the cavern she felt a small degree of security. With a little rationing, they could easily stretch out their stockpile of food to last them over a month. Her immediate problem was water. There wasn't enough to last a week and she didn't know how long it would take her to clear a path to the pit.

A few days went by. The clicking of boots and muffled voices filtered downward through the rock. Every helicopter that landed on the ridge meant an opportunity to hammer apart the tops of the large boulders that were blocking her way.

Making a narrow gap big enough to crawl through, took her longer than she initially thought. In the late afternoon of the fourth day, she heard a new sound coming from outside of the main entrance. It was the loud, twanging ring of a sledge hammer chipping away at the boulders blocking the entrance.

A few hours later, she heard the deafening banging of jackhammers as they turned the air inside the cavern into a cloud of dust. The echoing, loud, sharp banging exploded in her sensitive ears. Stuffing them with cotton from the first aid kits and tying one of Ryan's T-shirts around her head didn't bring her much relief.

She knew that her time was running out. Even if it took them a few days to get through, the painful, mind numbing ringing would drive her to kill herself first.

Working day and night, she frantically chipped away at the tops of the boulders and cleared a path that was barely big enough for her to squeeze over. After packing all the supplies she figured she would initially need, she used the nozzle of Ratlin's rifle to push the backpack over the boulders. Then it was her turn to squeeze through. The loose mass sticking out of her back made her feel like she was dragging a flimsy tarp behind her.

In front of the pile of rocks sealing the opening, there was barely enough room for her to squat in. Claraicy quietly removed them away from the pit's entrance while listening for any activity from both above and below. Not knowing how deep the pit was, she tied two ropes together and wrapped one end around a large boulder. After tying the backpack to the other end of the rope, she lowered it into the pit.

Hearing no clamouring beneath her, she told herself, "If there was anything down there, the bag would have attracted some kind of attention."

With the stock of Ratlin's assault rifle pushed in to make it less cumbersome, Claraicy slung it around her neck, turned around and slowly made her descent into the unknown. Jesse slowly followed her bit by bit down the rope. Every time the jackhammer stopped, so did she. She found the pounding sounds of the jackhammers above her a direct contrast to the eerie quiet radiating from below.

The bottom of the shaft sloped into a cave. As her foot touched the bottom, she let go of the rope and turned around. Stepping on the skin draping from her back, Claraicy lost her balance and landed face down into a thick puddle of bat guano.

The strong ammonia overwhelmed her lungs. As she fought to get up, a chunk of rope wrapped around her foot causing her to slip and fall on her side. It was the rope Ratlin had used. Frazzled, she wrapped her arm around her nose and wildly kicked the rope off her leg.

After carefully getting to her feet, she looked around. Removing her head wrap and cotton plugs, she found that her ears were still ringing. With the base of her thumbs covering her eardrums, she used the tips of her fingers to gently stroke her temples, in small, circular motions, until the ringing in her ears started to ease.

High above her, a few small, narrow cracks between the massive boulders that formed the exterior wall of the cavern gave her enough light to see. Looking around at all the bat guano, Claraicy commented, "So the creatures did have another way in and out."

A tiny stream of water ran down the side of the cave and into a half-moon shaped pool at the far end of the exterior wall. Next to the stream, she saw a trail of footprints that were almost wiped away by a pair of blood stained scrape marks, all of which disappeared into the pool. "I wonder who is dragging who, the soldier or the ghost?"

As she walked over to the pool, she noticed some small ripples along the edge of the water. She knew that something was agitating the water. "This is too far away for the jackhammers to be causing it."

Claraicy calmly told Jesse, "Stay here, I'll be right back."

Sliding into the chest-high, guano saturated water, Claraicy used her feet to feel around the mucky bottom. It didn't take her long before she discovered a stream of water draining into a large gap beneath where two of the massive rocks forming the wall met. "If they could get through, so can I."

Taking a deep breath, she dove under the water and pulled herself into the narrow gap. A few metres away, she could see daylight. After pulling herself through, she found herself outside in a small pool at the edge of a swamp, surrounded by thick brush and lush vegetation. A huge overhanging rock jutted out above the small pool of water, making it invisible to anybody on top of the ridge.

After shaking the water and guano out of her ears, Claraicy could hear the distant jack hammers along with the generators and compressors that powered them. Curious, she scaled a tall pine tree and looked around.

In the air above her, she saw the bright distinctive markings on the police helicopters. Claraicy didn't think anything of it when she spotted two drab coloured army helicopters in the distance. She could only pick up the odd word as people screamed above the machinery. As the two helicopters got closer, the machinery stopped.

Below her, there was no sign of the soldier that was in the cave or anyone else nearby. She felt relieved. She hugged the tree trunk and tried to relax as a light breeze rocked the tree back and forth. With the breeze came all the delightful scents of the forest. After being trapped inside of the cavern and breathing dust for over a week, she relished the fresh air and warm sun filtering through the branches.

Her brief moment of relaxation was short lived as her thoughts returned to Jesse. As she climbed down, the loose tissue-like skin dangling from her back kept getting caught in the branches and made her descent very difficult.

While stepping down onto a branch, a gust of wind blow some of the loose skin under her foot. With the skin drawn tight, another gust of wind turned the loose tissue on her back into a small sail and pushed her foot off the branch. Hanging with one arm, Claraicy tried to swing towards another branch.

The strain was too much for the small branch she was hanging from. It snapped. Despite grabbing at everything she could, she couldn't catch herself. With her hands full of twigs and the wind blowing her further away from the tree trunk, she began to free fall.

Like a parachute, the loose, tissue-like skin on her back fanned out and glided her to the ground. Seconds seemed to last forever as she landed on her feet and marvelled at what had happened. With the flexible skin still spread out, she looked from side to side. Brown, bat-like wings had extended out of a second set of shoulders protruding from her back.

Reaching over her shoulders, she felt the newly formed shoulder blades. The wings attached to her back were like a second pair of arms. Concentrating as hard as she could, she tried to make the wings move. She couldn't. Instead, they slowly relaxed and a long tail helped lift the ends of them off the ground and fold them into a giant mound on her back.

Snapping out of her bewildered daze, she shook her head and crawled back into the smelly pool. After retrieving the backpack and rifle, she went back for Jesse. While clinging to Claraicy's tail, some water had gotten into Jesse's lungs. On the bank, as Jesse hacked out the water, Claraicy lay on her stomach. Dragging the wings back and forth though the slurry had drained all of her energy. After catching her breath, she sat up and tried to let everything sink in.

"The bats. It all started with the giant bats. It wasn't until after that pair of giant, strange looking bats attacked me that any of this occurred. Maybe the bat I killed laid some kind of egg inside of me before it died." Claraicy turned her head and glanced at her wings. "I have no control over them. Maybe I'm a host for some kind of alien invasion or something. Could that be why soldiers are involved?"

Chapter Sixteen

The Goat

Hidden under some propped up netting stuffed with vegetation, Degroot leaned forward and softly spoke into his headset, "Is everyone alright?"

Doctor Stern looked at DeGroot. "Is there any response?"

"Sorry, he's still not responding." DeGroot looked up at the doctor and forced a worried smile. "I told you, those two could vanish anywhere up to a month or more and then suddenly pop out without a scratch. They must have turned off their transponders. After having their camp set on fire, the police are probably using everything at their disposal to find them. I wouldn't worry. This is child's play to those two. Just fun and games."

"It is not just them. My whole life is on the line here, along with Doctor Scott's and many, many others. You don't know how important this mission is. We cannot let our research be discovered by anyone. Nobody can know what we have done, or the scope of our research."

DeGroot grinned as he watched the frazzled doctor walk back to his tent flailing his arms. Shaking his head, he said under his breath, "You fool, you don't even know what is really going on out here."

Half way to his tent, the doctor bumped into Ann. She tried to calm him down with a few softly spoken words. DeGroot couldn't hear what she said, only the doctor's vicious response as he shoved her aside. "Listen, you are just a tech. Do your work, shut up, and leave me alone."

Ann walked over to DeGroot. "He's getting worse."

"He's okay. He's just blowing off some frustration, that's all."

"Yeah, but why me? What did I do?"

DeGroot turned and stared at her legs. "You were available, that's all. He knows better than taking it out on me. That makes you the only one left to wail on."

Ann knelt down and put her arms around his neck and shoulder. As she gave him a hug, she said, "Thank you."

With a wide grin, DeGroot gazed at her pitiful face and replied, "For what?"

After a short second hug, she said, "For being here. I've been watching you. You're always so level headed and you don't let anything rattle you, not even Duncan."

"I've too much to do. I can't afford to get rattled."

While watching a helicopter circle the lake, she told him, "Out here I feel like a prisoner. I'm alone, bored and coming down with cabin fever. I can only calibrate my equipment so many times a day. Can I sit here with you and read for a while? The doctor won't be any company for me today. I promise I won't bother you."

Feeling her soft breasts cradling his shoulder, DeGroot smiled. "Okay. Sure."

After giving DeGroot another hug and a small kiss on his temple, Ann slowly relaxed her clutching arms and gracefully sat down on the log next to him. After wiggling a bit to get comfortable, she pulled out a novel from a deep pocket in her tight cargo pants and opened it. Facing him, she smiled and repeated her delight. "Thank you."

Degroot could feel the warmth radiating from her leg as it rested next to his. Outside of coordinating their search, most of the talk over the police radio was idle chit-chat. Listening to all the police small talk started to bother him. Family, wives, girlfriends, sports and friends seemed to be all they talked about. Everything that he had to give up. The warm touch of Ann's leg was more than a pleasant distraction, it was a reminder of what could have been.

As Ann bent forward to read, the material in the front of her loose fitting sweater fell forward. Every time she turned a page, her head would tilt to the side. DeGroot couldn't avoid seeing everything that her bra was straining to support. He closed his eyes and tried to focus solely on the radio.

As Ann slowly read her book, DeGroot could hear her fingers separate the pages before turning to the next page. Between each chapter, she would close her eyes and stretch her neck, leaving very little for DeGroot's imagination. A few chapters had gone by before the conversation in his ear shook him to his feet. "Finally!"

DeGroot grabbed Ann's shoulder. "No questions. Go get the doc."

Ann ran to the doctor's tent and they both ran back. Almost out of breath, the doctor inquired, "What up?"

"They released the goat."

Ann looked at both of them with a questioning face as the doctor gave out a sigh of relief. "Great, now maybe they will leave us alone."

******

Steve McNab shook his head. He felt wet sand squeezing through his fingers as he clenched his fists. The sounds of wind rushing through the trees and waves coming ashore told him that he was no longer cooped up in his small dark cell. He tried to focus his eyes. A stinging sensation told him that someone had put drops in them. Trees and bushes were unrecognizable blotches of green. The gentle rolling dark blanket had to be the water. Still groggy, he rolled over and tried to wash out his eyes in the surf.

A loud humming pounded at his head. Another wave splashed more water into his eyes. The unmistakable beating sound could only be one thing. Looking up he saw the large ring from a helicopter propeller as it hovering above him.

He saw fuzzy blobs repell down ropes onto the shoreline. He tried to think. *Where am I? Who are they?* Scared, he scrambled into the water.

Weighted down by their heavy equipment, the men couldn't follow him. As soon as the second helicopter arrived, three dark, sleeker looking bodies splashed into the murky water, right next to him.

Instinctively, Steve's training took over and he reacted swiftly. He smashed the palm of his hand into the first man's face, shoving his nose upwards and into his brain. Blood gushed everywhere.

Sinking under the water, Steve held himself down by wrapping his leg and arm around a sunken tree. In the dark water, shadows were all he could see.

The two remaining divers swam to their dead comrade. As the water washed out his eyes, the shapes got clearer. The air in Steve's lungs couldn't support him for much longer. Using both hands, he broke a straight, arm's length branch off the submerged tree.

As the divers bobbed on the surface less than a few metres above him, he let go of the sunken tree and used his legs to push away from it as hard as he could. Darting to the surface, he struck the sharp end of the stick into the gut of one of the divers. It pierced his rubber suit, entered his abdomen, went under his rib cage and puncturing his left lung.

Reaching down, Steve took the diver's knife from his leg and slashed the last diver across his neck as he swam over to help. As small caliber bullets rained down from the helicopter and splashed into the water around him, Steve twisted the first diver around and used him as a shield.

After he removed the diver's tanks and flippers, he hid beneath the second diver as bullets continued to zip through the water. Steve cut the straps off the diver's tanks and removed his mask. With his vision almost fully restored, he looking around for any more pursuers.

The second diver held his gut and trying to contain the bleeding while he rolled around in the water. As their eyes meet, Steve looked away. That was when he noticed the insignia on the diver's suit. The Ontario Provincial Police decal was unmistakable. Who and what he was didn't matter. He had become a cop killer. That was a crime on which no one could shield you from.

******

Perched high in a pine tree next to the ridge, Claraicy peered through the branches and watched the police officers pack up. Without the banging of jackhammers ringing in the air, her acute hearing focussed in on their vociferous chatter.

Almost every other sentence contained the words 'cop killer' in it. It was as if what happened to her parents and Patrick no longer mattered.

Why would they totally abandon the search for me just because there is a cop killer on the loose? Claraicy thought a moment longer, then smiled. *Unless they think it's the same person. But why would they think that?*

It took only four round trips for the helicopters to relocate all of them along with their equipment. As the last helicopter disappeared, Claraicy worked her way along the limb she was on and leaped the short distance to a narrow ledge onto the side of the ridge. She found that moving on the steep sloping rock was harder then she first thought. There wasn't much for her to hang onto. She dug her hard claw-like nails into every crack she could find.

After a while climbing got easier for her. She managed to get to the various gaps where she thought the giant bats were using to get inside. Once there, she stuffed rocks, branches and anything that she could find into them. She even used almost two dozen clear, discarded water bottles that the police had chucked into the bushes. She flattened and jammed them into the cracks hoping to allow in some light while helping to seal them.

Convinced that the bats could no longer get through, she looked down. The side of the ridge was almost vertical. Without knowing how, her wings instinctively opened. As the breeze filled them, she could feel herself getting lighter. After taking a deep breath, in a leap of faith she jumped over the edge. The wings acted like a separate identity as they glided her safely down to a small clearing a short distance from the murky pool.

******

Duncan and MacNeil's locators started blinking on DeGroot's screen. He pressed his hand against the microphone on his ear. "Duncan, are you receiving?"

"We're back. What's happening? The police suddenly packed up and flew away."

"The goat was dropped at the lake you had previously picked out, and had no problem eluding capture."

The air went quiet. After a several seconds, Duncan asked, "Any casualties?"

DeGroot slowly replied, "You trained him to survive and avoid capture at any cost, and that's what he did. One cop is dead and two more are in critical condition. Being locked up didn't slow his reflexes." After a brief pause, he continued. "After the police regroup, they will be out for blood. They are going to use all their resources to hunt that bastard down and nail him to the wall."

"To bad about the cops but everyone knew the risks. So what's our position?"

"The police have left this entire sector and moved all their personnel near the lake where we planted the goat. They won't be able to catch him. It shouldn't take long before they realize that they are fighting a losing battle and finally allow the military to take over."

"In that case, we're coming in."

It took Duncan and MacNeil over five hours to make their way back to the camp. Covered in grass, weeds and mud, they looked like walking clumps of swamp sludge. Cold, hungry and exhausted, neither of them was in any condition to celebrate. Duncan lowered his head. "We couldn't find any trace of Ratlin. He may be trapped inside a cave or maybe held up in the swamp somewhere. We have to reequip and go back."

DeGroot stared at him. "You bull-headed bastard, how about you two replace me and Drake? We can search for Ratlin while you two recuperate."

Duncan looked up at DeGroot. "You know, if I had one ounce of energy left in me I'd whip your ass for talking to me like that."

"I know." DeGroot couldn't help but snort out, "But look at you. You're running on an empty tank. You've got nothing left."

Ann walked over and handed two hot mugs of coffee to the battered soldiers. They sat down and rested their backs against the same tree. As they sipped some coffee, Ann piped up. "I've got some food heating up in the tent. Where do you want it?"

MacNeil flopped unto his back. "Here's fine. I can't move."

In the two minutes it took Ann to return with two plates of food, they had both fallen asleep. Ann looked at DeGroot. DeGroot smiled back and told her, "Well, we have to eat too."

The two of them were half finished their meal when the doctor came out of his tent. "Are they back yet?"

"Yes, sir. You almost tripped over them."

The doctor looked around and spotted them. Duncan and MacNeil's attire had blended in with the surrounding vegetation. Their boots are what gave them away. "Well what's happening?"

"Nothing until they wake."

"Well, wake them."

DeGroot saw the doctor's foot go back. Dropping his food tray, he leaped up, grabbed his knife and knocked the doctor to the ground. "If you so much as try to kick them again, you won't have to worry about anything anymore."

Doctor Stern looked into DeGroot's eyes and saw nothing. The normally lighthearted soldier had turned to ice. Feeling the cold edge of his knife digging into his throat, the doctor replied, "All right."

DeGroot bounced up, sheathed his knife and smiled as he extended his hand to the doctor. "Great, we understand each other."

The doctor crawled away like a crab and then got up. Small drops of blood formed along a thin red line across his throat. "I'm in charge here."

"No you're not. How can you give the orders when you don't even know what's really going on out here?" DeGroot gave the doctor a wide smile and added, "Doctor Scott's latest experiments must be allowed to continue, no matter what the cost, human or otherwise."

Doctor Stern felt his neck and used his sleeve to wipe off some of the blood. Looking at the stain, he asked him, "So what is really going on out here?"

"That is strictly need to know. Just remember that we're all expendable, even you."

The next morning, Duncan woke to find a hot cup of coffee on the ground in front of his face. Perched up on one arm, Duncan took a drink. "Thanks."

Holding Ann's left arm around his neck, DeGroot kept her on her feet as he walked her past Duncan and MacNeil. "Ann was on watch. When I got up to relieve her, I saw you stirring. By the time I brewed some coffee and cooked up some grub for you, she was asleep."

After DeGroot returned from Ann's tent, Duncan questioned him. "It's Ann now? What happened to 'The Queen'? You better be careful. Feelings and our type can be a confusing mixture."

"Don't worry about me. Mission first, everything else second. Besides, this unit is all I have. Everyone else is either dead or think I am. That will never change. Not now, not ever. Especially not after this one is over."

"I'm the same. Even my brother assumes I'm dead. In the swamp, he once walked so close to me that I could've tugged on his pant leg. Emotions and our profession don't mix. Remember, we all volunteered for this assignment." Duncan took a few deep breaths. "Now, how has Drake been holding up?"

"He fine. His muscles are getting a little stiff from being confined, but he's all right."

"When MacNeil wakes up, I'll have them switch. He needs time to recuperate. It was tough out there. We were constantly on the move and spent most of our time in the water." Duncan took in a strong whiff of maple syrup. "Man, you had it good back here."

DeGroot gave out a subdued chuckle. "I made tonnes of pancakes and fried up a huge mound of bacon and eggs. I thought the smell and sound of sizzling bacon would have woken the pair of you."

"That sounds like you made enough for me, but you better be prepared to make some more when MacNeil finally gets up."

With MacNeil on watch and Drake back at camp, Duncan and DeGroot set out to find Ratlin. The police helicopters were keeping to a regular flight path to and from the lake where Steve was dropped off. That made avoiding them extremely easy.

It had been almost two weeks since Ratlin's disappearance. As the pair discussed where to search, Duncan told DeGroot, "He has to be injured."

DeGroot piped up. "In the length of time he has had, even with two broken legs, he could have waltzed a canoe past the police and around the lake unnoticed."

Duncan could see that DeGroot was worried. "All we can do is hope that Ratlin either hears or sees us, and finally reveals himself."

Foot prints of every shape and size littered the area at the base of the ridge. Some had treads simular to the same military style boots that Ratlin wore. A lot of the local search and rescue members were also members of the local militia and wore their government-issued footwear.

Duncan and MacNeil went through everywhere the police had searched. They also checked places the police would never have thought of. They checked beneath the muck at the edge of the water, in hollows at the tops of trees, under tree roots, the middle of thorn bushes, the places the police would never imagine anyone could squeeze into.

Duncan remembered MacNeil telling him that Ratlin's location sensor was strongest near a pit deep inside the crevice. "MacNeil would not have imploded the crevice if he thought that it would endanger Ratlin." Turning to face DeGroot, he added, "There had to be another way out of that tunnel."

Chapter Seventeen

Recovery

Claraicy needed time to digest everything that happened to her body along with her future. With the police gone, she no longer felt the urge to run.

She knew that she had a couple weeks' worth of food up in her cavern. There was plenty of clean water pouring out of the inside wall of the cavern. Getting in and out of the bat's cave was difficult, but it offered the protection and solitude she greatly needed. The light shining through the plastic bottles lit up the cave enough for her to see. She had plenty of room to walk around, plus food, water, tools, warm sleeping bags, mattresses, and Jesse. For the first time since she was abandoned in the woods, she felt somewhat comfortable and safe.

The bat guano wasn't hard to get rid of. Holding her wings against the wall, she collected water and poured it over the section of floor that she wanted to clean. The water flushed the guano into the pool. After a while the water washed it away, leaving only some of the heavier sediment behind in the basin.

Instead of swimming in and out of the mucky pool, she decided to wait it out. She needed time to think. Even though the pain was gone, the awkwardness of the huge wings sticking out of her back made it hard for her to move around. Her body needed time to adjust, and she feared that even more mutations might be cast upon her.

Claraicy's only uplifting moments came from Jesse. Watching her play at the edge of the pool and use one of the sleeping bags as a place to hide stuff in, brought a smile to her face. She suddenly realized that in her entire life, she never had so many reasons to be happy. No one was there to criticise and belittle her. She no longer feared being beaten and raped. She had a comfortable place to stay and someone to love that actually loved her back. That alone made everything that she was going through bearable.

Retrieving the supplies from the small cavern was easier then she expected. The tunnel was narrow enough that she could spread her arms and legs apart and climb it like a child on a doorframe. After carefully lowering the backpacks and camping equipment by rope, she simply tossed the sleeping bags and air mattresses down the hole.

Feeling exhausted, on her final trip down she wrapped the sling of Ryan's rifle over her shoulder and almost slid down the rope. With Patrick's single burner butane camp stove readily at hand, Claraicy boiled a pot of water and made herself a mug of tea. With the leftover water, she dumped in a bag of dehydrated potatoes and mixed in a can of flaked ham. The large meal made her groggy.

Too sore to move, Claraicy grabbed a nearby sleeping bag and used it as a pillow. Seeing her lying on the ground, Jesse crawled out from a narrow tunnel that she had been exploring and snuggled up beside her. Claraicy smiled and lovingly wrapped her arm around her grotesque daughter before falling asleep.

When she woke, there was almost no light coming into the cavern. Despite her entire body aching, she crawled over to the pile of camping equipment and pulled out a lantern. Turning on the gas, she pushed the igniter. The small ball of flames that puffed out told her that something was wrong. All of the shuffling and banging it had endured had broken its mantle. After fumbling through the backpacks, she found a package of mantles and replaced it.

It took time for her to get used to the bright light, but after she did, she didn't want to waste it. While unpacking the backpacks, she divided the cavern up into sections. She organized all the food in one area, camping equipment and tools in another and set up a comfortable sleeping area in yet another. Afterwards, she designated a small area next to the pool for them to use as a washroom. In front of it was a stream of water flowing from the wall. That made it was easy for her to flush their faeces and urine into the pool and let the constantly flowing water wash it away.

By the time daylight began to seep through the plastic bottles, Claraicy was sorting through all of the clothes she had scrounged. Using a sewing kit that her mother had packed, she sewed together a jumpsuit. The top section was made from a blue sweater with its back sliced almost to the collar, and the bottom from a pair of her mother's jogging pants that she had cut out the rear to allow for the tail. Held on by her legs, arms and collar, the outfit made her feel a bit more human. She looked at herself in a small mirror that she had stumbled upon in one of the backpacks. "It's a lot better than wearing furs."

As the days passed, she could feel almost every part of her body tingle. Her uncontrollable appetite had forced her to ration her food. Every time she got up to walk around the cavern she could feel more and more of her wings' presence. They were no longer foreign objects stuck on her back. They had become a part of her.

At the end of a week, she could look at her wings and they would slowly respond. Their bones grew harder and tissue tougher. Each of the wings stretched out over double her height. Inside the cavern, there was only enough room to fully spread out one of them at a time.

Standing beside the wall, she stretched out her wings in front of her. With their tips touching each other, Claraicy could see how massive they actually were. Her wingspan easily surpassed the width of the small house that she grew up in. They started at a second set of shoulder blades attached to her back, and ended at the tip of her curled up tail.

Hearing no activity going on outside, with Jesse in tow, Claraicy ventured into the pool and climbed out into the fresh air. As she spread out her wings, a faint breeze flowing through the trees was enough to push her backwards. With her wings folded up on her back she began her daily search for anything that could extend her dwindling food supply. As she rummaged through the forest, she could feel the short hairs growing through the cracks between her hard scales. They twitched and tingled, and she found that their roots were more sensitive than her old skin.

Within a week her wings had become a true part of her. A part of her that she desperately wanted to know how to use.

******

The glare off one of the plastic bottles Claraicy had shoved into the cracks on top of the rock caught Duncan's attention. DeGroot climbed a nearby tree to keep watch while Duncan worked his way up the steep rock. The faint aroma of cooked beans escaped through the opening he had made by removing one of the crushed plastic bottles. Peering inside, Duncan saw the small glow from a camp stove. "Ratlin, is that you down there?"

The soft blue light from the stove went out. Duncan lit a red signal flare and dropped it into the cavern. Not thinking, Claraicy threw a sleeping bag over it. A dark brown cloud rose up and started to fill the cavern as the fibres in the sleeping bag melted. The toxic smoke coming out of the crack temporarily blinded Duncan. After taking a deep breath, he shuffled his body over the crack. As the smoke found other places to exit, Duncan fanned it away with his hand. Through another plastic bottle, he got a fuzzy glimpse of Claraicy as she dragged the smothering sleeping bag over to the pool. After tossing both it and flare in, she looked up and saw him staring at her.

Claraicy instinctively grabbed Jesse and dove into the water. As she surfaced on the other side, DeGroot could hear some water splash. It didn't take him long to spot the hidden pool. He watched the dark blurry figure through the dense foliage as it got up and ran away. With Claraicy's wings flapping behind her, all he could see was a giant, undulating shadow as she disappeared down the narrow creek. "Duncan, that wasn't Ratlin."

"I know. It was our prey." Duncan quickly resealed the crack to prevent any excess smoke from escaping and drawing unwanted attention to the area. "Did you see where it went?"

"No, it was hiding under a cloak of some kind. However, a least we know the direction it was travelling."

Duncan and DeGroot both climbed down and met next to the murky pool. Duncan plunged into the water and emerged inside the cavern. Using his flashlight, he spotted Ratlin's pack and equipment. After briefly looking around, he swam back out and announced, "Ratlin must have been inside there at some point. We need to conceal this site. You stay here while I track down our prey."

The strange footprints led Duncan down a muddy creek bed. He found them very easy to follow until they came to a wall of thick, thorny brush. "If it could get through, so can I."

Taking off his backpack, he used it as a shield and forced his way through the tiny needles. The sound of rushing water made him grab a thorny branch with his bare hands as one of his feet slipped off the ledge. After regaining his balance he looked down the steep cliff at the wide, fast flowing creek below.

On the far side of the wide ravine, Duncan saw a large, shadowy figure staring back at him from behind some trees. It would take hours for him to get cross the deep gorge. "Any creature that could simply leap over a wide ravine would be long gone by time we got across."

Duncan slowly worked his way back to DeGroot, studying every footprint the creature made. They were neither human nor animal. It ran on two legs like a man leaving an animalistic imprint of only its toes. At places, the creature's strides were three metres apart.

In the deep muck, Duncan could make out the small slits extending above each wide toe. "Interesting, the humanoid creature has cat-like claws instead of toenails." Spotting signs of a huge dew claw extending a half metre away from its toes made he think. "That is one giant foot."

As Duncan walked through the narrow gap between the lush vegetation running along the banks of the creek, his foot got stuck. Looking down, he saw large fingers tightly wrapped around his ankle. Dropping to his knees, Duncan pushed aside the branches of a small bush with his forearm to get a better look at who was hiding beneath it. Ratlin's white eyes and teeth shone back at him. Pressed into the bank, his unrecognizable body was plastered in mud and vegetation. "About time you showed up."

"It's no wonder the cops didn't find you."

Duncan helped Ratlin work his way free from under the entwined tree roots and vegetation. Behind him, the lifeless body rolled out off a dry ledge and into the water. Ratlin smiled at Duncan, "Don't worry about him, he'll be fine. If it wasn't for the damn cops showing up, I would've had him back to camp and tested by now."

Duncan's torso straightened. "The cops have been gone for almost two weeks now."

Ratlin shook his head while replying, "Well, someone was out here beating the bushes."

"That was probably our prey." Duncan smiled and took a deep breath. "At least part of our mission is over. Now lets get you two out of here." Looking at the man's leg and arm, he added, "So, he was the one the cops had spotted on the rock."

"Sorry about that. I was trying to get him to the lake. I left him on the rock because the poor man just wanted a brief moment to soak in some sun. I thought he would be safe there while I prepared a hiding spot for him in the brush. Then the cops spotted him and everything went crazy. The helicopter wasn't travelling over its normal route. All the poor man wanted was to breathe in some fresh air before being crammed under a pile of bushes until we could transport him back to camp."

Bending over, Duncan used his fingers to peel away some of the mud from the man's face. "Surprise, surprise. I never thought I would see your face again."

Chapter Eighteen

David

From the outside, the doctor's newly constructed house didn't seem like much more than a quaint, ordinary cottage with an attached double-door garage. There was nothing extraordinary about it to draw unwanted attention.

The only unusual thing about the house was the strange way the garage butted up against the side of a huge hill that towered above the property. It appeared as if the garage was an afterthought, and the builders simply placed a beam from the roof of the house to the side of rocky hill, and then chiselled off what was needed to accommodate it.

Beneath both the house and garage was a thick, reinforced cement pad that formed the roof of the large open basement that Doctor Scott was turning into his laboratory. Inside, Jane was busy assembling the freshly unpacked lab equipment. With tubes of grease, several types of tape, wrenches, pliers, screwdrivers, and other various tools splattered over the U-shaped, stainless steel counter, the laboratory looked more like a workshop. It was full of all sorts of equipment in various stages of assembly.

Between the walls and the counter was a narrow walkway that allowed Jane to get to the wires and tubes at the back of the machines. At the open end were a couple of desks that were separated by a large sliding stainless steel door that led into a long underground hallway. The only other gap in the counter was the walkway to stairs that led up to door in the garage.

After helping Jane lift and position an autoclave onto the counter, the doctor told her, "You are much stronger than you look."

With droplets of sweat forming on her brow, she caught her breath and answered, "I get that a lot."

The doctor smiled at her. "Thank you for agreeing to help me."

Jane looked at the doctor. Dressed in paint smeared coveralls, unshaven and with his unbrushed hair pointing in every direction, he was still strikingly handsome. Aware of how she must appear, she looked away. "Thanks."

"How long do you think it would be before you can get the equipment ready for some samples?"

"I could have most of them put together in about two to three hours. After that, I still have to untangling some of the wires and figure out which one goes to each piece of equipment. Whoever packed them must have been in a real rush, I found wiring harnesses and various pieces of equipment packed in the wrong boxes."

Jane brushed some hair away from her face with her greasy hand while paced back and forth. "After I get all the equipment running, I will still have clean everything and flush out all the lines before I can start calibrating anything. I just hope that nothing got damaged in the move and that all the computer programs are still working."

Doctor Scott continued to smile at her. "So you are talking sometime tomorrow at the earliest."

Jane saw her reflection on the glass shield of a piece of equipment. Turning away from the doctor, she wiped away a smudge of grease from her cheek with a tissue from the side pocket of her lab coat. "After everything is set up, it could still take several hours to warm up all the equipment. During every stage of the procedure, each piece of machinery has to be thoroughly checked over to verify that everything is working properly. Once that is done, I can begin calibrating them. At the hospital I could do that in an hour and a half. Being a first start-up, we talking quadruple the work."

The doctor looked at Jane. Her hair was half pulled out of the elastic that tied it back in a ponytail. He knew that she was trying hard to impress him. Strands of hair were stuck to the sweat on her forehead. "Jane, you can finish putting the equipment together in the morning if you want. I wish that I could've been more help to you out here over the last week. I'm almost finished setting up the isolation rooms in the tunnel."

"When will I get to tour them? From the equipment that I saw you carry in, they must be amazing."

"Someday, but not yet." Before Jane could respond, Doctor Scott blurted out, "While I was back there, I got word that we should be expecting some samples around noon tomorrow. If we both get an early start and concentrate on just the equipment that we will initially need to use, we should be ready in time. We can finish setting up the rest as we need them. Right now, I think we both need a break." Rubbing his chin, he added, "And maybe a shave."

Jane leaned against the counter. She had been working steadily all day without a break. "Agreed, I am getting a bit pooped out." After taking a swig of water she added, "In fact, I'm all pooped out."

Doctor Scott smiled, not expecting such a low-brow expression to come out of her mouth. The doctor took off his coveralls and grabbed his jacket from the hook next to the door. "Good, I'm starved. Grab your coat, I know a nice place to eat."

******

After investigating the inside of the cavern, DeGroot began to crawl out of the murky pool. Looking up, he saw Ratlin smiling at him. Surprised, he lost his hand hold and slid back into the water.

As DeGroot stood up in the water, Ratlin commented, "That's a fine hello."

DeGroot scrambled out and hugged his mud covered comrade.

"Welcome back. Where's Stuart?" The words barely got out of his mouth before he saw Duncan plowing through the trees, carrying a mangled, naked man in his arms.

Duncan laid David down next to the water and washed the mud and muck off his body. When Duncan first met him, he was two hundred and fifty pounds of solid muscle. He was now less than a hundred.

Noticing DeGroot standing behind him, Duncan piped up. "DeGroot, meet David Rankin. He was one of the mercenaries who battled the creatures. Up until the time we found out that the creature was female, Doctor Scott thought that he might have even been the creature."

Ratlin piped up. "I thought that we were hunting for Sarah?"

"Not anymore."

David's eyes opened. "Duncan, you finally found me."

"We saw your trail through the fence and started to follow it, but between the ash and rain it petered out. Even though most of us thought the winter got you, we never stopped searching for your remains."

In barely a whisper, David said, "Ratlin had found more than just that."

Looking at the state of David's emaciated body, Duncan asked, "What happened to you?"

"I thought I heard a bear rustling in the woods and hid in a small cave for protection. I never saw daylight again until Ratlin rescued me."

Duncan looked around. "How did you survive?"

"Inside the cave where a series of cracks and tunnels that travelled throughout the surrounding rocks. What I had heard wasn't a bear. It was actually a few of the giant bats the doctors had used in the lab. For some reason, they wouldn't leave me alone. They nipped away at me with their sharp teeth and forced me deeper inside of the ridge. I couldn't escape them. When I got to the large cavern that Ratlin found me in, I covered up the tunnel's entrance and hoped that they couldn't get in."

David looked down at his deformed shoulder and briefly fell silent. "I was wrong. Those creatures could wiggle through anything." It took a while to muster up the strength to look at Duncan. "Did anyone else escape?"

"Doctor Scott and Doctor Stern were the only ones that survived the attack." Duncan continued to wash away the muck from of David's injuries. His severed arm had a film of skin over the wound and his leg had started to heal. Not surprised, Duncan asked him, "How did this happen?"

"While I was asleep, the bats had crawled through a crack in the outside rock. They dug out a large rock above me and worked it free. I was still half asleep when it toppled down on my leg. As I tried to push it off of me, they created a small landslide that pinned my shoulder. They knew exactly what they were doing."

As DeGroot hitched an intravenous drip to David's arm, he shook his head. "You are giving them to much credit. They are just bats."

David turned away from the orange fluid that was being injected into his veins and looked at DeGroot's face. "They held me prisoner for three-quarters of a year. I survived on bat guano and slime. I even ate dirt, just to stop my stomach from growling. Water seeping down the side of the cave wall at least gave me something to drink. The bats used me like a medicine cabinet. Every time one of them was injured they would gnaw away at either my trapped leg or arm and lap up my blood. The only good thing about it was that they would being me some food afterwards. It wasn't much, maybe a few berries, a frog or a small dead snake. Even when you are starving the taste of a raw snake can turn your stomach, but you force it down." Turning his head towards Duncan, he asked him, "Do you have any idea what it is like to be totally at the mercy of a pack of animals?"

"You may find it hard to believe, but yes, I think I do." Duncan looked at the scars on the back of his hands. He never considered the men that had taken pleasure in slowly cooking his flesh as human. They lived off of his pain like a wild pack of mongrel dogs. Looking back at David, he inquired, "How many bats were there?"

"Six. Eight at first. One vanished and another one would only occasionally reappear, usually after getting injured."

Ratlin spoke up. "I managed to shoot two of them when they attacked me in the cavern. After discovering that my rope had been cut, I decided not to stick around. I just grabbed David and got the hell out."

DeGroot spoke up. "I didn't see any remains in the cavern."

Duncan thought for a moment before replying. "Maybe the creature ate them." Looking at Ratlin, he continued. "You must have seen it? It swam out of the cavern and ran down the creek right past you."

"I saw a blur shortly before you ran by. Hidden under all the vegetation, I thought that was the wind playing tricks on me."

Drake saw Duncan and DeGroot carry David into the camp. Several metres behind them, Ratlin slowly came into sight. Without a word said, he ran to Ratlin and helped him into his bunk.

Ann held the big tent's flap open while DeGroot and Ratlin carried David inside. While DeGroot picked him up and placed him on a bed, Duncan removed two duffle bags from the stretcher and put them outside the tent. Doctor Stern quickly examined David and poked more IVs into his body. Turning to Ann, he told her, "His blood is too thick to take any samples. We may have to wait 'til tomorrow morning before taking any."

"All I need is a drop. Can't you squeeze that out?"

The doctor looked at Ann's frazzled face. "I think I can manage a drop or two, but that's all."

After the doctor gave Ann a small vial, Duncan pulled him outside. With no one else around, he told him, "The mission has changed. Several of the bats had escaped from the old facility. There may be up to seven of them on the loose. Ratlin shot two of them but until we find their bodies we can't discard them." After a brief pause, he continued. "The creature that we have been chasing has evolved. She is no longer human. DeGroot and I tried to take as many samples as we could. Hopefully one of them will shed some light on what is happening to her."

Duncan carried the duffle bags to the doctor's tent. The doctor waited until he left before opening them. They were full of plastic bags containing anything they thought might contain the creature's DNA. There were rags, bowls, sleeping bags, eating utensils and even bat guano. "There is too much for us to process out here."

In the middle of the night, Drake and DeGroot quietly left the camp with David and the two duffel bags full of samples. In the still night air, every minute sound echoed over the water. With barely a hum coming from the raft's electric motor, more noise was made from its wake splashing against the shore.

They quickly made their way out of the lake, down a creek, into another lake, through a swampy marsh and into yet another lake. By the time they got there, the crest of the morning sun glowed over the tree tops and made the water shimmer. A few trees had started to turn into their vibrant fall colours. David took in the spectacular view. It was his first real sunrise in almost a year.

A few flakes of snow drifted downwards as Marq's plane landed. Even though it was brief and was gone as quickly as it started, it was still the first snow of the season. Drake lifted David into the passenger seat of the plane and placed the two duffel bags in the back while DeGroot held the raft steady. As Marq secured David's IVs to a handle above the door, barely a word was said except, "Keep an eye on them and make sure they don't come out. The doc expects him to be alive when he arrives."

"Don't worry, I've transported more patients then I can count. He'll be fine."

The two exhausted soldiers sat in the raft and watched the plane fly away. DeGroot smiled at Drake as he turned on the motor. "With the money the doctor pays him, he should have a fleet of brand new planes by now."

"He's not stupid. He knows how to spend it without attracting unwanted attention. The planes he flies may look old, but their engines and equipment are all top of the line. That's why Duncan enlisted him. He's smart. He knows how to play the game."

******

Doctor Scott met Marq as he landed his plane. With people watching, he hugged David like an old friend and helped Marq get him into a wheelchair. As he wheeled him to his dark green Landrover and put him into the passenger seat, Marq carefully placed the duffel bags into the trunk. A local fisherman sitting beside the fuel pump next to the dock gave Marq a polite wave. Marq reciprocated the gesture.

As far as anyone was concerned, David was just a handicapped passenger being dropped off. After David was strapped into the passenger seat, the doctor patiently waited for Marq to finish tying up his plane. The small two-seater plane was dwarfed next to the larger twin prop that he normally used.

Before driving off, the doctor twisted around towards the back seat. He then pulled an envelope out of his breast pocket and passed it to Marq. "When we get back to my place, I need to go over some stuff with you. It should only take fifteen minutes or so. The way this is going, you should be able to afford that new jet you always wanted, maybe even a small commuter airline."

At the house, Marq helped the doctor place David into a wheelchair and then grabbed both duffle bags. After going through the man-door of the garage, they turned right and proceeded to what appeared to be an unused section of wall. The large steel door was carefully camouflaged. Behind a fake set of electrical outlets, the doctor both disarmed and unlocked the door. Marq pushed against the left side of it and let the counterweights and electric motors do the rest. The door sunk into the wall and then slid sideways behind a wall of heavy-duty shelving that extended from the floor all the way to the ceiling of the garage.

The doctor wheeled David inside and Marq followed him with the bags. They proceeded down the long corridor of secured rooms that were carved out of the rock. In the second room there was a bed and a complete living room setup including a wall mounted TV and a refrigerator. Still under the effects of the drugs in his IV, David opened one eye and looked at the view coming out of the panel of glass beside the bed. "At least there's no bars on the window."

"It's not a window. It is just a large monitor connected to a camera outside. You can use the arrow keypad below it to move the camera around to change the angle you wish to view. It was the best I could offer you."

Flopping his head to his chest, David muttered, "So I'm still a prisoner unable to breathe in fresh air."

As the doctor clipped the IVs to a stand, he replied, "I had excellent air exchangers installed. The air is as fresh as it is outside, only warmer."

The doctor secured him to the bed and covered him with a blanket. After hitching him to some monitors, he heard him ramble on. "At least it's better than being held captive by a bunch of bats."

Standing in the doorway, Marq had learned to tune out a lot of what he heard. After seeing Duncan alive, a man that was reported dead and even had a full military funeral, he knew better than to ask any questions. He knew that he was involved in something big. He just couldn't figure out why the army needed a civilian pilot. Unless he was just an expendable cover, and that meant he had to be extra careful.

As the doctor left David's room, he waved Marq into the room next to the exit. Sitting down, the doctor was unable to look at Marq's face as he spoke. "The man you ditched ended up killing that police officer that was on the front page of the newspaper a while ago. We thought the drugs in his system would make him want to ran and hide instead of attack. We wanted him out there to take the police on a wild goose chase. We were wrong." The doctor looked up at Marq. "I'm pretty sure your friend Ryan is now off the hook."

"So where does that leave me?"

"No one will ever touch any of us. We plucked that soldier out of a military prison. I'm only a paid-off pawn just a few levels above you in this operation. You're real smart and you're always thinking. Even right now, I bet that your brain is going a hundred miles an hour." The doctor stood up and added, "Duncan didn't recruit you because of your piloting skills. He knew that you were loyal, patriotic and would have made an excellent officer had you enlisted. I don't know much about his past but I trust his judgement."

The doctor looked down at his desk. "You probably know more about Duncan than I do. However, we both trust him. If you didn't, no matter how much money I paid you, you wouldn't have agreed to help me."

"Despite his brother, growing up, he was one of my best friends."

"He's not the same person anymore. Now he has strict orders to kill anyone that compromises the mission, and he would. My competitors have already tried to highjack and sabotage my research. If anything goes wrong, we may be taking everything to our graves or find an early one. The stakes are way too high, but I think you knew all of this, didn't you?"

With a solemn face, Marq answered, "When I was growing up, all of the kids relied on Duncan to protect them. None of the grownups cared about us. He was our one kid police force. None of us knew just how much we relied on him until he enlisted. When someone like that asks for your help, you know what you are getting into."

After a long period of silence, the pair started to quickly go over some flight schedules. With the maps tucked away in his pants pocket, Marq grabbed one of the duffel bags and helped the doctor carry them down a sloping corridor. At the end of the corridor was a door leading into the lab. Jane was sitting at her computer verifying the results of her trial runs. The clicking of the keys on the keyboard drowned out the door opening and the two men's footsteps.

The doctor leaned over her shoulder to see what she was doing. Startled, she jumped up. Her shoulder caught the bottom of his jaw. Blood started to pour out of the doctor's mouth.

Jane quickly grabbed the first aid kit hanging on the wall. Turning around she saw Marq. For a brief second, she froze and then smiled. The puzzled look on his face quickly returned her sober demeanor. She knew that he didn't remember her.

Shoving the cuff of his sleeve into his mouth to prevent blood getting everywhere, Dr. Scott mumbled, "Marq, this is Jane, my latest recruit."

Using the round shiny side of autoclave like a mirror, Doctor Scott examined the extent of his injury. He had bitten his tongue and cracked his lip. Jane handed him a compressed bandage to soak up the blood. "I'm sorry, you startled me."

"It's okay. I should have known better then to look over someone's shoulder when they are concentrating on their work."

The bleeding began to slow down and he could feel his lip swelling up. "Marq just flew in the samples we were waiting for. After my mouth stops bleeding, it could take me up to a few hours to prep the first batch for you to test. How about taking some time off? You have been working like a beaver." Looking over at Marq he added, "I know! Marq, you need a ride back. How about you take this nice, young lady up for a relaxing, scenic joy ride. My tab."

The doctor threw his keys to Marq before either could respond. "Jane can drive it back."

Still a little stunned, Jane looked at Marq and then back at the doctor. "Thanks, but are you sure that I can't help with the samples?"

Looking at the blood on the bandage, Doctor Scott answered, "No, I'll be fine. Go and have a good time. You deserve it."

Jane replied, "Okay, but we'll take my car. That way I won't have to be worried about scratching yours."

Marq looked at Jane and placed the doctor's keys on the counter. "All right, let's go."

At first Jane felt hurt and was a little angry that Doctor Scott had passed her off to another man so easily. Stopping for lunch at the diner next to the pier, Jane decided to stick to a bowl of soup. The thought of flying in a small plane with a full stomach made her queasy. As her nerves started to get to her, her skin began to turn pale.

Watching her try to steady her coffee with both hands, Marq smiled. "Don't worry. We'll be going up in my twin engine bush plane. I don't think you are quite ready for a two-seater."

"I think that would be much better." Jane took the elastic out of her hair and ran her fingers through it. Her long, straight black hair fell over the sides of her face and unto her shoulders. Marq suddenly remembered seeing her before, but where, when? It is hard to forget such an attractive woman.

Marq put his hand on Jane's slight waist and helped her into his plane. Not remembering the circumstances of how they first met, he decided to tread carefully. "You should wear your hair down more often."

"I would if I could, but I can't work with it down."

"You can't work all the time. What do you do for fun?"

"Read, swim and try to get skin cancer when there's some sun."

As he finished his preflight checklist, he asked, "How long have you been living here?"

She watched him put away his clipboard as she answered. "Three years."

Marq still couldn't remember where they had met. The last thing he wanted was to cause friction between him and Dr. Scott. Not knowing how to reply, he decided to say nothing.

Jane held on tight as the plane took off across the water. Still expecting to be on the water, she opened her eyes as Marq levelled the plane and flew over a small clump of trees. "That wasn't that bad, and a lot faster than I expected."

"The new high performance engines I had installed suck up the fuel during liftoff, but make a huge difference." Marq flew around in the same pattern he took almost all the tourists. The fall colours were not at their peak, but enough to make the rich, scenery absolutely magnificent. Jane's face slowly started to return to its normal colour. Marq took this as a sign to extend his flight. "I'll show you where I was brought up."

Marq flew over the house that he was born and raised in. He identified each house they drifted over, his uncle's, the Stuart's, the LeChasseur's and all the other families he was brought up with. On the edge of town, Jane pointed out a house decorated in Christmas lights and candy canes. "Who's that?"

"That's Satan Claus'. The Mitchell's leave their lights on all year long in hope that some dumb kid comes a knocking. That fat, lazy slob even bleaches his long hair and beard white at Christmas time. There are a lot of rumours floating around about him No one that knows him trusts him."

"Are you talking about Kerry Mitchell?"

"The one and the same. The fat, ugly, pervert, Satan Claus."

Chapter Nineteen

The cabin

A mere stone's throw from his cabin, Ryan lay under a bush and quietly waited. His sunken cheeks and taut skin portrayed only a part of his ordeal as sharp pains shot up from his badly injured leg. The deep gashes Claraicy had sliced into his arm and shoulder with her claws were minor compared to the severe muscle damage she had inflicted on his leg and the right side of his torso. It was dawn when he had first spotted his cabin from the far side of the small, long lake in front of it. It had taken him 'til mid-afternoon to hobble and crawl his way to the cabin.

The moment he saw the door, he knew that someone had already been there. The tiny twig that he had wedged on the top of it were missing. Unable to go anywhere, he hid under the bush and waited to see if anyone was still there. After a few hours, he saw a raccoon sniffing around the cabin's door. The curious animal showed no signs of anxiety, which it would if someone was inside. As the cold, damp night air crept in, he felt that he had no choice.

Since the attack, the only food he had to eat was a few insects, some scattered berries, the odd root and some disgusting vegetation that was only fit for deer. With his injuries he was barely able to move, let alone forage for food. The ordeal had stripped away all of his reserves and he desperately needed something substantial to eat.

Using a stick, he lifted himself upright and hobbled his way to the cabin. The racoon glanced at him and ran away. The inside of the cabin had been ransacked. Almost everything he owned was scattered over the floor. His walls were stripped bare along with his closet and cup-boards.

Whoever did it was long gone. On the floor was a can of sardines. Using his stick he slid it over to the side of the bed ahead of him. The mattress had been flipped into its edge against the wall. He used his stick to flop it down unto the wooden bed slats. With great care he slowly laid down.

With his good left arm, he reached over the side of the bed and picked up the can of sardines. Pulling back the peel top lid, he drank the salty sardine water and one by one devoured the small fish. He fell asleep within seconds after the empty tin rolled onto the floor. It didn't last for long. He was awoken by a sharp pain running along his side and down his leg.

He could feel the blood oozing out of his makeshift bandages of moss and yarrow leaves. His right side had been clawed at and both his shoulders bitten. His leg had received the most damage as he had tried to kick Claraicy away from him. Unable to get his pistol out of its holster, if it wasn't for his spear, he believed that she would have killed him.

Ryan got up and found his first aid kit along with some other medical supplies. With them spread over his bed and on the floor next to him, he began removing his makeshift bandages. First, he cut the bindings that held the protective outer layer of birch bark in place. Then he pulled off the moss and yarrow leaves he had used as a dressing. He had used fishing line to suture the more serious wounds. After he ran out of line, he was forced to use long thorns. By piercing them through both sides of the gash and wrapping the veins from the yarrow leaves around both ends of them in a figure eight, he had held the wounds together. As the thorns were disturbed, some of the newly formed scabs broke open and started to bleed.

In places, the fishing line had ripped through the skin, exposing sections of scabbed-over muscle. With some of the smaller gashes starting to heal, infection from the thorns made the skin around them swell. He flicked off a few maggots that had been feasting on sections of dead tissue. Without being able to properly care for his wounds, letting them eat the dead flesh had kept the wounds relatively clean and they showed no evidence of gangrene.

After cleaning and wiping the wounds with disinfectant, he began the painful process of restitching several of the large gashes. Running out of alcohol patches, he began using whiskey to disinfect his wounds. Not worried about excess bleeding, for every two to three shots of whiskey he used, he drank one to thin his blood and improve the circulation in his leg. Its numbing effect was both a bonus and a hindrance. It took away the pain, but made it harder for him to sew up his wounds.

The next morning, Ryan found his camouflaged fall hunting outfit and gingerly put on the pants, shirt and jacket over his bandages. After tying up his boots, he walked over to the table and felt something rubbed against his sore side. It didn't take him long to find and remove a small plastic bag glued inside the lining of the jacket. "Willy, you stupid idiot, you should have at least put it on the edge so I won't notice it so easily."

After dumping everything out of his backpack, he found another tracking device tucked neatly under a flap. Filled with paranoia, he checked everything. Tapping on a can of beans, he found one that had a false bottom that encased another device. He also discovered one of the devices glued into a deep tread on his left boot.

While heating up some water for tea, Ryan went through his refrigerator and freezer. By the time the fire in his stove had died, everything he could salvage from them was either cooked or dried into jerky. Anything that could spoil had to be either eaten or left behind. While re-packing his spare backpack with whatever he could fine, he sipped his tea and ate a couple platefuls of eggs, bacon and steak. After wrapping a steak sandwich and placing it on top of his bag, he stretched out on his bed.

Exhausted and full of endorphins, for a brief time he forgot about everything that was going on around him. The sound of a plane landing on the lake in front of his cabin snapped him back to reality. After stuffing the sandwich into his pants pocket, he grabbed his backpack and belt. As the plane turned around at the far end of the lake and taxied towards the cabin, he hobbled out the door before anyone inside the plane could see him.

With a sturdy walking stick and cloth bandages made mostly from bedding, he found it easier to move. He snuck behind the cabin and used it as a shield. As Willy ran towards the cabin, Ryan hopped past the narrow, neatly piled stacks of firewood.

A silent pressure alarm attached to one of the floorboards of the cabin had alerted Willy. Along with the tracking devices attached to various objects inside the cabin, he had also fastened motion-activated game cameras to various trees surrounding it. One look inside told him that Ryan had already left. As Andy approached, Willy ordered him to climb the trees and switch the SD cards in the cameras.

Using a viewfinder to flip through the photos, Willy got past the wildlife and smiled as the first picture of Ryan appeared. "I told you he would come back here." Excited, he proudly showed Andy the photos of Ryan. "Look, the sad-sac got himself badly injured. That could account for the blood on his canoe."

Andy piped up. "Why don't you give it up and leave him alone? It's wasn't Ryan that attacked those people and killed that officer. The real culprit is hiding somewhere around that lake."

With a smirk on his face, Willy told him, "But the piece of scum that I'm after is right here."

As Willy went back into the cabin, he took a closer look around. The piece left of the tracking devices that Ryan had found were sitting on the kitchen counter. With the toe of his boot, he spread out the mound of blood-filled moss that was lying on the floor. Grinning from ear to ear, Willy commented, "This is going to be easier than I thought. By the looks of things, I'd say the bastard is in real bad shape. Why else would he risk packing his wounds with dirty leaves?" Looking over at Andy, he asked, "What is all this bloody crap on the floor anyways?"

The young native easily recognized the various components of Ryan's discarded dressing. "The plant that look like feathers is called soldier's woundwort. You call it yarrow. Native warriors would put it on their wounds to help stop them from bleeding."

Kneeling over, he picked up a clump of moss. Two broken, scab-encrusted thorns were resting on top of it. "This man is a survivor. He is capable of anything." Shaking his head, he added, "You know what they say about a wounded animal. They're unpredictable and that makes them dangerous. To run them down is plain stupid. A smart hunter waits them out. If you give their injuries time to stiffen, their state of mind diminishes as the adrenaline wears off and the pain increases."

"Someone has to put them out of their misery and I say the quicker the better."

Shivers started running the length of Andy's back. "You just want him to fight back and give you an excuse to shoot to kill."

Willy smiled at Andy. "He's still a person of interest and if he resists, I won't think twice about defending myself."

******

Ryan knew every inch of the surrounding woods and exactly where to go. He had stacked firewood in various places throughout the area, waiting for enough snow to haul it out by sled. Ryan always liked to have his firewood cut a year or two ahead. He wanted to be sure he always had enough cured wood. Near several of the piles, he had made makeshift shelters. In most cases it was only a simple lean-to to protect him from the rain.

His wounds were patched up and he had plenty of medical and camping supplies in his pack. He knew that fresh water and shelter would not be a problem, but if he had to wait them out, food would be. Limited to carrying only what his bad leg could bear, he only packed enough food for a couple weeks. He could stretch that amount out for an extra week if he had to, but his body was already malnourished and needed time to recover. After his food was gone, he knew that he would have to rely on the land.

Ryan wasn't too concerned about Willy finding him. He knew more about tracking than almost anyone else in the area. That was why the authorities normally called on him for any search and rescue missions. He also knew how to avoid leaving a trail. In the open where he couldn't hide his tracks, he knew how to disguised them. He would convert the appearance of the tracks to mimic that of a bear's or another type of large creature.

His worst fear was being spotted by the plane that was buzzing overhead. The pitch of the plane's motor signalled its direction. As the pitch decreased, he knew that the plane was turned away from him. That meant that he was free to hobble his way towards a large and hopefully abandoned bear den.

******

From the backseat of the aeroplane, Willy and Andy studied the forest. With the leaves beginning to turn into their fall colours, it was hard to make out anything. With the sun heating the rocks and the abundant wildlife, the infrared heat detector installed in the plane was useless. Feeling discouraged, Willy screamed at the pilot, "How can we see anything from here, we are too far up."

The red-faced pilot yelled back at him, "If we get any closer to the ground, all you will see will be a blur and this plane can't fly any slower."

Andy looked over at Willy as he peered through a pair of binoculars. "This is stupid. A scared rabbit will never come out of his hole. Don't you get it? He's a ghost. If I couldn't even spot his trail on the ground, he's not going to let you see him from up here."

Willy dismissed his colleague's remark. "Listen, Brown, nothing is going to stop me from getting this guy." While lifting the binoculars back up to his eyes, he added, "And I mean nothing."

The pilot interrupted their conversation. "Nothing but time. We're running low on fuel and I'm being questioned about why I broke off from the main search. Your side adventure here is not cutting it with my dispatcher."

"Then drop us off. We'll find him on foot."

******

Inside the communications trailer that the army had airlifted into the forest for the police to use, Detective Arnold picked up the microphone. "How's the search going?"

A helicopter pilot flying over a creek leading away from the lake replied, "He simply disappeared. They've searched the entire lake three times. I think we have identified every fish, beaver and muskrat in that lake by now. Some of them fish are huge, I gotta come back here with a pole sometime."

Out of frustration, the detective took off his hat and vigorously scratched his head with both hands. Pounding his fist against the wall of the trailer, he exploded. "They can count the fish in the lake, but they can't find a warm-blooded object the size of a man?"

The army corporal sitting beside him spoke up. "This guy is more than just good. He has to be professionally trained."

The detective stood up and started to pace back and forth until he started to sweat. Resting his hand on the army corporal's shoulder, he inquired, "What if the army had trained him? What if he was one of yours?"

The soldier looked up at him. "If he's Special Forces, forget about him. He'll never be found nor captured. Those guys aren't even men, they are trained machines. The tans are the best in the world. Not even the Yankee green bonnets or the British SAS can touch them."

The pale corporal sat at his post as the angry detective continued to pace and rant. "If he is one of yours, maybe one of your best should get out there and search for him. Why should everyone be breathing down my neck? It looks to me like this may be more your problem than it is ours."

After a few minutes, the detective sat down along a counter filled with aerial photographs. A knock on the door sent the corporal outside. As the soldier returned, a large scruffy man followed him inside the command centre. "Detective Arnold, this is Colonel Stuart. He's here to evaluate the situation."

The detective turned away from the series of aerial photos he was studying. As he swivelled his office chair, his arm slid a couple photos onto the floor. The large man stretching out his hand looked more like a wild motorcycle gang member than a soldier. His clothes were tattered and covered in mud. The only sign of him being a Colonel in the Canadian Armed Forces were his dog tags, his domineering manner and the tan beret that he was wearing.

"Colonel Stuart?" The detective studied the man's face. Even with mud filling in most of his scars, he recognized him. "Duncan, I never knew that you were a member of the Special Forces."

"You were not supposed to."

The stunned detective soberly asked him, "What were you doing with Doctor Scott?"

Duncan coldly answered him, "The military saw some potential in his work, and you probably have a good idea of the rest."

Detective Arnold looked at him. "That's the problem, I don't, and you made sure that I didn't." Glancing at the corporal, he added, "Is he one of yours?"

"Of course." Duncan turned to the Corporal. "I'll need a copy of all the aerial photos taken to date, in chronological order. I want to start at the beginning."

"Yes, sir." The corporal wasted no time and began rummaging through the file cabinets.

Duncan studied the photos that were spread over the table. "Are these the most recent images?"

The detective turned his chair around to the counter. "Yes."

Over his shoulder, Duncan pointed at the corner of one of the photos. "What do you see?"

"Nothing. Nothing but bush and bulrushes."

Tipping his finger on the picture, he informed the detective, "That bush was me working my way here. I've been on the ground with two of my men for a few days now. We could've had a party out there and your people wouldn't have spotted us." Duncan picked up the photo. "Now, how could you expect your crew to find one man who doesn't want to be found?"

While resting his elbows on the table, Detective Arnold cradled his face in his hands. "So, what will you be needing from me this time?"

"First, get everything out of the air. He won't leave his hole if he thinks he's being watched. Second, I require your total and complete cooperation. The third and final thing will be for you and your men to leave us alone to do our job. That means I demand that you get everyone out of here, even you. There will be no more body bags flown out of here while I'm in charge. This is going to be a completely military operation. Got it?"

Detective Arnold glared at Duncan's cold, mud-covered face. "So it's just like before. You're going to fence everyone out and so you can have your own private war games."

******

Ryan deliberately travelled in intersecting circles so anyone good enough to track him wouldn't know where or even the direction he was heading. On a smooth, rocky ridge he veered off the circle in a fashion that no evidence could be left behind. Once he got to the entrance of a bear cave, he looked back. Through the trees he could see sections of the circle that he had veered off of. It would be easy to spot anyone tracking him. Between the rocky terrain and thick vegetation that should give him plenty of time to take whatever action he deemed necessary.

A steady rain had eroded almost all the footprints in front of the cave. What was left of the prints were smudged obscure depressions with no defining characteristics. Ryan couldn't even tell how old they were. Going onto his left knee, he shone his flashlight into the cave before crawling inside.

The cave was high enough that he could sit upright, and wide enough that he could stretch out his legs with room to spare. A familiar smell overtook him. Shining his flashlight to the back of the cave, he saw some movement coming from a narrow crevice. As it turned to face him, the reflection from a pair of big, round, bright green eyes glared back at him. They were the wrong colour for a bear.

The low rumbling words, "I thought I killed you?" vibrated through the cave.

Ryan froze. His flashlight slipped from his shaking hand and rattled down the side of a large rock. He was left in the dark.

Chapter Twenty

Close encounters

After the plane dropped him off, Willy blindly walked straight into the woods and crossed one of Ryan's paths without spotting it. No matter how quiet Andy tried to be, Willy's fumbling broadcasted their whereabouts to Ryan. With Willy only a fifty metres away, he glanced into the dark cave and knew that he had nowhere to go.

With his leg beginning to seize up, he knew that there was no way he could outrun Willy or the creature. He sunk into the shadows. Even as the temperature began to drop, Ryan started to sweat. All he could think of was to pacify the creature and pray that it knew that they both were in danger.

Ryan's head flipped back and forth from the back of the cave to the snapping twigs in the forest. The deep cavern appeared empty but he knew that the creature was still in there. There was only one exit and he was sitting in front of it. Facing the darkness, Ryan whispered, "One of the men out there is gun crazy and would love to put a bullet into me. You would be a witness. If he spots you, I don't believe he would think twice about killing you and throwing your body into a shallow grave right beside mine."

There was no response. Claraicy didn't move. Ryan rested his revolver on top of his upright knee and pointed it where he had seen her eyes. He felt that if she had wanted to attack him, she would have done it already. The sounds coming from the forest were getting further and further away. After a couple minutes of silence, Ryan whispered, "Why did you stop? Why did you allow me to escape?"

Ryan's questions made the blood rush to Claraicy's head. Who was he to question her? He knew nothing about her. Claraicy snapped back in a low, growling voice that rattled around the cave. "You are not the reason that I am out here."

As Ryan tried to speak, Claraicy's voice got louder, "You got it all wrong. You are the witness. That cop that is after you is nothing compared to the men after me." After a brief pause, she asked him, "Why didn't you leave when I told you? I didn't want to hurt you but you gave me no choice."

By the way her voice vibrated off the walls of the cave, he knew that she wasn't where he had thought she was. Ryan adjusted the muzzle of his revolver before answering. "I'm paid to protect the people inside the park and that is what I was trying to do."

With the muzzle of his revolver pointing at a large rock, Claraicy knew that he had no idea where she was. Projecting her voice off the rock, she replied, "And I'm just trying to stay alive."

With her voice echoing in a slightly different manner every time she spoke, he was leery of her location. "By mutilating people?"

Watching the tip of Ryan's gun travel back and forth, she lowered her voice and replied, "Only those that deserve it."

The subdued tone in her voice made him feel easier. As he tried to flex his stiff throbbing leg, he bit his lower lip. With some sunlight reflecting off the side of his face, Claraicy could see the pain he was under. In barely a whisper, she asked, "How is your leg?"

"Not as bad as I first thought. It must not have been as deep as it first looked because it's healing faster than I expected it would." Ryan shook some of the sweat away from his eyes and thought for a moment. "This is getting silly. My name is Ryan, what can I call you?"

"Claraicy." It suddenly dawned on her that this was the longest conversation that she had ever had with a boy. They normally ended after a short sentence or verbal wisecrack.

As Ryan's stomach began to rumble, the sound echoed in the cave and was amplified ten times louder than it was. He could hear sounds in the trees that indicated Willy was still out there. *Even a small herd of caribou or a large moose in rut with humungous antlers wouldn't make as much racket.* After his stomach rumbled some more, he detected movement from various sections of the far end of the cave.

He reached for his flashlight and then stopped. The sun was going down and any form of light could signal their location. Feeling like a rabbit hiding under a bush while a pair of dogs circled it, Ryan peered into the cave as he opened his pack. Scared and knowing some form of detente was needed, he asked, "Claraicy, are you hungry?"

"Yes."

"I have homemade jerky, trail-mix, nuts, raisins, dried fruit and some Chinese noodles. The rest of the stuff needs to be cooked. Does any of that sound good to you?"

Claraicy abruptly answered, "Noodles."

Ryan tossed a bag to the back of the cave. He could hear her crawl towards it. As she picked it up, the plastic wrapper reflected some of the limited light in the cave. In a rush to open it, Claraicy split the bag open and most of it scattered over the ground.

Ryan reached in his pack and pulled out a second one. "Here, try again."

Feeling humiliated she sharply replied, "No."

The sounds in the forest stopped. Ryan listened for about twenty minutes until they returned. He picked up a piece of jerky and started to chew it. All that time he could hear Claraicy as she gathered up the fine, broken pieces of noodles and crunched them between her teeth. As the sound echoed, Ryan got up the nerve to ask her, "Don't you care if you get caught?"

"No. Yes. I suppose so."

That night the pair barely moved. Claraicy hid in the shadows while Ryan crouched down by the entrance with his rolled up sleeping bag supporting his back and a blanket on top. With one hand on the edge of his blanket in case he had to escape and the other hand clutching his revolver, he spent a long, weary night. As the heat from the rising sun woke him, he wiggled his body deeper into the shadows. His movement woke Claraicy. "Don't come any closer."

"Okay, don't worry." Ryan wasn't as afraid of her as he had been. He had spent a lot of time with animals, and thought of this wild half-human creature as one of them. He knew that mutual respect, space and trust is all most domestic or wild animals require.

"You say don't worry, but why should I trust you? What makes you different than the rest of the men out there?"

"I didn't shoot you, did I?"

"No, but that could be because you were afraid the shot would pinpoint your location to the men that are after you."

Ryan couldn't respond. She was probably right. While sharing some jerky with Claraicy, he heard some scratching coming from along the wall of the cave. He picked up a pebble and tossed it at the sound. Claraicy screamed out, "Don't you dare hurt Jesse."

Ryan's neck stiffened and his face turned pale. "I'm sorry! I didn't know you had someone with you. I thought you were alone."

Every nerve in his body started to quiver. His heart and lungs raced. Ryan whipped his head back and forth trying to look both outside for Willy and at Claraicy at the same time. Claraicy slowly crawled toward him. Ryan pointed his revolver at her forehead.

As the sun slipped behind a cloud, the dim light and shadows gave her a mesmerizing appearance. Long, matted strands of dangling hair obscured her unusual, slightly deformed face with wide shadowy stripes. The hump on her back had been replaced by what looked like a crumbled up blanket. "If you think that I'm afraid of that thing, you're wrong. I could tear the head off your neck before you could empty that toy gun of yours." Claraicy placed her hand in front of the gun's muzzle. "Because, that's what it would take to stop me."

Ryan could see Claraicy's long sharp nails protruding out of the ends of her thicker than normal fingers. Her hands and claws had grown since she had attacked him. They were definitely not human, but they weren't canine or feline either. They were a mixture of all three. He carefully placed his revolver on the ground. "I didn't mean to harm your friend. I just thought it was a scavenger trying to get at the food."

Claraicy reached down and grabbed Ryan's ankle. "Don't forget whose woods we're in. It's not yours anymore." Claraicy sunk back into the shadows. "Don't piss me off. Next time, you may not survive."

Ryan tucked his knees against his chest. "I know that you could've easily killed me back there."

"I've changed a lot since then. I'm faster, stronger and with each day that goes by I'm becoming more animal than human. You saw my claws. Can you imagine me putting nail polish on them?" Claraicy looked into Ryan's enlarged eyes. "Relax, I'm not going to hurt you, at least not this time."

Ryan watched Claraicy as she crawled backwards into the shadows. "What happened to you?"

"I don't really know. All I know is that every time I look into a pool of water, I see less and less of myself."

Ryan could hear a change in Claraicy's voice. It was no longer cold and angry. It was sad.

Claraicy continued talking. "All I see is this monstrous creature slowly consuming every cell of my body. I don't know if I'm even human anymore."

"Of course you are. You just have some strange medical condition, that's all."

Ryan could hear some sobbing in Claraicy's voice. "When you saw me on the rock beside the lake, I was still somewhat human. Now, I'm more monstrous, and part of me is starting to like it."

"Monsters don't have emotions. You obviously do, therefore you can't be a monster."

Claraicy never replied, instead she tossed a handful of dirt into Ryan's face and hid in the shadows. After dusting the dirt from around his eyes, he could hear half-muffled whimpers coming from the back of the cavern. He knew better than to say another word.

Picking up his revolver, Ryan looked outside. He couldn't hear anything out of the ordinary. Birds were singing and he saw squirrels chasing each other through the branches. If anyone was out there, the woods would be much quieter. Ryan looked back towards Claraicy. He instinctively knew that she didn't want to harm him, but like dealing with any frightened, wild creature, he had to tread carefully.

An hour had passed before Ryan uttered a word. "I don't think the cops are out there anymore." With no response he added, "They are not looking for you, so who are you hiding from?"

"The soldiers."

"So that's why they showed up here. I saw a plane dropping off a squad of Special Forces, along with a couple of civilians."

"They chased me out of the cave I was living in, but I'm too fast for them." After a brief pause, she continued, "No one will ever hurt me again. Never again."

Memories of the deformed figure that he saw on the rock came back to him. "I know how fast and agile you are."

Trying to calm her back down, Ryan asked in a gentle voice, "How is your back? It looked like it was causing you a lot of pain when I first saw you."

"Much better." Claraicy's voice began to get lower. "At least it doesn't hurt anymore."

Ryan looked down at his swollen leg and started to wonder. *Did she pass on whatever had infected her?* A tremble ran through him. He thought of this wild girl like he would a cornered bear. She could turn from hot to cold, then back to a boil within a flash.

Ryan nervously turned away and tried to refocus his attention to what was going on outside the cave. In the forest, he knew what to do and had more control over everything around him. With his binoculars, he systematically scanned the surrounding area. Everything appeared normal.

"The army may be after you, but I don't think they are interested in me? I gotta find out if anyone is out there." Not getting any response, he added, "I'll be coming back."

Ryan snuck out of the cave. Using a stick to prop himself up, he quietly made his way through the brush. He easily spotted almost every footstep Willy and his companions made. *A herd of rooting hogs would have been harder to follow.*

It didn't take him long to discover their abandoned campsite. A few of the bigger coals in their fire pit were still warm. By the way the dirt sunk into the ashes and their temperature, he determined that they had left shortly before sunset. Their trail led straight back to the lake next to his cabin. "They must have flown out."

A large shadow had suddenly blocked out the sun. Ryan looked up. Standing on a tree branch above him was Claraicy. One of her gigantic, light reddish-brown wings was spread out as far as it could go and blocked out the sun. The wing appeared to start at her neck and end a metre below her feet, near the tip of a clawed, mace-like tail. She stood there with one elongated foot gripping a branch and the sharp claws of the other foot deeply embedded in the trunk. The dew claw on each heel securely anchored her feet in place as the gentle wind fluttered her wing like a huge Chinese sail. Pressed against her chest she held a young creature that looked like a small, deformed ape.

The wind pushed the hair away from her face. Speechless, Ryan was fixated on her protruding jaw and reptilian skin. Claraicy's big eyes gave a cat-like appearance to her long rough face. Even in the open air, her voice still rattled as she told him, "There's no one out here but us. We're all alone."

Ryan bounced his head around in every direction as the words echoed through the trees. Claraicy quickly folded up her wing and released the blinding sunlight into Ryan eyes.

With a bit of a chuckle, she said, "If you had your gun in your hand right now, would you pull the trigger?"

Chapter Twenty-One

The Cells

Jane graduated at the top in her class and could easily identify every cell in the human body along with most plants, animals and micro-organisms. As she viewed a strange cell under the microscope, she was bewildered. They were so uniquely different from anything that she had seen before that she had to dissect one of them and catalogue all of its unusual features.

At first, she thought it was a mutated white blood cell, but its golden hue and the shape of its nucleus was completely wrong, even for a mutation. When she discovered more identical cells on the slides that Doctor Scott had prepared for her, she knew that it was not a fluke. The only time she seen anything close to it was when she was studying the copper-rich blood of horseshoe crabs.

On one slide, the strange cells grossly outnumbered the regular white blood cells. Taking the tube of blood that accompanied it, she transferred some of it into the small centrifuge vial. After letting it spin for a few minutes, the blood was separated into several layers that ranged from almost clear at the top to gold at the bottom, with various coloured layers in between. Using a syringe, she extracted the golden substance from the bottom of the vial and examined it closer.

To her surprise, when she viewed the golden substance under high magnification, she discovered that the nucleus of each golden cell was centred on a minute identical, golden crystal. Full of excitement, Jane picked up the phone and rang Doctor Scott. "Doctor, I found something really bizarre. Can you come to the lab?"

The doctor had been only two rooms away. One look at her confused face was all it took. The handsome man Jane admired had vanished. Both fear and a bit of glee radiated from him as he grabbed her shoulders. "You discovered the crystals?"

"Yes, but how did you know?"

"Because that is what I have been looking for. I'm sure that you heard what happened a few years ago."

Jane didn't know how to react. All the excitement that she had felt had been squashed by the doctor's subdued reaction. It took a moment for her to regain her thoughts and finally break the silence. "Sure, what you were doing was never a dark secret. It is just the obscure particulars that were a mystery. Everyone in the hospital had their own theories behind how you were growing your own stem cells, and how you were using them in your DNA research."

"That was only a part of my research. A very small hurdle that we had to overcome before we could proceed up the huge staircase of steps that followed.

That was why I needed my own research facility. As long as everyone thought that cloning stem cells was all I was doing, my true research was safe."

The doctor took a deep breath and with a half grin, continued, "It seemed like every small step took years to accomplish." Pointing to the microscope, he smiled. "But you can see the results."

Waving her hands in front of her, she told him, "But, I don't know what I'm seeing. Tell me, what am I looking at?"

"My third generation of genetically modified stem cells."

Out of frustration, the doctor had to look away. As he looked around the room at all of the lab equipment, he apologized to Jane. "I'm sorry. I guess that I shouldn't have to be so secretive about what I got you into."

Shaking her head, Jane bellowed out, "So spill it."

"The team that I put together had found a way to incorporate chemically reproducible, minute crystals into the nucleus of stem cells. They are capable of collecting and storing information at a sub-atomic level. Think of them like the smallest microchip imaginable. They are capable of holding vast amount of information. In its own way it treats the DNA information that we programmed into the crystals like the normal DNA of any other living cell. The biggest difference is, it doesn't deteriorate over time."

It didn't take Jane very long before it dawned on her what that meant. "So they don't age."

Doctor Scott broke out laughing. "Age? You don't get it. Stem cells are programmed to replace damaged cells. They are capable of replacing any cell in the human body. With them, a person could even regrow organs and limbs."

Jane was bewildered. With her jaw hanging open, the doctor smiled as he continued. "We originally designed the cells as a cancer treatment. Our modified stem cells can identify cells that are not compatible to the DNA profile that was programmed into the crystals, and eradicate them. Before my facility was destroyed, my research had reached the point that the modified cells could not only reverse the effects of AIDS, but destroy the virus itself."

With the modified cells being completely different from regular cells, Jane had to question him. "Why don't the patients' bodies reject them like any other foreign body?"

The doctor grinned from ear to ear. "That was my doing. If you truly researched my background you would have found out that cellular enzymes was one of my specialities. Using them, I managed to give the cells a means to control any living tissue they come in contact with. Along with the ability to cloak themselves from the body's own defences, the cells can excrete various enzymes capable of both killing and simulating the cells around them."

Jane went over to the centrifuge and pulled out a small vial. "This is gold. I extracted gold from your cells. By my calculations, just from the samples you have given me, there is enough metal in these vials to kill someone."

"We needed a way to restrict the reproduction of the cells in a controlled environment. In order to multiply, the main thing that the modified cells needed was a constant supply of soluble gold. Our biggest problem was getting over the hurtle of heavy metal poisoning. That could've severely damaged the patient's liver, kidneys, brain, skin and prevent bone and tissue growth. We ended up using low levels of a gold and chloride mixture. To our surprise, we found by simply controlling the length of time the metal is in the body, the effects of metal poisoning can be reversed."

"That's not what I'm seeing."

Doctor Scott walked over to the microscope and tapped on its eye piece. "That's why you are here. I need help. We need to find out why both the cells and patient are not only surviving on their own, but thriving."

Jane knew that without some additional background research, the doctor's work was far above her understanding. Instead of contemplating how he dealt with the effects of the metal poisoning, she thought about the patient. "So, what happens to the patient after their cured and the cells are no long needed?"

"We had planned on simply inhibiting the cells from being able to reproduce. The cells are living organisms. Without the proper nutrients, they should just die out naturally and leave the gold behind in the liver. Then all we would have to do is flush out the patient's liver. In the soft tissue, we figured the process might take a few weeks. If the cells were in the bone marrow, it could take months to extract all the heavy metal."

Jane crossed her arms and slowly tilted her head. "We wouldn't be setting up an entire laboratory in your basement unless this patient was special. You had the full use of all equipment in the hospital."

The doctor looked away as he told her, "Everyone knew about the facility that was destroyed. That was actually my second facility. In fact, there had been three of them. Before the last one went up in flames, we had upgraded all the methods we had pioneered. They were supposed to be more reliable and easier to control, but we never had time to test the results."

After turning around and facing her, he added, "When I was told that my cells were still alive, I knew that I could not risk losing another chance to save my research." Shaking his head, he continued, "The mental and physical effects from heavy metal poisoning alone should have killed him. How and where this subject had got all the nutrients and minerals to imitate the proper environment needed to grow the cells is absolutely mind bending."

"Maybe he was at a rival research facility?"

"No, impossible. I am the only person left that knows the chemical formula required to keep the cells alive. That is why I decided to set up this lab." Doctor Scott closed his eyes.

After a few seconds that seemed like an hour, he confessed, "A patient had escaped the fire that destroyed my last lab. Apparently, he had managed to survive. That bothers me. Until I can thoroughly test the new cells, I am not totally sure what they are truly capable of. I became a doctor to help people, not to create a new life-form."

"If all of the cells are contained inside of a single patient, they cannot pose any outside danger."

"But they are not. The cells have been transmitted into another human and that subject is still roaming around in the woods right now. We have to discover how that could have happened. If the cells can be easily transferable, they are not only useless to my research, they are a potential nightmare. We can't have infected people roaming the forest, or even worse, infected wild animals."

"I'm confused. Let's back up a bit. These cells are designed to attack and destroy mutant cells in humans. How can they live in any other organism that doesn't match the DNA programmed into them?"

"Bingo, now you know part of my problem. The other part is that the person these samples came from is mutating."

"Into what?"

"We don't know. So far, we know that her present DNA is no longer what I would even consider to be human. Every new sighting of her indicates that she is mutating at an alarming rate. Her body has not only accepted all the heavy metal in it, but has obviously adapted to it. We need to find out how the cells have adapted to an incompatible host. That could be the key to understanding why she is mutating."

Jane turned around and looked at the tray of slides on the counter. "If she is no longer human, what is she?"

The doctor was afraid to mention the fruit bats that had also escaped the lab. He didn't want to frighten her. "I believe that she is reverting backwards. Our DNA holds not only what we are, but also what we were. If the signals coming from the crystals are scrambled, she could have cells with thousands of different DNA profiles coexisting inside of her. She could be both a walking laboratory and a zoo pressed into one body."

Picking up a vial of blood, Jane held it in the air. Even without a microscope, the odd glitter of gold caught her eye. "Has this happened to any of your other patients?"

Doctor Scott abruptly replied, "One." The doctor didn't want to talk about Sarah, nor the creatures from the mine. "She died in the fire."

Jane place the vial back into the tray and faced the doctor. "I would imagine that a lot of your patients ended up dead."

With his arms crossed in front of him, he told her, "They were all next to death before they knocked at my door. They were all volunteers and most of them were only given a few weeks to live."

Jane needed time to think. Walking across the room, she sat down at her desk. Turning her chair to face the doctor, she told him, "So, if your modified cells are creating mutated cells, they in turn will create more mutant cells. You have created a new form of cancer."

The doctor gave out a sigh and placed his hands behind his head. "But this one doesn't kill the host. It turns them into a monster."

Jane sat at her desk and nervously tapped the point of her pen against the metal table. After she took some time to reflect she stood up and screamed, "You needed my help. You tricked me into helping you. You created an infectious organism of unknown potential that could put people's lives in jeopardy. I got into the medical field to help people. Now, I feel like you have given me no choice. I can't just look the other way."

Dr. Scott dropped his arms to his side and walked over to Jane. In a soft voice, he told her, "Jane, I admit, I need help. After we first met, I researched your background. You are an extraordinary technician and I believe that you could've been an excellent doctor or even scientist if you wanted to."

Jane put her hands on her hips. "So that was a job interview?"

Dr. Scott shook his head and smiled. "The people that are presently funding my research have also checked into your background. They are willing to pay you generously for your time. You can start at triple your present wage, including all the time you have already put in. However, you would have to sign a binding legal agreement that would demand your complete silence."

Bewildered, Jane lowered her voice. "You expect me to help you fix your mistakes?"

In the same timid voice, the doctor replied, "Yes."

Jane watched the doctor as he rocked back and forth on his heels with his hands behind his back. "If I help you and agree to stay, will I get any credit for my work?"

"They're may not be any. Right now, all I can offer you is tax free cash with absolutely no paper trail. It could even be directly deposited in a safe off-shore bank account if you want."

"How much time am I looking at? Will I need to get an extended leave of absence from the hospital so I have a job to go back to?"

"I don't know how long it will take. If my research can be saved, you may have a full time job for years to come. You may even be able to start a luxurious retirement before you hit forty."

Jane put her hands over her face and considered her present life. Her work was her life. All she could think about was the cells' ability to cure cancer and old age. "Okay, I agree. I'll stay, but I need to know what I'm dealing with."

"Fine." Dr. Scott pulled out a document from the filing cabinet. "I need you to sign this first."

Jane glanced at the document and looked up at the doctor. "This is a government form. Is the government actually funding your research?"

"Indirectly. It is an obscure branch of the Canadian Armed Forces. Those cells can quickly heal any damage caused by bullets and shrapnel. It could saves a lot of lives in the battlefield. For a huge country, we have a small regular army. We need to keep our trained soldiers alive and healthy."

"We are neutral. We're not going to war."

"We have a lot of natural resources. With global warming melting the ice caps, there are a lot of countries wanting to make claims to Canadian soil. The government needs to be in a position to enforce our claim."

Jane took in a deep breath. "So, this is all about patriotism. I take it that you are aware that both of my brothers are in the services."

"Yes." The doctor smiled. "Think about it. Without the constant fear of dying or losing limbs, our soldiers could be unstoppable. A squad of our super soldiers could go up against an entire company of equally trained and equipped soldiers, and without the fear of dying, take the risks needed to beat them. If we can utilise it to cure diseases at the same time, maybe someday we could even get some recognition for it."

"So in a little over ten years I can retire?"

"Probably less than that. However you won't be allowed to discuss anything that goes on in here with anyone. That would constitute treason. That means absolutely no one without clearance, not even your brothers. If anyone finds out about our research, not only would our work be in jeopardy, so would our lives."

Jane stretched her left hand flat against the table. "I get it."

Dr. Scott watched as Jane nervously clicked her pen before signing the document. "Now, Jane, I need you to start up another battery of tests for me. We need to discover how and why the cells accepted a different host."

"Do you have any theories?"

"My original theory was that if a host's body was too weak to fight off infection. The modified cells would have been unopposed. Like a tumour, they would mass in a localized area of infection until they cloned enough cells to expand further into the host's body."

Jane interjected. "So you believe that they converted the local cells into stem cells and cloned them in order to infiltrate the host's body like a cancer. By overwhelming the host's defences, they would take over."

"The problem is that my theory doesn't explain why the cells' DNA programming had changed. It should still be human. I think that there were hormones in the recipient that we didn't anticipate, and they interfered with the transfer of information from the crystals to the stem cells."

"If that is the case, we'll need a steady supply of live cells to test."

"That's not a problem. I think that it is time for me to introduce you to David."

Jane followed the doctor through the stainless steel door and into a tunnel carved into the hill. On top of a short incline, the doctor entered his security code and opened a door. Beyond it was an adjoining tunnel with over a half dozen stainless steel doorways and half as many windows inside them on each side. Jane was shocked by its hospital-like appearance. Everything was either stainless steel, reinforced glass or freshly painted concrete.

The doctor stopped in front of a panel of tinted glass and Jane looked through the one-way window into David's cell. Without looking away from the window, the doctor told her, "Jane, this is David. He was the patient that survived the fire, and for now, our only source of modified cells."

As they entered the room, David simply blinked and turned so they couldn't see his face. Jane stared at the mangled man lying on the bed and asked, "How is he doing?"

"David isn't completely happy about being locked up." The doctor walked over to the computer next to the bed and looked over David's vital signs. "Unlike the other subject, he has developed multiple signs of heavy metal poisoning. It has gotten visibly worse since he arrived. The strange thing is that when he first arrived, he was alright. Now he is physically going downhill. His bones and soft tissue have stopped growing the way they should and even his brain has been affected by the excess gold in his system. He can still remember everything, but to formulate new thoughts is extremely difficult for him."

"Those are all signs of heavy metal poisoning. Why can't you just cleanse his body of it? You have the technology, I know it."

The doctor turned the chair and faced her. "Then we wouldn't have a reliable source of modified cells."

Jane saw the mess David's body was in and recalled the newspaper article about a mangled man sighted in the woods. The police were unable to recover the body. Turning to the doctor, she asked him, "How many people are involved and just how big is this operation?"

"Including us, right now they are only a couple dozen people that know anything about my research."

Jane started to regret signing the document. "Is this the mangled man the police were searching for?"

"Yes."

"Is the mutated monster you were referring to earlier the one responsible for mutilating the people in the park?"

The doctor stood up and took one step towards her and then stopped. Looking at David, in almost a whisper he answered, "Yes."

Jane grabbed her hair and aimlessly walked around the room. "So, is that why you asked me to have breakfast with you?" Releasing her hair, she clenched her fists in front of her and bellowed out, "You used me. You needed to know if you were partly responsible for what happened to the Mitchells."

The doctor took another step towards her and replied, "Yes, and yes to a lot more that I think you are just afraid to mention."

Chapter Twenty-Two

First kill

Patrick used his elbow to knock on Kerry's back door. Hearing no response he became impatient. With most of his hand still supporting his injured gut, he gingerly opened the door with his fingertips. He saw Kerry sitting at the kitchen table nursing a glass of whiskey. With both hands supporting his gut, Patrick he gave out a painful groan. "Damn you. You couldn't even get off your fat arse to open the door for me."

Kerry looked at him and said, "Sit your arse down. If it wasn't for you, I'd still be a man, not a castrated eunuch."

Grabbing the back of a chair, Patrick bellowed out, "And if it wasn't for you, I wouldn't have shit pumping out of my gut and into a bag right now."

"Okay, fine. The bitch did a number on both of us. Now sit down."

Patrick slowly sat down and leant back as far as he could to relieve the stress on his stomach. "Now, what is our situation with the cops and what are we going to do about that damn daughter of yours?"

"I've been told that the police have pulled our and the military have taken over. They are looking for a man a long ways away from where Claraicy attacked us. As I see it, we have a chance to go back in and get rid of her once and for all. If she talks, I could be charged with attempted murder."

Kerry looked away from his glass and pointed his finger at Patrick. "I'm sure that she knows what really happened to your wife. You talk too much when you drink and she was always around. They will arrest you too."

"She knows. She mentioned my wife before she left me to die." Patrick wrestled with the pain in his stomach and released another small groan before continuing. "She knows it all. She knows how I cooked and fed her flesh to the dogs. She also knows that the rose bushes have been feeding on her crushed bones for almost two years now. There is nothing left for the police to find. The wild ramblings of a demented child doesn't scare me."

"So you won't help me?"

"I had my belly full of her, thank you. You're the one that screwed her up, not me. After all, the way she is now, who would believe anything she said? My only problem is with LC. With him still out there, I may not be able to get to my stash. My buyer had already paid me half in advance. If I don't retrieve it soon, I'll be the one ground into fertilizer and planted in the ground."

"I heard that they found what's left of LC's canoe sunk in the lake?"

Patrick shook his head, "You don't know him like I do. He's still out there."

"So how much time do you figure your fence will give you? He can't be stupid. He has to know what's going on out there. It's all over the press."

"He won't wait too long, maybe a week or two if I'm lucky. They don't care about my problems. I'll have to find a way into the park and get it."

******

Perched on a branch behind the green and red foliage of a maple tree, Claraicy watched Ryan as he slowly walked through the forest foraging for food. She saw him gather fungus, worms, bugs, plants and things that she never would have imagined anyone could eat.

Hidden high in the forest's canopy, she felt safe. She knew that Ryan wasn't her enemy. What scared her the most about being around him was the fact that she knew that her mind could snap at any time, and his death would be added to her nightmares. Still, she felt a growing desire to be near him.

As Ryan turned and started to wander back to the old bear den, Claraicy held Jesse in her arms and leaped out of the tree. Her massive wings flapped twice and vaulted her above the forest canopy. As she glided above the tree tops, her dark shadow made Ryan cower under a bush. Within a few seconds she disappeared behind a clump of trees.

She wanted to fly over the lake but knew that she couldn't make it. She had to go around it. While running through the clearings, she loved the way a simple jump would spring her into the air, and a few flaps of her wings would lift her over large groves of trees. It was a powerful rush, but it quickly drained her energy. She couldn't stay aloft for any extended length of time.

Her wings and everything to do with flying was still new to her. She was still trying to figure out how her wings even worked. Flapping them bounced her up and down into the air. Her tail acted like a rudder and changed the direction she was heading. Facing the wind, she could spread her wings and fly like a kite. That was all she could figure out, so far.

Taking a break, she munched on some trail mix that she had taken from Ryan's backpack and watched some birds fly from tree to tree. Even the insects could gracefully dance around in any direction they wanted. She had these huge wings and it was very frustrating that all she could do is bounce around on them. As birds flapped their wings, dived and twisted through the tree branches, Claraicy grew even more frustrated.

The long, narrow lake took the entire afternoon to go around. It was nightfall by the time she spotted the pool outside of the concealed cavern. She felt funny. Something inside of her froze. Looking around, she saw nothing unusual in the trees or bushes. The birds and animals were chattering away like normal.

She tried to move, but her body refused. Suddenly she saw some leaves on the ground move. Her brain tried to dismiss it as a mouse or squirrel scavenging for nuts. The leaves moved again. It was too big to be a squirrel.

Her large ears twisted forward to help her focus on the unusual movement.

Well below a whisper, she made out a muffled voice. "Drake, is anything happening there?" The sound was so low, her brain tried to dismiss it as an audio elusion. Then, in even a lower voice, she distinctively hear the word, "Nothing."

Claraicy crouched down behind some bushes and waited. Moments later a head and an arm from a soldier appeared out of the murky pool and pushed a small sack under the pile of leaves. She heard a "Thank you", as the arm sunk back into the pool. She saw the warm air twirl above the pile of leaves as a burst of steam rose from under them and mixed with the cooler night air.

The smell of coffee filled Claraicy's lungs and made her furious. They were waiting for her to come back. The food she had escaped with had been eaten. The rest was in the cavern. Her starving body demanded to be fed and so did Jesse. Given no choice, she retreated into the woods.

As hunger dominated her mind, Claraicy was no longer in control of her actions. Dusk was approaching and pure animalistic instinct began to take over. On a branch a few metres above an animal trail, she patiently waited for anything to appear. As hours went by and the pains in her stomach began to tighten, she would've been happy for even a mouse. Along with the first sign of daylight, the rattling of branches caught her attention.

Below her a large skittish buck wandered slowly down the path. Leaping out of the tree, Claraicy grabbed a hold of its antlers with both hands and twisted its head upward. After wrestling the buck to the ground, she adjusting her grip on its lethal antlers and sunk her teeth into her prey's exposed neck.

The harder the buck fought, the deeper Claraicy's enlarged canine teeth worked their way into its neck. The buck's legs wildly flailed about and its sharp hooves sliced chunks of bark off of the nearby trees. Blood started to squirt out of a severed artery in its neck. Claraicy's mouth clung onto the deer's neck as she sucked in as much of the deer's rich blood as she could. It took almost two minutes to slow down to a trickle. By that time, the buck had stopped kicking and its muscles went limp. It was over.

Jesse jubilantly watched as her mother had savagely killed her first deer. With a burst of energy flowing through her, Claraicy clawed into the creature's belly and began devouring the animal's liver and heart. With her head submerged into the deer's belly, her wings spread over the carcass and concealed her gruesome meal as she gnawed away at it.

Jesse crawled under her mother's wings and bit into a ripped off piece of liver. Claraicy turned her head and viciously snarled at her. Surprised at her reaction, she froze. Jesse had run into the forest by the time she could get to her feet and cry out, "Jesse, I didn't mean it. Please, forgive me."

Claraicy looked down at the dead deer and wondered. *Could that have been Ryan? Was my hunger the reason that I couldn't keep my eyes off of him?* As a soft drizzle made its way through the forest canopy, Claraicy curled up under a nearby cedar tree to let her swollen gut digest the meat.

It was only after Claraicy's eyelids had closed that Jesse dared to approach the deer carcass. Paying most of her attention to Claraicy, she didn't notice the crow pecking at the carcass. As the startled crow cawed and flew away, she tore off a hunk of meat and ran into the forest.

Looking back, she saw that her mother hadn't moved. It was the first time that she had threatened her and Jesse didn't know how to react. The strong bond between them had been crushed. Even though her mother was metres away, she felt isolated and scared.

The demand for the massive amounts of protein that their developing bodies required had turned the pair into rivals. If they both ate their fill, the carcass would barely last them a week. Despite this, Jesse was so afraid of her mother that she barely ate enough to keep her stomach from growling. Even the crows were stealing more meat than Jesse was consuming.

After only a few days, Claraicy noticed that Jesse was getting weaker. Her once round belly had started to shrink. With the birds going after the tender meat that was beginning to spoil, she tried to entice her daughter to eat more by increasing the distance between her and the half-eaten carcass. Even then, Jesse would only venture near it when she thought her mother was sleeping.

Out of desperation, Jesse supplemented her diet with worms, insects and anything else she could find. After a few days, Claraicy noticed Jesse leaping out of a tree and turning a frightened rabbit into her first meaningful kill.

A sense of pride came over Claraicy as she approached her daughter. Jesse returned her delight with a snarling growl. Despite her offspring's demeanor, Claraicy proudly sat back and watched her consume over half the rabbit. As Jesse glanced at her mother, she was no longer afraid of her. She could defend herself and even kill if necessary.

That night, after she finished eating the rabbit, she came up to Claraicy and gingerly snuggled up next to her. They were no longer competitors. She no longer needed her mother to provide for her, but she somehow knew that they still needed each other.

As the deer's carcass disappeared, Claraicy went back to the pool. She could still sense the sentry's presence. In the dark, she climbed the giant mound of rocks and peered through the small cracks. She could only see one soldier inside of the cavern. Slipping down into the forest surrounding the pool, she patiently waited for the right time.

The sun was rising high in the cloudless sky when it finally happened. A soldier crawled out of the pool and passed the guard a thermos of coffee and a container full of stew. Feeling safe that no one was watching, Drake stood up. "It's too bright out. Nobody is going to sneak around when there are no shadows to hide in."

Crawling out from the plastic lined, leaf covered trench, MacNeil told him, "It's my turn to stretch my legs and get some more supplies."

As MacNeil ate his breakfast, Drake slipped under the leaf covered mesh. MacNeil kicked some leaves on top of him. With his rifle slung over his shoulders, he stowed the containers in his pack and informed him, "I'll be back before you can get snuggled in and comfy."

"Is that even possible?"

"Sure, after the leeches excrete enough dope into your blood that you can't feel your muscles cramping up."

"You're joking?"

"Got yah."

Claraicy quietly snuck away and returned carrying a large bundle wrapped in the dead deer's hide. The sun was directly overhead and its bright reflective light even illuminated the forest bed beneath the dense evergreens. The overhanging ledge cast a shadow over the pool.

Knowing the direction Drake was facing, she stealthily work her way behind him towards the edge of the water. Next to the vertical rock face, there were several large bushes that hung over the edge of the pool. After slithering between them and the rock, she quietly slid under the murky water.

Inside the cave, Claraicy poked her head out of the water. Once she was sure that no one was there, she crawled out. While putting down the bundle she looked around.

Most of the food that she had left behind had been consumed by the soldiers. The camping supplies were shoved into a corner along with almost everything else she had salvaged. The only exception was Ryan's rifle and ammunition. It was stored with their stuff on the other side of the cave.

Claraicy went over to their bags and emptied them out. Using her claws, she ripped, bent or broke apart everything she could, including a padded aluminum briefcase full of liquid filled darts. Using a rock, she crushed them. After disassembling and mangling their stash of weapons, she twisted apart all of their bullets, and carefully poured the gun powder out of them.

Feeling satisfied, she started to lick some clean water that was coming down the side of the rock. The taste of the minerals in the rock behind the water compelled her to smell it. Her nose lead her downward towards a pile of dirt clinging to the side of the rock. She picked up a handful and tasted it. Something inside of her forced her to shove it into her mouth, then another and another.

When her stomach couldn't hold any more, the feeling of despair and hunger finally left her. It was like she had taken a tranquillizer and all she wanted to do was lay down and take a nap. Fighting off the drowsiness, she grabbed a backpack and Ryan's rifle before wading into the pool. Causing barely a ripple, she pulled herself out in the same spot that she had entered.

******

After returning, MacNeil surfaced from the pool and shook the muddy water away from his face and eye brows. Seeing the mess Claraicy had created, he yelled out, "Drake, you blind fool!"

Their bedding, cook stove, clothes and equipment where all destroyed. In the middle of the floor, written in gunpowder, bullets and empty cartridge casings was, "LEAVE ME ALONE".

Carefully placed above the message was the remains of the buck's head. It's sharp, seven point antlers, defleshed cheeks and hanging skin added to its ghastly, eyeless appearance. MacNeil knew that it was left as both a warning and an indication of what she was capable of.

Chapter Twenty-Three

Flight

Claraicy circled back around across the lake. Looking down at the old bear den, a sense of contentment overcame her as she nestled into the branches of a large maple tree. Even with a few large gaps in the tree's canopy, she felt safer and more comfortable the higher she got. Curled up with her back against the tree trunk and her wings wrapped around her, something inside of her needed to know that Ryan was alright. With a quarter of the leaves missing from the tree, the morning sun shone through the branches and warmed her dark wings.

Within half an hour, Ryan crawled out of the den, stretched and with barely a limp, walked over to a nearby bush and urinated. The crackling voice radiating above him caught him off guard. "A little jumpy are we? So, how have you been? I see your leg is much better."

Ryan did up his zipper and looked up. "I didn't see you up there. I'm doing fine, and yes my leg is much better. How have you been?"

"I'm not sure. Lately, I've been feeling like I've already lost the fight. I feel that it's just a matter of time before the beast growing inside of me takes over. Right now, I'm more savage than human. If I was standing next to you and the urge to kill you came over me, I don't know if I could stop myself."

"You obviously don't want to kill me. In the first place, you climbed that tree to separate us. That demonstrates that you can control your actions, doesn't it? As long as you think like a human, you are still human."

"I don't know if you are right or wrong, but I don't want to take that chance. I don't feel human anymore. What if the animal inside of me wanted me up here just to pounce on top of you and snap your neck?"

Claraicy stood up on the branch she was on and yelled out. "Look at me. What part of me is human? Is it my tail, my wings, my claws, my fangs, my giant pointy ears or is it that rattling sound that comes out of my mouth? I know, it has to be my smooth soft skin. Every girl wants to be covered in hard, scaly skin like this."

Not wanting to rile her, Ryan replied in a calm voice, "No, none of that. The fact you can question yourself about being human proves to me that you still are. You just have a terrific Halloween costume, that's all. Some people would pay a small fortune to look like you."

Claraicy sat down on the branch and babbled out, "You don't understand the cravings I am having. They are not normal."

Ryan walked through some dense bushes towards her. When he looked up, she was gone. Resting against the tree trunk were his rifle and backpack.

******

Duncan paced in front of Drake while he screamed out, "How could you let her just waltz past you?"

Drake rigidly stood there at attention. "I don't know, sir. It has never happened before."

"I'm sorry. Rest easy." Duncan knew Drake was one of the best lookouts he had ever encountered. "We have to find out how she did it."

"We already figured that out." Drake led Duncan to where Claraicy slithered into the pool. "See these tracks? She had simply pulled herself over the slime covered gravel next to the rock using what looks like claws attached to her fingers. Her body and legs have to be extremely smooth to push the brush aside without getting caught on any twigs. The only thing we found were some clumps of deer hair."

While studying Claraicy's tracks, Duncan told Drake, "So we have a target that can fly, run like a cheetah, and slither like a lizard. I wouldn't be surprised if she has even more animal characteristics like acute hearing, eye sight and smell." Duncan stood up and faced Drake while he added, "She knew exactly where you were and utilised your blind spots."

"I know, I should have cleared those bushes."

"If you had, it would have been like painting a huge sign, 'We are here watching you'. Duncan started to pace back and forth. "The best defence is a good offence. That is why she is mutating into a predator. She wouldn't just hide. If she feels threatened in any way, she'll attack. We have to be smarter then she is and treat her with respect. If we ever hope to capture her alive, we have to break down her defences."

******

Jane called Doctor Scott over to her computer and informed him, "Doctor, I believe I know what's going on inside the creature. All the crystals look identical, but they're not. There are two unique types of them. One is bigger than the other. Judging from the size difference, I suspect that one is human but the other's not. With both sets of crystals sending signals to the creature's stem cells, the conflict has allowed the creature's own nervous system to step into the mix. Our DNA contains everything we have evolved from right back to the primitive ooze that made up the first protein. If the crystals contain the same information, her body may be picking and choosing whatever she needs to survive."

"So you are telling me that you believe this girl has chosen to become this creature?"

Jane looked up at the doctor as he peered over her shoulder at her computer monitor. "Yes."

"That's impossible." The doctor studied the results from both sets of DNA on the monitor. "Look carefully. This crystal's DNA is that of a bat. We had used fruit bats to test the cells on. They are only a shade further away from us than an ape."

"That explains the smaller set of crystals, what about the larger ones? Wouldn't that indicate that she was infected by two different sources?"

"At the time of the fire, there was a pair of bats that we had scheduled for dissection." Looking down at the floor, the doctor continued to pace the room. "During one of the tests, the technician didn't fasten the intravenous needles into a couple of bats securely enough. Long story short, they came out. In a hurry the technician mixed up the tubes when she reinstalled them. One bat was being used to grow modified cells for harvesting, and the other was being tested for cell growth."

"So there was cross-contamination going on in your lab."

"The tags were damaged and the technician misread a nine for a four on the first bat and didn't look at the second bat's tag. As soon as she discovered her mistake, I was immediately informed. I had a lot of money invested in those bats. I decided that it would be a shame to kill them and get nothing out of it, so I let them live to find out what would happen. They were not even scheduled to be tested until the week after the fire destroyed the lab. I wanted to give the cells plenty of time to grow to make it easier to spot any changes."

"So you never found out what damage the cross-contamination had done to the bats."

The doctor smiled. "No, but I do know that some of man's greatest discoveries came from accidents."

Jane was shocked by the comment. "What good could come from this?"

The doctor put his hand on her shoulder. "A better understanding of what the modified cells are truly capable of."

Jane didn't know how to react. "I guess knowledge is power, but in this case, I am still not sure how it is beneficial."

"Our first cells lacked control over the DNA information. It was like going to an electrical box and randomly flipping all of the switches off and on. Our last attempt tried to solidify the dominant and subordinate genes. When the bats got cross-contaminated, I thought that it was a great chance to test how stable the latest modified cells were. I was hoping to find pockets of cells that were identical to the DNA of either one or the other of the modified cells. If the cells came in direct contact with one another, there was also the possibility that either one could become dominant, or they could even fuse together."

Jane thought for a moment to let what the doctor told her sink in. "So basically you wanted to give the cells time to battle it out."

The doctor smiled and told her, "Exactly, plus contrive a way to extract one set and not the other."

Jane looked at her monitor displaying three different sets of DNA. "That's like playing God."

The doctor carried on as if he didn't even hear Jane's comment. "The creature roaming around out there is basically a symbiotic triplet, with each jousting for dominance. In order to survive, her brain has been constantly pumping adrenaline into her body. The 'flee or flight' mode that she has been in is a very primeval response that is deeply embedded in all three DNA profiles. Her body's hormones must be going berserk. Right now, the bat's genes are winning because she is frightened. I think that her physical changes could be a result of all the hormones excreted from her own cells."

After a brief pause, the doctor slapped his hands together and added, "Right now, it is possible that her body could contain thousands of different DNA profiles."

The room went quiet. Jane got off her chair and paced the floor as the doctor rocked back and forth in his chair. After a few minutes, Jane broke the silence. "So, if this creature didn't have anything to be afraid of, her hormones could stabilize and she could revert back to normal."

"Yes, but we would have to have complete control over her environment." The doctor grinned and gave a small chuckle. "We don't even need to capture her. All we need to do is pamper her a little and give her body time to relax."

With images of what Claraicy had done to Patrick and the Mitchells running through her mind, Jane coldly replied, "Why should we? Wouldn't it be more prudent to capture her?"

The doctor stood up and grasped the back of his head with both hands. "And waste this great opportunity to study the modified cell's true potential?"

******

The diligent soldiers made no attempt to conceal what they were doing as they packed up and left the pool. Drawn in by the ruckus, Claraicy watched them from the protection of the forest and followed them to the lake where they got into their canoes.

Within an hour, two of the soldiers returned sporting florescent orange hunting vests. After unpacking their raft, they placed two large packs on their backs and carried a stretcher full of bags and boxes to the small clearing next to the pool.

After putting down the stretcher, they slipped off the packs and immediately left. From Claraicy's vantage point high in the forest canopy, their bright orange vests made them easy to spot. As they got into their raft, she jumped out of the tree that she was in and glided onto the rocky ridge.

From the top of a large boulder she peered through the treetops and saw them beach their boat on the far side of the lake. Curious about what they had left behind, Claraicy jumped off the boulder and floated down to the clearing.

After poking the bags with a long stick, she noticed a note tied loosely to one duffle bags. Afraid it was booby trapped, she carefully ripped it off and unfolded it.

In large bold type it read, 'We do not want to harm you. We want to help you. We truly believe that our doctors have the means to cure you. There is still time. Please think about it. We will respect your privacy and provide you with everything you need. In this bag, there is a radio that is preset to a private frequency for you to contact us. Please let us help you. If you agree, we can also protect you from the police and any others that want to harm you.' The note was signed 'Doctor Michael Scott'.

As Claraicy crouched down and reread the note, she looked at the tips of her wings as they rested on the ground beside her. Part of her relished the excitement of flight and the wild, while part of her longed to be normal. The note gave her a lot to consider. "Is being human all that great?"

Thoughts of her parents and Patrick ran through her head. They were followed by the wide range of feelings she had toward Ryan. "How can anyone protect me from myself?"

Chapter Twenty-Four

Normality

The first box Claraicy opened was stuffed full of books, teenager magazines and a calendar. She picked up the calendar and flipped through the pages. Each month had a beautiful painting that represented the season. January had people skating, February people were tobogganing, March had people shopping for spring clothes, and on and on. When she got to December, there was a painting of Santa Claus surrounded by a flock of adoring children.

In a violent rage she tore apart the picture and flung the entire calendar into the woods. After spending a moment to cool down, she pulled one of the packs to where she was sitting and opened it. It contained a wide assortment of food, fire starter, matches, a hair brush, a metal mirror and the radio.

A few flakes of snow floated down and landed on her hands as she unpacked the stretcher that turned out to be a camp cot. It melted as soon as it landed. After a few minutes it stopped. It was just another reminder of the frigid season that was quickly approaching.

Spread out on the ground were a few heavy blankets, a pillow, a small wood stove, flashlights, lanterns, a double burner camping stove, camp fuel, dishes, cookware, what looked like a bag of tarps, poles and almost anything she needed to set up camp. Claraicy sat down and read the note a few more times and tried to digest exactly what it was saying. She glanced at the mirror lying on the ground in front of her. Twice she reached over and tried to pick it up, but something inside of her wouldn't allow her.

Using the instructions they had supplied her, she set up the metal poles and attached the tarps to the sides and roof. The tent wasn't originally designed to be put up by a single person, however both it and the instruction had been modified to help her. The front of it had a zippered door and its walls had clear vinyl windows sewn into them. After shoving a piece of stove pipe through a hole in the roof that was surrounded by fireproof material, she fastened it to the stove. It took Claraicy only a few minutes to collect some kindling and start a fire.

At first it was heaven. As the warmth radiated from the stove she looked around at the bags and boxes. Suddenly the walls started to close in on her and she couldn't breathe. She felt as if she was locked in her room and her father was standing outside of the door.

In a panic she ran outside and leaped into the air. She tried to land on top of the ledge above the pool but didn't quite make it. As she grabbed anything she could, she flapped her wings and pulled herself onto the ledge. Folding her wings around her, she sat there facing the tent. In a tight ball she rocked back and forth. All she could do was stare at the tent and think. *Who am I? What am I? Should I let them try to cure me? Can they? What will happen to me if they do cure me? Will I end up in jail for what I've done?*

As Claraicy watched the smoke drift away from the chimney pipe, a cold breeze made her shiver. Knowing that warmth was so close played on her mind. Finally, she jumped down and went back into the tent. The fire had burned down to a few glowing ambers. All it took was a few broken sticks to bring it back to life. After collecting some more firewood, she brought everything inside and sat in front of the stove.

Jesse cautiously snuck into the tent and curled up under the cot as her mother quietly leafed through some magazines. Claraicy felt childish as she became fixated at the way the boys in the silly photos looked at the girls. She wondered if Ryan would ever look at her that way. At that moment, all she wanted was to be just a normal teenage girl.

Outside of collecting firewood, all Claraicy had to do was cook her meals and tend the fire. In her free time she read some of the romantic teenage drivel the soldiers gave her and flipped through the magazines. It took a couple days before she got the nerve to turn on the radio and press the button. "I want to be a normal girl. I don't want to become a hideous monster."

After a couple seconds, a soft female voice answered back, "You don't have to. We can help you." In the background, Claraicy could hear scuffling sounds as if somebody was moving some furniture and then some deep breathes, before she heard, "My name is Ann. What is your name?"

With tears running down her face, she answered, "Claraicy."

"That's a pretty name. Well Claraicy, I think we are going to become good friends over the next while."

"Are you a doctor?"

"No, but we have one at the camp with us, plus a complete research centre at our disposal."

Claraicy wiped her cheek before asking, "Do you know what is happening to me?"

"You have acquired a very abnormal infection. This unusual medical condition is normally host dependent and considers your body's DNA as a foreign threat. Think about it like a parasite growing inside of you, fighting to stay alive. We need to control the infection before we can even attempt to extract it from your body. Afterwards, your normal cells should simply regenerate back to normal. It won't happen overnight. The entire procedure will take time. You will have to trust us. We honestly don't want to hurt you."

"Your soldiers had a lot of bullets. How can I be certain that you are not just wanting to turn me into an easy target?"

"The soldiers that were following you had tranquillizer darts loaded in their rifles. The real ammunition that you found was only in case of emergency. It was only to be used if they felt their lives were in danger. I bet that the boxes of ammunition that you found were all full."

Claraicy remembered breaking the darts she had found in the case and opening the full boxes of ammo. At no time had they fired even a single shot at her. At no time did they truly threaten her. After shaking her head, she sat up straight and asked, "What do I have to do?"

Ann put down the neatly typed card she was reading and took another one from Doctor Stern. She barely glanced at it before reading it to Claraicy. "For now, nothing. We want you to relax and not have to worry about anything. We need you to give your body's natural defences the opportunity to fight back. It cannot maintain the rigorous demands you are putting on it. You have to allow it to fight this parasite-like infection. Right now your body is stressed out and is allowing the infection to spread. If you keep on running, given time, the infection will take over and Claraicy will no longer exist."

Claraicy paused for a moment before questioning Ann some more. "I have never heard of anything like this happening to anyone else. Where did these parasites come from, another planet?"

The doctor found the appropriate card and handed it to Ann. "First, they are not what you would consider to be normal parasites. Like cancer, they are mutated cells that somehow got infused into your body. As far as I know, you are the first person that these cells have ever attempted to mutate. The fact that they are transmitted by blood and cannot live outside of a living body is puzzling."

"What kind of cells are they?"

After accepting another card from the doctor, Ann continued. "Think of them like white blood cells on steroids. They heal wounds, fight off any type of infection you may get, and in general, fix you." Ann closed her eyes and added, "This apparently includes changing any part of you that they felt could help you survive."

Doctor Stern tapped his finger on top of the cards and whispered in Ann's ear, "Stick to what is written on the cards."

Claraicy looked at Jesse. Without telling Ann what was really going on in her mind, she asked, "Are there others walking around with these cells inside of them?"

"Yes. In fact we rescued an infected man from the same cave that you were staying in. We believe that he was the original source of some of your parasitic cells. Were you ever in direct contract with him?"

Claraicy put down the radio and looked up at the roof. She didn't know how to respond.

"Claraicy, are you still there?"

"I'm still here."   After a brief pause she slowly continued, "I heard someone, but I never saw who it was. At first I thought the moaning sound was from the wind blowing through the cracks and tunnels. When I heard the odd scream, I started to believe that the place was haunted. At the time I was in no shape to crawl around hunting for its source. When I found the tunnel the ghostly sounds were coming out of, I piled rocks in front of it to muffle them."

Ann looked at Doctor Stern as he flipped through the cards. After dropping them on the floor he quickly typed out a response.

As he typed it out, Ann read it off his monitor. "The place wasn't haunted. He wasn't a ghost. He was trapped in the cave under some rocks. Unlike you, his infection did not allow him the ability to adapt. We had been searching for him for almost a year. The specially modified cells inside of his body had kept him alive. The doctor believes that his body will fully recover. The mental trauma he endured was horrendous and could take several years to get over. When we found your blood on the rock beside the lake, we initially thought that we had found him. That was why the soldiers were pursuing you."

"I didn't know. It is hard to believe that anyone could suffer that long without dying." As soon as the words left her mouth, Claraicy thought of all the times that she had wanted to die. She should have died at least a dozen times over the past year. Despite the horrible conditions she had put her body through, she managed to gave birth to Jesse and mature over six years in less than one.

Ann listened to the blank static coming from the radio. "Claraicy, are you still there?"

Claraicy waited. She had a lot to digest.

"Claraicy are you still there?"

Claraicy slowly picked up the radio. "Why soldiers? Why the secrecy?"

On his knees, Doctor Stern picked out the appropriate card and passed it to Ann. The sudden appearance of Duncan towering behind them made Ann twitch.

After taking a couple seconds to compose herself, she read the card to Claraicy. "When the infected cells were discovered, the doctors thought it was best to avoid any public hysteria. The cells are host reliant and were not considered to be a threat to anyone. They felt that professionally trained soldiers were the best way to quietly find and retrieve any infected victims without the press whipping the country side into a panic."

"It's still all very confusing."

"Claraicy, you have gone through a lot and this is a lot to digest."

Duncan handed Ann a piece of paper. After glancing it over, she added, "It is October now and winter is coming. We would like to offer you a warm cozy trailer to live in. No more firewood to worry about. It will help you relax and let your body take back some control. Fear is your enemy, not us. Think of us as your personal body guards. We will protect you from the public, police and anyone else that wants to harm you. All we are asking for in return is that you allow us to take some samples from you in order to monitor your progress."

From the forest, Claraicy watched the soldiers dismantle her tent. Hours later, a couple army helicopters guided a big camo painted trailer down into the same clearing. As they pulled out the wings on its sides, the trailer grew wider and formed a cross. Large propane tanks were brought in by another helicopter along with a huge wooden crate by a fourth.

Claraicy got excited as they unscrewed the box and all the furnishings were carried into the trailer. The wood from the crate was neatly laid out in front of the trailer and converted into a patio. With some scraps of wood, two soldiers screwed together a bench. Other soldiers were busy setting up solar panels and a wind generator on top of the ridge.

Over the next week Claraicy felt that she had found a friend. Ann was never more than a push on a radio's button away from her. Sitting in front of the television with a full stomach and Jesse curled up on her lap, Claraicy felt more comfortable then she had at any point in her life. The trailer was like her own private apartment. With shelves full of books to read and all kinds of shows and movies downloaded onto a server, she had lots to occupy her time.

Claraicy tried hard to suppress all of the animalistic urges she had festering inside of her. She had to consciously think about everything she did and told herself, "I am not an animal. I am a human being."

At times it was hard for her to pass by a window. If she looked out, her eyes would search for any source of meat that scurried, hopped or flew. Drool would drip from her mouth at the thought of biting into their flesh. Most of the time, she could simply draw the blinds and suppress her urges.

At other times the excitement was unbearable. Despite her desire to be human again, she had to go outside and feel some freedom. As she leaped into the sky and become a part of the natural order of life she felt like she was in control of her life and she could do anything she wanted.

******

"How is our subject doing?"

Ann watched Doctor Scott's image break out a smile on the computer screen. "Claraicy is improving. Her human food consumption is increasing and her raw meat consumption has decreased like you predicted. Her hunting sprees are getting further apart but she still has to fight off her urges to fly. I think it may be an addiction. A lot of people out there wish they could do what she can. Other than that, I see a lot of slow but steady progress."

"Have you been able to get samples from her?"

"So far we have only managed to get some stool and urine samples from the trailer's holding tank. Things should improve tomorrow. She has finally agreed to let me see her and take a blood sample."

"That's terrific but remember, if she starts to panic, the creature inside of her could turn on you without any warning. Keep me informed of any progress or changes in her development. Now put on Duncan."

Whenever the doctor asked for Duncan, Ann knew that it was a private conversation. As soon as Duncan grabbed the phone and sat down, Ann left the tent. "Yes, sir."

"Is everything secure for a prolonged stay? We don't know how long this process could take."

"Yes, everything is in place."

"That's good. How are we doing with keeping track of the goat and the park ranger?"

"Steve's tracking device is working great. He has given us enough that we can put together something to keep the police and newspapers happy. We have to make the public think that we are serving their interests and have just cause to keep the area under quarantine. As far as the park ranger is concerned. We found him hiding in a cave. He has made himself pretty comfortable and I can't see him changing locations. We are closely monitoring him from a safe distance for now."

"With the injuries that had he endured, there is a slight chance that he could be infected. If he shows any signs of abnormality, you know what to do."

"Do you really think he could be infected?"

"No, but we still haven't found out why Claraicy's body accepted the modified cells in the first place. Our last tests confirmed that they still contain the original DNA profiles we programmed into them and they are operating properly. There must be something that we are missing." Jane watched the doctor pace up and down the lab.

As he stopped in front of a rack of test tubes filled with blood, he told Duncan, "If we discover that the cells can be easily transferable, you know what that does to the program, and to us. We have to verify the ranger's condition."

Duncan coldly informed him, "I know. I've already begun putting steps in place."

******

"Finally." Ryan was delighted to see a small rabbit suspended in the air. It had been days since he had caught anything and he made short work of putting together a backwoods rabbit stew. With water lily tubers instead of potatoes, cow-parsnip, mushrooms, rock tripe, a few berries and a variety of chopped up greens from the forest, his largest pot was filled to the brim.

After his second bowl, he started to get drowsy. After taking the pot off of the fire, he put a rock on top of the lid to prevent insects and rodents from wiggling their way into it.

From a cliff a half kilometre away, Ratlin looked through his spotting scope and saw Ryan curl up and wrap a blanket around him. After watching his motionless body for a few a minutes, he announced over his radio, "Tell the doctor that the subject is out cold."

Ratlin crawled into the bear den and he glanced back at Dr. Stern, "He's dead to the world all right." He had Ryan's pants pulled down to his ankles before the doctor got inside. With Ryan's knees tucked into his chest, the doctor inserted a needle into his back and extracted a sample of his spinal fluids. Next, blood and tissue samples were taken from Ryan's injured leg where the puncture mark wouldn't be easily noticed. After that was done, Ratlin cringed as Dr. Stern inserted a catheter into Ryan penis to collect a clean urine sample. After all the sites stopped bleeding, the doctor gave Ryan an injection of antibiotics.

As the doctor packed up, Ratlin pulled up Ryan's pants and placed him in the same position that he was found in. After all signs of their presence was cleaned up, Ratlin used his toe to tip over Ryan's stew. "I'll leave a couple rabbits in his traps tomorrow to make up for it."

Chapter Twenty-Five

Halloween

When Ryan woke, the side of his leg felt damp. Resting beside it was the overturned stew pot. Scavengers had taken all of the meat and starchy components of the stew. The only thing left was some mud covered greens and a puddle of dirt soaked in broth. At the back of the small cavern he could hear the faint echoes of something breathing.

Thinking Claraicy had returned, he turned on his flashlight. When he spotted a fox curled up in a crevice, something inside of him sank. He poked at the small beast with the barrel of his rifle. No response. He poked it harder. It still didn't move. With his hand tight around the fox's muzzle he put his ear against the creature's chest and listened to its shallow breathing. It had been either drugged or was very sick. Picking it up, he carefully carried the fox out and laid it down under some bushes a couple dozen metres away from the den.

After returning to the den, Ryan began cleaning up the mess. The fox must have eaten some of the leftover meat. He tried to think. After pouring a second cup of coffee he had to take a leak. As he tried to urinate a sharp burst of pain ran up him. His kidneys emptied gradually but at a high price. It was as if someone was tightly squeezing his penis.

Ryan immediately took note of how the rest of his body felt. His tail bone hurt and he had a strange twinge in his thigh. After pulling down his pants, his fingers led him to the tender sites on the back of his leg where the doctor had taken tissue samples. With the aid of a mirror, he noticed a small round bruise next to his tail bone with a bright red dot in the middle. His mind started to race. "Even Alien abductions aren't this secretive. At least none that I have read about."

******

Claraicy heard Ann humming as she walked along the path that the soldiers had hacked through the thorn bushes. In front of her, a tall, muscular soldier hacked off the odd protruding branch with a machete. As they approached the trailer, Claraicy thought Ann looked incredibly beautiful. Even dressed in bush gear with her hair tied back and wearing thick rimmed glasses, she was everything Claraicy wanted to be.

She watched the way the soldier smiled at Ann as he removed his backpack and handed it to her. As Ann turned and walked towards the door, Claraicy watched the soldier admire her curves. His glowing smile made her heart sink. *No man will ever look at me like that.*

As Ann knocked on the door, Claraicy looked around and saw Jesse hide under the bed. Panic stricken, she yelled through the door, "He's not coming in, is he?"

"No. He is just here to help me carry my equipment and make sure that I got here safely. You know, bears and such. He has strict orders not to even peer through the windows. It will be just the two of us."

Ann left her bag outside the door and walked in. Despite seeing photos of Claraicy's grotesque appearance and mentally preparing herself for their meeting, the sight of her terrified Ann. She couldn't let Claraicy know. As she tried to control her breathing, she saw Claraicy's head and shoulders twitch. She was just as nervous as she was. Trying to relieve the tension, Ann put on a wide smile and extended her hand. "It is so nice to finally meet you."

Ann's hand disappeared as Claraicy reluctantly reached out and wrapped her fingers around it as gently as she could. Claraicy's hands were extremely long, rough and a lot stronger than most of the men she knew. As Claraicy released her, Ann felt the scaly skin on the forearm. Claraicy saw the puzzled look on Ann face. "I know, it's harder than leather. The mosquitoes and black flies had given up trying to penetrate it."

"It's more reptilian." Ann picked up Claraicy's hand and looked more closely at the skin. The odd small hair had worked its way through the cracks between the armour plated skin cells. "Hair cannot grow on hard surfaces. Your normal skin must be still growing underneath it."

The hair follicles allowed Claraicy to feel Ann's soft smooth hands as she studied her arm. "Unlike you, I was never beautiful and over the past year I've grown uglier and uglier every day." After a brief pause, Claraicy inquired, "Do you actually believe that you could make me look human again?"

"After seeing you and examining your skin close up, we believe we can. We believe that most of your changes are superficial. Despite the layer of reptilian-like scales growing over your skin, oversized ears and a pair of wings, you are still human. Once your body begins to realize that these changes have become a nuisance, it will simply shed them. If our theory is correct, you should see signs of it starting to revert back within a few months."

Claraicy cocked her head to the side and asked, "Why are you saying we and our?"

Ann took off her glasses and showed Claraicy the camera and ear piece. "I'm sorry, I meant to tell you about this as soon as I introduced myself, but I forgot. With these glasses, I can relay everything that I see to two doctors that are standing by. They have been analysing everything and relaying the information back to me. Is that all right with you?"

Claraicy took a couple step backward and screamed out, "I told you no men!"

Ann distanced herself from her and had her back to the door. In a low calm voice, she told her, "They are research scientists trying to help you the best they can."

After taking a few deep breaths Claraicy harshly asked, "How many people can see me? I'm not being broadcasted all over the planet, am I?"

Ann frantically answered, "No one else, the only people watching are the two doctors that I told you about and maybe one nurse. It's on a very secure feed. We don't want anyone or anything to hinder your recovery."

Claraicy walked over to Ann and placed her hand over her glasses. "I don't want anyone else to see me, not like this."

"Okay, I'll just put on my other set of glasses." Ann showed Claraicy the off and on switch on the side of the glasses and turned it on the off position before setting them on the coffee table. After retrieving the backpack, she found her regular glasses and put them on. Looking at Claraicy, Ann smiled. "How about washing and brushing your hair before we go any further?"

Claraicy couldn't remember the last time anyone washed her hair for her. Even her mother refused to do it. As Ann chatted away about lotions and creams that she might consider using to soften her skin, all she could do is revel in the pure pleasure of having a scalp massage and clean hair.

Afterwards she sat down on a stool while Ann ran a brush through her long, course hair. "Next time I come, I think I will bring some of those lotions to try on your skin. I should get someone to drop some off at your door along with some hair supplies." While trying to work her brush through a large knot in Claraicy's hair, she added, "Men don't understand women's needs at all, do they?"

Claraicy lowered her head and mumbled out, "I wouldn't know, I just turned fourteen a couple months ago."

As Ann sealed the hair matted brush into a plastic bag, she turned her head and looked at the size of Claraicy. "Wow, I would never have guessed. You look so mature for your age."

Claraicy glared at her while spewing out, "Last year I was just a child."

In a calm voice, Ann told her, "A lot has happened to you in the past year." With the glasses sitting on a coffee table facing them, Ann gingerly proceeded to examine Claraicy. From her heel to the claws on her foot measured 75 centimetres. "We measured some of your footprints in the mud about a week ago. Your feet have already shrunk a few millimetres." Ann held Claraicy's foot and smiled. "Congratulations, you are already showing signs of converting back. This proves that the doctors were right about you."

Claraicy smiled as Ann cheerfully measured various body parts including her wings and the second pair of shoulders they were mounted on. In an upbeat tone, she asked, "Has anything else changed?"

Smiling back at her, Ann replied, "I don't know. This is the first time we have properly measured you." She was glad that Claraicy was finally in a good mood because the next thing she had to do was inject a needle into her. "Now, we need some blood and tissue samples from you. It is going to hurt. Are you feeling up to that?"

Claraicy took a deep breath. "Sure."

Ann watched Claraicy closely for any sign of anxiety as she took out a handheld rotary tool and drilled a millimetre wide hole through a scale on her arm. After forcing a needle into the narrow hole, Ann poked around for a vein. Claraicy barely flinched. Without being able to see through the scales Ann had to go by feel. Eventually a thick orange fluid began to come out. Doctor Scott had told Ann what to expect. With gold replacing the iron in the blood's haemoglobin, Claraicy's red blood cells were slowly turning yellow.

Claraicy glared at the fluid and inquired, "Is that my blood?"

Ann calmly answered her, "Yes and no. The strange colour that you are seeing are the parasitic cells that I told you about. When mixed with your regular cells they turn your blood into a different colour." After labelling the sample, she smiled at Claraicy. "Now that wasn't so bad, was it?"

Claraicy shrugged her shoulders. "No, I hardly felt it."

"Good because the next needle will be a little bigger, and you may feel a little more discomfort. Do you want me to put something on your skin to dull the pain?"

"No. It should be all right."

After drilling a three millimetre wide hole through one of the scales on Claraicy's thigh, Ann twisted a long, thick needle into it. As she hit the femur, she saw the pupils in Claraicy's eyes grow and a huge gasp of air swell up her chest. As her claws dug into the arms of the chair Ann jumped back. "Are you okay?"

The claws on Claraicy's fingers began to retract as Claraicy answered. "Yes, I guess you should have used some of the stuff to dull the pain. I'm sorry, I thought that I could handle it."

"Next time I will." While keeping an eye on Claraicy's face, Ann gently pulled out the needle containing the tissue sample. "We are all done."

Before saying goodbye, Ann switched her glasses. With DeGroot standing outside, Claraicy didn't want to walk Ann to the door. After the door clicked shut, Ann passed her bag to DeGroot and started to walking towards the path. As soon as she was sure that Claraicy couldn't hear her, she asked, "Did you swap all the collection boxes?"

DeGroot handed her a plastic jug and a bag full of filters. "Yes, the trailer's modifies septic system separated out everything even some of the dead cells. It's like a cross between a primitive water purification unit and a gold miner's wash board. I'm just glad that they incorporated water jets into her toilet to wash her down like a bidet. If she had to use toilet paper, collecting samples would've been messy."

"Well with her tail, they had to customize the design of the toilet anyway. Plus, they felt that the system needed more water to separate all the crap in the faeces and urine." Out of sight of the trailer, Ann switched the audio on her glasses back on. "So what did you think?"

Doctor Scott spoke up. "We'll discuss it when you get back to camp."

A little further down the path, Ann asked DeGroot, "Before I forget, when Duncan measured Claraicy's foot print, how long did he say it was?"

"75 centimetres."

"That's what I thought he said."

DeGroot chuckled. "A little white lie won't hurt her."

******

Claraicy laid back on the sofa and flipped through the movies and shows they had compiled for her to watch. She started to watch a silly movie about a crazy ghost coming to life for a few hours on Halloween and reliving what it was like being a normal teenage boy again.

Claraicy scratched behind Jesse's ears. "I wonder why they choose this movie? I guess they just like rubbing it in."

With Jesse resting on her lap, they both chewed on sticks of jerky while the opening credits were being shown. As the ghost in the movie was granted his wish, Claraicy looked at her hands. "Only in the movies." Most of the movie occurred in a large house during a teenage Halloween party. Seeing the outlandish costumes that the actors were wearing, Claraicy looked at her arms. She recalled Ryan's spiel about her looking like a girl dressed up in a terrific Halloween costume. "I look a lot better than they do."

Glancing at the calendar hanging on the wall, she realized that Halloween was only two days away. Claraicy got up and went to the mirror. With her hair brushed behind her ears, she looked like a Hollywood creation. Looking at herself in a new light, she reached down and picked up Jesse. Staring at the pair of them in the mirror, she commented, "Who needs a costume?"

Every dream she had that night had to do with Halloween. The following morning, she looked into the mirror and studied her profile. To her surprise she noticed a loose scale under her arm pit. Using a claw, she scratched off a few of the surrounding scales. "I'm shedding! Ann was right."

Gazing into the mirror she told herself, "This could be my only chance to go out and have everyone wish that they could look like me. Who cares that it's Halloween and it isn't really a costume? The only thing that matters is that everyone, even the rich snobs, would be envious of me for a change."

It had been a year since her father had left her to die. Now, she was about to face the outside world alone. *What if I discover that I don't want to go back?*

After sleeping all afternoon, she left Jesse with enough open cans of meat to keep her content. With a full stomach and several meals packed into a bag wrapped around her neck, she flew through the night. Not wanting to be sighted, she weaved between the tree tops and soared barely above the surface of the lakes and foliage in the clearing. In the first eight hours she managed to travel over hundred kilometres.

At daybreak, despite the houses along the road being kilometres apart, Claraicy felt as if everyone was watching her. She was no longer able to fly. Dropping to the ground she ran through the forest. At the outskirts of Sioux Lookout she slowed down to a fast walk and followed the roadways. Several drivers smiled, waved and honk their horns at her as they drove by. To onlookers she was just someone in a costume.

A couple stopped their car and asked her if she needed a lift. With a shake of her head and a polite 'No thanks', they drove off.

By the time she reached Sioux Lookout, school was over and many of the parents were starting to show off they young children's costumes to their friends and neighbours. As dusk approached the older children started to flood the streets, running door to door gathering pillow cases full of candy. The decorated streets were full of children of all ages. Comical graveyards, cobwebs and blow up monsters were everywhere.

Claraicy semi-enjoyed the stares she got as she slowly walked through the streets. She had never been allowed to go out on Halloween and everything seemed surreal. It was as if she was watching it on TV. Parents and older siblings walked beside the younger children as they went door to door. Flashes from cameras lit up the doorways as neighbours recorded the festive event. The night was full of wildly, vocalised glee and excitement.

As Claraicy walked down the middle of the street, a couple of older girls dressed like rock stars walked past her. "Nice costume. You must have spent a bundle." The tallest girl asked, "Do I know you? I'm Nancy."

Claraicy didn't need the introduction. Everyone knew Nancy. She was seventeen, stunningly beautiful and had her choice of any boy she wanted. "I'm new to town."

"You should come to our park later." Nancy eyed Claraicy up and down. "Nice wings but you could have made your face a little more scary."

Claraicy smiled. "Thanks, but I thought that I would go with something more subtle this year."

Noticing the empty bag in Claraicy's hand, Nancy informed her, "People here are still giving out stuff to older kids too, or are you planning to rip off some greedy young brats later?"

Claraicy looked around at the kids collecting all the goodies they can. As the pair walked away, Claraicy approached the nearest house. An old lady opened the door and looked at Claraicy's empty bag. "Are you on your second bag already? You should save some for the little kiddies you know."

Claraicy took a half step back and answered, "No, it just took me a lot longer to get ready then I had expected."

"Well then." The lady put a can of pop in her bag. "There you go."

As she walked away, Claraicy heard her mumble, "That'll start to weigh her down. Older teenagers shouldn't be out trick or treating. They should leave more for the younger kids."

The rest of the block was more receptive. A few houses had their porch lights turned off, but most were very warm, cheerful and very generous. Between houses, she ate what she could without slowing her down. At one door, a young woman in her late twenties dressed as a stylish witch stared and marvelled at Claraicy's appearance. "Where did you get it?"

"Toronto." In Northern Ontario, Toronto was like saying New York or San Francisco. Everything obscure and foreign comes from of Toronto.

A few more idolizing compliments made Claraicy's spirits soar. As streets and time passed by, the younger kids started to disappear. At the end of a long street she found herself facing a house lit up in red, yellow, blue and green lights. A sleigh with nine reindeer decorated the front lawn. Down its walkway two rows of giant candy canes were lined up to form a runway. A fibreglass elf holding a pair of signal flags stood next to it, as if he had just guided Santa's sleigh to a safe landing. On top of the roof, standing next to the chimney, was a huge Santa Claus. She dropped her bag. Every muscle inside of her started to twitch.

The next thing she knew, she was on the roof and had put her fist through Santa's fibreglass chest where his heart would have been if it had one. Strands of the chicken wire used in its construction scraped off some of the scales from her hand and arm. After dislodging the metal straps securing the figure in place, she heaved the large monstrosity into the air. Landing head first into the wooden sleigh, it smashed into pieces. Jumping down, she drew out her claws and ripped apart the rest of the display. Nothing was spared.

Looking around snorting, Claraicy saw a couple recording her on their cell phones. The sight of Claraicy running towards them made the boy drop his phone. Without missing a step, she swooped it up and threw it against the side of a brick house. Leaping into the air, Claraicy pounced on the back of the girl.

She looked around but couldn't see the phone. Flipping the frightened girl over, Claraicy began to run her claws over the girl's pockets. "Where is it?"

The frightened girl pulled the phone out of the sleeve of her jacket, "Is that what you are after?"

Claraicy wildly grabbed it and snapped it in half with her bare hands. Shards from its shattered screen sliced the girl's cheek. Her eyes bulged out so much that droplets of blood started to form.

Claraicy's deep breaths made her sound like a snorting bull. Still focussed on the girl's face, she could hear the footsteps of people running towards her. Jumping up, she took a few giant strides and then ducked between some houses. After running along the tops of fence posts, through backyards and past a half dozen dogs, Claraicy was several blocks away before she ventured back onto a road. She slowed down and walked at the same pace as everyone else. She tried hard not to draw any attention to herself.

Claraicy saw Nancy and her friend running towards her. "What's all the commotion going on?"

Claraicy replied, "I heard that someone wrecked somebody's Christmas display."

"Good. Who did they think they are pretending it's Christmas all year long."

Nancy looked at Claraicy's skin. A large section of it was peeling off down her entire side and across her stomach. The girls started to giggle at the sight of the pink skin showing through. Claraicy couldn't stop herself and released a wild growl.

As the girls casually walked away, Nancy snickered, "Nice sound effects, but still a lousy costume." Turning to her friend, she added, "And to think that I wanted her to come to our party. How embarrassing would that have been. If I was her I would be demanding my money back."

Nancy's friend looked back at Claraicy. "Ya, but you have to admit that those wings were absolutely gorgeous."

Chapter Twenty-Six

Fugitives

The hairs on the back of Ryan's neck stood erect. Somehow he could feel the invisible eyes of someone spying on him. Despite being in the middle of a vast wilderness, he felt like a caged animal. With the police gone, the only other people in the forest that he was aware of were the strange party that Marq flew in. He thought of Duncan. They had grown up together. Ryan tried to dismiss his involvement. "There has to be someone else out here, but who?"

Both scared and confused, Ryan carefully scouted around the area for more clues to their identity. Instead of concentrating on sources of food and animal pathways to lay traps, he scoured the rocky ridges and thick brush for places where someone could watch him without being seen.

It took him only half an hour to find a freshly dug out trench under some thorn bushes on top of a hill almost half a kilometre away. Despite the distance, if there was no wind to disturb the bare tree branches and distort the view, someone could easily see the den's entrance along with a couple of the paths he sometimes used. Taking out his binoculars, he could even make out a couple red embers from his morning fire along with his backpack. The den was much more open than he thought it was. In fact, without the leaves in the trees, his hiding spot wasn't hidden at all.

Sweeping back and forth over the entire area, Ryan spotted another possible lookout. It rested on top of a ridge with a small patch of brush to hide behind. The closer he got to the obscure location, the more he realized that it possibly had a better view of the bear den.

By the time he climbed up a rock face to get there, the patch of brush on top had vanished. Ryan bent over and felt the stone. It was still warm. Faint lines of black shoe polish marked where the person's boots would have been. After examining the area, a few overturned pebbles that still had dark specks of moisture on them were enough to lead him down the ridge.

The large bare rocks along the ridge made the tracking difficult. A careful person could hop from one to another without leaving any trace behind. The time it took for Ryan to find the scant signs that were left behind, he knew his prey was getting further and further away.

Ryan knew that it would be a waste of time chasing after them. Standing up, he looked around one last time before carefully veering off of the ridge and running back to the den. If the fleeing spy believed he was still trailing them, they would be trying to escape. They won't be able to watch the den at the same time. After gathering up all his stuff, he ran away as fast as he could.

If his pursuers were like most trained trackers, they would expect to find him hidden in the forest, in view of the den, because it is human nature to need to know who or what is after you. Ryan wasn't about to be caught so easily. He knew that his best hope was to go back to his cabin and retrieve more supplies before they figured out he had left.

At the cabin, Ryan didn't want to use the door. It was too exposed; too easily watched. Mounted to the bare trees in front the cabin he could see Willy's cameras. They were easy to evade as he made his way to the back of the cabin. The hinges on the window above his bed were well-oiled and its pins were easy to pull out with the pliers on his multi-tool. Wiggling the window, he created a gap large enough that he could insert the blade of his knife and dislodged the hooks that held it shut. After reattaching the hinges, he propped the window open with a chunk of firewood, climbed on top of the woodpile under the window and crawled inside.

Ryan stuffed his backpack with all the food and supplies he could find. Rapidly looking around, his eyes stopped at the headboard of his bed. He had specially designed it himself. It looked like it was made of thick heavy timbers, but a knot in the wood next to the wall held the truth. He had hammered it out and transformed it into a spring mounted button. Pushing the knot in the length of his first finger, a series of cables, pulleys and levers released the pins that held the plywood centre onto the frame of the headboard. Hinged on the bottom, the foam backed plywood fell forward and revealed a secret storage cabinet.

An empty cabin can be used by anyone wandering through the forest. Providing protection and food to a hungry traveller was one thing, but supplying them with expensive equipment was another.

Secured inside of the small cabinet was an assortment of knives for hunting, survival and throwing, along with extra ammunition, his pellet pistol and an air-powered tranquillizer gun. Everything was held in place with Velcro straps. The thick foam glued to the hinged plywood prevented anything from rattling. Ryan packed up some snare wire, several knives and his Beeman P1 .20 caliber air pistol along with all the pellets he had for it. He couldn't rely on snared food anymore. He may have to keep on the move. The powerful, single shot pistol could semi-quietly kill small game like rabbits and grouse with a head shot, or even something larger if hit in the temple at close range.

******

Doctor Scott called over the lab's PA system, "Jane, have you got any results yet?"

Jane put down her clipboard and replied over the voice activated PA system, "The results of the first two sets are already off."

Five minutes later the doctor walked into the lab. "Are any more off?"

Jane looked at him shook her head. "Only one more. You have to give the equipment time to do its job. It can't be rushed."

The doctor eagerly walked over to her. "I know. Now, show me what you have?"

Jane handed the doctor her clipboard. "The samples are from a human male. The cells had been altered by what I presume were the cells from the escaped bats. They were almost all dead before I received them."

The doctor caught the sarcasm in her voice. "Yes, I know that you have a good handle on what's going on."

Jane passed the doctor the second set of results. "Just remember, if you want me to do my job, I have to know what I'm actually searching for. None of this 'need-to-know' crap."

"Okay, I know that you are not an idiot. I will fill you in with what is really going on later. For now, I have let the team in the field know how to proceed."

As the doctor looked at the second set of results, he glanced over at Jane. "By the way, the man's name is Ryan. The contaminated girl had attacked him. Her name is Claraicy Mitchell, the daughter of Kerry Mitchell."

Shocked, Jane blurted out, "The man that was castrated."

"Claraicy's father had bought a very sizable insurance policy on her just before she was reported missing. Because of the huge amount, the insurance company refused to pay anything without a body. For all they knew, she was a runaway. The man she gutted was Patrick Leer, her neighbour and a very close friend of her father. Both men had a history of violence and suspected criminal behaviour. It's a small cruel twisted world, even in this small town."

Jane passed the doctor the third set of results. "These are from Ryan's stool sample. It contains crystals from a few modified cells. All the results are showing that they are dying off."

She lowered her eyebrows as she continued. "I wouldn't have expected anyone could receive this amount of contamination from some blood splatter during a fight. The cells had to have to be multiplying in order to get the amount we are finding."

"The attack was violent and there was evidence that they were both bleeding rather heavily." Shaking his head, he added, "But I have to agree that the amount we are finding is way too high. It has been well over a month since the attack. They should've all died out by now. We shouldn't be getting anything." The Doctor scratched his head. "What puzzles me is that without being properly nourished, the cells should not be able to reproduce in his body at all."

Jane took back her clipboard and went over the results for anything she could have missed. "Do you have any theories?"

The doctor smiled as he vigorously paced around the floor. "I suspect that the cells are doing exactly what they are designed to do: survive. After rapidly repairing any tissue they came in contact with, they probably formed a wall between them and the host body's white blood cells. Now that his injuries have healed, his white blood cells have turned their attention to their tiny fortresses. The modified cells that have not died from starvation are slowly being killed off. It should be just a matter of time before the cells that they had mutated succumb to his body's vast army of defences and be replaced with normal cells."

A buzzer on the computer signalled that the fourth set of results were completed. Jane turned around and sent them to the printer. The anxious doctor demanded, "Which samples are these?"

"The spinal fluid." A glimpse was all Jane needed as she passed the results to the doctor. "There goes your theory."

The doctor's jaw dropped as he read the results. "Some of these are freshly formed cells. They are not fortifying themselves, they are attacking the white blood cells at their source. By stopping the creation of white blood cells, they could freely travel anywhere in Ryan's body."

Jane cocked her head and told the doctor, "Our tests show that his body is expelling some of them. As their numbers dwindle, it will be only a matter of time before it is game over."

Doctor Scott glanced at a sample lying on the counter. After reading the name on it, he concluded, "David lucked out when he started eating dirt. It was rich in fine gold particles and other minerals that his cells needed. The area that they are in has pockets of soil containing higher than normal levels of gold. The trace particles are too sparse to mine. Like David, Ryan could be eating dirt to fight off hunger."

Jane shook her head. "I don't think so. It would have shown in his urine and stool samples. He has had plenty to eat."

Putting his hands on the back of his head, the doctor rambled out loud, "In a couple of our early test subjects, after their bodies began to reject the cells, the cells grouped together and began to cannibalize each other."

The doctor stopped pacing and looked at Jane. "The cannibalising of the cells had actually halted the effects of heavy metal poisoning. As long as Ryan's body has enough cells to fight off his immune system, they can survive. Just in case, I think that a mineral analysis of his stool is in order, and try to separate the discarded crystals if you can. He consumes a lot a local vegetation. Maybe some of the plants contain enough minerals to keep the cells going."

"What about Claraicy?"

"She's a real mess." The doctor looked up at the ceiling. While staring into a light, he announced, "There may be some new and unexpected changes in the cells' behaviour that we haven't thought of."

The phone rang and Doctor Scott answered. "Hello?"

A deep voice blurted out, "Did you see today's paper?"

The doctor stood up straight. "No General, I haven't."

"Someone has snapped a picture of what looks like your creature running around Sioux Lookout. In the article, it says that your creature had demolished someone's entire Christmas display. What is going on there? If it wasn't for the fact that it's Halloween and the perpetrator was reported as wearing a demon costume, we'd be in real big trouble."

"I wasn't aware of anything going on."

"I'll send you a copy. But right now, I want you to either insert a tracking device into her or bring her in. Those are your choices."

Jane was standing close enough to the phone that she could hear both sides of the conversation. "There is no way that we can bring her in against her wishes. With the amount of cells in her, drugs are useless. In her mental state, any stress we put on her could tip the balance in the modified cells' favour. There won't be anything left of Claraicy to study and research. The only way to safely bring her in is dead."

"Then we study the creature she has become." Expecting a violent backlash, the doctor took a step back. To his surprise, all Jane did was shake her head.

After a minute of silence, Doctor Scott asked her, "Now, how about the test results from the samples taken from her?"

Jane took a couple deep breaths and tried to regain her composure. "They were the last ones that I prepared. They will not be fully completed for at least another hour."

Like clockwork, Doctor Scott returned in exactly an hour and dropped the newspaper on Jane's desk. "Are they ready?"

"They are starting to come off now." Before Jane could get the first set off the printer, the doctor's hands were on the corner of the paper. "The blood sample that you gave me was orange. Gold had already replaced two thirds of the iron in her blood. It is just like a horseshoe crab's blood being blue when copper is used instead of the iron in the haemoglobin."

The doctor grabbed the second set before Jane could even glance at it. "Are you sure these tissue results are accurate? These results are showing a huge decrease in the amount of crystals in her system. That indicates that our plan was actually working."

Jane looked at him. "What do you mean, was?"

"According to that newspaper, something must have erupted inside of her. In the article, people commented on how timid and polite she was when she went door to door. A couple people even took a picture of her smiling for the camera. Something must have flipped a switch inside of her to trigger such a response." Looking a Jane, he added, "We have to cool her down somehow. If we can't, with her temper she could blow up and take everyone with her."

A photo of Claraicy popped up on Jane's computer. Even in the hastily taken picture, Jane could see the cracks in Claraicy's outer skin and her exposed pink inner layer. "We were so close."

******

Claraicy landed on top of the ridge overseeing the trailer. She examined the split and dangling outer skin on her side and across her abdomen. The yellowish skin beneath it was white from the cold air. Seeing no one around she hopped down. Instead of rushing into the warm trailer, she dove into the frigid pool.

She slowly crawled out of the water and into the cavern on all fours. At the edge of the wall adjacent the pool, she began sniffing the ground. Drool dripped from her corners of her mouth as she brushed away the top layer of dirt and began digging a small hole. After removing a handful of dirt from the hole, she shoved it into her mouth. She then licked some water off of the cavern's wall to help wash it down.

A few shiny sparkles twinkled on her face and hands. "Ahhhh, that's good." Crouched on her hands and knees, she started gnawing at the ground like a starving dog on a fresh bone.

******

In the communication trailer that they had setup beside the lake, DeGroot announced, "Duncan she's back." DeGroot got up from his chair and let Duncan review the different cameras on his monitors.

Wildly flipping through the screens, Duncan asked, "Where is she?"

"She's in the cave. All that was caught on camera was a large shadow darting into the water."

Doctor Stern looked over Duncan's shoulder as he repositioned the camera inside of the cavern. As he watched her lick the stone wall, he muttered, "Like African elephants that travel hundreds of kilometres in search of salt and mineral deposits, Claraicy's senses are telling her where to find the minerals her cells need. She is no longer human. She has become a wild animal driven by pure instinct. This has gone on long enough and she's getting too dangerous."

"Forget it, Doc. I know what you are thinking." Duncan grabbed the doctor's shoulders and looked straight into his eyes. "She's unique. We need to harness her abilities. With them, we could form a small regiment that could dominate any battlefield it entered. With the precision that only hand-to-hand combat can provide, it would give guerilla warfare an all new meaning. No bombs, no friendly fire, no civilian casualties, just total destruction of the enemy. It would be unstoppable. No one would dare oppose us."

Doctor Stern snapped back, "But she is actually three creatures in one. She can't be controlled. I know enough about medicine to tell you that this is one experiment no one would be allowed to do inside of any government regulated lab. Not even a military one."

Duncan's face turned cold. "Doctor Scott needs to find out everything about her and I'm here to make sure he does."

Defiantly, the doctor snapped back, "We don't need her, we have David."

Duncan's grin made the doctor briefly stop talking. "What Doctor Scott is finding out from David is great, but if he could find a way to utilize Claraicy's abilities, that would be beyond all of our expectations. For that, he needs to find out exactly how the modified cells are functioning inside of her and harness their true ability."

Doctor Stern shook his head and crossed his arms. "You expect to use her like a reproducible biological weapon. I've heard of using elephants, dogs, dolphins, monkeys and even rats, but that is ridiculous. Her behaviour is too erratic."

Over his headset Drake announced, "Duncan, we have more trouble. Your brother is back. So much for the police blockade. I spotted his canoe creeping along the south-west bank of the lake."

"I told you that he wouldn't let it go." Duncan walked down to the lakeshore. He saw a small speck bouncing around in the waves pounding the shoreline. "He is probably lake hopping. There are some streams at that end that lead into a few other small lakes. I'll have MacNeil keep an eye on him."

DeGroot walked over to Duncan. "We're spread too thin. We have Steve, Claraicy, Ryan and now your brother to keep track of. We need some reinforcements."

"I know. Thank goodness the tracking device we injected into Steve is still working. You can monitor him from here. For now, Ratlin and I will deal with Claraicy, Drake can track Ryan and MacNeil can keep an eye on Willy. We will just have to hold everything together the best we can."

By the time Duncan and Ratlin got their canoe half way across the lake, DeGroot informed him that Claraicy had already left the cavern. "She's gone. I reviewed the footage and saw her staring into the camera while she was taping her loose skin together with some duct tape that we must have left behind. Within a half of a minute after that, she had filled a bag full of soil and dove into the water."

Duncan placed his paddle across the canoe, put his head down and closed his eyes. "There goes any chance of trapping her inside the cavern."

Ratlin looked at him and shook his head. "Capturing her is not going to be that easy."

Chapter Twenty-Seven

Payback

Rubbing the back of his neck, Ryan felt that lying still under an insect-infested bush was emotionally much harder than running through the woods. He had patiently watched over his cabin for days and saw nothing. In a moment a frustration, he broke his silence and muttered to himself, "Surely they would have expected me to show up here sooner or later."

It wasn't until the fifth day that he saw anyone. From out of the forest, two men carrying rifles sneaked around to the back of the cabin and peered into the window. Even from a distance, Ryan easily recognized Patrick. He was thinner and had a bulge under the front of his jacket. It took him a bit longer to recognize Kerry. His face looked a lot different from the last time he had seen him. *Those two can't be the men that were watching me. If Patrick had seen me all alone out there, he would have pulled the trigger.*

Ryan lay still under the bush and watched the pair enter the front door. Within fifteen minutes, Patrick came back out carrying an aluminum briefcase. Ryan had never owned a briefcase. Kerry slowly followed Patrick to the back of the cabin.

Putting down the briefcase, Patrick turned to him. "You were there when I told Willy to look under the cupboards. That nitwit just looked inside of them. It's no wonder he didn't find anything to frame Ryan with."

When Kerry caught up to him, he said, "In his defence, no one ever looks in the boarded-up gap between the floor and the bottom of the cupboards. You could've made the opening a little more obvious."

"And risk having Ryan find it? No way." Patrick picked up the briefcase and surveyed the area. "Cops are just plain stupid, that's why they are cops. I could've painted a big yellow 'X' over it and he still wouldn't have found it."

After Patrick handed him the brief case, Kerry asked, "What do you want me to do with it?"

"Hang on to it and follow me. If LC knew that I had hid my entire stash right under his nose, he would've puked."

Patrick only walked a few metres into the woods behind the cabin before he took his folding shovel out of his backpack and started to dig. Crouched on his knees, he pushed and piled the soil on top of a flat rock. It didn't take long before he struck the blocks of wood that protected the large plastic cooler he had buried. With the cooler still in the ground, he pried open the lid and removed six more briefcases.

After closing the lid and burying the cooler, he stood up and looked back at Kerry. "If you want to hide something from someone, just put it right under their nose. They will never find it. If they do just say it is their's."

Kerry picked up two briefcases in each hand. "They ain't that heavy."

Patrick snickered. "My cut alone is worth over two hundred grand. The Asians are willing to pay a small fortune for high quality bear parts. Most of the weight is from the drying salts that they were packed in." Picking up the last two briefcases, he turned to Kerry and added, "Are you ready?"

Kerry caught something in the corner of his eye. While turning around and looking through the trees, he whispered, "I thought I saw something in the trees."

Patrick grinned and told him, "Your daughter has you running scared."

With his eyes still roaming through the trees, Kerry stated, "Just remember your promise. She's next."

Patrick put one hand on his ostomy bag. "How can I forget? When she gets hers, she'll find out the true meaning of payback."

As the two men disappeared into the forest, Ryan quietly followed them into a soupy marsh. When the pair reached their large rubber raft, they tossed the briefcases into it and began to push it into the water.

By the time they finally got aboard, all of the splashing and banging of paddles had drowned out the recoil of Ryan's well placed shots. He had managed to hit the air chambers that ran along the side of the raft five times.

As the two men turned the raft and began to paddle away, Ryan put three more small holes into the back of the raft. His last shot sent a pellet into a previous hole, through the inside rubber and struck the heel of Patrick's boot.

Looking down, Patrick saw half of a pellet sticking out of his heel. As he looked through the trees, he proclaimed, "Ryan's out there and he had shot holes in the boat. I may not be able to see him, but I know it's him."

The back end of the raft slowly started to fold in on Kerry. "We're sinking!"

"No guff!"

The escaping air whistled as it rushed out of the small holes. As the raft sank and rubbed against the debris on the bottom, Patrick proclaimed, "There is no way that he's going to get the better of me." After dumping out his backpack and filled it with the contents of the briefcases, he grabbed his rifle and jumped into the swamp.

As Patrick waded through the waist high muck and scurried into the woods, Kerry paddled towards to shore. A submerged branch hooked the raft and spun it around. Stuck in the middle of the swamp, Kerry shoved the butt of his shotgun tight against his shoulder and searched through the trees.

Seeing some movement in the trees, Kerry quickly turned around. The momentum was too much for the sinking raft and the fully inflated side flipped into the air. Splashing head first into the muck, Kerry wasted no time in getting to his feet and grabbing the side of the raft. Fighting his way through the mud and sunken debris, he dragged the raft behind him with one arm while holding his shotgun above his head with the other.

Ryan wasn't interested in Kerry. It was Patrick that he wanted. As Kerry waded ashore, Ryan went after Patrick. Patrick wasn't nearly as nimble as he once was. As he ran through the trees and brush, he didn't notice a long, sharp thorn digging its way through his jacket until it pierced his ostomy bag. The putrid smell of the oozing liquid slurry and ripe gases filled the air around him. He couldn't hide. All Ryan needed was his nose.

Exhausted and knowing that Ryan wasn't far behind him, he leaned against a tree and aimed his rifle at every sound he heard. "Ryan, I can hear you coming for me. With this damn shit bag, I can't hide from you anymore. It has ruined everything."

From a branch high above Patrick came, "It has also ruined my hunt." Claraicy looked down at the cowering, frightened man. "I guess I will have to finish the job I had started."

Patrick fired a couple shots into the branches. With Patrick's full attention focussed on Claraicy, Ryan rushed in and grabbed his rifle. "It's over."

Ryan looked up and saw Claraicy poke her head out from behind the tree trunk. "I need him to clear my name."

"When you're done with him." Claraicy grinned before slowly adding, "I need him to pay off the debt that he owes his late wife."

Ryan looked at Claraicy as drool hung from her mouth in anticipation of a kill. In his eyes, she was no longer just a crazy, deformed girl. She was a monstrous, twisted creature. "No, he belongs in jail."

Enraged, Claraicy took flight and began to fly in big circles over their heads. Ryan turned to Patrick. "You are lucky that I got to you when it did, 'cause she is no longer playing games."

Claraicy's nose flared as she flew over the marsh. She could smell and hear her fat shivering father trying to patch the holes in the raft with rubber cement from the repair kit. Hovering over the small, dry clearing, she grinned. "Ryan can't protect both of you. You're mine."

Kerry grabbed his pump action shotgun and fired three quick shots. Two tore holes into her right wing and the third peppered her chest. He barely had time to get another shell into the chamber before Claraicy dove on top of his shoulders and knock the gun out of his hands. Her sharp claws pinned him face first into the ground.

Infuriated, she pulled his right hand to her mouth and began to gnaw off his fingers one at a time. As he screamed, she told him, "This will stop you from diddling another helpless child."

After she was finished with his right hand, she pulled his left arm from under him. "You can't hid it from me."

As she spit his last finger out of her mouth, Claraicy stood up and watched her father get up and try to run away. Running through the trees around him, she herded him back to the same clearing, and then pounced on him again.

The game of catch and release continued until he started to slow down to a crawl. After dragging him back to the clearing, Claraicy tore off his boots. Through his socks, she started biting off his toes.

Sinking back into the woods, she waited for him to try to get away. He didn't move. He refused play anymore. Kerry twisted his head and faced her. "Just get it over with."

Claraicy rushed in and slashed him across his chest and then retreated back into the woods. He started to crawl away on his back. He got third-quarters of the way under a bush when Claraicy grabbed his legs and turned him over. After tearing open the back of his pants, she shoved the barrel of his shotgun deep inside of him. The more he screamed the further she shoved it in.

By the time his screams stopped, over half the barrel had disappeared. With blood bubbled out of his mouth, Claraicy grabbed his face and told him, "You just can't take what you dish out, can you?"

With the shotgun still inside of him, Claraicy rolled him over and looked into his face. There was nothing left. A couple blinks, that was it. "You can't die on me yet. I have much more planned for you."

On the far side of the swamp, Ratlin huddled under a spruce tree and peered through the branches. As soon as he got his binoculars out and saw what was happening, he put down his rifle loaded with tranquillizer darts and unholstered his pistol. Despite the cool air, sweat started to drip down his forehead as he realized what he was witnessing.

Kerry opened his eyes and saw the dark clouds rolling in and blocking out the sun. The soft rain that accompanied them washed away some of the blood that was coming out of his mouth with every breath he took. When Claraicy returned she was carrying a four litre jug of camping fuel and a small bag.

He felt helpless as she rolled him over and dragged him on his belly to the remains of a large, hollowed-out pine stump. He had no fight left in him. With a few bashes with her fists, she created a big cavity on the side of the stump. It looked like a large, hollow, high-back chair. After flipping her father over her shoulder, she flopped him down into the cavity. His torso sank into the hollow centre and his legs dangled outside of cavity. The sides and back of the stump wedged him tightly in place.

After dousing him with fuel she asked him, "Isn't this what you wanted to do to me?"

He blinked. Despite the rain, it only took one match to send flames almost to the tree tops. The bubbles of blood oozing from his mouth muffled Kerry's final scream before his head fell to his chest. Claraicy gathered everything she could, even the rubber raft, and threw it on the fire.

The shotgun shells fastened to Kerry's belt began to go off, blowing apart the burning ambers and creating a mystical light show. As the sides of the stump slowly burned away, what was left of her father's body sunk inside of it.

Then it finally happened. The shell in the shotgun's chamber exploded, blasted through Kerry's neck and blew apart his skull. Jumping around in jubilation, she screamed out, "Freedom! Finally I am free of you forever."

Frightened, Jesse watched with from under the protection of a dense spruce tree. Despite her fear of fire, Claraicy's bizarre behaviour terrified her even more.

******

Despite the dark clouds and rain, the funnel of black smoke coming from the burning rubber raft was hard to miss. Ryan chuckled, "I think your partner is being reacquainted with your late wife."

Patrick looked at the smoke. "I guess he deserved it."

After Ryan ordered Patrick to remove his boot laces, he wrapped his arms around a tree and tied his hands together. "That should hold you until I get back."

Astonished, Patrick looked at Ryan and cried out, "You can't leave me. What if she comes back?"

"If I were you, I'd pray she doesn't." Ryan ran back to the marsh, hid behind a bush and began watching Claraicy dancing in front of the fire. *Surely this should attract some attention.*

Claraicy tried desperately to keep the fire going, but after a few hours the rain finally won. Ryan's mind began to sink. *Maybe they were too far away to see it? Maybe they just need more time to get here?*

Eventually, the rain stopped and Ryan watched Claraicy sift through the ashes. As she collected the remains of her father's charred bones, she laid them beside a rock. While she used another rock to pound and grind the bones into powder, she began to sing. "This is the way we crush his bones, crush his bones, crush his bones. This is the way we crush his bones, isn't it a beautiful morning?" She sang the same verse over and over, each time with more and more glee.

Ryan was mesmerized by Claraicy as she ground her father's bones into ashes and tossed them in the marsh. She seemed to do it so calmly, like a small girl making mud pies. He shook his head and tried to think about what he should do next. He had to get back to Patrick before she was finished.

When he got back to the tree, he found Patrick trying to cut through the boot lace with the edge of a stone. As he untied him, Ryan said, "We are getting out of here."

After retying Patrick's hands behind his back, Ryan forced him southward through the forest towards the nearest road. He didn't care how many days or weeks it would take. Knowing that Claraicy was in the forest frightened him even more then the possibility of going to jail for crimes he didn't commit. At least in court he had a chance to defend himself.

Stopping to shoot a grouse or rabbit for supper or pick a handful of berries were the only breaks they took. From sunup to sundown, Ryan kept nudging Patrick ahead of him. Fearing what Claraicy might do to him, Patrick didn't fight back.

Just after daybreak on the third day, they got halfway across a clearing of tall grass and shrubs when Patrick abruptly stopped. Ryan pushed his shoulder. "Come on, we still have a long way to go yet."

Suddenly Ryan felt something jabbing him in the back. "Not so fast."

Ryan knew Willy's voice. "Why am I not surprised? You always liked to bushwhack people."

Willy started to laugh. "Why should I give you a fair chance? Now put your hands behind your back." As he put handcuffs on him, he added, "You've become a nuisance that we can no longer tolerate."

A shadow came over them and instinctively they all looked up and saw Claraicy using her wings to block out the sun. Resting on two small branches near the top a tree, she relaxed her wings. The three men initially froze. Ryan tried to escape, but Willy jumped on top of him and hauled him to his feet. Seeing Willy's pistol pressed into Ryan's back, Claraicy screeched out, "Don't touch him."

"So the rat has a girlfriend. I find it hard to believe that even someone as ugly as you could fall for the likes of him. Don't you have any standards at all?" Willy waved his pistol in Claraicy direction and added, "How about you just fly away like a good little demon."

Claraicy started to laugh. "Fire, and you and your friend will become meat for my table."

After pushing Ryan in front of him, Willy pressed his gun against the back of his head and told her, "Fly away or he dies."

Suddenly, blood splattered out of Ryan's side and he dropped to the ground. Willy immediately backed away and pointed his pistol at Claraicy. "It wasn't me. I didn't shoot him."

She had heard the impact of the bullet that hit Ryan but not the gun being fired. She quickly looked around. On a distant rocky ridge she spotted a tiny flash as another bullet was silently fired.

Chapter Twenty-Eight

Revenge

The erratic breeze that was swaying the tree back and forth along with the shock of spotting another bullet being fired caused Claraicy to lose her footing. As her body turned and fell, the bullet narrowly whizzed by her shoulder. The pellet holes in her wing from the shotgun caused her to twist in the air and land on her side.

Getting to her feet, she looked around. Willy and Patrick had run into the swamp that bordered one side of the clearing. Their bobbing heads and torsos were barely visible above the vegetation as they struggled through the soupy muck. She went over to Ryan and dropped to her knees. She held him in her arms and she cried out in pain. "What has he done to deserve this?"

Poking her head above the tall grass and brush, she gazed towards the ridge where the shot came from. Another dim flash of light made her jerk away from Ryan's still body.

This time, the bullet went through part of her wing. Getting to her feet, she threw her fists into the air. Her fiery eyes glared at the ridge where the bullet came from.

Engulfed in rage, she bolted through the meadow towards the sniper's position. Her long feet and muscular legs acted like giant springs. Each stride she took vaulted her into the air and over the fallen trees, rocks and small bushes. She bounced from place to place, not giving the sniper an easy target.

It was over two kilometres to the edge of the ridge. It took Claraicy only a few minutes to get there. By the time she climbed up the side of it, all that was left was the scent of a man and the lingering fumes of gunpowder.

She followed the man's scent all the way to a small lake. It was connected to several other lakes. Without the normal use of her wings, she felt both handicapped and lost. By the time she got back to where Ryan was, his body was gone. There were boot prints all over the area. Raising her head, an angry deafening roar echoed throughout the forest.

Claraicy leaped high in the air and jumped around the meadow shaking her fists in rage. Suddenly she heard a volley of rifle fire. There was a large florescent orange dart in her leg. Another hit her neck, and a third hit her arm. Confused, she ran towards the trees as fast as she could. More bursts of rifle fire bellowed behind her. Several darts had impaled her wings as they flopped from side to side with every stride she took.

Despite feeling drunk, she kept running. She stumbled her way through the trees and over the stone outcrops that dotted the landscape. It got harder and harder to keep moving but she knew that she somehow had to escape. As she ran along a long rocky cliff she glanced back to see if anyone was in sight before springing into the air and landing on a branch of a tall tree.

Through the bare entwined branches that stretched over a small gorge, she saw a dense grove of pine trees. She climbed, crawled and clawed her way through them towards the grove. Her head was spinning as she leaped through the air and grabbed a hold of a branch of one of the pine trees. She could barely see as she fumbled her way behind its protective canopy.

Once safely hidden high within the lush sticky branches, she sat at the base of a branch and wrapped her legs and arms around the tree trunk. The sap oozing from the bark of the pine tree acted like a sticky glue and helped hold her in place as her body finally succumbed to the drugs.

******

One by one the soldiers made their way back to base camp. Ratlin rolled Ryan off of his shoulder and onto a cot. Doctor Stern ran over to examine him. His white skin and open eyes and mouth said it all. "He's dead?"

Ratlin shrugged his shoulders and looked at Ryan's face. "Claraicy wouldn't leave him. By the time we separated them, too much time had passed. The stuff in the needle that you gave me didn't work on him. All we could do was patch him up and haul him in."

The doctor looked over at Duncan. "And Claraicy?"

Duncan reluctantly answered, "It looked like her father had peppered her with buck shot. I saw the sun shining through a bunch of holes in one of her wings."

Shaking his head, he added, "She's tough, she ran off with at least three darts in her. We trailed her for over ten kilometres before we finally lost her."

DeGroot approached Duncan and informed him, "The choppers will be here in fifteen minutes with some reinforcements."

Turning to the doctor, Duncan said, "They have finally given us the manpower to launch a capture operation. We'll find her, even if we have to search every rock and tree in the region."

Ratlin looked out the window. "The sooner she's caught the better. I saw her chew the fingers and toes off a man and sodomized him with his own shotgun. You don't want a creature like that running around loose." He turned to Duncan. "Even after the man's flesh was burnt off his bones, she actually sang while she was grounding his charred remains into dust. What kind of monster does that?"

Duncan was slow to respond. "Something inside of her brain isn't normal. I don't think it has anything to do with the modified cells. She doesn't think or react like a normal person. That will make her even harder to capture."

Ratlin's stomach couldn't handle any food. All he could do was watch as the rest ate as much as they could before the helicopters arrived. Each helicopter had a net dangling from it carrying in a wide assortment of supplies. After detaching the nets, Ratlin and MacNeil climbed up a rope ladder and got aboard one helicopter while Duncan got into the second.

Drake waved to them from the canoe as he set out to check up on Steve. They needed him to be hiding close by. They don't want him to be scared enough to bolt away. Without him running loose in the park, the cops and local officials could be pressured into reopening it to the general public.

DeGroot stayed behind to tend to the camp. He also had to properly pack Ryan's body before it is shipped to Doctor Scott.

The helicopters had barely left before DeGroot spotted Marq's plane. With Doctor Stern and Ann's help, he emptied a large refrigerated crate of groceries and lab supplies. They then folded the body bag containing Ryan's naked corpse into it. Ann and the doctor lifted one end of the crate and DeGroot the other. Together they managed to carry it to their makeshift dock as the plane taxied towards shore.

Not wanting to risk damage to his plane, Marq carefully maneuvered its hoist to lift the crate off the lashed together logs that formed the dock. "Do I want to know what is in it?"

"Nope." As the crate was set down inside the plane, DeGroot hitched up its motor's air and exhaust hoses. "All you need to know about it is that it has a short life expectancy. Make sure the refrigeration unit stays running. I installed fresh propane tanks. Remember that every second counts."

As soon as Marq's plane left the water, DeGroot started to prepare the camp for an attack. They were aware that Claraicy had known where the camp was for a long time. Not knowing her physical condition or how she would react to the shooting, he concentrated on making the camp extremely difficult for her to penetrate.

******

Doctor Scott used a small, highly sensitive metal detector to scan Ryan's naked body. He picked up a marker and placed a small circle near the bottom of Ryan's spine. Jane helped him flip the once strong, muscular body over onto its back. Wearing magnifying goggles, Dr. Scott sliced open Ryan's abdomen and started pulling out his intestines.

Jane had to look away. The young, handsome man lying dead in the table was about her age. In the hospital, she had seen a lot of dead people and had even assisted in a few autopsies, but they had been either sick or in a severe accident. For some strange reason, Ryan's healthy looking corpse made her feel vulnerable.

As she turned back, the doctor said, "Jane, go to the autoclave and get a glass canister full of the sterilized medium."

The doctor smiled as he cut and peeled the tissue away from the small cluster of cells that were pressed against Ryan's spine. "There may not be many of them, but I believe I've located a few survivors." Jane's face had lost most of its colour. As she watched the doctor coldly mutilate Ryan's body, she wondered if her own lifeless body would ever be laying on his table and treated in the same fashion.

"Got them!" The doctor quickly placed a small cluster of cells into the liquid media. He then held it up to take a good long look at them. "The injection they gave him may not have saved him, but it gave my cells a fighting chance. Look at them. Aren't they absolutely beautiful?"

Looking closer at them, his jaw dropped. "I would never have guessed it was even possible. Jane, come here. You won't believe what the cells have done."

Jane walked over to the doctor and took the canister. Red strains led away from the tight group of shimmering cells. At first the cluster looked like a colourful jellyfish. She looked closer at it. Under the bright lights of the operating table, the cluster's unique formation caused her face to turn pale. The cells had formed an embryo. "The cells were acting like a true parasite. They not only found a way to feed off his body, they found a way to multiply."

The doctor's eyes twinkled as he tried to hold back his joy. "I would never have believed it if I hadn't seen it with my own eyes. Do you have any idea what this discovery could lead to?"

Jane turned to him and abruptly said, "And do you know what dangers it could unearth?"

******

Ann watched as DeGroot unravelled rolls of razor wire and attached them to a series of metal posts pounded into the ground around the perimeter. He stacked one roll on top of the next. As the sunlight hit the sharp edges, they looked like huge strands of Christmas garland. She was amazed by DeGroot's ingenuity as he devised some unconventional ways to get the job safely done.

Several time she offered to help but was refused. "You would just make it harder. My mind is programmed to do things in a certain fashion. If you don't fully understand the technics involved, you could get seriously hurt."

Jobs that normally took three men to do, DeGroot rigged up ingenious ways to get them done all by himself. Ann watched him work and tried to help when she could. Most of the time it was only pass this and hold that, but it made her feel like she wasn't just a useless bystander. It took DeGroot time to finally except her assistance. Together they quickly erected a tall wall of razor wire around the camp. It had only one gateway that opened from the inside.

DeGroot could only smile as he looked down from his makeshift ladder. Ann was saturated in sweat. She was not use to doing hard manual labour under the hot sun. She had the tails of her top tied around her waist and her hair in a pony tail. The sweat made her clothes stick to her skin. With the top buttons on her blouse undone she looked like a pin up girl from a magazine.

Night came and the helicopters dropped the three weary men off outside of the compound. The doctor never had to ask. Their tired, joyless heads said it all. Duncan came up to the doctor and said, "I saw her with the infrared. She was so deep under everything that I couldn't get a good shot. We ended up losing her in the swamp next to where we got the park ranger. Tomorrow is another day. Don't worry, we'll get her."

As Duncan turned away, the doctor commented, "You know, you may end up needing to use live ammunition."

Duncan looked at the doctor and studied his smug face. "No way, look what happened to the ranger. I can't risk killing her. We need her alive."

With one side of his mouth twisted upwards, the doctor told him, "You tried to shoot her before with real ammo, what has changed?"

Duncan snapped back, "Trying to carefully maim a still target with a sniper rifle isn't the same as shooting at someone with an automatic from a moving helicopter."

Shaking his head, the doctor stubbornly replied, "But, her body heals really fast and you know how hard it would be to kill her. You know what those cells are capable of. Knocking her out of commission could be your only way of capturing her."

"We can't risk losing her. At least not yet."

******

The next morning, after the rest left, Ann kept busy by hauling away the branches from the trees that DeGroot stripped. He left the trunks of the trees still standing. Using them as posts, they began draping huge, overlapping sheets of nylon netting laced with fine copper wire over the camp. Doctor Stern just sat back and watched.

Along with an assortment of winches, blocks, tackle and rope, DeGroot relied on Ann's determined assistance. With her cranking the winches and hauling the rope through the tackle, he guided the netting into place using several long poles as fulcrums. The edges of the mesh were simply tossed over the top of the razor wire and snared in place by its teeth.

Besides the gateway, the only opening into the camp was an open two metre high by three metre wide tunnel of razor wire that led into the water for about five metres. With the wire preventing her from climbing in, her only other option would be to swim in. When DeGroot and Duncan discussed the fortification, they felt that it could act as a trap. If she tried to swim in, her waterlogged wings would slow her down enough that a single sentry would be able to put enough tranquillizer darts into her to stop and subdue her.

Once the perimeter was completed, both Ann and the doctor helped him move all the tents closer to the middle of the compound. As the doctor helped tear down and set the equipment back up, Ann did some of the grunt work. The last thing to be done was to setup three machine guns nests, one by the water and the other two at the far corners of the camp. Even with Ann's help, the entire process took them over four exhausting days. All that was left was the tedious job of trimming, separating and joining the wires in the netting to electrify them.

******

It had been a couple hours since Claraicy last heard the constant beating from the helicopters' propellers that had been combing the park. The only sound that she could hear was the sweet chatter of birds as she poked her head out of the old bear den. She was a bit surprised that nobody searched inside it but she was glad they didn't. Ryan's scent was still in the air and that made her feel both sad and furious at the same time.

Walking outside, she spread out her wings and looked at the new growth that had filled in the holes from the shotgun pellets. With Jesse's arms wrapped around her neck and claws digging into her tough hide, Claraicy flapped her wings twice. That was enough to lift both of them off the ground. Despite Jesse weighing two-thirds her weight, Claraicy's large wings had no problem carrying both of them over the treetops.

The soldiers weren't her only quarry. She had another. If Willy hadn't arrested Ryan and made him into an easy target, he might still be alive. The words that she had overheard him saying still bothered her. 'You've become a nuisance that we can no long tolerate.'

She knew that Willy was about to coldly execute Ryan for doing his job. Thinking about the pair made her insides boil. As they glided over a small lake, Claraicy looked at Jessie and declared, "They must think that I'm some kind of freak that they can just shoo away. Maybe the old Claraicy, but not anymore."

******

Willy and Patrick's trail was almost a week old by the time Claraicy finally found it. They had a good head start, but drudging through swamps while dodging army helicopters slowed them down considerably. Knowing that they had probably stashed their vehicles along the nearest roadway beside a waterway made it easy for Claraicy to track them down. Swamps that took them hours to cross, took her only a couple minutes to fly over.

Every time she flew above the trees, she saw helicopters in the far distance crisscrossing the forest. As she hid in a tall, dense evergreen she smelt a familiar scent. Despite the hole in Patrick's ostomy bag being sealed with duct tape, the breeze had carried its putrid scent for several kilometres. In six days, the pair had barely managed to travel forty kilometres. It was about three in the morning when Claraicy spotted a few stubborn embers from their campfire.

Inside their tent, the two exhausted men were snoring like chainsaws. Seeing the cut branches draped over the tent for camouflage, Claraicy grinned. While the pair soundly slept, she quietly collected big bushy wads of dry wood and gingerly placed them along the sides and back of the tent. Uncertain of what was going on, Jesse climbed a nearby tree and watched her mother rekindle the fire. Her long limbs and sharp claws made her ascent easy.

Collecting and airlifting additional wood to stack around the tent had eaten up a little over an hour. The sun was far from rising and the tired men's snores had never wavered. The pile of mostly loose kindling and dead pine branches was higher than the tent. She placed the last armful of kindling she collected, next to the small fire, to connect it to the pile.

Fanning her wings softly, she guided the flames towards the dry kindling surrounding the tent. As she stood back and watched, above the loud crackling fire she could hear the men starting to cough.

Within a matter of seconds, the nylon tent melted away along with the outer edges of the men's sleeping bags. The men got to their feet and poked their heads above the fire. Pulling their sleeping bags over their heads, they flopped over the stack of burning wood and rolled away from it. On hands and knees they crawled out of what was left of their bags, and started to hack the smoke out of their lungs.

Claraicy walked over and lifted Willy's head by his still sizzling hair. With a quick jab to his chest she smashed through his rib cage and pulled out his heart. "You don't need this." Looking at the bloody, beating organ, she added, "I'm surprised. I was under the impression that you never had one."

Willy's eyes stared at his slowly beating heart. Looking up at Claraicy's smiling face, the last thing he heard was, "It still beats, but like you, it doesn't feel anything." As she squeezed his heart and tossed it to the ground, his lifeless body collapsed.

Spotting Patrick trying to run away, she pointed at him and declared, "You're next." With one giant leap into the air she managed to land face to face in front of him. "You are one stinking piece of shit. I'm not sure that I even want to touch you, you turd."

"Then don't. Let me go. You'll never see me again."

"Liar." With one wide swing of her arm, her sharp claws ripped his head off his shoulders.

As Claraicy stood over the bodies, Jesse climbed down from the tree. "You can have them. They are just soulless animals disguised as humans."

Jesse put her head into the hole in Willy's chest and pulled out a large hunk of Willy's lung. She briefly stopped chewing and looked at Claraicy. She needed to be sure that it was alright to eat her kill.

Claraicy grinned. "That should hold you for a couple days." Content on her mother's acceptance, Jesse ripped Patrick open and worked herself into a wild, eating frenzy.

******

Daybreak saw three helicopters arrive at the barb wired fortress. Duncan, Ratlin and MacNeil each climbed aboard them in order to broaden the search for Claraicy. DeGroot turned and saw Ann staring at the helicopters as they left. Her slight shiver wasn't from the cold. "As long as they are the ones doing the hunting, Claraicy is no threat to us."

With her arms tightly squeezing her chest, Ann blurted out, "Even Duncan said that her actions are irrational. No one can guess what she'll do next. If she comes after me, I'm totally defenceless."

DeGroot walked over to the doctor's tent and returned carrying Ryan's P1. Handing it to Ann, he told her, "Practice with this one first. I'll make sure that Duncan gets you a real one when you can prove to him that you can handle it."

After studying the pistol, she told him, "Even if she thinks it's real, it won't stop her."

DeGroot had been on sentry duty all night. As Ann plunked away with the pellet gun, he took the opportunity to take a short nap. Expecting Claraicy to come after them, the doctor spent most of his time inside of the machine gun nest next to the water. Duncan had shown him the basics on how to operate it. Despite never expecting to actually use it, the doctor felt safer being next to it.

As they lifted off, the helicopter pilot told Duncan about an isolated fire that his equipment had detected as he flew in to pick him up. Comparing its coordinates to Willy's last sighting, Duncan suspected it was his campsite. Tapping the pilot on the shoulder, he told him to do a quick fly-by.

By the time they reached it, the fire had almost burnt itself out and a flock of hungry birds were busy pecking at the remains of two bodies. The hovering helicopter scared away most of the birds. Without their flapping wings distorting his view Duncan saw that one of the bodies had been decapitated. He ordered the pilot to get lower to the ground.

Duncan crawled into the back and tossed a rope ladder out of the side door. While climbing down the rope, he spotted two poles sticking out of the ground. Patrick's head was struck on top of one of them. A defiant crow was picking at the human heart that was impaled on top of the other.

Tears began to form in his eyes as he saw the remains of his brother's torn apart corpse. Leaping from the rope, he ran over to his brother's remains and fell to his knees. As he pushed some of his brother's body parts closer to his torso, he began to sob. "I knew that you were a stupid asshole but you didn't deserve to die like this."

Chapter Twenty-Nine

Declaration of War

While they ate their lunch, two police officers manning a road block leading into the park watched as a swarm of army helicopters flew over their heads. Even at the speed they were travelling, the officers saw machine guns sticking out of their side doorways of some of them. As the flotilla disappeared beyond the tree tops, the male officer turned to his female partner. Without swallowing the food in his mouth, he mumbled, "I wonder what kind of body count has been racked up to demand this kind of a response."

Lowering her coffee mug, she said, "I'm just glad we are out of there."

Her partner finally swallowed the morsel of sandwich he had been chewing, and said, "He's a cop killer. I hope they blow so many holes through him that they will only need a shoe box to take his remains."

Over the police radio, reports of more army helicopters flying into the park were coming in from various roadblocks around the park and officers on patrol. It didn't take long before suspicions and rumours worked their way through their ranks. With that much firepower involved, most of them smiled after hearing the news. Believing that the soldiers had the suspect cornered and given up hope of capturing him alive, their wishes of a lethal end to a cop killer may be finally granted.

At the police station, Detective Arnold sat at his desk and studied a map of the park. With a pencil and ruler he drew lines on it indicating the direction the helicopters were travelling. After seeing that almost all the lines converged over one section of the park, he stood up and looked out the window. "Duncan, I wish you would just tell me what is really going on." Shaking his head he added, "Whatever you are hiding from me has gone on far too long."

******

It had been a long sleepless night. Tired, Claraicy and Jesse stopped to take a short nap under a tree next to a shaded stream. Along the narrow gorge the creek was in, trees with intertwining branches lined the cliffs on both sides. Despite the helicopters weaving through the sky like vultures, they felt relatively safe.

Claraicy was only able to sleep for a few minutes. Going to the stream, she splashed water over her face and tried to clear her head.

While kneeling at the edge of the water to take a drink, she heard the echoing roar of a small two man helicopter as it slowly made its way down the gully. As its shadow preceded it around a bend, the water she had cupped in her hand poured through her fingers. Claraicy got up and ran to Jesse. She quickly picked her up and ran as fast as she could into the trees.

As the pilot pushed on his throttle, the co-pilot announce over the radio, "Duncan, I see her. She is in the small canyon north-east of you."

Her sudden burst of speed caught them off guard. They lost sight of her and began flying just above the tree tops to see if they could regain a visual.

As Claraicy neared the top of rocky outcrop above them, she put Jesse down, grabbed a large rock and leaped into the air. Below her, the soldiers in the helicopter were busy searching for her in the trees along the near side of the gully. Flapping her wings as fast as she could, she hovered above the slow moving helicopter and dropped the rock into its props.

Flying so close to the trees, the pilot was helpless. He had no room to manoeuvre as the rear of the helicopter spun into a grove of tall pine trees. As the mangled craft rolled down the side of the gully, Claraicy landed on a rocky outcrop above the carnage and yelled out, "Leave us alone!"

Without a distress signal being issued, the crews of two larger nearby helicopters were surprised to see the massive fire ball from the crash. The sun radiating behind Claraicy confused the helicopters' infrared detectors as they flew past her to investigate the crash. Looking around she spotted a boulder a bit bigger than the last one. As she lifted it into the air as high as she could, she told herself, "It worked once, why not a second time?"

The pilot of the rear helicopter abruptly slowed down. "We have an unidentified flying object on our screen. I have no visual. How do you want us to proceed?"

Over the radio came back, "We have no other craft near that sector. Treat object as hostile. Bring her down, but remember that we do not want a kill."

The pilot of the lead helicopter replied, "Message received. Injure only. Shoot off every limb but her head and try to leave her torso intact."

The rear helicopter rose slightly into the air and its crew began adjusting its equipment, while the lead helicopter sped out of sight. Claraicy beat her wings as hard as she could and tried to manoeuver herself above the stationary helicopter.

She noticed the other helicopter reappeared from the direction of the sun. The helicopter below her twisted and a sudden burst of bullets blazed from the machine gun mount by it side door. Claraicy dropped the boulder. The sudden weight loss bounced her above the craft. Caught in the turbulent airflow created by the craft, she folded her wings into a dive and narrowly missed its propellers.

As the pilot twisted the helicopter to keep her in sight, she managed to swoop under it and latch onto its belly. The two soldiers in the back heard her claws dig into the outer skin. The helicopter's bulletproof belly prevented them from shooting at her through the floor.

Digging her claws into the craft's outer skin, Claraicy worked her way towards its rear and ripped open one of the engine's inspection doors. Reaching inside, she pulled, sliced and yanked on everything she could grab until the engine finally started to sputter. With her arm covered in fuel and hydraulic oil, Claraicy released her grip and used the downdraft from the propellers to catapult her into a controlled dive. As the helicopter sunk into the ravine, the seasoned pilot had managed to level the craft and began guided it towards a small rocky clearing next to the stream.

Fifteen metres above it, an arc from a stripped wire ignited the fuel spewing out of a ruptured fuel line. With the entire engine compartment on fire, the two soldiers in the back along with the pilot and co-pilot prepared themselves for a crash landing. A small explosion in the engine compartment sent the large craft into a tailspin. Its nose bounced off the side of the ravine and flipped it upside down onto the rocks.

Spreading her wings like a parachute, Claraicy floated down and disappeared beneath the forest's thick canopy. As she got to her feet, she saw the last helicopter rushing toward her. With bullets whipping through the branches, she picked up Jesse and ran as fast as she could. Targeting the heat radiating from them, the bullets from its machine guns cut through branches, thick limbs and any small trees in its path. Claraicy knew that she couldn't out run them forever.

Every time the bullets got close, she would use her powerful legs to bounce to the side and change direction. With Jesse clinging to her neck, she turned left, right, right, left, right, left, left, trying to confuse the gunner. Unable to outguess her, the gunner rocked the machine gun from side to side and sprayed the entire forest.

She felt burning sensations as a couple bullets nicked the side of her right arm and leg. Jesse's sharp claws worked their way through Claraicy's thick outer hide and cut into her flesh. Running to the edge of a cliff she jumped and went into a free fall to gain speed. Just as she was about to hit the water, she cocked her wings and zoomed down the creek bed. As she approached a long tunnel created by the entwined trees on both sides of the fast flowing water, she folded her wings and began running though it.

The speed of her escape stunned the pilot. All he could do was weave back and forth along the creek and hope to pick up her heat signal. The pilot shook his head and reluctantly reported, "She got away. Last sighting had her heading north down the creek bed. There is wildlife all over the place. No sure target."

Duncan rubbed the back on his neck and told him, "Keep searching. I'll send out some more helicopters to assist you."

Sitting on a branch above a small herd of woodland caribou, Jesse watched the helicopter slowly make its second pass over the creek bed. Far in the distance, she saw additional helicopters approaching from every direction. As the helicopter continued along the ravine, Claraicy wiggled out from between two large boulders. Glancing at the blood dripping from her arm, she gave out a roar.

As the startled herd bolted away, she leaped into the air and sunk her claws into the back of one of them. The creature twisted and kicked as hard as it could as Claraicy lifted it into the air.

She barely got airborne before a buzzer on the radar started to blare. The pilot turned the craft around. With only a dozen metres separating them, Claraicy saw the horror in the pilot's face as she used her powerful legs to catapult the poor creature upwards towards the helicopter's propellers. The strong downdraft they created deflected the hind quarters of the flailing beast into the windshield.

The caribou's head was tossed over the nose of the helicopter and was impaled by the equipment sticking out of it. Inside the cockpit the instrument panel started to sizzle as the blood from the caribou seeped into the cracks.

The pilot fought to see where he was heading. With his co-pilot spraying fire retardant foam over the panel, the pilot aimed the helicopter upward and climbed out of the ravine. He rocked the craft back and forth and then twisted it forward. He finally dislodged the dead caribou. Flying purely on instinct and under the protection and guidance of three helicopters, the pilot carefully landed safely on the ground.

"What were you thinking of?" was yelled into the pilot's ear as he took off his helmet. Duncan stood solidly in front of him. "You just made this into a war. Have you any idea what that creature is or what she means to the Canadian military?"

The confused pilot took a step back as he answered, "No, sir. All I know is what was told to us in the briefing. She is a dangerous, secret military weapon on the loose."

Duncan shook his head. "No, she's your replacement. Have you ever tried to shoot down a bat with a BB gun?"

"Yes, sir."

"Could you?"

"No, sir."

"Exactly, and neither will the enemy. She is just learning how to fly. Imagine what she could do when she discovers what she is truly capable of."

The white faced pilot turned and looked at his damaged helicopter. "That is scary, sir."

Duncan lowered his voice and shook his head. "You just gave her the experience she needed to fine-tune her skills. Now that she has tasted her first blood, she is going to be even harder to capture." Duncan looked down at the pilot's name tag, 'Lt. D. Grant', and asked, "What does the 'D' stand for?"

Looking square at Duncan's face, he replied, "Daniel."

Duncan took a few seconds to calm down. "Well Dan, at least you survived and that makes you one hell of a pilot."

******

Jane's face had turned pale as she handed Doctor Scott a clipboard. "I have finished the tests you asked for on Claraicy's blood."

"Thanks, Jane." The doctor smiled as he looked at the results. "I knew it. It had to be. It was the only way it could have happened. She was pregnant when she got contaminated. How else could her body willingly accept foreign DNA? As long the modified cells remain inside of her, her body will keep on producing hormones. Her body thinks that she is still pregnant. By now, her confused, overstimulated brain considers her entire body an extended uterus."

Jane stood beside the doctor and mumbled, "What about the child?"

Chapter Thirty

Defiance

Steve looked up from behind some bushes and saw several helicopters circling a small section of forest. He had spent his first month in the park avoiding them. Since then, he had hardly seen any come anywhere near where he was hiding. He took out a pair of binoculars he had stolen from the police. His suspicions were right. They were no longer police, but military.

A sudden chill made the hairs on the back of his neck stand straight out. "Man, I'm such a fool. They know exactly where I am. They have been deliberately avoiding me." While watching the helicopters twist and turn around the contours of the terrain, he shook his head. Not worried about being heard, he yelled out, "I was planted here as a decoy. They are manipulating me like a marionette. Those helicopters are not even searching for me. They are looking for something else."

The army had given him enough rope to make him think he was safe. Like well trained sheep dogs they herded him around the forest. They had nipped at his heels until he was exactly where they wanted him to be. After taking time to collect his thoughts, he spoke out loud, "It is obvious that the police are gone. I wonder why they are still allowing me to roam free. They are spending a lot of resources. Something really big must be going on out here."

Steve knew that when play time was over, he would become a liability. This time he would not have anyone to protect him. He also knew that they had no aspirations of sending him back to the prison they had taken him from.

After he was convinced the helicopters weren't creeping any closer, he crawled back to a dense grove of cedars. The exterior of his shelter was made from woven branches stuffed with grass, mud and twigs. Its main framework was constructed from trimmed bent limbs covered in bark. Steve needed it to be small enough that his own body heat could keep it warm. The walls were about twenty centimetres thick and well insulated to help prevent heat detectors from finding him.

After stripping off his clothes, he very carefully ran his fingers over every muscle of his body. He repeated the process over and over again until he finally felt a tiny bump.

From the supplies Steve had stolen from the police, he pulled out several mirrors, a sewing kit, a first aid kit and a fishing knife. He opened up the first aid kit and placed it neatly in front of him. After threading the needle he wedged several small mirrors between two twigs in the wall behind him. After folding his leather belt, he placed it into his mouth.

Lying on his back with his left leg folded above him, he couldn't see the tiny scar. With his fingers, he double checked its location on the back of his left thigh. Beneath it he detected something hard. After disinfecting the blade with alcohol, he bit down on his belt and used the sharp point of the fishing knife to slice a small incision into his thigh. The mirrors were almost useless and he proceeded mainly by feel. He used two fingers from his left hand to guide the blade of the knife as he pushed it slowly further into his thigh with his right hand. After hitting something solid, he wiggled the knife from side to side. He could feel the tip of the knife moving it.

He sliced the hole a little wider. By wiggling the transmitter back and forth with the tip of the knife it began to dislodge itself and begin to move more freely. Tears began to run down his face.

With the knife sticking out of his thigh, he selected a long pair of forceps from the first aid kit and disinfected the end of it with an alcohol pad. He bit down on his belt even harder. The tip of the knife was resting on the side of the transmitter. Using it as a guide, he slid the forceps along the blade. With the forceps resting on something solid, he opened up the jaws. He could feel them sliding over the edges of the transmitter. With the forceps locked in place, pulling it out was the easiest part. After dosing the wound with tincture of iodine he proceeded to stitch up the incision. It took several more minutes before the pain had subsided enough that he could remove his belt from his mouth. Even longer before he could breath properly.

Steve stared at the transmitter, wondering what to do with it. If he destroyed it, they would know that he found it and come after him. If he threw it away, it would stand still and they would know something was wrong. No matter what, he had to leave his shelter. They knew where it was. He also needed time to assess his situation and consider his options.

Before dawn he had set several rabbit snares along a well used trail with piles of rabbit droppings deposited all along it. It was midafternoon when Steve heard a rabbit snapping branches and hopping around in terror. A knot in the line prevented the snare wire from strangling the beast.

Steve quickly ran to the poor animal and grabbed it. After getting the rabbit out of the snare, he held it between his legs. He cut a small incision into the loose skin around its neck. While holding the terrified rabbit with his left hand, he took the transmitter from his pocket and carefully squeezed it under the beast's skin. When he was sure that it could not work its way back out, he released the frightened creature.

Steve gave out a sigh of relief as he watched the rabbit bounce through the dense brush and disappear. Looking around he couldn't see any movement whatsoever. After he ate and packed up his meagre belongings, he strapped on his backpack and ran through the woods as fast as he could go. Occasionally, he ducked into a hiding spot and listened for any sounds of pursuit. He heard nothing. After four such stops and still nothing, he slowed down to conserve his energy.

******

In the command trailer, the radio operator turned to Duncan. "Sir, the police have inquired about a missing officer that they believe may have entered the park without their permission. They want to send in their own search party to look for him."

Duncan stood behind the radio operator. "Is he still on the line?"

"Yes, I put him on hold."

"Good, patch me through to him."

While standing up to let Duncan use his chair, the soldier pushed a button on the side of the phone and then passed the receiver to him. "Sir, he is now on the line."

Duncan sat down and leaned back. "Colonel Stuart speaking."

"This is Detective Arnold. Colonel Stuart, one of my men is missing, a Corporal William Stuart. I did my homework. I know that he is your brother."

Duncan hesitated before answering. "There is no need to send anyone into the park to look for him. We found his body along with a Patrick Leer's. They were both badly mutilated. With them was a backpack full of skilfully preserved bear parts. I can only assume that they have been poached."

"I'm sorry for your loss. He was probably trying to bring Patrick Leer in when the maniac that has been eluding you caught up with them. This is getting way out of hand and you are too personally involved. I think we should be taking over the investigation from here."

Duncan sat up straight and defiantly told him, "Sorry, no one is entering this park!"

The stubborn detective quickly replied, "Well, I certainly am!"

After a deep breath, Duncan lowered his voice. "I'll tell you what. I'll personally pick you up and show you what we found. Then we can discuss it. Where is the closest heliport that we can pick you up?"

A small crowd formed around the heliport next to the police station. The detective wasn't expecting to be picked up in an assault helicopter. On the way into the park, Duncan had Daniel fly over the disabled helicopter and the two downed ones. "This is what we are up against. So far two highly trained soldiers have been killed and four more are in the hospital. Do you really want your inept pencil pushers to come in here and multiply the death count? Didn't you learned anything back at the Devil's Claw?"

"That was different. This time we are dealing with a cop killer." The detective thought about the creatures back at Devil's Claw Ridge. "Our officers are a lot better trained than some of your guards back at the ridge."

Looking straight into Duncan's eyes, he added, "After Doctor Scott's medical facility was burnt, I saw some aerial photos of a few downed aircraft before their wreckage mysteriously disappeared. This is getting old and I know that you and the doctor are hiding something from me. Regardless what others believe, I know that a single man couldn't do this much damage."

Shaking his head, Duncan calmly told him, "You have no idea what you are up against. Those helicopters were armed with fifty caliber machine guns. What do your helicopters have?"

As they got closer to the campsite, the detective paid close attention to the surrounding terrain. The wind had blown the charred remains of the men's sleeping bags against the bushes. Beside the large blotches of dark red sand were a couple of huge adjacent blood stained rocks. Written on the rocks in bold letters were the words, 'Leave me alone'.

After circling the area a few times, Daniel decided it was safe to lower the helicopter. As it neared the ground, Duncan leaped out of the side door.

Not wanting to be rushed, the detective tried to take his time. He barely got one foot out of the helicopter before it started to take off again. Tumbling to the ground, he looked at Duncan and yelled above the helicopter's loud engine. "All my gear is still aboard the chopper."

Duncan screamed back, "You fool, he has to get back into the air A.S.A.P. If he is caught on the ground he could be a ripe target. Besides, you won't need any of your gear."

The detective looked at Duncan and then at the fleeing helicopter. "What's going on here?"

Duncan walked up to him and said, "It is not a man we are after, it is a highly advanced instrument of war."

The detective stared at Duncan with a confused look on his face. "What are you talking about? With all your resources, you should have captured what ever it is long before now. Instead, I see your men fleeing from this cop killer."

Duncan snapped back, "We are up against an adversary that can destroy armed helicopters and mutilate people without a lick of remorse. Capturing such a foe isn't easy. It takes time."

Looking around the camp site, the detective was shocked at the amount of blood that was splattered everywhere. He found himself unlatching his holster. With one hand firmly on his pistol's grip he walked around and started to examine the scene up close.

The letters written on the rocks were done in blood. The small particles of human tissue that were embedded in it, told him how it was done. He felt a bit light headed and had to sit down. "This animal used chunks of the victims' bodies to write with."

Turning towards the rocks, he picked at a embedded tissue. "Judging from the colour and cell structure, I would say this section was smeared on by using either a kidney or piece of liver,"

Duncan looked down at him. "I was informed it was mostly from my brother's liver."

Once Detective Arnold got back in the air, he started to regain some of the starched composure that he had compromised at the site. As the helicopter approached the compound he was amazed at how heavily fortified it was. It had manned machine gun nests, barbed wire fencing, a half dozen trailers and manned lookout towers. A strange netting covered the entire area above the compound. "What is all this for? What is really going on out here?"

Duncan ignored his questions. The helicopter just tapped on the ground outside of the camp. Both Detective Arnold and Duncan quickly jumped off. As soon as their boots hit the ground the co-pilot threw their bags off and the helicopter jolted upwards into the air. DeGroot was standing next to the barbwire gate with a key to unlock it. "Welcome back, sir."

Duncan returned DeGroot's salute as he walked past him. The detective looked around and counted over two dozen armed soldiers. It wasn't until he saw Ann break the barrel of the air gun across her leg and load in another pellet that he ventured another question. Dressed in a tight fitting sweater and blue jeans, she looked out of place. "What's the girl doing here?"

Putting his arm across the back of detective's shoulders, Duncan kept him walking towards a large trailer with a red cross on the door. "She's a highly specialized lab technician. We brought her in to assist our medical staff."

Looking back at Ann, he inquired, "What's she doing with a pellet gun?"

As he opened the door of the trailer, Duncan chuckled, "Because I wouldn't issue her a real one until she proved to me that she could handle it."

Inside the trailer Duncan led the detective through the small infirmary. It had ten empty neatly made cots, all set on an angle to make it easier to get patients in and out. Above their pillows were shelves of medical supplies and various medical apparatuses.

At the far end of the infirmary Duncan opened a thick door. As a cloud of fog rolled out, he told the bewildered detective, "This is our morgue."

Looking back at the empty cots, Detective Arnold asked, "Where are the injured soldiers you were telling me about?"

Duncan put his hand on the detective's shoulder and guided him into the morgue, while answering him, "They were airlifted back to base. This is basically a triage, not a hospital, although we do have a fully functional operating room at the other end of the trailer in case of emergencies."

The detective reluctantly looked down at Willy's remains. "Where is the rest of him?"

"Eaten." Duncan pointed to some tears in Willy's flesh. "The doctor figured that after his main organs were removed, a creature or creatures ripped him apart. When we found him, a flock of birds were fighting over his remains."

Detective Arnold looked up at the massive soldier and saw his eyes water. As a tear zig-zagged down the ridges of his scared face, he asked him, "Were you close?"

Duncan look down at what was left of Willy's face. Despite his plucked out eyes and missing cheeks, all he saw was his younger brother. "Not very."

"So what are you planning to do when you catch this guy?"

Duncan turned to the detective and sharply replied, "My job. My orders are to hand over the perpetrator to the proper authorities. Alive if at all possible. Despite my feelings, I do have orders and I will follow them."

Once outside the hospital trailer, Drake pulled Duncan away from the detective. "New images are coming in from the drone that was launched this morning."

Duncan took the tablet from Drake and scanned through the photos. After closely studying one, he directed Drake to request for an Aurora surveillance aircraft to be deployed and search the area in the photo in more detail. The inquisitive detective overheard enough to inquire, "The military is throwing a lot of money into this. Any chance I could see that picture?"

Duncan smiled at him. "None."

Smiling back, Detective Arnold smugly told him, "Then I will just have to get a court order for you to release everything you have. This has gone way too far. I requested military assistance in the case, not a military takeover."

Duncan chuckled and tried hard not to laugh. "Try anything and I will have martial law declared over this entire region. As I told you, you do not know who or what we are dealing with. Do you think I would endanger my men for nothing? And by the way, if anything you have seen today makes its way to the press, I'll have you locked up. You didn't know what went on back at the ridge, and I've no intention of letting you know what is going on here."

Detective Arnold shook his head and wagged his finger at Duncan. "We'll see about that."

With the raising and twirling of Duncan's left arm, two soldiers ran behind the detective and grabbed his arms. "Take this man into custody."

Detective Arnold screamed as loud as he could. "You can't do this!"

Duncan smugly replied, "Your superior will have a memo from Ottawa laying on his desk within an hour stating that you are staying with us as an observer. You won't even be missed."

Locked inside a large aerated shipping container, the detective paced three steps back and forth. Within an hour, the door to Detective Arnold's small prison opened. Duncan stepped inside and abruptly handed him a clipboard. "Call your superior and read exactly what is written on these papers."

The detective quickly read the papers as Duncan punched a number into the phone. The detective took it and put it to his ear. "Hi, this is Detective Jack Arnold."

The reception wasn't the greatest, but through the static he heard, "I didn't expect to hear from you so soon."

With Duncan and two guards standing over him, the detective didn't know how to respond. After glancing at the papers, he told his captain, "I was handed a phone and told to check in."

"I received a memo that you are to be at the military's disposal. They have issued a gag order on everything. Can you tell me what is going on?"

Looking down the barrel of Duncan's pistol, Detective Arnold dropped the clipboard and told his Captain, "It's extremely complicated. I can tell you this, if we don't fully co-operate with them, neither one of us will see our pensions."

"What about Corporal Stuart?"

Sweat ran down the detective's nose and landed on the phone. "The dumb fool stumbled across the wrong bear. What's left of him wouldn't fill a carry-on bag."

******

Posted on the bulletin board at the police station was, 'We are all sorry to hear that Corporal William Stuart was recently killed in an animal attack while off duty. His remains will be flown to Souix Lookout later today. A tentative funeral service is being planned for this coming Thursday at six pm. Further details will be posted.'

After reading the memo, Andy stormed into the Captain's office. "You mean to tell everybody here that Willy was killed by an animal? I despised him more than anyone else here but I find that hard to believe. Has anyone done an autopsy?"

The Captain put the memo in his top drawer and stood up. "So do I, but when the time is right we will be doing a full investigation."

Andy cocked his head and asked, "What's wrong with right now?"

"Everything." The captain placed both of his hands on his desk and looked at Andy. "Because we both know that it was a two legged animal that did it."

Chapter Thirty-One

Life and death

Drake used a stick to spread apart some wolf faeces. "Duncan, I found the goat's transmitter. Somehow a wolf ate it. We may have been monitoring a decoy."

"That means he could be anywhere. We have to find him."

******

Steve stood under a hanging rock as a drone flew about a hundred metres overhead. It was the third time he saw it within a three hour span. Using a pair of binoculars, he searched through the clouds. "Where did it go?"

Flying high above the clouds was an Aurora surveillance plane with its distinctive long spike extending from its tail. Even with an altitude of several kilometres, he easily recognized its distinctive markings. "The Canuck military was getting serious. Whatever is going on is big, real big."

******

Jane's breathing became erratic after reading the results that came off printer. Looking at the glass container in the incubator next to her desk, she crossed her arms and started to rock from side to side. The small cluster of cells were easily identifiable. The tiny embryo had become a small, living being. As she put her hand onto the glass and smiled, her breathing began to relax. It had become her child.

Over the intercom, Dr. Scott interrupted her. "Are the results finished on the saliva collected from those mutilated men?"

Jane snapped out of her special bonding moment and answered. "The first series of them are off. I was just about to call you. Do you want me to send them through to you?"

"You know that I don't trust electronic systems. People are always finding new ways to intercept them. I'll be right there."

The doctor only took a minute to get to the lab. Jane handed him the printout. "The saliva wasn't Claraicy's. It was her offspring's. There was no sign of any modified cells, but that doesn't mean that the creature doesn't possess them."

"You could be right. Though, if the creature's body felt that it didn't need the cells, they may have simply died out, or went into some kind of hibernation." After studying the results, the doctor was puzzled. "What I find fascinating is that the creature's cells all contain the same DNA."

Jane checked the progress of the next series of tests before answering, "It is also very possible that the creature that Claraicy gave birth to isn't like her."

Under his breath, the doctor mumbled, "Just like the creatures in the mine." Turning to face Jane, he inquired, "Have you put the creature's DNA into the computer to figure out what it would look like when it is completely mature?"

"Those results will be ready this afternoon if we are lucky. The entire process of unravelling its DNA is quite complex. There are a lot of different programs that the data has to weave in and out of before we can even run the simulator."

At two o'clock, the computer had generated all the stages of growth up to its present appearance. It took a couple more hours for the computer to extrapolate the growth of the creature all the way to its adult form. When it was finished, Jane and the doctor were glued to the computer monitor. They watched in amazement as the creature slowly morphed through the different stages of its life.

As an infant, it resembled a baby ape with large ears and huge cat-like claws. In its adolescent period, wings had started to sprout out of his back. As an adult, its body became more feline and its mouth resembled a lion's with large thick teeth designed to tear apart and consume anything they dig in to.

Images of the winged lion-like creature that led the assault of his facility flashed through the doctor's mind. Feeling himself becoming fixated in the past, he flicked his head back and forth and broke the silence. "This creature is destined to be a pure alpha predator. At the computer's projected rate of growth, it would take less than three years for it to become fully mature. Come spring, even as an adolescent this thing could be uncontrollable. It will be worthless to us. At least its mother has some human traits that we should be able to manipulate."

In a timid voice, Jane looked at the incubator. "If Claraicy was pregnant before she was infected, the modified cells could have seen the fetus as a threat and tried to correct its DNA. Theoretical speaking, the corrected DNA could have completely taken over and redesigned every cell in the fetus."

Jane turned to the small cluster of cells in the incubator and added, "Fetuses with incompatible blood types and even those from a different species can grow inside of a womb. Medical science has proven that. The only problem is, if there is no flow of cells going to and from the fetus, how could the cells make the initial corrections?"

The doctor looked over her shoulder at the incubator. "That small cluster was capable of creating its own womb. The modified cells were designed to manipulate and grow whatever tissue they wanted. If they felt that the host needed a second heart to stay alive, they would create one."

Jane looked away from the incubator and told the doctor, "But this fetus was a separate identity, it was never a part of the host. The young creature out there was."

Putting his finger across his lips, the doctor replied, "What if the fetus was infected at the same time as Claraicy? By the speed her cells have mutated, we know that when she got infected, there were a tremendous amount of modified cells transferred into her body. It must have been an extremely violent encounter."

Jane could see the doctor's point and told him, "I guess if some modified cells got into the embryonic fluid, they could have reconfigured the fetuses DNA." Jane looked away a moment, then turned to face the doctor. "But that doesn't explain how the different DNA strains became one completely different, uniform strain."

In a revelation, the doctor slapped the side of his head and told her, "Somehow the modified cells must have created their own filtering mechanism. If I am right, the young creature has an organ somewhere in its circulatory system that monitors its DNA. That means that it may have the ability to never grow old. Without cellular degeneration, it could live forever."

******

Two soldiers dressed in full spit and polished uniforms, side arms and ear phones, removed the small plain wooden coffin containing Willy's body out of the plane while four more stood in line at the bottom of the ladder. The police captain noticed that all of the soldiers wore reflective mesh over their faces, preventing them from being identified.

Undaunted by the soldiers' bayoneted rifles, six police officers in parade dress marched towards the plane. The four soldiers on guard immediately formed a human wall in front of the ramp and pointed their bayonets at chest level. Pushed from behind, the lead officer was almost skewered by two of them.

Seeing the soldiers standing firm, Detective Arnold climbed over the side of the ramp and tried to defuse the situation. "It's okay. These guys have strict orders to protect Willy's remains until they are cremated and his ashes are secured in an urn."

A few drops of blood trickled down the left side of the large officer's shirt as he yelled out, "Without an autopsy?"

Placing his hand on the barrel of one of the soldiers' rifles, Detective Arnold announced in a calm voice, "There is no need for one. I saw what was left of his remains. The wild animals destroyed everything. There wasn't enough left for the coroner to examine. Just look at the size of the coffin. Doesn't that tell you anything?"

The disciplined, steadfast soldiers never uttered a word as the press filmed everything. The large police officer was trained to take control of rowdy people, not the other way around. After seeing no name tags on the soldiers' uniforms, the officer demanded, "Take off those masks so I can see your ugly mugs."

The officer behind him noticed the distinctive red chest and dagger on their sleeves and gave him a nudge. "Look at their badges. They are Special Forces. They can't be identified."

As the burly officer tried to force the bayonets pointed at his chest aside, the soldiers jerked them back in place, slicing the officer's jacket. With the tip of the bayonet pressed against his chest, the officer tried to study the soldier's face through the mesh. "I'll remember you. You can't hide from me."

As he tried to extend his arm towards one of the soldiers, his lapel was pierced by another soldier's bayonet. Stunned that the soldiers showed no remorse, he stepped back and saw the police captain shake his head.

As the six disgruntled officers returned to their ranks, the police captain bellowed out, "We will honour our own."

Detective Arnold went up to the captain and whispered into his ear, "Not this time. Just tell the men to stand down."

The detective rubbed the stitches behind his right ear. The small bump under his skin left him with no doubt of who is really in control. While glancing back at Duncan, he told his captain, "I'll try to fill you in as much as I can. How about we just honour Willy without turning his funeral into a media circus." In a voice loud enough to be heard by the media's delicate microphones, he added, "And tell Clyde to sober up. I don't care how many mints he chews on, I can still smell it."

The captain looked him in the face and whispered, "You know that he doesn't even drink."

The detective stiffened his neck and informed him, "If anything develops from this incident, they will turn him into the biggest lush in Northern Ontario."

"How?"

Detective Arnold smiled and patted him on his back. "You don't know who and what you are dealing with. How many strange orders have you received lately? Open your eyes. Can't you see that we are merely puppets to them?"

After listening to the captain discreetly address his men, the detective went over to the rope that cordoned off the reporters from the air field and fed them a statement. "Hello, my name is Detective Jack Arnold, and I have been given the job as spokesman for both the police department and the army. Corporal William Stuart's closest relative was a high ranking soldier that was attached to the man hunt going on in the park. As such, he has every right to decide how to best put Officer Stuart to rest. As you have witnessed, there has been some confusion about who was going to be carrying the coffin. This is a small town and some of the police officers were greatly offended. For that, we are greatly sorry and extend our deepest apologies to the deceased's family and friends."

The detective looked over the flabbergast reporters before continuing. "Corporal William Stuart, the police officer killed in the park, died while attempting to visit his only surviving family member. To the best of our knowledge he was trapped inside a tent when one or even two bears attacked him in the middle of the night. From what I saw of the campsite, he never stood a chance. The soldiers here are from the Canadian Special Operations Regiment out of Petawawa, and as such can not be personally identified. Corporal Stuart's next of kin has expressed his desire for a private funeral ceremony, and is working with the police department to arrange a separate police ceremony. If you have any more questions, I will gladly answer them after the funeral."

Out of respect, the police honour guard formed two rows leading up to the hearse. While the officers stood at attention, the two soldiers carried Willy's body through them to the back of the hearse. Clyde opened the back of the hearse and let the pallbearers in along with two other soldiers. Before closing the door, he mumbled, "I apologize for my behaviour. I was under the impression he had no family. When a person puts on a uniform, he automatically becomes a member of a large extended family. When a fellow officer dies, we have always guarded and honoured his remains. Your involvement had turned everything upside down."

"You're forgiven." Drake saw Clyde stare at the drop of blood on the tip of his bayonet. "We feel the same way. I'm sorry for your jacket. I'll see that you get a new one on me."

One of the two remaining soldiers went into the front passenger seat of the hearse. As it started to drive away, the last soldier walking behind it was picked up by the first of two military vehicles that had been parked behind the hearse. Police motorcycles merged in front and behind the strange procession and gave them a police escort. As Detective Arnold crawled into the backseat of a police cruiser, he looked at the captain. "My orders have been changed. They no longer need me out there."

The captain turned to him and asked, "Do you know what is really going on out there?"

The detective could only imagine the position the captain was placed in. "Not really."

Two soldiers stood at attention outside of the crematorium's door while another stood in the hall next to the corridor leading to it. The two soldiers inside of the crematorium oversaw and double-checked every step the lone funeral worker made. Through a glass porthole in the furnace, they watched the coffin and Willy's body slowly crumble into a pile of ashes. Afterwards, a special metal vacuum cleaner was brought in and the oven was vacuumed out. The funeral worker extracted the metal canister from the vacuum, removed the vacuum's filter and placed it on top of the ashes.

While screwing on the canister's metal top, he told the soldier next to him, "That's everything." After the canister was placed into a specially made wooden urn, the soldiers escorted it to the funeral home's waiting room. "Here you go, sir. Your brother's remains have been secured."

Duncan accepted the urn and cradled it in his arms as he sat down. "Wait outside, I would like some time alone with William."

As the soldiers left the parlour through one door, the police captain entered through another. "Who do you think you are? He was a police officer and deserves some respect."

With a mesh screen coving his face, Duncan stood up and bellowed out, "I'm his brother. I knew that stupid idiot better than anyone, so stop pretending that he was a good cop just because he is dead."

******

"Becca are you coming or not? According to the weatherman, this warm weather will only last four days before it starts to get cold."

Dressed in a snug sweater that made her breasts pop out and a pair of tight jeans, Becca flung her long blonde hair to one side, and asked. "Randy, are you sure it is safe?"

With a large grin on his face, Randy told her, "Sure, my brother Andy along with all the other cops will be attending the funeral. Nobody will be guarding the park today."

Biting the side of her bottom lip, Becca asked, "What about the killer and the bear that ate that cop?"

Grabbing the back of his head, Randy looked up at the ceiling. "Come on, if they haven't caught the killer by now, it's because he is long gone. As far as the poor bear that killed that cop, he probably died from food poisoning. Besides if they thought there was a real threat, they wouldn't allow anyone to leave their posts, not even to attend a funeral."

"Okay." Becca reached down and shoved her wallet into her backpack. "Any word from Kevin and Amanda? Are they still coming?"

Randy quietly stood in the doorway looking at Becca's cute little butt as she bent over. As she stood up, he smiled, walked over and gave her a kiss. "They'll be waiting for us on the old logging road."

Becca looked at him and twisted the side of her face in disappointment. "Shucks."

While picking up her stuffed backpack, he told her, "Don't worry. We'll have plenty of time together. While they are snuggled in their tent, it's going to be hunky old me keeping your sweet, little, sexy body warm tonight."

Becca ran her hands up and down the curves of her body, "Are you sure that you are enough for little old me? This tiny body has a huge amount of needs. Maybe I should tell Amanda to take a hike. It may take both of you to satisfy all of my needs."

Randy chuckled as Becca placed her forefinger in her mouth, "Just me babe, I'm all you'll ever need."

Chapter Thirty-Two

Food

The funeral parlour looked lopsided. Duncan and a few veiled soldiers sat on one side, and the police fill the other. As the preacher started his sermon, a soldier dressed in battle fatigues stepped into the room at stood by the door. Duncan noticed him right away. With a simple nod of recognition the soldier, stepped outside of the door and waited.

******

The smell of citronella floated over the campsite as the four, college students finished setting it up for the night. As a gentle breeze pushed some fallen leaves against the red and yellow tents, the tents almost vanished in the richly coloured forest. It wasn't until they lit a fire that the camp became truly noticeable from any real distance. The smell of roasted wieners, freshly brewed coffee and bug repellant blended together into a strange exotic aroma.

Randy began tickling Becca as she bent over to unroll their sleeping bags. Her high pitched laugh drowned out a nearby loon as it called for its mate.

Despite being several kilometres away, the strange ruckus caught Claraicy's sensitive ears and woke her from her midday slumber. Jesse was already awake. Claraicy saw the drool dipping from Jesse's mouth as the strange foreign smell drifted through the air. Claraicy took a deep whiff and could smell the bug spray. "No. Leave the humans alone. We can't fall into one of their traps. They want to kill us. Do you understand?"

Jesse nodded. In a low harsh rumbling voice, she told Claraicy, "I understand but humans tasty."

******

After the funeral, Duncan walked up to Detective Arnold. The detective's face turned pale. "What do you want?"

With nobody in earshot, he told him, "Your officers allowed four civilians to enter the park. Our drones spotted their canoes an hour ago. If anything happens to them it'll be on your shoulders."

With sweat beginning to form on his forehead, the weary detective replied, "The captain was the one that allowed the men to attend the funeral, not me."

Duncan snapped back, "It was your job to keep him in line. Just because he is your superior doesn't mean you can't tell him what to do."

After seeing the police captain on his cell phone, he added, "Your captain is probably talking to my superior right now. He'll have a fun time explaining his lax attitude and inability to be cooperative with us."

As three officers walked by, Duncan lowered his voice to a whisper. "If we can get to them in time, I'll have my men escort the hooligans out. What you do with them after that is your business."

With his teeth clenched together, the detective sharply replied, "Why can't my men do it? Those kids couldn't have gone that far into the park."

Duncan put his hand on the detective's shoulder and coldly told him, "Because if they do, I can't guarantee their safety."

As soon as Duncan got into his vehicle he phoned the camp. "Give Ratlin two squads of men and tell him to surround the intruders' camp. We can use the kids as bait. I've made the police aware of their presence and hinted that there was a possibility of potential fatalities."

Stunned, DeGroot questioned him. "So we are not going to extract them?"

"No, they knew the risks when they entered the park. By tomorrow we should know if the creatures are going to bite or not. If they are not interested in them, we might as well fly the young brats out and continue our hunt."

******

As the sun started to set, curiosity got the better of Claraicy. With the flames of their roaring fire beckoning her, she slowly crept towards the jubilant, noisy campsite. To get a better view, she climbed a large tree and found a sturdy branch to sit on. From there, she quietly watched and listened. The joyful sounds of laughter, flirting and kidding around were broadcasted throughout the area and over the lake they were camped beside. Claraicy closed her eyes and wished that she could join them.

A small movement from under a bush woke her from her fantasy. With the faint aroma of gun oil in the air, she knew that it wasn't an animal. If the soldiers knew she was sitting above them, they would have already reacted. As long as she didn't move, she was safe. Not wanting to leave, she closed her eyes and pretended the soldiers weren't there. While listening to the lively revelry, she dreamt of what her lost childhood could've been like.

Sitting on a log next to their roaring fire, both couples cuddled under the bright stars that filled the dark, almost moonless sky. The Earth had blocked out all but a tiny sliver of it. Protected under heavy blankets, each pair went quiet. Amanda's bra was the first thing to be slipped out from under their blanket. Two pairs of pants and underwear closely followed. As the log began to rock, Randy piped up. "Go to your tent will you?"

Kevin and Amanda spoke up almost at the same time. "Spoil sport." Then they began to laugh.

Becca watched the bare-backed couple dash into their tent with their blanket flapping to one side. "You know, Kevin does have a terrific ass."

Randy smiled and began to chuckle. "And I thought you were looking at Amanda's."

Becca gently slapped Randy on the side of his head and smiled. "Hey, I'm not you."

With his arms wrapped around Becca, he gently squeezed her far breast. "And she is definitely not you."

Becca shimmed onto his lap and began to moan as Randy gently massaged both of her breasts. Just above a whisper, she got out between her deep, pleasure filled breaths, "You got that right."

Turning around to face Randy, Becca wrapped one arm around his head and smothered him with her lips. Her other hand made its way down the small of his back and down into his pants. After several hard squeezes on his firm butt, her hand migrated around to the front. Randy moved his right hand under her sweater and carefully undid her bra before travelled back to her front to resume massaging her left breast. While his thumb and forefinger rolled her nipple back and forth, Becca gave out a loud moan.

"Keep it down out there," Kevin bellowed from the lively tent.

Randy yelled back, "You are just jealous that I got the golden prize."

Claraicy opened her eyes. The more Becca moaned, the more bewildered Claraicy became. *Was the young woman actually enjoying it, or was she being raped?* To Claraicy, sex was a painful, barbarous act of torture that men cruelly inflicted on women and children. Baffled, all she could do is watch.

Despite the cool night air, between soft passionate kisses, the pair slowly peeled off their clothes. First he took off his shirt, then she removed her unbuttoned sweater and unsnapped bra. The kisses got more intense as she slipped off her jeans. Randy looked down at her panties. "Are we a little shy?"

"Hey, it's cold out here. I had to wear something to keep it warm for you. Besides, I bet that you wore something to keep your little fellow from getting cold." Becca smiled and bit her bottom lip as she undid his belt. Looking down she noticed a small bulge in his pants pocket. "So what do you have here?"

"A surprise that I was saving for the right occasion." Randy reached into his pocket and unfolded several tissues. "Sorry for the way it is wrapped but the box it came in would have been too hard to conceal."

Becca's jaw dropped and her eyes bulged out as he revealed a gold ring with three sparkling diamonds. She couldn't breathe as Randy placed the ring on her finger and softly whispered to her, "Becca Bealer, will you marry me?"

At the top of her lungs, she screamed frantically. As the almost naked Becca jumped around screaming, Randy leaped up and grabbed her by her shoulders. With his arms around her head and waist, he held her tightly until she stopped.

Becca's wild outburst shook Claraicy out of her confused state. As Becca stepped back to get another look at the ring, Claraicy dropped out of the tree and smash the side of Randy's head in with one swipe of her claws. Claraicy turned to Becca. "You're free. He can't hurt you anymore."

Becca screamed even louder than before. Delirious, she shook her head and punched Claraicy in the face. "Free? You stupid, hideous monster, he finally gets the nerve to ask me to marry him, and you kill him! How does that make me free? Why don't you just kill me too?"

Breaking twigs and the crunching of fallen leaves made the woods almost come alive. Claraicy batted Becca aside, and stepped back.

With her eyes bulging, Becca rolled up her lips and revealed her bright, white upper teeth. Without showing any sign of fear, she jumped up and dashed towards Claraicy swinging both of her arms. As one of her fists hit the side of Claraicy's face, she was swept away by a dark figure as it zoomed through the camp in a blur.

Six soldiers jumped out of the surrounding brush. Claraicy heard Becca scream as she was dragged through the dark brush with her legs and arms wildly flailing away. Amidst a volley of volley of tranquilliser dart, Claraicy jumped into the air. Her huge flapping wings knocked the darts aside as she rose into the air and became part of the dark night's sky.

As beams of light criss-crossed the sky, she peered down and saw four soldiers running after Jesse and the ungrateful wench. The other two campers never got the chance to look outside of their tent before the soldiers fired two darts through the thin fabric and put them asleep. Inside their tent, their two entwined naked bodies laid motionless as the remaining soldiers swarmed the camp.

Claraicy saw Jesse running along a ridge that lead to a high rocky cliff overlooking the lake. Even with Becca flung over her shoulder, the soldiers couldn't keep up with her. She could hear the distinctive beating sound of a helicopter in the distance. Jesse stopped at the summit of the ridge and tossed the frightened girl to the ground. With water beneath her and the soldiers approaching fast, Jesse shook her head in frustration.

She grabbed Becca by her hair and began dragging her back and forth across the cliff while she tried to figure out what to do. The sharp rocks poking through its surface of the water below meant that jumping off the cliff wasn't an option.

Jesse ignored the shallow moans and tearful pleadings coming from her captive. As Becca tried to free her hair from Jesse's grip, her high pitched screams made it easy for the soldiers to pin point her location.

Seeing her daughter being surrounded, Claraicy swooped down and grabbed Jesse by the shoulders. As Claraicy tried to lift them off the ground, Becca quickly wrapped her legs around a tree root and struck Jesse hands with her fists. In desperation, Claraicy yelled out, "Let her go."

The blood covering Becca's legs made the tree root hard for her to hang onto. As it slipped through her entwined ankles she let loose another shrilling scream. Jesse glanced down at the terrified girl and rumbled, "My food."

While Claraicy began to carry them away, Jesse grabbed Becca's shoulder and lifted her high enough to bite into her exposed left breast. After ripping off a large chunk of skin along with Becca's nipple, Jesse barely chewed it before she swallowed it. Her next bite sank her huge canine teeth deep into one of Becca's silicone implants and pulled it out from her trembling body.

The bitter taste of the implant made her want to gag. Violently tossing her head back and forth, she tried to expel the disgusting stuff from her mouth. With some of the silicone still stuck between her teeth, Jesse unknowingly loosened her grip.

In desperation, Becca swung her knees upwards and kicked Jesse in the chest. The force of the blow tore Jesse's claws out of Becca's shoulder. As her hair slipped through Jesse's fingers, Becca tumbled downwards to the rocks below. The sudden weight loss jolted Claraicy and Jesse into the night air.

With her hands free, Jesse used her claws to scrape the awful tasting goo from between her teeth. After spitting out some of the small remaining particles, Jesse grabbed Claraicy's feet and tried to pry her mother's claws out of her sides.

Claraicy tried to hang on to Jesse the best she could while not wanting to pierce her sharp claws through her daughter's tough hide and hurt her. As Jesse got one of Claraicy's claws free, Claraicy reached down and tried to grab Jesse's arms. She was too late.

Jesse had squirmed herself free. As she fell towards the sloping branches of some pine trees, she yelled, "My food. All mine."

Chapter Thirty-Three

Wounds

Ratlin was the first on the scene. The young traumatised girl lay on her back shaking with her eyes wide open. Blood poured out of her chest, shoulder and the back of her head. That made the rocks surrounding her very slippery. MacNeil and two other soldiers held their flashlights on her while Ratlin examined her wounds. Becca looked at him. "Are the creatures gone?"

As Ratlin bandaged her head, he answered, "Yes, now let me patch you up. We need to get you out of here."

Becca stared at the sky. "Why, Randy's dead."

While Ratlin placing a field bandage over what was left of her left breast, Becca looked at the soldiers holding the flashlights. "He had just asked me to marry him."

MacNeil answered her. "We know."

Three large field bandages wrapped around her chest and shoulder, it was not enough to cover the wounded area. MacNeil and a couple other soldiers passed Ratlin the bandages from their personal emergency supply. After applying two more field dressings, he taped a few of the plastic wrappers that the dressing came in overtop of her chest to help prevent any infection and provide the young girl with a little dignity. The deep gashes around her waist and wrists used up the rest of his supply of bandages. The multiple cuts and scrapes down the length of her arms and legs would just have to wait.

As Ratlin tied on his last bandage, the helicopter that was hovering above the middle of the lake approached the shore. Slowly it lowered a caged cot full of supplies to the ground. With the help of four other soldiers, Ratlin removed all the medical supplies. Then they carefully placed Becca on the padded board inside the cage and immobilized her limbs using blocks of foam.

Jesse ran as fast as she could to get back to the cliff. It wasn't fast enough. Becca was being hauled into the helicopter when Jesse ran blindly onto the cliff. The soldiers saw her, turned and immediately opened fire. The mere speed of their action made the soldier in front slip in a pool of Becca's blood. He tumbled backwards and crash against two others. As the trio fought to recover their balance, they blocked everyone else's shot.

Seeing the helicopter crew fighting to get Becca aboard, Jesse bolted through the group of soldiers and almost collided into MacNeil. As she skirted around him, DeGroot could only get off a couple shots before MacNeil and two other soldiers were in the line of fire. As Jesse disappeared into the brush, the soldiers quickly formed an armed circle with everyone shining their flashlights into the trees.

They heard the word "Mine" coming from the dense, dark forest. DeGroot yelled out, "Can you spot it?"

The infrared viewer in the helicopter had no trouble seeing Jesse. "The creature is on the right side of the pine trees in front of the big rocky cliff. You'll have to take it. If I fire, the debris from my fifty cals hitting that sloping rock behind her will tear your men apart."

Three soldiers slapped magazines of live ammo into their rifles and sprayed the grove of pine tree with bullets. As they reloaded, the rest of the soldiers lined up behind them and took turns shooting apart the trees and chipping at the rocks behind Jesse. Claraicy could only watch in horror as the barrage of rifle fire showered shrapnel, rock shards and flying splinters of wood onto Jesse.

High above the action, Claraicy looked down and felt that her child was about to be killed in front of her eyes. She had to do something. After climbing as high as she could into the air, Claraicy waited a brief moment to focus before falling downwards into a blurring dive. She caught the soldiers in the rear of the action off guard. As she smashed her chest against the back of Ratlin's and another solder's helmets, the claws on her feet latched onto the shoulders of a third. As the two soldiers fell onto the kneeling men in front of them, most of the gun fire stopped.

Claraicy lifted her flailing prize into the night sky. Off to the side of the mayhem, two soldiers redirect their fire at her.

Without giving them a chance to regroup, she circled around and dropped the struggling soldier in front of the trees Jesse was hiding behind. Claraicy then disappeared behind the rocks. The thrashing limbs of the gasping soldier prevented a single shot from being fired at them.

With most of the soldiers shining their flashlights in the sky, DeGroot called the helicopter and asked, "Where did she go?"

"All I got was a streak of light on my screen. She could be anywhere."

One of Jesse's shoulders was smashed by a falling rock. Splinters from the trees had pierced almost every part of her body. Despite her injuries, she used the lull to try to crawl around the large pile of rocks that she was pinned against.

Claraicy saw some rubble being pushed to the side and snuck around a boulder to get a closer look. From under a pile of debris, she could make out Jesse's fingers clutched around a tree root. Picking up a hunk of wood, Claraicy tossed it into the forest. As the soldiers refocused their attention, she ran into the debris field and grabbed Jesse's arm. Before the helicopter could pin point her, she ducked around a tall grove of pine trees and disappeared.

Lying in a gully under a fallen tree, Claraicy picked up her injured child and scolded her. "You have to learn. Sometimes your food isn't really yours."

In a tired but defiant voice, Jesse forced out, "No, my food. My food."

******

As more soldiers arrived, MacNeil looked around and saw Ratlin lying on the ground with his neck twisted to one side. A medic had already placed a cloth over his face.

MacNeil fell to his knees and started to rifle through a small emergency pouch that he always carried on his belt. He stabbed a needle through Ratlin's pants and directly into his femoral artery. Pulling back the plunger, he saw red swirls coming into the cylinder. Knowing he had a direct hit, he slowly pushed the plunger and emptied the needle's contents directly into Ratlin's bloodstream. Turning to the medic, he yelled out, "Why was this man's face covered?"

"He was showing no signs of life. I'm sorry but he is dead."

"No, he's not. Treat this soldier as if he was still able to talk to you, and be careful with his neck. I don't want him to end up paralysed."

"Yes, sir." The medic knelt over and placed a shoulder and head splint behind Ratlin's back. As he secured it in place, he almost jumped as Ratlin blinked his eyes. "He's alive! He was dead!"

MacNeil looked at him and smiled. "I told you. Now get him back to camp on the first available helicopter. Don't send him to the base hospital with the others. This soldier requires immediate treatment. I'll call Doctor Stern and make sure he has everything ready to receive him. Got it?"

"Yes, sir."

******

Leaving a trail of blood behind her, Claraicy glanced down at Jesse as she ran through the thick brush. Her body had been impaled by a well over hundred splinters. The two largest ones stuck out of her chest and were almost a half a metre long. Claraicy became wary of them getting snagged on the branches. She knew that if she didn't stop the bleeding, her injured offspring would die.

As soon as she was safely away from the helicopters' searchlights, she took to the sky. Spotting a familiar overhanging rock that protected a large diagonal crevice, she glided in front of it and landed. She had used the shelter once during a bad storm. The armour-like skin that cover her arms, legs and chest was covered in her daughter's blood. As she laid her down, she started to cry.

With no time for self-pity, Claraicy flew away and returned with all the first aid supplies she had collected and stashed away. If she tried to remove the two large splinters from Jesse's chest, she could bleed to death. She had no idea what organs may have been pierced. In Jesse's thigh was a smaller but more frightening splinter. The way blood poured out every time it moved meant that it had pierced either a major vein or artery.

All she could do was pack gauze soaked in iodine, alcohol and antibiotic around them. For the rest, she simply pulled them out, stitched and bandaged them the best she could. Looking down at her motionless child, she felt that she needed help, but from where?

Despite the beating hum of the helicopters filling the night air, Claraicy knew of only one place to go. The soldier's encampment was about ten kilometres away. Following the creeks and gullies meant she had to travel over twenty. She ran most of the way. With her enormous strides, it took her only an hour and a half to reach the razor wire that surrounded the fortress.

******

Ann held Ratlin's head while the doctor adjusted the support rods between his head and his shoulders. After that, they encased his upper body in a large cast that went from his chest, under his armpits and all the way to the top of his head, with only his face left uncovered.

Turning to Drake, Doctor Stern commented, "Despite having three smashed vertebrae in his neck, a broken collar bone and an almost severed spinal column, you can inform Duncan that Ratlin will live. Fortunately, he still has control over his vital organs. He was lucky. A normal man would be in a morgue by now."

Ann thought she was witnessing a miracle. She had spent a few years in emergency before transferring to the lab and dealt with a lot of automotive crash victims. She had never seen anyone survive such a severe head, neck and spinal damage so calmly. As she finished sealing the cast, Ratlin couldn't keep his eyes off her face.

To her surprise, Ratlin managed to mumble out, "You're as beautiful as any angel I could imagine." The cast held his jaw tightly in place and slurred his speech as he added, "It's no wonder DeGroot likes you as much as he does."

Ann's cheeks turned almost red as she smiled at him. "When you talk to him next, tell him that I really like him too. For now, you need to rest."

As she was about to leave, Ann looked back at Ratlin from the doorway and smiled. "Try to get some sleep. I'll see you in the morning."

Next door, she shared a trailer with seven female soldiers. At the other end of the medical trailer, Ann saw Doctor Stern sitting outside his trailer with his head sunk into his hands. Two female soldiers exited the women' trailer with their rifles slung over their shoulders ready to depart on the next helicopter. Ann smiled at them but her kind gesture was ignored. To them she was an outsider, a mere civilian that they were forced to tolerate. The women were worse than the men. At least the men would smile and acknowledge her.

Under Ann's lab coat, she wore a holster containing the pellet gun that DeGroot insisted she carry at all times. He promised her that on the next supply drop there would be a real pistol with her name engraved on it. Ann released the flap on the holster and put her hand on the gun's handle. *I hope he keeps his word. I'm getting tired of feeling like a helpless princess.*

As she put her hand on the door handle, sparks started to fly above her. Claraicy had landed on her hands and knees on the electrified netting three metres over her head. Her bulging, bloodshot eyes were stuck wide open with tears of desperation. "Ann, you have to help me? My daughter needs you."

Without hesitation, Ann instinctively pulled out the pistol and fired. Everything felt like it was in slow motion. She could see the pellet splat into Claraicy's eye and watched as she covered it with her hand, trying to stop the vitreous humor from gushing out of it.

As the machine guns started to zero in on her, Claraicy vaulted into the air. As she circled around, Ann could hear her scream out, "You traitor. You lying traitor."

Chapter Thirty-Four

Vision

Ann looked up at the night sky. Fine droplets of the clear jelly from Claraicy's eyeball dropped off the netting and landed on her shoulders, hands and face along with the surgical cap that she was wearing. She looked at the droplets that had landed on the back of her hand. Still dumbfounded by what had happened, she walked over to the laboratory trailer. Reaching for the handle, she realized that she was still squeezing the trigger of the pistol. She sat down on the steps and looked at the gun in her hand. "What have I done?"

DeGroot saw her crying on the steps and went over to her. "It's okay. It was the first time that you had to shoot at someone. You'll get over it. At least you didn't kill her."

"You don't understand, I shot a mother begging me to help her daughter. I'm a nurse. I'm supposed to help people, not shoot them."

******

Claraicy returned to the crevice and found Jesse where she had left her. Her bleeding had mostly stopped, but her breathing was shallow and irregular. Claraicy went over to one of the first aid kits and retrieved a mirror.

The pellet had pierced the eyeball but was still lodged in the eye's ciliary body. Setting the mirror on a rock, she used the long nosed forceps from Patrick's first-aid kit to pull the pellet out. Looking through the injured eye, she could still make out various shades of light. Relieved that she still had some sight in it, she pulled her eyelid over her eye and taped it shut.

******

Daybreak broke and Duncan knew that everything had changed. Wounded and nursing an injured sibling, Claraicy could simply go into hiding and the hunt could go on indefinitely. Over the radio he inquired, "Did anyone up there get a good fix on where she went or even which direction she was last heading?"

The co-pilot of the Aurora replied, "North-east. She only stayed in the air long enough to clear the camp's perimeter. We used her heat signature to follow her for about five kilometres. She was travelling a lot slower and much more erratically than before. After that, she played one of her old tricks. She found and scattered a herd of deer to confuse us. That is when we lost her."

Duncan turned and faced DeGroot. "She's travelling more and more by foot through the ravines. When she runs down these creeks she must leave behind a distinct splash or rhythm."

After thinking for a moment, DeGroot stated, "If she travels at a constant speed I would imagine that the Aurora has some kind of sonar that could detect her. The way her feet hit the water and the steady rhythm of her strides could give them a good trace signature to follow."

"Work with the Aurora's crew and find a way to make it happen. If they can't find her, nobody can. Remember, we have all the data collected from the drones and helicopters still at our disposal." As soon as Duncan turned away, he stopped. Turning halfway back around he added, "Get a pistol from the armoury and give it to Ann. She has earned it."

Knowing Duncan's low opinion of Ann, DeGroot questioned him. "Why the change of heart?"

Duncan studied DeGroot's face for a few seconds before answering. "That creature is full of rage and wouldn't think twice about seeking revenge."

DeGroot looked at the women's trailer while stating, "She shouldn't have anything to worry about as long as she stays in the camp."

******

Not being able to see out of both eyes confused Claraicy's judgement as she tried to manoeuver around the small crevice. With her head throbbing, she tripped over a branch and smacked the side of her head against the wall. Landing on her hands and knees, she began striking the ground with her fists.

Even the pain and agony of being shot and drugged wasn't as disorienting as losing the sight from one of her eyes. She felt that all the control that she had gained over her life had been stripped away by that tiny pellet.

After shutting her good eye, her headache slowly went away. With both of her eyes shut she felt her way around the crevice. Needing to look after her daughter, she opened her good eye. Her headache quickly came back. With the canteen resting on Jesse's lower lip, she shut her eye and tried to get her to drink by feel and sound.

While concentrating on Jesse's image, Claraicy opened her mouth slightly and a strange clicking sound emerged out of it. To her surprise, dream-like images instantaneously flashed in her head. Her mind could see the large splinters move as Jesse breathed and even the water pouring out of the canteen.

After spending a couple hours with both of her eyes wrapped in a bandage, Claraicy discovered that she didn't need her eyes to get around her small shelter. However to survive, they needed more than just shelter. They needed food and water. Looking at Jesse, she knew that meant lots of freshly killed meat. For that, she had to see more than just outlines and obscure images.

******

As Steve looked out from behind the tarp he had slept under, he saw that the ground was covered with snow. Crawling from under the cedar tree, he took out his binoculars and painstakingly searched the sky above him for any signs of a drone or any other manmade craft. Nothing. Not even a misshapen cloud caused by something flying amongst them. All of his pursuers' attention seemed to be focussed to the distant north-east region of the park. Only the odd craft ventured his way. Even then, they were just circling around to approach their search area from a different angle.

It had been almost a week since he had removed the transponder from his leg. Spending most of his time hiding had used up most of the stolen rations. There was very little time to gather food. At the snail's pace of only five kilometres a day, his slow trek south-west to the trans-Canada highway may take him well over a month to complete. He had to speed up.

Even after drastically cutting his rations, he had run out of food. He had already lost a lot of weight and needed to stay in one place long enough to set snares, plus hunt and gather the food he needed to survive.

Hunger had already started playing tricks with both his mind and body. Fatigue, paranoia and his irrational thinking made him second-guess everything he did. Knowing that one aerial photograph could give away his location eroded the thin line between extreme paranoia and being careful.

The light snow that covered the ground made his tracks both easy to spot and hard to hide, so Steve stuck to the heavily wooded areas. It was midafternoon when he started to circle around a large rocky outcrop surrounded by thick vegetation.

The mid-day sun had melted most of the snow and made travelling easier. Along what looked like an animal path, the distinctive clean cuts from a machete caught his eye. The ends of the cuts were old and had turned brown.

Along the path, Steve saw a variety of different animal tracks, but nothing human. At the end of the kilometre-long trail stood a camo painted trailer. The heavy rings welded to the sides of its flat roof told him how it got there. Steve circled around the trailer. He saw plenty of signs of animals, but nothing indicating any human traffic anywhere near the structure. It was deserted.

With the sky clear of any air traffic above him, he cautiously approached the doorway. He opened the screen door with only a slight squeak and found the main door unlocked. Walking inside, he could tell that the trailer had been barely used. The weird design of some of the furniture made him curious. The strange clothes in the closet had also caught his attention. There were mainly jumpsuits with no backs.

The only thing in the closet that was semi-normal was a lovely long, red, backless dress with shoestring straps designed to be tied behind the woman's neck. Taking it out, he took a closer look at the provocative dress and found that even that had the back cut much lower than a normal woman's hips.

Returning to the kitchen, he found the cupboards half full of cans of soups, stews, pasta, vegetables and canned meat. He was well aware of the various tricks that could be played. After grabbing a can of Irish stew, he checked to see if it had been resealed. Feeling confident that it was not tampered with, he cut it open with his knife. It wasn't until he started to rummage through the draws for a spoon that he even thought of using a can opener.

Despite being famished, he slowly swallowed down small mouthfuls of semi-frozen stew while filling his backpack with all the food that he thought he could carry. After eating half of the can, the sharp pains in his gut made him feel like vomiting.

He knew that he had to lie down. His shrunken stomach needed time to adjust. With his head swirling in circles, he fumbled his way into the bedroom and curled under the covers. Slowly the pains in his stomach eased and the endorphins from the food along with the comfortable, semi-warm bed lulled him into a deep sleep.

The beautiful northern lights danced in the sky as Claraicy climbed on top of the ridge above the trailer. Lifting up the bandage covering her good eye, she looked around. The single set of footprints in front of the trailer gave her all the warning that she needed. Someone was inside. The pool of water beneath her had an undisturbed layer of snow and ice along its edges. There was a small ice free opening in the middle of it about a metre round, and a narrow patch next to the mouth of the creek flowing from it.

Knowing that there was no way to enter the pool without cracking the ice and making a lot of noise, Claraicy went down stream and snuck into the ice free creek. After quietly creeping along it, she carefully wiggled her way around the thin ice at the edge of the pool. As soon as the water got halfway up to her thighs, she cover her eyes, took a deep breath and quietly lowered herself under the ice. In the opening at the centre of the pool, Claraicy poked her head out of the water and took another look around. Everything was quiet. While she pulled the bandage back over her eye, she took another deep breath and swam through the water trap into the cavern.

The soldiers had left almost nothing behind except for some clothes that Claraicy had taken from her parents and Patrick. Grabbing a couple cotton T-shirts, she dried herself off. It was a lot warmer inside the cavern and there wasn't any ice at all.

Claraicy grabbed one of her father's long sleeved shirts and tied the cuffs. She sniffed at the dirt at the edge of the walls until she found some that was suitable. After filling the arms of the shirt with dirt, she tied the shoulders together. She repeated the process with the two more long sleeved shirts and then draped them around her neck. Claraicy stepped back into the water and covered up her eyes.

As soon as Claraicy sensed that she was below the hole in the ice, she used her strong legs to hurl herself upward. With her torso above the water, she spread her wings and lifted herself out of the water and into the air. The loud cracking sound from the breaking ice jolted Steve to the window. Along with the saturated dirt around her neck, the water and ice clinged to her weighed her down. Gently flapping her wings a few times above the pool just to keep airborne, she shook off most of the water and ice off her.

With the multicoloured Northern lights glowing behind Claraicy as she rose out of the pool, Steve could see how her wings extended down the entire length of her tail like a bat and left only her feet dangling below them. With only two powerful flaps of her wings, Claraicy lifted herself above the overhanging rock that protected the pool. After swinging the large, scorpion-like claw at the tip of the tail to the side, she changed directions and disappeared into the colourful evening sky.

******

Duncan heard a knock at the door. MacNeil had already rolled out of his bunk. Outside the door, an excited private blurted out, "Tell the colonel that the Aurora had picked up something."

Duncan heard the message. He was used to being woken up in the middle of the night and slept with his clothes on. All he had to do is put on his coat and boots. He rushed into the communications trailer and blurted out, "What is it? What did they find?"

The young corporal passed Duncan the message. He extended his left arm and pointed his first finger into the air. He didn't want to be interrupted as he read the message to himself. "Get them on the phone. I need to talk to them."

The corporal handed Duncan the phone. "They are already on the line."

"Why didn't you say so?"

"Sorry sir, you never gave me a chance to."

Duncan put the phone to his ear. "Is this the person in charge of the sonar?"

"You got her."

Duncan yawned and closed his eyes. "Are you sure it's our creature that you have identified?"

The female technician turned away from the screen that she was glued to. "Pretty sure. I detected a steady clicking sound. It was like a bat's but a lot stronger and unique in itself. It didn't match anything we had ever encountered. Since your creature is one of a kind, we figured that's what it was. When we circled around, our radar picked up a large creature flying over the lake in front of your camp. I'm surprised that your sentries didn't spot it."

Stunned and not completely awake, Duncan shook his head. "Did you capture any video?"

"Yes sir, we caught everything we could. We followed the creature for about fifteen kilometres before it landed. We tried to detect a pattern in its running but it was too erratic. Even our infrared cameras and heat sensors lost it after a couple kilometres."

Duncan commented, "She's smart. From what the helicopter pilots are telling me, that creature has developed its own bag of tricks to evade us. Our high tech equipment can barely cope with them."

The female technician smiled as she told Duncan, "Trust me, we love a challenge. All she is doing is making us more determined to find a way to track her down."

Thinking about how desperate Claraicy was when she confronted Ann, Duncan inquired, "Where did you first pick up the clicking sound?"

"The big rocky ridge on the other side of the lake."

Duncan covered up the receiver and swore. "Shit. How stupid could I've been? Her spawn was injured and it needs the minerals in the dirt inside the cavern." Duncan slammed his fist against the wall of the trailer. Placing the receiver against his ear, he said, "I really appreciate everything you guys are doing up there. Thank you very, very much and keep up the great work."

The technician quickly blurted out, "Don't hang up, there is one more thing I should tell you. Inside the trailer next to the ridge, we detected a heat signature. We have already sent you some still photos."

Duncan turned his head and looked at the cork-board above his computer. Pinned on an area map were some fresh pictures of Steve and Claraicy at the trailer. Along the side of the cork-board were three rows of photographs of the downed helicopters and all the people that Claraicy had killed, injured and mutilated. "Make finding a way to track that creature your top priority. When she comes out of hiding, we'll need to be ready for her. There is no way of telling what she will do next."

After thanking the Aurora's crew again, Duncan got off of the phone and sat in front of a computer. Flipping through the links from the different hidden cameras set up around the ridge, he found two that were still functioning. One was inside of the cave, and the other one was hidden under the rocky overhang above the pool.

Reviewing the digital recording he saw that Claraicy had always kept her injured eye covered up. "That pea shooter must have caused more damage than I thought."

The freezing temperature turned the grease on the gears inside of the camera into a gooey putty. With the low battery signal on, Duncan slowly repositioned the outside camera towards the trailer.

As Steve looked out the window the flickering of the Northern lights made the night sky shimmer. As the light reflected off of the pool, he saw the twinkle of something shiny beneath the overhanging rock. Taking out his night-vision binoculars, he easily spotted the camera as its cold gears caused it to shake and wobble as it was being repositioned.

Duncan grinned as he saw Steve look into the camera lens through a small window in the trailer. "Well, at least we found you."

Chapter Thirty-Five

Traitor

Steve heard the approaching helicopters as he frantically tried to escape through the forest. He knew that all their high-tech equipment would give them a huge advantage. It took only fifteen minutes for a pair of small helicopters to reach the trailer. Five minutes after that, soldiers started to rappel down ropes hanging off the sides of several large helicopters. Lowered in groups of three, they creating a large semi-circle around Steve and began to push him towards the cliff above the deep ravine like a deer.

Instead of hiding or trying to force his way through them, he tied a rope around his waist. After wrapping the rope around the trunk of a big smooth birch tree, he began to rappel down the side of the steep ravine. He went as fast as his arms could manipulate the rope, and his legs could traverse through the jutting rocks and trees. At the bottom he yanked the soft nylon rope down and left almost no trace of his descent except for a smooth indent from the rope on the back of the tree and some disturbed soil along the edge.

Over hundreds of years, the spring floods had carved long, shallow grooves along the sides of the rocky walls. After spotting one of the cut-outs, Steve stuffed his gear inside of it. As quietly as he could, he rolled a piece of driftwood in front of it.

Despite the babbling creek, he could hear every sound he made echo off of the far side. A half dozen paces upstream he found another large cut-out. Laying on his back, he wiggled his body into it as far in as it would go. He was invisible to anyone looking over either side of the ravine.

The beating of the helicopters' propellers shook the sides of ravine. Small landslides and clouds of dust followed them. Covered in gravel, Steve knew the cold rock would help shield him from most of their equipment. As the helicopters took a second pass down the ravine, Steve took a mental inventory of his equipment. Tucked behind him was his rifle. His pistol was in his right hand next to face. His left hand rested on his chest, enabling him to choose between the knives fastened to his leg and vest, or one of the four flash grenades he stole from the police camp.

Steve held his breath when he heard stones clicking together. He knew that they had to be human footsteps. The fur on an animal's paws would muffle the sound and the clicking of hooves was quite distinctive. They stopped about five metre from him.

Only two pairs of boots were visible from his limited vantage point, but it sounded like there may be more. Steve pointed his pistol at the closest pair of boots. *A crippled man can't chase after him.*

An old familiar voice spoke out, "You gave us a bit of a run, but this part of your mission is over."

Steve's trigger finger, along with the rest of him, froze. He had only served under Duncan for six weeks, but his voice was unforgettable. "I thought you were dead."

"Not as long as you are still alive. As I told you before, 'If you want somebody dead, make sure they die.' Now you are going to find out why."

It took a while for Steve to get over the shock that Duncan was still alive. After tossing his pistol out a couple metres, he began to wiggle out of the groove. "I surrender. I know you. You won't kill an unarmed man."

With only his shoulder exposed, Steve reached over and stuck his fingers into the pins of a couple of flash grenades. While pushing on the rock to get out, he ripped the grenades from his vest and tossed them in front of the soldiers. The loud bang and bright flash reeled them backwards.

Steve rolled out of the groove and grabbed his pistol. As he started to run down the bank, his lower legs buckled and he fell to his knees. With the blasts from the grenades still ringing in his ears, he never heard the shots that crippled him.

Steve looked back as Duncan tore the pistol from his hand. When he saw Duncan's scarred face, he froze. Duncan squatted on one knee so Steve could get a good look at him. "Don't you remember me?"

Duncan's face, neck and ears were scarred to the point that Steve couldn't identify him. With his hearing partially restored, he tried to talk. Seeing his mouth begin to open, Duncan interrupted him. "Did you know what they did to me?"

Duncan showed him his hands. "Piece by piece they slowly cooked my flesh, then they let the maggots eat away at it a while before they decided it was time to cook it some more. It was weeks before their camp was overrun and I was rescued."

While working his fingers along his leg towards his knife, Steve pleaded, "I didn't know."

"Bullshit! You knew what those heathens would do to us. They gave a person a choice between telling them what they want to hear and receive a merciful death, or being brutally tortured. You must have turned your coat inside out and gave them everything in order to get out both alive and intact. Between torture sessions, I was forced to watch my men being abused, humiliated and raped before they were beheaded. Unlike you, none of us talked. We didn't know that you had already told them everything. At one time, those men and women were your friends."

Drake came into Steve's view and hit the side of his face with the butt his rifle. "You monstrous traitor." Drake waved the end of his rifle under Steve's nose. Smoke was still curling out of the end of his barrel. "Let's see if you can magically walk away this time. We're not M.P.s. You got lucky when they arrested you before we caught up to you."

Duncan grabbed Steve's face. "The hospital staff needed my dental records to confirm my identify. With my body burnt from head to toe, the nurses treated me like I was a refugee from hell. It took years and a miracle of science to regenerate the nerve endings that those bastards had fried."

Steve spit in Duncan's face. "You could have just given them what they wanted. It didn't have to end the way it did."

Outraged, Duncan smacked the side of Steve's face and looked up at the sky. "So you actually think it's all my fault? My men would still be dead." Duncan faced Steve and added, "For some strange reason, you are the only prisoner that I ever heard of them releasing."

"Well I'm not responsible for everything that happened over there."

Seeing Steve pulling out his knife, MacNeil kicked his back and knocked him face first into the ground. Picking him up by his shoulders, MacNeil tossed Steve head first against the rock wall and shouted, "You back stabbing piece of shit. There are now only five Green Dragons left because of you. Don't try to point the blame on anyone else. You still had a bandage covering your fresh tattoo when you gave up our position along with several other units."

Steve bounced off the rock and landed on his back. Shattered pieces of the bones protruded through the lower part of his pants. Blood gushed out of his ripped open forehead and flattened nose. From a dozen metres away, DeGroot piped up. "Leave something for the rest of us."

MacNeil smiled at him. "Fine. But if a single girl on this entire planet can stomach looking at him without puking, he's mine again."

DeGroot came over and sat on Steve's chest. "You've seen the creature that we are after, haven't you?"

Spitting out blood, Steve answered him. "Sure, I saw the winged demon."

DeGroot grabbed Steve's chin and smiled. "This unit was trained to tackle the spawns of Satan himself. Up to now, you have been the scape goat. Along with being a cop killer, the police firmly believe that you are responsible for every atrocity that that creature has committed. Welcome to hell."

With a twisted grin, DeGroot stood up and looked at Duncan. "Honestly, what good is he to our mission? The cops won't bother us anymore. We could put his remains on ice and thaw him out when it's over. We could tell the police that a bear got him before we could. They wouldn't care. They want him dead as much as we do."

Steve quickly grabbed the knife hidden in his vest. Before the blade was unsheathed, Drake had his foot on top of his hand. "I'm with DeGroot." Looking at Duncan he asked, "What do you think we should we do with him?"

Duncan knelt down and stared at Steve's face. "The conniving coward can't even look at me. He's not even a man. I say we castrate the goat like any other farm animal before its sent to slaughter."

Before Duncan could stand up, Drake had flipped Steve over and DeGroot was pulling Steve's pants down to his ankles. Not wanting to feel left out, MacNeil plopped down on Steve's shoulder blades and grabbed his knees. With his legs straddling Steve's body to get more leverage, he leaning back and bent Steve's body into almost a 'U'. "Come and get them."

Seeing Steve's testicles dangling in the air, DeGroot pulled out his knife. "I've been waited a long for this moment. A long, long time."

As Steve started to defecate, MacNeil called out, "Hurry up, he's getting shit all over them."

"Fine." DeGroot bent over and grabbed a testicle and sliced it off along with over half of his scrotum. "That was for Paul Lyons. He was the closest friend I ever had."

Drake pushed DeGroot aside and cut off Steve other testicle along with most of his remaining scrotum. "That was for Pamela Gurney. She was one terrific woman and one great soldier. She didn't deserve to be violated and have her naked, mutilated body put on display that way." Throwing the testicle on the ground, Drake stepped on it and rubbed the sole of his boot against it until it was a mashed into paste.

MacNeil dropped Steve's legs and flipped him around. He wanted to see Steve's face as he reached down and cut deep into his groin to sliced off his penis. "That was for Bobby Hicks. He may have been a bit of a prick and a card cheat, but he didn't deserve to die that way. None of them did."

Standing over Steve, he added, "You never were a real man. Now, you can't even pretend to be one."

Spurred by the unshackled rage of the others, Duncan walked over, reached down and grabbed Steve's hair. "You slithering snake. This is for blabbing your mouth off just to save your own scaly skin."

With Drake and MacNeil holding him down, Duncan put his knee against Steve's forehead and forced his jaw open with his left hand. Pulling out his knife with his right, he pressed the blade along the centre of Steve's tongue until it split it apart. The two halves twisted around like two wiggling worms in a pool of blood.

Steve looked into Duncan's cold eyes and tried to grab his arms. Duncan stood up and left Steve's outstretched arms dangling in the air. Coldly staring at his blood covered face, Duncan shook his head. "We took you in and treated you like family. How could you betray us like that? Did you really think that your life is worth that much more than theirs?"

Duncan waited for a reply that Steve wasn't even capable of giving. With all hope lost, all he could do was rock his head back a forth.

MacNeil and DeGroot took turns grinding what was left of the discarded organs into a slimy paste with their boots. Drake roughly tied field dressings to Steve's groin and legs to keep him from bleeding to death. As Duncan walked over to the jubilant pair, over his headphone he could hear Colonel Kevin Conway ask, "What's going on down there?"

Duncan replied, "Finishing an old mission."

The rough seasoned colonel knew about Duncan's past and easily surmised what had happened. After stroking his mustache with his forefinger he yelled down, "Is he dead?"

"He's not going to cause anyone any problems, ever again."

Colonel Conway called to have his unit extracted. It didn't take long before Duncan's squad was all that remained. By the time the helicopter came to pick him up, Drake had placed Steve's body into body bag and injected enough drugs into him to put him into a coma. Leaving the bag partly unzipped, he was airlifted to the camp.

As Drake and MacNeil carried him to the hospital trailer, Duncan walked beside them. Whispering so none of the other soldiers could hear, Duncan told MacNeil, "Tell the doc to patch him up just enough to keep him alive. I also want him to insert a transmitter into his gut, preferably his liver."

MacNeil glanced at him and asked, "You have something in mind, don't you?"

Duncan smiled and said, "Oh ya. That snake is going to get what he deserves." After a walking a few steps further, Duncan's face turned cold. "I have to go and make some arrangements. Tell Doctor Stern to leave his tongue the way it was meant to be. After all, snakes are supposed to have forked tongues so people can tell that they can't be trusted."

******

That night Drake answered another knock on the door. "Tell Duncan that the captain of the Aurora needs to talk to you ASAP."

Duncan looked up at Drake and rolled out of bed without saying a word. Walking through the ankle high snow that had fallen overnight, he told Drake, "I hope it's more good news."

"This time of day, it normally is."

After climbing into the communication trailer, the corporal handed Duncan the phone. "This is Colonel Stuart. What have you got for me?"

"The creature's sonar is unique, but she doesn't use it much. Fortunately for us, the few times that she has were enough for us to triangulate the approximate position of her lair. We have already passed on the location and vital information to the officer overseeing the drones. He had informed me that they should be ready to go up at dawn."

With an inquisitive look, he asked, "You said approximate, how close is that?"

"We got it down to about one and a half kilometres long and three-quarters wide. When she lands, we seem to lose her fairly quickly. Her skin has taken on some stealth qualities. Whatever it is made of seems to be eluding our instruments."

A bit puzzled, Duncan inquired, "Then how did you figure out her location?"

"By the way she runs. You were right. We were able to formulate a distinct trace signature from her gait. With the way her wings shift from side to side, no other creature could possibly replicate the same rhythm and sounds that she does as she runs. Unfortunately, we lose track of her when she slows down."

******

Lying in the hospital trailer, Steve was just like the other patients except his name wasn't on his chart, only 'XXX'. To most of the other patients he was just another injured soldier. As he opened his eyes, Ann got up from her chair and checked his vital signs. It had been a long night.

As Ann changed the bandages on Steve's groin, she noticed DeGroot standing by the door. Steve saw him and began to sweat. Ann looked at his eyes and then over to DeGroot. "What's wrong with you? He is not going to hurt you."

With his jaw wired shut, Steve blinked but didn't mutter a sound. When he came in, his body had been covered in a blanket. Drake had pushed to the side. All she saw was the condition of his face as he was carried into the operating room.

With a broken nose, chipped teeth and lacerations all over his face and mouth, she didn't question the doctor's reasoning behind wiring his jaw shut. However, she was shocked that Doctor Stern didn't want her assistance in the operating room. It must have been very difficult for him to wire Steve's jaw shut by himself. At least he asked for Drake's help to set the broken bones in Steve's legs.

Before Steve could wake up, Drake had strapped his arms to the side of the hospital bed. Seeing Ann coming over with a tray of soapy water, he told her, "Under no condition are you to release him. If you give him half a chance, he'll cut you to threads without batting an eye."

As Ann washed off the disinfectant that the doctor had used while stitching up the skin graft on Steve's chest, she saw what was left of the tattoo over his heart. Although the centre had been cut out, she recognized the green and red edges. It was the same fiery green dragon standing in front of a large red maple leaf holding a knife and smoking pistol, that Ratlin and DeGroot had.

In fact, every member of Duncan's elite unit had one.

Seeing him open his eyes, she commented, "So you had the same tattoo as the others. I love the fire bursting out of the dragon's mouth." After pausing for a moment, she added, "You must've all served together."

Steve blinked. Ann thought for a moment. "Did you once serve under Duncan?"

Steve blinked again. Ann got curious, "Does one blink means yes, and two mean no? If that is correct, blink twice."

Steve blinked twice. Ann sat on the edge of Steve's bunk and noticed DeGroot standing next to the door. "He had nothing to do with what happened to you, did he?"

Steve blinked once. DeGroot saw Ann talking to Steve and saw the deliberate blink. Walking over to Ann, he rubbed her shoulder. "No sense asking a traitor any questions. They are nothing but snakes. They will tell anybody anything they think you want to hear, no matter what the cost." Putting his hand on Ann's shoulder, he said, "Let's go. I only have three quarters of an hour before my shift starts."

Ann got up and pulled up Steve's blanket. His icy stare and the fact that he was both shivering and sweating at the same time left her not knowing what to think. Watching her leave, Steve noticed the bulge her pistol made under her lab coat. Flexing his hands, he started to think.

As they ate their breakfast, Ann was unusually quiet. DeGroot tried hard to break her silence by asking her questions about her new pistol, the weather, what she was reading and anything else he could think of. She turned and looked at him. "What happened to patient triple X?"

DeGroot smirked. "You mean the goat?"

Shocked by his response, she stood up and bellowed out, "He served with you. Doesn't that mean anything?"

"Sit down." In a low harsh voice, he added, "The Green Dragons had a perfect record before we were betrayed by that traitor. We had always looked out for each other and nobody was ever left behind." After taking a deep breath, he told her, "Don't get caught in the middle. He is not worth it. His treachery got a lot innocent people killed. Some of them were dear friends of mine. Cop killers don't go free and neither do traitors. If you like it or not, either way his fate is sealed."

******

Claraicy crawled out of a freshly dug hole in the side of a small hill and stretched. The black bear that had dug the den was no match for her. All she had to do was wait for him to go out scrounging for food to move in without a fight. Despite being outweighed, Claraicy refused to allow him anywhere near his winter den. With her giant wings she had no problem scaring him away.

It took time for the splinters in Jesse's chest and leg to fester and become loose. Not wanting to cause any further damage, it took over a week for Claraicy to gingerly work the two shattered chunks of wood out. The large splinter in her leg took longer to extract. Every time she touched it, more blood would gush out.

When she finally got the splinter out, Claraicy went outside and tossed it into the forest. Afterwards she looked up saw something twinkle in the morning sky. The rising sun had reflected off the windshield of the Aurora plane as it circled around to make another pass over her position. Figuring the plane was too far away to bother her, Claraicy went back to work.

Her injured eye was no longer sore but she still had to keep it shut. After applying some ointment over it, she wrapped a rag around her head and under her ear to cover it up. She had finally got comfortable using only one eye without getting headaches or getting dizzy. Looking back at the den, Claraicy knew that Jesse would wake up hungry and that meant that she had to hunt.

Climbing through the trees, she found a nice spot overseeing several animal trails, while still within earshot of the den in case the bear came back. It wasn't long before a rabbit appeared.

Crawling through the bare branches, she repositioned herself over its path. Using the claws on her feet, she clung to a branch with her hands dangling a metre above the path of her unsuspecting victim. As it made its way around a bush, Claraicy dropped hands first on top of the rabbit. While standing up, she twisted and pulled off the creature's head. Before any blood was wasted, Claraicy shoved the creature's neck into her mouth and elevated it over her head. With her neck as far back as it would go, she sucked out all of the creature's warm, nutritious blood that she could. To her it was as stimulating as drinking a cup of coffee.

Claraicy walked back to a large fallen tree in front of the den. While sitting on top of it, she rested against the sloping branch and let her wings fall to the sides. After ripping off the fur, Claraicy pulled out the rabbit's guts and put them aside for Jesse along with the hind legs.

Over the next hour, she slowly consumed the rest of the rabbit raw. Afterwards she flung the bones behind the tree with the other scraps and hung the rabbit hide over a tree branch.

Claraicy's dark wings were spread out soaking in the warm sun when Jesse crawled out of the den. Three ugly scabs covered the areas where the large splinters had been. She went over to Claraicy and smelled the rabbit guts. With a shallow growl, she ate the guts and reluctantly took the hind legs with her into the snow covered forest. Claraicy knew that she probably wouldn't see her again until dusk.

Despite still recovering, Jesse wanted to hunt down and kill her own meat.

Knowing she couldn't, Claraicy made sure she didn't go to sleep hungry.

The trees surrounding the den protected Claraicy from the cold breeze. With her wings folded around her like a blanket, soaking in the warm sun, she took a short nap. The buzz of a drone flying overhead only slightly stirred her senses. From the air, her furry, dark boney wings helped her body blend into the coarse bark of the fallen tree.

******

Ann couldn't strip off her smock and crawl under the covers of her bunk quick enough. Most of the other women in the trailer were gone and only one remained. The soldier's shift had ended an hour ago and she was already fast asleep. DeGroot had been the only one in camp that she felt comfortable talking to, and now she felt that she had no one. She saw what remained of triple X's groin when she changed his dressings and catheter. She saw what the soldiers had done to him. After only a couple hours sleep, her nightmares about DeGroot savagely castrating him woke her up yelling, "How could he."

Ann looked over at the sleeping soldier. "Good, she's still asleep."

Not able to get back to sleep, she got dressed and went for a walk around the camp. As she walked by the doctor's trailer, she glanced in the window and saw him sitting at his table. After knocking on his door, she announced herself. "It's Ann. Can I come in? I need to talk to someone."

When the doctor said, "Come in," Ann froze for a moment. She knew that he never wanted her to be anywhere near Triple X, let alone talk about him.

Doctor Stern was sitting at his table staring at the bottle of wine gripped in his hands. Another empty one was on the floor beside him. As Ann closed the door, he turned off his tablet and told her, "I've been half expecting you."

Ann looked at him. "How, why?"

After taking a gulp of wine, he looked at her and said, "I checked on our star patient. I told you not to change his dressings, but you did it anyway."

"I had to, it needed changing. I'm a nurse. I can't just ignore a patient in need of care." Seeing the shape that the doctor was in, she knew that it wasn't in his nature either. "How could you go along with them and say nothing?"

The doctor took another swig before answering her. "Steve was brought here as a sacrificial goat. I knew that he wasn't going to get out of here alive. I knew how Duncan and his men felt about him, but what they did to him was inhuman. Something must of snapped when they caught up to him. That's not who and what they are."

Ann sat down at the table and took a swig of wine. "I have to agree with you. I don't understand how can feel that what they did to him was justified."

Doctor Stern took his bottle back and took a large swig. "Steve was a self-centred turncoat. Apparently, he was out scouting when he was captured. The mob that nabbed him were well known for their ruthless treatment of prisoners.

Before they could even tie his hands, he had them convinced that he was actually one of their spies. While Duncan's platoon was being tortured and butchered, he walked away without a scratch on him."

Ann took the bottle and took a large swig. "That seems a little far-fetched."

The doctor looked up at her. "I read the transcription of his court martial. They found most of the Green Dragons stripped naked, beheaded and chopped into pieces. The heathens had stuck the heads of the men on pikes. I'm not going to tell you what they did to the women. During the trial one of them testified that Steve had told his leader the location of every gun placement and dugout. Duncan was taken prisoner, dragged back to their camp and repeatively tortured. DeGroot, Ratlin, Drake and MacNeil were out on patrol when the ambush happened. By the time they got back, it was all over. They tracked the heathens back to their base and helped organize a strike. Duncan was the only prisoner that survived."

The doctor handed Ann the bottle. It took her only two swallows to finish it. "That still doesn't justify what they did."

"No, it doesn't." The doctor went over to the cupboard, pulled out another bottle and filled two glasses. "It doesn't justify it at all. They are trained professionals. What they did goes against everything they believe in, especially Duncan of all people."

Sipping on her wine, Ann spilled out, "Those men must really love Duncan to blindly do his bidding like that."

"You got it backwards. Duncan is like a machine. That is why it is so hard for me to believe he took any part in it. Those heathens had wiped out almost all of his emotions. I was shocked that he even cared at all when his brother was killed. The others are the ones that are still having nightmares. Finding their comrades' dismembered and mutilated bodies must have been horrific. They're the ones you need to watch out for."

Ann took a large mouthful of wine before replying, "I guess we have all changed."

"The difference is, we're not soldiers."

******

Inside the communications trailer, the operator yelled out, "Get the colonel."

A soldier ran out of the communication trailer and within seconds Duncan appeared. "What is it?"

The corporal that was attending the phone told him, "It's the base. A drone picked up something. Last night's snowfall worked to our advantage. The drones spotted some footprints that they believe came from the creature we are after."

The soldier showed Duncan the short video on the computer monitor.

Whatever made the footprints was walking on two legs. Animals walking on all four create a completely different set of overlapping footprints.

After going over two hours' worth of video, Duncan stopped it and zoomed in on one frame. Claraicy was almost invisible against the fallen tree. If it wasn't for a sudden breeze blowing some of her hair across her face, he may not have picked her out. "I have yet to see a tree that grows hair."

Chapter Thirty-Six

Bait

Through a window, Duncan watched Steve flex his fists. Entering the hospital trailer, he walked over to him and smiled. "I think you are well enough for your final mission."

After seeing MacNeil standing behind Duncan with a needle in his hand, Steve desperately tried to wiggle free from his restraints, but couldn't. As the drug cocktail rendered him unconscious, Duncan and MacNeil dressed him before dragged him outside by his arms. As the pre-formed casts on his legs smashed against the metal stairs, his face shrivelled up in pain.

Ann heard the commotion and looked out of the window. Seeing them dragging Steve towards the gate, she rushed out of the doctor's trailer and yelled out, "Where are you taking him? He shouldn't be moved. He has only been here a few days and his injuries haven't even started to heal yet."

As they dragged him through the gate towards a waiting helicopter, Duncan told her, "It doesn't concern you."

Running after them as fast as she could, Ann barked out a word for every step she took getting to the gate. "He's, my, patient. That, makes, him, my, concern."

By the time she caught up with them, they already had Steve aboard the helicopter. Duncan looked at Ann as she caught her breath, and coldly told her, "Not anymore."

Climbing into the helicopter, Ann defiantly said, "I'm coming with you."

Duncan grinned for a couple seconds before his face went back to stone. "Fine, but I warn you, don't get in our way."

The ride was only half an hour long, but to Ann it had dragged on for hours. At times the undercarriage of the helicopter was rubbing against the top of the odd tall pine tree. Biting her bottom lip, she tried to keep silent. Duncan and MacNeil strapped a parachute and a small pack onto Steve. When they started to unfasten the pre-formed casts on Steve's legs. It got too much for Ann and she exploded, "What are you doing? His bones will fall apart without them."

MacNeil quietly tied a pair of boots onto Steve's feet as Duncan snapped back, "None of your concern."

Ann yelled back, "Anything and everything you do to him is my concern."

Duncan could smell the alcohol on her breath. Shaking his head, he grinned. "I told you to keep out of our way. You weren't invited on this mission and you have absolutely no input on what happens. You should've stayed put and had another glass." Putting his hand on her shoulder, he told her, "This is war, that means some people die so others can live. My advice to you is shut your eyes and cover your ears. Once you witnessed it, your mind will never allow you to forget it. It will become a part of you for the rest of your life."

Too scared to reply, Ann started to shiver. Thinking that she was cold, MacNeil took off his jacket and handed it to her. "Here, put it on."

Outside the helicopter's window, the trees were dusted with snow and small patches of ice were lining the sides of the waterways. Inside the helicopter, Duncan leaned into the cockpit and pointed to a small clearing, "There, that should be perfect."

As the pilot yelled, "Hang on," the helicopter vaulted into the air. After the helicopter was stabilized, Duncan and MacNeil opened the side door and pushed Steve out. His chute barely had a chance to open before getting hung up in the trees. MacNeil smiled at Duncan. "If that isn't a good invitation, I don't know what is."

It took a while for Ann's brain to digest what she had witnessed. Appalled, she gasped, "What have you done?"

"He was serving a life sentence when we got him out of prison." Duncan turned and smiled at her, "Traitors shouldn't be allowed to die of old age, they should pay for what they did."

As soon as the helicopter landed, MacNeil walked towards his trailer and saw Drake painting 'Green Dragons' above the door. "What's this?"

"Justice has been served, and I thought it was finally time to honour our dead."

MacNeil looked at the fresh paint. "You may be right, but green paint on a green trailer doesn't really stick out."

Drake smiled at him as he replied, "It was all I had. Besides, we're Special Forces, we are not supposed to stick out."

After entering the trailer, MacNeil walked over to Ratlin's bunk and bent over. The metal halo that kept Ratlin's neck straight with his spine had prevented him from seeing MacNeil approach. "It's done. The goat has been delivered. By the time the creatures are finished with him, he'll be ripped apart even worse than what those heathens did to our friends."

Ratlin smiled. "Good. I wish I could be there. You should have set up a camera so we could all watch. I would pay to see that slimy snake being torn apart, one mouthful at a time. I just hope that he's still alive while they do it"

In the communications trailer, Duncan sat down in front of a computer monitor. The transmitter placed inside of Steve's liver was working great. Not only was his position being transmitted, but also his vital signs and any sounds its microphone could pick up.

From Steve's vitals, he could tell that the drugs had not worn off yet. The images relayed to Duncan from the drone circling overhead showed Steve's right arm twisted in an unnatural position over a branch. Zooming in, he saw that it was broken in at least two places.

******

Needing to get image of Steve plummeting to the ground out of her head, Ann methodically checked her patients. Her last patient had broken his leg slipping off of a pile of rocks. As she pulled back his blanket, she remembered MacNeil removing Steve's cast. As soon as she was finished with the injured soldier, she walked over to the doctor's trailer and knocked on his door.

"Who is it?"

With her head resting against the door, she replied, "It's me, Ann."

"Thank god it's only you." After a few seconds the door lock clicked. As the door opened, he added, "Please come in."

As Ann began to push on the door, the doctor lost his balance and fell behind it. Rolling onto his side, he made enough room for Ann to squeeze through. After helping him to his chair, she sat at the table across from him. His stubble, messy hair and red eyes told her how he spent the rest of the morning. She felt that she was lucky that he was even dressed.

He looked down at the almost empty glass of whiskey in front of him and sighed. "I watched you climb into the helicopter with them. What did they end up doing to the poor goat?"

With tears streaming down her face, Ann told him everything and left nothing out. The thought of DeGroot being involved in castrating Steve horrified her. "DeGroot is a good decent man. How could he be a part in all this?"

"He is a soldier. A military unit is like a family. If almost all your family was brutally violated, mutilated and beheaded, what would you want to do to the man responsible for it. They were just given a golden opportunity to fulfill that desire and they took it."

Ann took the bottle of whiskey and pour herself a couple ounces. After taking a sip and forcing it down, she said, "Never the less, what I witnessed was pure insanity. He was still a human being."

The doctor threw back his glass and licked his lips. "Only to us. To them, he was less than nothing. He was a gangrenous limb that needed to be hacked off and cast away. Have you looked outside? Everyone is rejoicing." Raising his empty glass, he added, "The goat has been sacrificed and the Green Dragons can once more hold their heads up high."

Ann looked at the half conscious doctor and questioned him. "If you knew how vile the goat was, why are you drinking alone? Is there something that you are not telling me? "

The doctor tried to pour himself some more whiskey but spilled most of it onto the table. "Because I did my job, and now I'm trapped in this wilderness with nowhere to go."

While wiping off the table, Ann inquired, "What job? What did you do?"

The doctor looked up from his glass. "If you don't know, then maybe he doesn't either. Maybe I'm worried for nothing."

******

The same smell that made Claraicy retreat into the den drew Jesse outside. Her wounds were almost completely healed and she wanted to hunt and kill her own food. The sight of the helpless man dangling above her made her drool. With large snowflakes floating to the ground, Jesse never saw the plane flying amongst the snow clouds above her.

Food was all Jesse could think of from the time she woke to the time she fell asleep. She was growing fast and almost outweighed Claraicy. Fish, frogs, birds, rabbits, mice and venison all added to her rapidly increasing girth and across her huge, strong shoulders. It was like everything she ate was being converted into bone and muscle.

Steve's eyes were barely open when one of Jesse's claws swiped across the laces of one of his boots. The shattered bones in his leg twisted and popped through the skin. Looking down, he saw her jump up trying to grab his dangling foot.

He bent his knees to get his feet out of reach. Jesse got frustrated and almost ran up the tree. No matter which limb she was on, she still couldn't reach him. Steve's parachute was caught-up on several branches. Chewing the cords and shaking the branches proved to be a waste of time. Climbing down, she returned with a sharp edged stone.

Climbing from one branch to another, Jesse chopped away at the cords and material. One by one the cords began to snap. The added stress on the parachute made it began to rip apart. As one side of the chute suddenly collapsed, Steve grabbed a hold of a branch with his good arm.

He weighed too much for the small limb to bare. Steve helplessly watched as it snapped and twist downward. As he fell, a cord wrapped around one of his legs and twisted him upside down. Landing on his head, his neck snapped back and his twitching body flailed about. Despite his jaw still wired shut, blood spewed out of his mouth with every defiant twitch his body made.

Jesse quickly made her way down and heard a deep growl from a large black bear. Hesitating, she waited. It was the same bear that her mother had chased away from the den. Looking at Jesse, he stood up on his back legs and roared. Jesse felt that she was ready to take on such a large predator. She backed up slowly, turned around and climbed back up the tree.

As Claraicy's wings darkened the sky above them, the bear dropped on all fours and turned silent. As the huge bear looked up, she dove towards his head.

The bear twisted sideways to escape being hit. Landing next to Steve's twitching body, Claraicy looked around. Jesse leaped out of the tree and ran to her side. Claraicy could see the hunger in her daughter's eyes.

Jesse looked up at her. "Food. Both eat?"

Claraicy looked down at the twisted man. "Humans are bad food. They are lots of better food out here that you to eat."

"No, human good food."

Claraicy reached down and grabbed Steve by the cheeks. His eyes were still blinking as she used her claws to slice his head off where the neck was broken. Holding his head in the air, she told Jesse, "Humans make lousy food. Kill one, and the rest will come after you." After tossing Steve's head into the woods, Claraicy leaped into the air.

With the male bear pacing back and forth at the edge of the small clearing, Jesse cautiously leaned over Steve's body. She ripped open his stomach and pulled out some of his intestines. Seeing her mother flying above her, she proclaimed, "This good food."

Hovering overhead, Claraicy thought about Jesse's almost cannibalistic behaviour. *I was still human when I gave birth to her. Doesn't that count for anything?* Watching her rip Steve's torso apart, she asked herself, *If it was me lying there, would she eat me too?*

As Claraicy flew away, the large male bear stood on his hind legs and started to growl. Jesse looked down at the carcass and then over at the bear. As it stepped toward her, she stood her ground and screamed out, "No, my food."

******

Claraicy stayed within ear shot of Jesse. Between the bear's low, rumbling growls and Jesse's higher, shrill hisses, Claraicy could hear the pair verbally jostle for superiority, predatory rank and dominance. Without any sounds of actual fighting, Claraicy hoped that Jesse would safely back off and leave the human for the bear.

Claraicy waited until everything was all over before returning to the site. Human remains were scattered all over the small clearing. Almost all the flesh had been either torn or chewed off the bones. Bear prints over Jesse's and Jesse's prints stepping over the bear's indicated to Claraicy that they both took turns ripping the body apart. While one carried off of limb and was busy eating it, the other tore off a piece to eat. Neither wanted to risk getting injured. With winter almost upon them, the bear was only interested in storing more food, while Jesse just wanted to satisfy her constant hunger.

Claraicy rummaged through the man's equipment. The material from the parachute had multiple uses. She felt that she could make use most of the stuff from his pack and pockets. While sitting down and going through the small pack she found an old newspaper. It was a week old. She thought that it was put in for emergency kindling.

On the bottom of the front page was a large advertisement. Below a sketch of a smiling Santa with a young girl on his lap was written, 'The world's greatest job could be yours. If you would like the thrill of having an innocent child begging to get on your lap, call us.' After reading it, Claraicy sprung to her feet and violently threw the newspaper to the ground.

******

At his computer, Duncan went over the distorted images being relayed to him from the Aurora and the pair of drones they had deployed. The large snowflakes falling to the ground obscured his view. As his frustration mounted, the corporal sitting next to him announced, "The transmitter is on the move."

Duncan wheeled his chair over to him. "Finally, something that we can use. How's its reception?"

"Great."

After going over the incoming data, Duncan smiled. "It's doing everything it's supposed to do. Now all we have to do is retrieve the remaining body parts. If we don't pretend we cared about him, Claraicy and her spawn may suspect it was a trap."

After the snow stopped falling, Duncan had the Aurora thoroughly scanned the area before allowing any helicopters to approach the area. Two birds of prey guarded the transport helicopter. The helicopter whipped the snow from the trees into a mini blizzard as the ropes were dropped out of the side door. After repelling down, Duncan and MacNeil quickly scouted around the site.

Amongst Steve's scattered remains, MacNeil identified some bear tracks and called Duncan over. Judging from the layers of snow it was clear that its tracks were on top of Jesse's. "It was probably just scavenging for leftovers. It looks like the spawn got to him first."

Something inside MacNeil made him ask Duncan, "Shouldn't the bear be hibernating by now?"

"It should." Duncan thought for a brief moment. "Maybe it hadn't put on enough weight, or maybe its den was stolen. The prey was last sighted outside of one. It could've been his."

After quickly collecting what was left of Steve and placing the various parts into a body bag, they scouted around the site. Pieces of newspaper were scattered beside a bush. He walked over to it and saw it had been crushed in the middle.

He smiled as he saw a cross-ways crease in the paper. That meant that it had been deliberately folded to make it easier to read the ad for the Santa's workshop. "I guess Claraicy didn't like our ad. We'll leave the paper here in case she wants to read some more."

Getting out his locator, Duncan found the small pack that he had strapped to Steve buried in the snow. Most of the gear was gone, but the tracking devices he had embedded into them had been discarded. While trying to retrieve them, he used his foot to push away the snow on the ground and found Steve's severed head. The bandages had fallen off and the wire attached to his jaw had come loose.

Picking up the head, Duncan got a surprise. The tongue was neatly sewn up. It was no longer forked like he had ordered the doctor to leave it. Without saying a word, he slammed the head into the open body bag and zipped it shut. MacNeil had seen Duncan's violent reaction. "What's up?"

Duncan shook his head as he tied the bag to a rope dangling from the helicopter. "Let's get out of here. We have enough of him to put on ice in order to convince the police that he's actually dead when this is finally over."

As they landed, Duncan tossed the bag carrying Steve's remains over his shoulder. Instead of taking it to the small morgue in the hospital trailer, he walked straight to the doctor's door.

Ann saw Duncan in the window. "Doc, Duncan's back and he is mighty pissed off about something."

As Ann dashed into the doctor's bedroom, the doctor poured another glass of whiskey. Duncan didn't bother to knock. Barging in, he plopped the bag down on the table and unzipped it. After pulling out Steve's blood soaked head, he shoved it into the doctor's face and bellowed out, "What is this? Did I not give you a direct order or not?"

The doctor cocked his head to the side and looked up at him. "Yes, you gave me an order. Too bad it wasn't one that my conscience would allow me to follow. I am a doctor. He had lost a lot of blood. I was worried that he would bleed to death. I had to sew it back together."

Duncan almost touched noses with the doctor as he told him, "So you admit that you disobeyed me. This is the one and only warning that I'm going to give you. If you disobey me again, you may find yourself stuffed in a bag that weighs a lot less than this one."

Duncan left the bag on the table and slammed the door after him. Ann peeked out of the bedroom. "Are you all right?"

With his entire body shivering, the doctor replied, "Sure, for a dead man."

Locking the door, Ann rubbed the back of her head. "He is losing it. This is not what I signed up for. We have to get out of here."

The doctor looked at her and chuckled. "Believe it or not, he actually likes you. You have nothing to worry about. He wouldn't hurt you."

While retrieving a blanket from the bedroom, Ann commented, "I wouldn't be so sure about that."

The doctor closed his eyes. "I don't really know what we are doing out here, or what our true objective is anymore." Opening his eyes, he saw Ann's face as she wrapped the blanket around him. "But I do know that if Duncan actually thought for one moment that he couldn't trust me, I would become an expendable liability."

******

Claraicy heard the helicopters and worried about Jesse. She still hadn't returned. After they had flown away, she crawled out of the den and raced to the small clearing. All of Steve's remains were gone along with what was left of his gear. Looking around, she spotted the newspaper wrapped around the bottom of a bush.

Picking up the paper, she read some more of the ad. The line, 'No criminal checks are required' made her proclaim, "They are training paedophiles on how to get their jollies." On the bottom left hand corner of the ad was a small map with direction to 'Santa's College'.

She tore off the ad and took it back to the den. The cave was divided into two parts by a large overhanging rock. The extra pair of shoulders jutting out of her back made her frame too boxy to crawl past it. When Jesse wanted to be left alone, all she had to do is crawl into the back portion of the den and hide.

After squeezing her head into the back section, Claraicy was relieved to hear heavy breathing. Making her voice click, she saw a mental image of some fur that was mostly hidden behind a boulder. Feeling contented that Jesse was safe, Claraicy pulled her head out and sat near the entrance of the den where the light was brightest.

Claraicy refocused her attention on the ad. After a few minutes, she dumped out the backpack containing most of her camping gear. Rummaging through the mess, she pulled out a watch and looked at the date. Despite the newspaper being old, the graduation date was a week away. Squeezing the watch, she raised it into the air in glee and muttered, "No more."

Chapter Thirty-Seven

The hook

Jane made some small adjustments to the amounts of the various nutrients being fed into the fetus' artificial placenta. After carefully documenting the changes, she placed her hand against the glass. She smiled as the rhythm of its heart changed. "You know I'm here, don't you?" It was growing at two, almost three times the rate of a normal baby. As she hummed a lullaby, she wondered how the speed of its growth would affect its mental development.

The phone rang and startled her out of her day dream. "Is Doctor Scott there? He is not answering his cell phone."

"I'm sorry Duncan, he is still asleep. Is everything alright? You sound a bit edgy. Is there anything that I can help you with?"

While pacing up and down the length of the communication's trailer, Duncan told her, "Wake him up. This has to do with the side project that you were helping the doctor with. I need to talk to him as soon as possible. He's expecting my call."

"I'm sorry, but I when I arrived this morning I found him asleep at his computer. He must have been up all last night. I helped him into one of the beds a couple hours ago."

Duncan's voice mellowed down a bit. "How about letting the doctor sleep 'til noon. If he isn't up by then, wake him up and tell him that Claraicy has taken the bait. We have no idea how fast things could unfold. We also know that the implanted transmitter had been ingested. Unfortunately, she had discarded all of our other tracking devices. "

Curious, Jane asked him, "So I take it, the fake newspaper and sick Santa ad that I made up was the bait?"

"It was. We had to plant something that would draw her out of hiding. From what we can tell, when she saw it, she reacted exactly like the psychiatrist said she would. Tell Doctor Scott that the small fortune he paid him was worth it." Duncan hesitated a bit before adding, "I also have another delicate problem that I have to discuss with the doctor, but I think it can wait for now."

The doctor only slept for a couple hours. As soon as he woke, Jane handed him a coffee and filled him in. Handing his cup back to Jane, the doctor grabbed his phone and called Duncan. "I hear it took the bait."

"Hook, line and sinker."

While stretching his neck and arms, the doctor asked, "Have you been monitoring the transmitter's signals?"

Duncan looked at the monitor. A graph on the bottom corner showed movement over time. "Sure, we have been tracking it but it hasn't moved for quite a while now."

"Have there been any changes in the creature's breathing?" After yawning, the doctor told him, "Never mind. I'll have Jane patch set up the link."

Jane quickly flipped through the breathing history recorded from the time it was ingested. "Good news, the creature's breathing is slowing down. You were right, its body wants to hibernate. If it does, you should have no problem capturing it."

"Great, then we can concentrate on its mother."

******

It was one in the morning when Claraicy woke. All she could think about was her father raping her while dressed in his Santa suit. Bouncing young children on his lap all day, turned him into a twisted sexual monster by the time he got home. When he left her to die in the forest, he had actually saved her from another season of torture. Remembering him in that red suit infuriated her. Pacing back and forth she worked herself into a frenzy. She couldn't reason herself to stay and do nothing about it. She looked at the claws on her hands and finally decided. She was given this body as a gift that she had to use.

Her eye was almost back to normal. It was okay when she was on the ground, but when flying she couldn't accurately judge distance with it. Claraicy tied an olive green triangle bandage over it. Both of her large, pointed ears stood out of the sides of her head.

Since being shot, the scales that covered her body had grown harder. That increased her overall weight. It was her wide turned-up nose that bothered her the most. It seemed to help sharpen the images that she saw in her mind. At the same time it shattered her fantasies of growing up into a normal, happy woman. She could no longer look at herself in a mirror.

While chewing on a piece of dried meat, she placed a lanyard around her neck. Attached to it was a compass, and a plastic luggage tag containing the map to the college. Using some Velcro straps from a sleeping bag, she fastened a small pack to her forearm.

After listening to the soft snores coming from the back of the den, she was reassured that Jesse would be fine until she got back. Crawling outside, she leaped into the air. From a distant bush, a pair of tired eyes watched her vanish into the night sky.

******

Sitting at her station in the Aurora, the sonar technician looked at the blinking dots on the screen in front of her. "She's on her way. She is travelling in a straight line directly towards the coordinates you gave us."

Sitting in the communication trailer, Duncan replied, "Has everyone been alerted?"

"Yes sir. All of our teams are briefed and ready to lift off. Before she reaches the target, our drones should be in the vicinity to help pin-point her position."

******

In the middle of an abandoned mining town stood an old wooden church. While most of the surrounding buildings were falling apart, it was freshly painted with bright red trim around the windows, doors and soffits. With a spired bell tower on one side of the double front doors and a turret enclosing a stairwell on the other, the tall structure was easy for Claraicy to spot with her sonar.

Below the steeple, a pair of bright spotlights beamed out of the shutters of the bell tower. With every rotation they would change from yellow, green, red and blue, giving off a different appearance to the surrounding landscape with each pass. Stripes of red and green decorated the outside of the tower like a candy cane. In contrast, the stair turret looked like a brick chimney with a giant blown up Santa Claus standing on top of it. From the wrought iron gateway to the steps in front of the church were two rows of sparkling red and silver garland held up by large, plastic candy canes. A huge green sign above the front doors displayed 'Santa's College' in gold letters. In addition to the festive building, a dozen or more of the trees surrounding the church were decorated in colourful lights, balls and stars.

With the light reflecting off of the snow, the only place on the church that was not illuminated was the corner of the roof that was the furthest away from the spire. As a dark snow cloud blocked out the moonlight, Claraicy gently landed on the subdued corner.

The roof of the building had been neglected for decades. As she crawled over it her claws dug through the shingles and rotten wood. Small pieces of shingles broke off and fell to the ground. As she pried apart a small section of the roof, Claraicy listened for any reaction. *Everyone must be asleep.*

Past the shingles, wood and insulation, Claraicy got to the drywall. With one of her claws, she whittled a small hole in it and peered inside. A huge decorated chair stood at the head of the old church next to the pulpit. Draped over the pulpit was a scroll with a long list of names written on it. In front of the chair was a guide rope covered in red felt.

Everything was still and quiet. Claraicy decided to wait. With her head and torso lying inside the hole that she had created in the roof, she spread her wings on the outside to conceal the damage. The rising heat kept most of her warm. Outside, the falling snow covered her wings and body along with concealing the small pile of debris she had created on the ground.

******

A worried Drake asked, "Where is she?"

"We don't know. We lost her shortly after she was in sight of the trap. I guess once she saw her target, she stopped using her sonar. For some reason, even the drones couldn't pick her up. It is almost like her body absorbed their sonar and prevented anything get back to them. With her ability to control both her body temperature and the rhythm of her heartbeat, she's not giving us much to work with."

Drake looked at his watch. "It is almost daylight. Keep trying. Men's lives are at stake. We need anything you can give us."

"We have three hours of fuel left. We'll stay up as long as we can."

Duncan had only listened to the conversation up until then. "Drake, she's out there somewhere. With her enhanced senses, she will be aware of everything that's going on. At eight o'clock I want you to start school. Remember she is out for revenge. She will probably try to attack the Santas in mass to achieve maximum damage. Colonel Conway's men are well-disciplined and will do what has to be done. If they can put on a good show, they should be able to coax her out into the open."

Claraicy was awoken from a short nap by the clanking of dishes and chatter of a host of voices radiating from the basement. Shortly afterwards, two dozen, plump, velvet covered Santas strolled up the stairs and into the main hall. Each Santa carried a life-like doll about the size of a five year old girl, dressed in a short dress and tights.

One by one they took turns sitting on the huge chair and were scrutinised by three instructors. "Bounce that gut when you Ho, Ho, Ho... You can smile better than that... Curl that mustache and brush that beard. Any kid could tell it's a fake looking like that... You will never get a decent feel if can't get her on your lap. ... How are you going to get a girl to do exactly what you want if she doesn't believe that you're the real thing? You want to make her believe that all of her presents could be in jeopardy if she doesn't do what you want."

Claraicy grew angrier with every sly, sexual innuendo that was uttered. Using the claws on both her hands and feet, she ripped open the ceiling and swooped down on the trio seemingly in charge.

The instructor that she landed on never had a chance. Two lightning fast swipes from her claws cut through both of his cheeks, snapping his neck.

Claraicy then leaped onto the pretend Santa sitting on the chair. She slashed her claws across his neck and then bit into his arm as he tried to protect his face. She couldn't. There was no blood. Her sharp teeth couldn't penetrate his kevlar suit, neck guard and thick padding.

Confused, Claraicy looked at the crowd of Santas, as they pulled out the pistols and assault rifles that they had hidden in the dolls. Claraicy yanked the Santa out of the chair, flung him around and used him as a shield.

In the front row, to save time, some of the soldiers fired their weapons while they were still inside of the dolls. Their heads were blown apart and their stuffing was strewn everywhere. As a cloud of stuffing obscured their vision, they stopped shooting.

Colonel Conway yelled out, "Now!"

Some of the pews opened up and soldiers with net launchers popped out of them. One fired a large net toward Claraicy.

Claraicy quickly spread her wings and batted the electrified net away from her. With her wings spread out, she became too huge a target for the nets. The Colonel quickly yelled out, "Fire at will."

Several bullets tore into her wings before she could draw them back in. Grasping the bullet-proof Santa, she tossed him into the air as another net was shot out. Before the net encased soldier toppled the soldiers in the first two pews, Claraicy pounced into the air. She barely had time to flap her wings a second time before her arms started pulling her through the hole in the ceiling.

Amongst the chaos, she swung the claw on her tail against the side of a soldier's face. It hooked him under his upper jaw behind his molars. As she climbed through the hole his oversized Santa's suit twirling like a dancer's dress. Only a few soldiers had any shot at all.

It barely took Claraicy a second to pull herself through the hole. The jolt drove the sharp scorpion-like claw on her tail further into the soldier's skull. His puffed out suit got stuck between the rafters.

With the soldier's eyes staring at her, she reached down and grabbed a hold of his head. One powerful twisting tug was all it took to rip off his head off along with pulling out the upper part of his spine.

The headless soldier fell lifelessly to the floor amidst the crowd below. One quick flick of Claraicy's tail sent his soldier's head into a tree. Still wearing a beard, the new gruesome ornament hung just below the star on top, with its frozen dead eyes looking downwards.

Claraicy could see at least eight helicopters approach her from all sides. All she could do was fly straight up. The gunfire from one of their .50 caliber machine guns nicked two bones in her wings.

A sharp pain surged through her body as the first bone broke. Her body was still numb as the second one snapped. She had no choice but to go higher. Her head grew foggy. She could barely breathe as she levelled off and looked down at her pursuers. She was well above the dark snow clouds. The helicopters formed two large rings, circling below her.

For the first time, Claraicy could clearly see the large plane that was circling above them. She thought how unusual it was for it to be flying so low. Tucking her wings next to her body she dove downward. Gaining speed, she flashed between the two rings of helicopters and rocketed away as fast as she could into a nearby heavily treed valley.

Duncan got on the intercom to cool everyone down. "Don't worry, we know where she is heading. She isn't getting away. Plan 'B' will clip her wings for sure."

Claraicy's broken bones crackled as she landed. Confused and shaken she ran most of the way back to the den. Something didn't feel right as she crawled inside. It smelt funny. Sniffing around, she found several bags containing explosives. All she could think about was Jesse. Not thinking about her wings, she tried to squeeze into the back of the den. 'Kaboom'.

From outside the den, two sets of eyes watched as the den imploded.

"Sir, it's over. We got both of them."

Duncan picked up the phone. "Doctor Scott, the hunt is finally over."

Chapter Thirty-Eight

Taken

The camp was all smiles with a few exceptions. Duncan walked over to the hospital trailer and walked in. The doctor and Ann were making their rounds. Duncan looked straight at the doctor and said, "We need to talk."

The doctor nervously answered, "Fine, give me a few minutes so I can finish up here."

Duncan left and waited outside the door. The doctor's face was grey as he stepped out. "I heard the news. So what now?"

"First, I have to say that I'm sorry for putting you in the position that I did. As long as no one else knows or ever learns about you disobeying my order, I'll consider the case closed." Duncan studied the doctor's face and saw his eyes twitch.

Getting no verbal response from the doctor, he added, "Now get some coffee in you. I will need you at the dig when we extract the bodies. There is a very good chance that Claraicy is still alive. Piled under that much rubble, it should be easy to subdue her. I need you to put together all the drugs and equipment that we will need to render her unconscious but still alive. Doctor Scott feels that there is a lot of information that we can extract from her. If she happens to die, she'll be useless to him."

As Duncan walked away, Ann cracked open the door. "I heard. Can you trust him?"

As the doctor watched Duncan give out some orders to a few soldiers, he said, "He is more concerned with keeping the respect of his men than making an example of an old civilian like me. Yeah, I trust his word, for now, but that's just because he still needs me."

Ann crossed her arms. "Well I don't trust him anymore than I would use salt to sweeten my coffee, never again."

At the site, Drake, MacNeil, DeGroot and Duncan were unpacking and setting up tents when Doctor Stern and Ann finally arrived. As Ann walked towards the tents, DeGroot smiled. "You should be happy. The carnage is over. No one else will be getting hurt and you'll have no more patients to tend."

Ann looked at him. "We'll see."

Duncan walked over to the den and looked at the rocks blocking the entrance. A couple had been moved. The ape-like impressions on the ground left him with no doubt as to who moved them. But how? He had seen the spawn's fur and heard it breathe while he planted the explosives around the den. After glancing over at Ann and the doctor, he took a deep breath and kicked some dirt over the prints.

"Drake, MacNeil, come here." Duncan whispered in a steady voice, "We may have got Claraicy, but her spawn is still out there. I don't know how, but I just covered up some of its prints. Drake, scout the area and come back with some firewood. MacNeil, when he comes back you do the same. I want one of you out there at all times protecting the perimeter. Right now, the others don't need to know they are still in danger. We need them here mentally as well as physically to extract Claraicy from under that pile of rocks."

MacNeil questioned Duncan, "What about DeGroot?"

"He's compromised. He has gotten too close to Ann."

As soon as he turned to walk away, Duncan remembered the bear prints. *The bear must have eaten the transmitter. With them gone, he simply crawled back into his den in an attempt to reclaim it.*

Hidden behind a thick cover of pine needles, Jesse watched the soldiers as they used jacks, winches, pulleys, levers and brute force to carefully remove the rocks that had fallen on top of her mother. The tree that she was in gave her a great vantage point. As a large rock was rolled away, Jesse could see one of her mother's massive hands.

Lying on her side Claraicy raised her arm. Most of the small rocks and debris that had covered it fell off. As her arm got a bit higher, a couple larger rocks rolled away from the side of her face. Jesse's eyes grew as she realized that her mother was still alive.

Seeing Duncan, Claraicy's first instinct was to swiped at him. Duncan quickly leaned backwards and easily avoided the attack. "Doc, come here. She still has a lot of fight left in her."

As the doctor ran over, DeGroot and Duncan wrestled with Claraicy's free arm. With all the weight of both men on top of it, Doctor Stern aimed his rifle at her inner elbow and shot a high powered dart into a groove a .50 calibre bullet had dug into her tough skin. After pulling out the dart, he hammered a needle through the small hole that was created, connected a syringe and injected Claraicy with a strong sedative.

A minute later, the two soldiers were still struggling with her. The doctor administered a second dose. It took over five minutes and three injections to calm her down. As Claraicy's head bobbed around, the doctor capped and taped the needle onto her arm to use as a shunt until a proper one could be installed.

Rock after rock was either tossed, rolled or winched away until both of Claraicy's arms and one of her legs were unearthed. Both of her wings plus her tail were still buried. To speed things up, Duncan waved the doctor over. "Cut them off and cauterize them. She won't be needing them anymore."

The doctor looked at Duncan's stern face. "Fine, if you say so."

"I say so."

After going through three grinding wheels, the doctor found one that worked on Claraicy's tough skin. Slowly, the doctor cut away the wing tissue that was attached to her sides. After cutting a short strip, he would cauterized the wound with a soldering iron. Twice he had Ann inject Claraicy with blood coagulates to help stop the bleeding.

As the smell of burning flesh filtered through the forest, Jesse grew wilder. After seeing Ann walking away from the harsh smoke to breath in some fresh air, she could no longer control herself. Jumping to the ground, Jesse ran through the camp and grabbed Ann by the waist without even slowing down. Jesse was in and out of the camp before any of the soldiers could draw a bead on her. The shots fired after her were all in vain.

Despite being violently tossed around, Ann tried to reach for her pistol. She couldn't even get the catch off the holster. Her head, hands and feet were battered against the rocks and trees as Jesse ran through the forest. As Jesse stopped to find out if she was being followed, she curled up in a ball and cried out in pain.

Jesse jumped down from a tree and turned towards her. Somehow Ann got the courage to unlatched her holster, drew her pistol and wildly fired. Shocked, Jesse kicked some dirt into Ann's face and snuck away. Seeing Ann using both of her hands to pull herself to her feet, Jesse leaped on her back and sunk her teeth into her neck. Ann reached around and tried to shot her, but Jesse grabbed her arms.

Sucking in her rich warm blood gave Jesse the additional strength she needed to restrain Ann's arms. Supporting all of Jesse's constantly shifting weight, it didn't take long for Ann's legs to give out. As she fell forward, Jesse dug her teeth further into her neck and crushed her windpipe. Unable to breathe, Ann had no choose but to succumb to her fate.

The bear had robbed her of a large portion of her last meal. Jesse rolled Ann's body over. She ripped Ann's blouse apart along with her bra. Jesse smelt her large bare breasts. Carefully she sliced one open and smelt it. Remembering what happened last time, she licked her claws to find out what they tasted like. Satisfied, she bit into the sliced open breast and chewed off one large chunk of the fatty flesh after another. After finishing the juicy flesh, Jesse continued to eat her way down into her stomach and vital organs.

Jesse had barely bit into Ann's thighs when a bullet whizzed by her. "There it is."

Jesse threw Ann's body over her shoulder and darted off through the woods. DeGroot and MacNeil tried to chase after her. Needing to catch his breath, MacNeil told DeGroot, "She's gone. We'll never catch it." After a deep breath, he added, "It can run twice as fast as we can."

DeGroot bent over with his hands on his knees trying to catch his breath. "I can't. I can't just leave her." After a few more breathes he added, "Go back, they need you. As long as I'm chasing the creature, it won't be able to attack the rest of the team."

MacNeil stood up and told him, "I can't leave you."

Shaking his head, DeGroot emphasized, "This isn't your problem, she's not one of us. You can't risk your life for a civilian. I loved her. I don't have any choice, but you do. I have to see this through."

Back at the den, Doctor Stern looked at Duncan. "You knew that it was still alive didn't you?"

Duncan shook his head. "Not until after you arrived." Duncan looked straight into the doctor's face. "This was our best chance of capturing Claraicy alive and I wasn't about to lose it."

"So you were willing to risk our lives? Is human life that meaningless to you?"

Duncan hung his head down and thought for a while before answering. Over the past while, he had did things that he wouldn't have ever done before. "I know that some of the decisions I had made lately deeply bother you, but they had to be made. This is war."

"You have changed. You never used to be so callous" Dr. Stern turned away from him. "One of the last things that Ann said to me was that she would never trust you. I guess she was right."

Duncan and Drake used a long steel bar to pry a rock off Claraicy's leg. Then they repositioned Claraicy's body so the doctor could get at her tail. Duncan never said a word as he handed the Doctor his tools.

Dr. Stern cut, hacked and cauterized as much of Claraicy's tail and wings off as he could before standing up and walking away. "I think that is enough butchering for one day."

Duncan and Drake each grabbed one of Claraicy's arms and yanked the groggy Claraicy free. They wrapped tape tightly around her claws and strapped her on a stretcher. They were lifting Claraicy into the helicopter when MacNeil walked out of the trees.

MacNeil walked straight to Duncan. "He's obsessed. He's gone after the spawn. You were right. He was too close. He wouldn't listen to reason."

"That's love for you. If it won't kill you one way, it will kill you another." Turning to Drake, he said, "Load up everything you need. I want you to go back with MacNeil and get DeGroot. If the opportunity arises, feel free to kill the beast, she is of no great use to us. I'll be back as soon as I'm sure that Claraicy is safely secured. I'm done making assumptions."

******

Eager to finally see Claraicy, Jane stood next to the doctor as the van pulled into Dr. Scott's garage. She was disappointed when she saw Claraicy's body her wrapped like a mummy. Dr. Scott looked at Duncan and Dr. Stern. "Was this necessary?"

Duncan smiled. "I don't think that anyone could explain her appearance to any accidental bystander. Wrapped like this, she could be easily passed off as either a crash or burn victim."

Dr. Scott turned to Jane. "Go and make sure that everything is ready in the operating room."

Dr. Stern followed as Jane led the way. Dr. Scott guided the front of the stretcher as Duncan pushed it down the corridor. "Duncan, Dr. Stern is worried about you. In his daily reports, he had mentioned how the demeanor of both you and your squad has changed over the past while. Is everything going all right out there?"

"We have everything under control."

"Not according to him. He said that you and your squad have gotten much more callous and animalistic since Ryan's death. Is this true?"

Duncan crunched up his face and thought about what that doctor had said. "Maybe the demons inside of us got caught up in a little blood lust. When you are trying to hunt someone, you try to think like they do. Maybe some of Claraicy's ability to free her nightmarish, uninhibited desires had rubbed off on us." Turning to the doctor, he added, "I'll try to keep it contained from now on. We're not turning into wild animals. We'll be fine."

"What about Dr. Stern? A lot went on out there. How he doing?"

"Right now, I think he'll do anything to get out of his contract." Duncan thought of the flight there. "He and Ann got pretty close. When that spawn took her, something inside of him snapped."

"Do you think he could harm either Claraicy or the project?"

Duncan shook his head. "First and foremost, he's a doctor. Second, he is scared to death of what I'd do to him if he did anything."

The doctors cut the wrapping off of Claraicy and rolled her over onto her stomach. Dr. Scott studied how her extra set of shoulders were attached to her back. Dr. Scott looked over at Jane. "We need a complete CAT scan of her back. We have to know how everything is connected before we can finish cutting them off. We wouldn't want to sever a major nerve or artery by mistake."

It was hard for Jane to look away from Claraicy's deformities. "I'll go and get the equipment ready."

As Jane left, Dr. Scott asked Dr. Stern, "What did you use to cut with?"

"I went through several types of blades. The one that I thought worked the best was a fine toothed diamond edged blade. It seemed to work well on both the skin and the bones, but it is a slow process."

"Okay, get my grinder, it is hanging on your side of the table."

Dr. Stern set up the grinder while Dr. Scott injected some serum into Claraicy. "I gave her enough to heal quickly, but hopefully not enough to cause any regrowth. That way, I can study how the modified cells react within her body." Dr. Scott held up one of her hands and bent it towards the head of the table. "Strap it in place."

Both hands were strapped securely to the table with only the tips of her fingers extended over it. Dr. Scott plugged in and tested his grinder. One by one he cut off Claraicy's claws along with the tips of her fingers.

While Dr. Stern stitched them up, Dr. Scott prepared her toes. Duncan held down her legs. Even in the drugged up state she was in, her wiggling body wanted to put up a fight. By the time Jane had returned, the doctors had already begun grinding down her teeth. She was suddenly glad that she had saw Claraicy beforehand. Without her claws and canine teeth, Claraicy appeared almost helpless.

First, they x-rayed Claraicy and then wheeled her stretcher over to the CAT scan. Afterwards, the two doctors discussed the entwined blood vessels, extended spinal column and vertebrae. Knowing that great care was needed, they used the grinder sparingly. One wrong slip with it could paralyse her. That would render her useless for some of the tests Dr. Scott had lined up for her. Around delicate areas they were forced to use small hand saws and files.

Hours started to drift by. On one side of the table Duncan assisted Dr. Stern the best he could. On the other, Jane attended to Dr. Scott's every need. Duncan's presence in the operating room made Dr. Stern nervous. The doctor knew that Duncan wouldn't think twice about snapping his neck if he did anything to jeopardise the operation.

Jane looked at the sweat on the Dr. Stern's brow. "Are you okay?"

He glanced back at Duncan before answering. "Fine, I'll be fine."

Duncan put his hand on the doctor's shoulder. "You'll do great. Just remember, I'm right here behind you to make sure everything goes the way it should."

******

Jesse ran as far and as fast as she could. Her full extended gut plus the weight of Ann's remaining corpse slowed her down. It wasn't enough for DeGroot to catch up to her. Every time she stopped to rest, she could hear him clamouring his way further and further behind her. Each time, she got a longer rest than the last. After a while it become a waiting game for Jesse.

Wanting to stay within her regular hunting grounds, Jesse began leading DeGroot in large circles. She could see him getting weaker and weaker.

However, by not wanting to venture away from her territory she made it easier for Drake and MacNeil to catch up to them. Their fresh footprints were easy to spot in the snow. Even with some of their footprints on top of each other, the blood dripping from Ann's body made Jesse's trail impossible for them to miss.

Jesse chewed off another piece from Ann's thigh as it dangled over her shoulder. She went for another bite when she heard a disturbance in the woods. *It was too soon for him to catch up to me.*

After ripping off some more of the tender meat, she could hear the disturbance getting closer. Jesse put her arm around what was left of Ann's legs and ran away. Coming to a steep cliff, Jesse threw Ann's remains over the edge. As nimble as a mountain lion, she worked her way down the cliff. On the bank of the icy river below, she saw two soldiers walking along the edge.

After she retrieved Ann's body, Jesse pulled it under a pine tree and started to devour as much of it as she could. Her feast was interrupted by the sudden appearance of two ropes bouncing around in the air. Jesse looked up and saw the two soldiers repelling down the cliff. She ran over and grabbed one rope in each hand. Pulling, yanking and whipping the ropes from side to side, Jesse tried to make the soldiers fall off them. Drake's feet slipped on some ice and the side of his head smacked a rock jutting out of the cliff.

With Drake hanging motionless above her, Jesse redirected all of her attention to MacNeil. As she started to swing the rope, he wrapped his arms and legs tightly around it. Even with his face tucked into his arms to protect his head, he could feel the sharp rocks cutting into the rope. As Jesse pounded his body against the rocks, pieces of his gear were shaken free. The falling ammo clips, knives and other debris only added to Jesse's pleasure.

With MacNeil's limbs firmly secured around his rope, Jesse returned to Drake's rope. Swinging it from side to side, she pounded his body against the rocks. As his legs bounced off them, his feet became untangled. Seeing the barely conscious man left with only one arm wrapped around the rope, Jesse cried out in delight. "More food."

Noticing that Jesse's attention was solely focussed on Drake, MacNeil pulled out his pistol and started shooting at Jesse. Infuriated, she ran over to MacNeil's rope and wildly swung it about. A section of frayed rope above MacNeil began to break apart. With MacNeil's weight, the frayed rope took only a few seconds to snap. Jesse watched him fall over ten metres and bounce off the ice and rocks below.

Jesse tossed the rope aside and ran to MacNeil. He was still alive. Jesse grabbed and tugged at his arms, trying to get them away from his throat. She slashed him with her claws as he rolled around the frozen, rocky river bank.

Drake's shoulder was dislocated. Grabbing the rope above where his injured arm was wrapped around, he pulled himself up and managed to free it. Using his legs and good arm, he eased himself down. He was almost at the bottom when Jesse saw him. In two bounding leaps she was under him.

She only had to whip the rope once to cause Drake to fall the remaining three metres. As he landed, Drake rolled onto his back and reached for the knife attached to the front of his vest. Jesse opened her mouth as far as it would go while pouncing on him. She went for his throat. Her jaw was slammed shut by Drake's razor sharp knife as he jabbed it though her jaw, tongue and as far up into her head as he could push it.

With Jesse's weight on top of him, it took all of Drake's strength to keep the butt of the knife from digging into his chest. Jesse rolled away from Drake and tried to pull the knife out, but the teeth of the saw-edged backside of the knife acted like dozens of fish hooks. Without knowing what to do she tried to run away. Disoriented, she stepped backward, slipped and fell through the ice. With her hands still fighting with the knife, the fast flowing river pulled her under. Drake sat up in time to see her bobbing through an open section of fast flowing current.

After finally getting to the cliff, DeGroot grabbed a hold of Drake's rope and carefully repelled down. Once down he saw MacNeil spitting up blood and ran over to him. DeGroot could hear the broken ribs grind with every breath MacNeil took. One of his legs was broken and the other shattered. Jesse had torn apart sections of his arms, legs and the sides of his face.

Drake didn't try to get up. Between his shoulder, smashed face and badly battered body, sitting up was hard enough. As DeGroot turned to him, Drake finally spoke. "It was right behind you. Unfortunately, it was a matter of you or us. We thought that we stood a better chance."

Covered in MacNeil's blood, DeGroot stared at him. "I didn't mean for anyone to get hurt. It was my fight, not yours."

Drake slowly rocked his head back and forth. "We're a family, and as a family we have to look out for each other, even the stupid ones that can't listen to reason."

DeGroot bandaged them up as best he could. It was only after the helicopter came into sight that he walked over and saw what remained of Ann's body. The only thing left that told him it was really her was a small section around one of her eyes. Jesse had eaten away her chest, stomach, thighs, buttocks and even the cheeks on her face. Like a bear, she had systematically ripped open and consumed every area on her body that stored fatty tissue.

Behind him he could hear Drake say, "Is that what you risked your life for?"

DeGroot turned around and looked at him. "No, it was for love, revenge and pure stupidity. You were right. I was a total fool. There was no way I could have saved her." Looking back at her corpse, he started to cry. "Now, instead of remembering a bright, beautiful woman, I will be remembering a mangled mess of flesh and bones."

Chapter Thirty-Nine

Recovery

Claraicy woke up screaming in pain. She felt like her body was on fire. The first thing she saw were the bars of the giant cage that surrounded the bed she was strapped to. Lying on her belly with her arms and legs lashed to the bed, her head was the only thing she could move. Along with her entire back, a shearing pain ran down both of her arms and legs.

Not being able to see her wings, she tossed her head from side to side trying to get a glimpse of them. Even though she could feel them burning, they weren't there. They had been replaced by a large sheet of thick padding that was taped across her back, down her sides, and ended where her tail should have been.

As rage overtook her, instead of extending her claws, another burst of burning pain shot down the length of her limbs all the way to her brain. Claraicy screamed out, "You bastards. I'll kill every last one of you for this."

Her long, seemingly endless screams turned into high pitched squeals. As windows and glass started to shatter, Jane ran over to check on the incubator. She grabbed every towel that she could find along the way. Draping them over the incubator she attempted to muffle the sound. Sitting down at her computer, she watched the fetus' heart beat on the monitor. It was racing, but all his vital signs appeared to be slowly returning to normal. After she released a sigh of relief, Jane tried to calm herself by slowly breathing in and out, while saying, "It's all good. It's all good."

Duncan ran through the doors, shutting them as he went until he reached Claraicy. Seeing Dr. Scott frantically trying to calm her down, he told him, "Doc she's not a baby. You can't go 'shush'. How about you go away and give me a try."

The doctor threw his hands in the air and announced, "Fine, while you try, I'll go and get a stronger sedative for her."

After the doctor left the room, Duncan waited a few seconds for the door to swing shut. Wanting to make sure that the doctor was really gone, he walked over and looked through the small window in the door. The doctor was nowhere in sight. Returning to Claraicy's cage, he asked her, "Don't you want to be human again?"

As the piercing screams continued to echo off of the walls. Duncan doubted that Claraicy even heard him. Bending over and looking straight at her face, he yelled out, "Claraicy, don't you want to be human?"

Claraicy stopped her screaming long enough to yell back, "But I'm not human."

Duncan yelled back at her between her renewed screams, "You are still human. Your body still contains human DNA. It just needs time to revert you back to normal. The doctor is just trying to help you, but he needs your cooperation."

Claraicy's screams turned into moans. "I'm not human. I am better than that. I'm stronger, faster and more agile than any human being on this planet."

Duncan's voice lowered to match Claraicy's. "Being on top of the food chain has its disadvantages. Especially when you are the sole member of a unique species. You have no one to keep you company."

Claraicy tried to spit on Duncan before telling him, "I have Jesse."

Duncan rocked his head back and forth. "Sorry, your daughter is dead."

Claraicy remembered the first explosion and the fur that flew into her face before the second explosion. It didn't smell like Jesse's. Claraicy glared at Duncan. "She's still out there."

"After the explosion, she snatched and killed Ann, the nurse that visited you. My men tracked her down. She severely injured two of them before they ended up killing her. It was strictly done in self-defence."

Claraicy went quiet. She studied Duncan's grim face. "So you are telling me that she is really dead."

Showing Claraicy a little pity, he lowered his head. "When she pounced on one of my soldiers, she left him no choice. It was self-defence. Her lifeless body was last seen floating down a freezing river with a knife inserted through her jaw all the way to her brain."

As Claraicy's sobs turned into relentless crying, Duncan tried to ease her pain. "I'm sorry. She was out of control." Leaning against the bars, Duncan added, "Right now, you have been given a second chance to turn your life around. Trust me, we never wanted to harm you or your child. Remember the trailer we gave you. Remember all the work my men did to try to make you feel comfortable. When Dr. Scott found out about your problem, he sent us out to find you. He only wants to help you get better. If you didn't snap and start attacking everyone, the doctors wouldn't have reacted the way they did."

Claraicy looked at Duncan. His rough, scarred face seemed incapable of showing any emotion, but somehow it did. Feeling helpless, she reluctantly told him, "Do I have a choice?"

Duncan slid his hands up the bars until they were above his head. In a gentle voice he told her, "Claraicy, I'll be back, and I'll make sure you are properly treated, but you have to do your part and let the doctors help you."

As he turned to leave, his body's movements twirled his scent through the air in the room. Claraicy got a good whiff of it and her stomach started to growl. She couldn't figure out if he made her hungry or if there was something else about him.

Duncan visited Drake and MacNeil before leaving. MacNeil was heavily sedated and in a body cast. Hoping that he could hear him, Duncan wish him a speedy recovery while signing his cast, 'Get back on duty you lazy bastard, best regards Colonel Duncan Stuart'. Peering into Drake's room, he caught him reading. With his encased leg tied in the air and his right arm wrapped to his chest there was little else he could do.

Seeing Duncan, he asked, "Well, how is he doing?"

"MacNeil will recover. The ribs punctured one of his lungs. If he was anyone else, a fall like that would have killed him." Duncan smiled at Drake, "The immediate question is, how are you doing?"

Pointing to the image on the wall, he told him, "Wishing I was out there." As Duncan looked at the wind and freezing rain that a camera was relaying, Drake asked him, "Did you find the spawn's body?"

"Not yet," Duncan turned towards him, and added, "When the weather clears, I'm taking DeGroot back out to search for the body. I know how fond you are of that knife, and I want to get it back for you."

Drake gave out a subdued chuckle. "Good luck. If her body is trapped under the ice, you may not find it until spring."

With his hand on Drake's good shoulder, Duncan told him, "I know, but I'm keeping my fingers crossed. I would really like to put this nightmare to bed. Plus, I think I need some time alone with DeGroot. We need to have a good talk."

******

Large flakes of snow were fluttering down when Duncan returned to the bustling camp. The electrified wire mesh above the camp had already been removed. While one of the trailers that had been used as a bunk house was being airlifted away by helicopter, a squad of Colonel Conway's men were packing up and securing everything inside of the hospital trailer. The rest were busy taking down the barbed wire fence, turrets and machine gun emplacements.

Only the communications and Dr. Stern's trailer remained untouched. DeGroot stood outside of the communications trailer. His boots and uniform were parade ready. As Duncan approached, he snapped to attention and threw him a salute. "Welcome back, sir."

Duncan looked at him and grinned. "I'm not going to Court Marshall you."

DeGroot never moved. "Sir, if I was in charge and someone foolishly endangered the lives of the other members of his squad, I would."

Duncan shook his head. "No, a Court Marshall is too easy. I don't want the tax payers of this country to regret all of the money they spent on training you, then turn around and give you free board. No, you're going to work it off and regret what you have done. A good soldier puts his comrades first, mission second, self third and any personal life they have is to be disregarded until he is out of uniform, and far away from the theatre of operation. You screwed up. That spawn almost had you for dinner. Instead, you are walking around without a scratch while two of your team mates are bedridden, one of whom is still in serious condition. They are the ones you will have to answer to."

DeGroot threw Duncan another salute. "I'll make it right, sir. I promise. You won't regret it."

After returning his salute, Duncan brushed some snow off his shoulders and told him, "Well, I'm going in where it is warm." As he walked past the staunch soldier, he asked, "Now, what intelligence do you have on the spawn?"

Following him inside, DeGroot told him, "Nothing. The drones are still doing fly-bys, and the Aurora swept the area a few times. They spotted a few dead animal carcasses along the river bank, but that's all."

Duncan, Degroot and two squads of soldiers were airlifted to the river. The freezing rain and snow had erased all signs of Jesse. The men were divided into three groups, one on the top of each bank, while the rest joined Duncan and DeGroot along the river bank. With the waders and gaff hooks issued to the soldiers working the river banks, they systematically broke through the ice and checked every possible place that her body could either wash up or be held under.

By the afternoon of the second day, they had pulled several caribou carcasses, the remains of a black bear and numerous smaller dead animals out of the icy water. As the sun was starting to set, a soldier on the ridge saw a glare reflecting out of the water. "Colonel, I see something in the river."

The soldier on the ridge, patched through directions to the soldier wading in the water. As he felt along the bottom of the water, he quickly found that his long insulated rubber gloves were useless for identifying small objects. "Am I close?"

The soldier on the cliff patched directions via Duncan. "To your left."

After moving slightly, the soldier sent out a cry, "Awwwooo!"

Duncan yelled out, "What is it."

Holding the blade of the knife, the soldier quickly transferred it to his other hand. "It's a bloody sharp knife, that's what it is."

Twirling his arm, Duncan gestured to him and said, "Bring it here."

The soldier shook off the cut open glove while he waded out of the water. A constant flow of blood dripped out of two of his fingers as he handed Duncan the knife. "I was expecting another shiny dead fish or maybe a pop can, not a razor sharp knife."

Duncan glanced at his hand and told him, "Get that attended to. With the number of carcasses we have dug out of this creek, you don't know what pathogens are in that water."

Forming a fist in hopes that it would slow down the bleeding, the soldier replied, "Yes, sir."

Duncan looked the knife. The only thing shiny on Drake's black titanium knife was the cutting edge. He had a unique way of filing hook-like teeth into the back of the blade. They were designed to rip apart any flesh or bone that the knife came in contact with. Their sharp edges had kept the fish from eating the small red particles clinging between a few of the teeth. Different scenarios ran through Duncan's his mind.

After grappling with all of them, he determined that Jesse must have pulled the knife out of her jaw. The only question left was whether she's dead or not.

After leaving the river bank, Duncan's gut compelled him to go back to the bear den where they had captured Claraicy. Looking inside, he found that the Claraicy's wings were no longer there. The large rocks that had covered them had been rolled away. As Duncan crawled out of the den, DeGroot spotted a familiar set of footprints in the snow and yelled, "Duncan, she's still alive."

******

It took only a week for Claraicy's surgery to heal enough for her bandages to come off, and the agonizing pain to almost disappear. The energy her body needed to recover from her surgery made her hunger pains grow. With the soundproofing the doctor had installed, her cries of anguish went unanswered. Her solitary confinement was only broken at meal time.

No longer strapped to the bed, Claraicy would paced back and forth. Sometimes she would climb the bars and try to hang from the ones on top by her feet. Without her claws, she couldn't. At other times, she would vent her frustration by jumping around the cage, bouncing from one side to the next.

The meals that were slipped through a slot next to the floor were less than desirable. At first, she consumed enough to settle her stomach. After a few more days went by, she stopped eating completely and ignored her growling stomach. None of the food tasted right. Jane had even brought in a pot of beef stew, dished some out and ate it in front of her in an attempt to convince her it was safe. After a couple mouthfuls, Claraicy felt like vomiting.

As Jane and Dr. Scott opened and shut the door, sometimes Claraicy would detect a faint aroma that overwhelmed all of her senses. The smell would drive her wild. She knew that somewhere outside of her room was the food that her body was craving.

Duncan came into Claraicy's room. She pushed herself next to the bars with her face sticking through them as far as it would go. He looked at her frail body. She had lost a lot of weight. "What has been happening to you?"

With her eyes shut, she breathed in Duncan's scent as she told him, "They are starving me. Sometimes after the room is filled with gas, I wake up with new bandages taped to me. They knock me out and do whatever they want to me. I'm nothing more than a lab rat to them."

Duncan took a step closer to Claraicy's cage. "You are not the easiest patient to work with. Maybe the doctor figures that lulling you to sleep would be the least traumatic. Would you rather be strapped to the bed and not be able to move at all?"

Duncan shook his head and stepped closer to Claraicy. "The doctor called and told me that you are refusing to eat."

Claraicy took a deep whiff of Duncan's scent before answering him. "When I eat that garbage, I can't breathe. It's like ingesting poison."

Duncan put his hand on one of the bars. Claraicy immediately turned and starred at it. Spotting a little drool on the corner of her mouth, he pulled it away. Gazing into Claraicy's wanting eyes, Duncan nervously told her, "I'll find out what is going on."

As Duncan was about to leave, Claraicy asked him, "Why do you care?"

Duncan stopped and turned around. "I'm a soldier. When given a mission, I do whatever is necessary to win. The conflict between us was never personal. Out there, you did everything you could to survive. I admire and respect you for that. In a lot of ways we are exactly alike. That's why I care?"

"You are nothing like me. Your scarred face doesn't make you a mutated monster like me. It just makes you a grotesque misfit."

Before he left, he told her, "That's your opinion. Personally, I don't see that much of a difference between us. We are both killers that cannot escape our pasts. In a strange way, that makes us both monsters. Normal people don't kill one another. They find a peaceful way to work things out." Duncan grinned as he added, "But that's not what we do. That's not us."

As he went out the door, Claraicy yelled out, "What about your brother and the soldiers I killed?"

Duncan froze. As the door closed behind him, he answered, "That was war."

******

Down the hall, Jane and the Dr. Scott were in the operating room removing Ratlin's metal halo. Duncan watched them through the door's window. Seeing Ratlin's smiling face was reassuring.

Checking on his men, Duncan felt like a bit of a hypocrite. They were all there because of either Claraicy or her spawn. They knew that in a soldier's world, yesterday's foe could easily become tomorrow's ally. In combat, nothing should be taken personally.

Duncan stepped into the room as the doctor finished bandaging Ratlin's head where the halo had been attached to his skull. Leaning over the edge of

Ratlin's bed, he tried to smile. "How's your neck?"

"Stiff."

Duncan turned to the doctor. "So, how long before he is one hundred percent and can be put on active duty?"

"Physically, his muscles are still going to need some work to get back into shape. He was lucky; his neck and spine weren't as bad as we first thought. Needless to say, it'll be a while."

Looking back at Ratlin, Duncan told him, "I'll talk to you before I leave. Right now I need to discuss something with the doctor."

Jane chatted with Ratlin while she wheeled him back to his room. At the same time, Duncan walked beside Dr. Scott to the lab and asked him, "Claraicy doesn't look that good. What's really going on inside of her?"

"We have been trying to starve the cells out of her, but she isn't eating or drinking enough for her body to excrete them. They are just being reabsorbed and recycled. Claraicy's body is resisting any kind of change. We have to find a way to reverse her body's dependency on gold and revert it back to iron. We have even put her asleep and pumped iron rich food into her stomach. As soon as we remove the tube from her mouth, she throws it all up. At the rate it's going, it could be a long time before we see any results."

The doctor paused and smiled. "But, by the time we are done with her, we will have a much better understanding of what the cells are truly capable of, plus how they function, and how to control them. Isn't that why all those men and women were sacrificed? We have to find the cells and be able to harness their true potential, and have complete control over it."

Duncan crossed his arms and nodded his head in agreement. "If Claraicy doesn't have to endure the harsh wilderness and fight to survive, why should her body feel the need to mutate?"

Dr. Scott stopped and looked at him. "Her upbringing also contributed to her changes. Any badly abused kid would do almost anything not to be victimized again. In severe cases like Claraicy's, many are incapable of having a normal relationship with anyone. In her mind, every person she meets is secretly just like her father. Inside of her, her raging hormones are that of a scared adolescent child. She doesn't need to be under attack to desire claws to help defend herself, wings to escape and body armour to protect herself with. In her imaginary world, everyone is her enemy."

"It is hard to imagine anyone that can fight like she can as a sick, confused child. In battle, anyone that attacks you is the enemy. Their sex and age is irrelevant." Duncan looked back at Claraicy's door. "So what's next?"

The doctor also gazed at Claraicy's door. "We will have to place her into a drug-induced coma and run her blood through a filtering system that is specially designed to extract the cells. Then we'll insert a batch of modified cells, programmed with her own DNA." Glancing towards the lab, the doctor added, "We have already extracted some of her original DNA from her stomach tissue. Jane has been helping me grow enough stem cells to work with."

Duncan inquired, "Are you sure that the cells you took are original? If they are mutated, it could change her into yet another type of monster."

Doctor Scott rocked his head back and forth. "Stomach cells almost never change. Jane is very thorough. She has checked and double checked the cells we had extracted to make sure."

Still looking at Claraicy's door, Duncan asked, "She has lost a lot of weight."

"She will put some back on after we get all the tubes into her. Once she is in a coma she'll be easier to monitor. Maybe by shutting down her fractured mind, we'll find a way to actually control the cells. After all, our original goal was to create a better, more perfect human, not rogue monsters. If all we could produce were monsters, who in their right mind would back our research?"

That night after Claraicy fell asleep, gas was released into her room. Claraicy woke up and covered her face. She had no choice but to breathe it in and slowly sink into a coma. After an hour, the doctor turned off the gas and ventilated the room. When it was safe, Dr. Stern and Dr. Scott entered Claraicy's cage. After drilling holes through her armoured skin, they inserted needles and tubes into various blood vessels and organs. Claraicy's tough skin made it easy for them to look after her. They didn't have to worry about her getting bedsores, rashes and other ailments that most coma patients are inflicted with.

As part of her daily routine, Jane replaced the filters on the equipment that Claraicy was hitched up to. The large monitor in Claraicy's room displayed a snowshoe rabbit hopping across the clearing outside of the building. Jane watched the nervous hare stop and stand upright to look around. Being a lower member of the food chain, it had a very good reason to be scared. After replacing the last filter, Jane looked up at the wintery image on the wall and watched as a few fluffy flakes of snow floating down. Noticing something moving along the edge, she went over to the screen and panned it over to the side. Almost buried in the snow, she could see the head of a young bobcat as it licked blood off its paws. It wasn't much bigger than the hare, but deadly enough to turn it into a feast.

Jane turned around and looked at Claraicy's hands. The ends of her fingers had started to grow back. After verifying that Claraicy's straps were secure, she studied her extended jaw, large eyes and wide turned-up nose. "You probably wish that you were that cat."

Stepping back from the bed, Jane added, "Growing up, I was never scared of boogie men or monsters. I knew that my dog and father would protect me from anything out there. My father never missed when he shot his gun. To him it was always one bullet, one kill. I wish that he was with me right now, because knowing that another creature like you is out there is absolutely horrifying."

New Years was over before the filters stopped showing any traces of the modified cells. Even without the modified cells freely flowing throughout her bloodstream, her body still refused to let go of its newly acquired form. The doctors extracted tissue samples from Claraicy's body on a daily basis. The results continued to worry them. Despite the lack of modified cells, her body was desperately trying to regrow the limbs and tissue that the doctor had cut off, including her oversized canine teeth.

It was mid-January before Dr. Scott had produced enough modified cells that he could start injecting them into her. With new batches available on a weekly basis, the doctor expanded his inject program.

Two days after her third injection, Claraicy woke from her chemically induced coma screaming as loud as she could. "What are you doing to me?"

Jane ran to Claraicy's door and looked inside. Claraicy was violently thrashing about the bed, desperately trying to break free from the padded nylon straps around her wrists and ankles. Her entire bed was rocking from side to side. Despite the wheels being locked, the sheer force of her flailing slowly bounced her bed about the room.

Drake hobbled behind Dr. Stern down the corridor. Dr. Scott wasn't far behind them. With his hands grabbing the back of his head, he announced, "This is what I was afraid of. The cells must be fighting off the drugs instead of correcting her body's cellular DNA structure."

Drake and Dr. Scott held Claraicy down while Jane and Dr. Stern fastened six more straps to the bed. Two additional straps crisscrossing her chest and shoulders holding her shunt steady. Two more straps were attached to each leg, holding them slightly apart so they could check her catheter. As Drake stepped back, Claraicy looked at his face. "You are the one that tried to kill my daughter, ain't you? It was your knife that stabbed her."

Drake's face turned pale. "You mean killed her, don't you?"

"She's not dead. I would know. I'm her mother. I would feel it if she was dead. The same way that I know that it was you that stabbed her? I just know."

******

DeGroot crawled out of another bear den. Duncan and Ratlin were waiting for him and helped him to his feet. While stretching, he blinked to help him get used to the difference of light. "She wasn't in that one either. It looked like a big male this time. How much time does the doctor figure we have before the creature could wake up?"

Duncan sighed. "If we are lucky, maybe three more months. We should have plenty of time to check all the other caves and dens in this area and recheck them if necessary."

"What if she is already dead?"

"Until we find a body, we must assume she is still alive. Right now, her body could be regenerating itself into something that could make her mother look like a harmless butterfly."

Chapter Forty

The Awakening

Jesse stirred out of her slumber. Even in her groggy state, she could smell and hear the soldiers outside of the den. As she raised her head to hear them better, the head of the dead bear that had occupied the den flopped to the side. She waited until their voices faded away in the distance before lowering her guard. With the bear's skin wrapped around her to keep her warm, she slipped back into a deep sleep.

******

Another month had gone by and still no change in Claraicy. Standing behind Jane, Doctor Scott watched the monitor as another series of tests were being analysed. The newly modified cells had managed to block Claraicy's body from regenerating her wings and tail but hadn't been able to revert any cells back to normal. Knowing more tests were needed, Dr. Scott felt that he was overlooking something.

Operating the MRI unit, Jane noticed something strange as Claraicy's head was being scanned. "Doctor, I found something."

Towering over Jane's shoulder, Dr. Scott watched the monitor as she pointed out a bright red blob on the screen. After kissing the side of her forehead, he ecstatically announced, "That's it. That growth is the problem. The cells needed to find a way to coexist so they formed their own command centre at the top of her spinal column in order to coordinate cell reproduction. The DNA in the new modified cells are being suppressed by this new appendage." His voice dropped as he added, "We must figure out a way to either neutralized it or we will have to surgically remove it."

April had brought with it an early spring. The trial period was up. The radiation treatments Dr. Scott was using to shrink the appendage wasn't working. He was left with no alternative but to prepare for brain surgery. As the equipment needed for the specialized surgery was being shipped, the doctors practised on live animals to fine tune the proper technics they would need for the delicate upcoming surgery.

Their practice paid off. The long, six hour procedure went forward without any problems. Afterwards Jane handed Doctor Scott a welded stainless steel cage to go over and protect Claraicy's skull. It was placed on Claraicy's head and locked into position by two bolted on metal straps under her ears, plus over a dozen stainless steel screws into her skull. To suture her tough skin in place, the doctors were forced to use adhesive strips and glue.

Using a variety of different drugs, they managed to keep Claraicy in a coma for two weeks after the surgery. For the first time the results of Claraicy's tests came back positive. The surgery seemed to be paying off.

The first real change they saw was in Claraicy's skin tissue. As she started to shed her armour-like scales, Dr. Scott examined her thoroughly. Scans of her head showed that the portion of her brain dedicated to hearing was shrinking along with the size of her ears. Knowing that it would take months to physically see any change in Claraicy's bones, they measured her X-rays in thousands of a millimetre.

Without a layer of tough skin to protect her, Claraicy's newly formed skin began to suffer from bedsores. Keeping her mildly sedated, Dr. Scott felt that it was time to take off her straps and let her freely walk around her cage. The drugs kept her unusually calm and docile. A week later, she was moved into a new room with all the convenience of a small apartment. Only a locked door separated her from everyone else.

Jane peered into the window from the hallway. On the inside of the room, the small window appeared to be mirror and Claraicy was surprised to see it suddenly turn into a window. Walking over to it, Claraicy saw Jane cradling an infant in her arms. Jane's face was glowing as she looked down at her young charge. After pulling back the blanket to reveal his face, she lifted him up so Claraicy could get a better look.

At first, Claraicy was amazed at all its small perfect features. In a blink of an eye her mood changed to rage. "Why was your baby born normal and not mine? Are you trying to rub it in or something? Is this some kind of new torture you conjure up?"

Picking up a chair, Claraicy flung it at the window. It bounced off its thick, protective layer of plexiglass and struck her knee. As Claraicy screamed in pain, Jane ran down the hallway with the infant pressed against her chest. Everything was caught on the monitors. Lying on the floor in agony, Claraicy's screams caused almost everyone to come running to her room. Drake helped Dr. Scott put her onto a stretcher and wheel her into the X-ray room. The crack in her kneecap was clearly visible.

After elevating Claraicy's leg for several hours, Dr. Scott rechecked her swollen knee. "She will need surgery."

While he waited for some medical supplies to arrive, Dr. Scott extracted the fluid that was collecting in the knee. What should have been a simple operation, was complicated by Claraicy's dense gold saturated bones. The war between the modified cells had left behind misshaped bones that were neither creature nor human. Using fine wire, the doctors carefully tied the cracked kneecap together as best he could.

Jane was waiting outside with a dolly as Marq's truck drove down the driveway. As he got out, he asked her, "I hope everything is going all right in there."

"I goofed up and caused a slight mishap. I didn't mean any harm. Sometimes you can't predict how someone is going to react to something." Jane faced Marq and gave him a soft peck on his cheek. "I'm sorry, I didn't mean to rant."

After putting two boxes on a dolly for her, Marq wrapped his arm around her waist and gave her a gentle squeeze. "It's alright. Will I be seeing you later?"

"Not tonight. I'll let you know when I can get some time off."

Marq watched Jane as she wheeled the two light but awkward boxes through the door. As the door was shutting, he smiled and turned away. Inside the boxes were all the parts for an adjustable, plastic and metal, full-leg cast. Within an hour, the two doctors plus Drake had the cast securely fastened to Claraicy's leg.

*****

As Jesse opened her eyes, her first thought was of her mother. She was starving, but somehow she knew that wasn't what woke her. Something in side of her knew something was wrong. After pushing the thick, heavy bear hide off her, she crawled out of the den. The glare off the few remaining patches of snow hurt her eyes.

Trying to stand, Jesse's legs started to wobble and she tumbled to the ground. Over the winter, she had lost most of her girth and had doubled her height. Her entire body felt awkward and very strange. Every movement she made required her to think and retrain her muscles. Clawing her way up the side of a tree, she finally managed to stand upright. While leaning against the tree, she examined her new body. Her fur had been replaced by the same tough armour that had protected her mother. The claws on her hands and feet were long and sharp. Reaching around to her back, she could feel the bones inside of a huge hump. *I'm turning into my mother.*

She looked around at the patches of snow and barren trees. Inside her head she could hear her mother screaming in agony. Sniffing the air she slowly started to stagger into the forest. She slowly regained her balance and began to walk. Her pace got steadily faster, until she was finally running through the woods. On pure adrenaline, her giant strides glided her through the forest and vaulted her over fallen trees and rocks.

Spotting a deer, she quickly veered off course and ran it down. Leaping on top of it, she dug her claws into its nose and pulled its head back, exposing its slender neck. With one vicious bite to the neck, blood started pouring out of it. While sucking the rich, warm, nutritious fluid, Jesse was oblivious to everything else.

The poor creature bucked, kicked and fought as hard as it could to break free. Jesse's claws and teeth only sunk in deeper. The deer eventually collapsed. Jesse continued to suck and suck until the deer's heart had no more blood to pump out. She remembered her mother's thirst for blood. Her mother would sometimes kill an animal just to drink its blood, than give her the carcass to eat. She needed something in the blood. Now, Jesse needs it.

Standing up, Jesse noticed the fluid flowing down her leg. It was coming from her back. The huge capsule had cracked open during her struggle with the deer. Jesse stretched her arms into the sky as her wings fell to the ground. With blood dripping from her mouth, she threw her head upwards and gave out a rejoicing howl, "AAAOOOWW, AAAOOOWW."

Jesse looked down at the dead animal and dropped to her knees. Within seconds its stomach was ripped opened and she was gorging herself on its heart and liver. With her head buried inside the deer's chest, her hunger overwhelmed her. She hadn't eaten anything for months. Every mouthful she took primed her body for more. Her stomach extended as far as it could. Her tough skin acted like a corset and wouldn't let her swallow any more.

Pulling her blood drenched head out of the deer carcass, she caught her breath. Her huge ears were drenched in blood and had pieces of deer guts hanging off them. Between her long hibernation, the gruelling run, the kill and all she had eaten, her body needed a rest. Lying down next to the warm carcass, she pulled one of her wings over her and fell asleep.

When she woke, she found herself covered in snow, twigs and several small broken branches. Unknowingly, she had slept through a wild, two day long storm. The bones in her wings were no longer as flimsy as they were before, and with the aid of her tail she was able to lift them off the ground.

After quenching her hunger by gnawing on the frozen deer carcass, Jesse thought of her mother. Jesse pulled out one of the deer's kidneys and ate it like an apple as she tried to get her bearings. A gust of wind coming from the south-west caused her to close her eyes and take a deep breath. Her mother's scent relaxed every muscle in her body causing the remaining hunk of kidney to roll off his finger tips and into the snow. The odour was extremely faint but to Jesse it was like she was standing next to her.

Knowing that the wind could change at Mother Nature's whim, Jesse ran through the forest with her nose in the air. Her partially folded wings flopped around and frequently got snagged in tree branches. Forced to go around the denser parts of the forest, her mother's scent would sometimes vanish. When that happened, she would have to wander around until she smelt it again. With each passing hour, the scent got stronger and easier to detect.

******

Ratlin looked down at a strange set of tracks in the snow. A scale from Jesse's new armour clung to a sharp thorn next to her trail. Like a newly hatched butterfly, Jesse's skin was still soft and pliable when the thorn had ripped it off. As the frozen scale thawed in Ratlin's warm hand, he could tell how vulnerable she was. "Duncan come here. The spawn isn't sleeping anymore."

Duncan ran over and glanced at the tracks. "Judging from these, she's even bigger than her mother. I'm afraid that we may have another bloody battle ahead of us."

Ratlin handed Duncan the scale. "She may have woken up early. The scales protecting her are not fully hardened. If we can find her before they do, we might stand a better chance. We need to kill her before she kills any of us."

Chapter Forty-One

The Siege

The bones in Jesse's wings no longer flopped around like rubber dowels. As she jumped over rocks, fallen trees and other obstacles, they helped her gently glide back to the ground. Leaping from the tops of cliffs gave her a rush. Unlike her mother, Jesse found manipulating her wings very easy. She used them to lift herself over small gullies. Travelling around dozens of small lakes, dense thickets, swamps and ravines, it took Jesse over a week to get to Doctor Scott's house.

Standing on the cliff beside the house, Jesse looked at her scratched scales. Most of the marks occured before the storm. Afterwards, her armour had deflected almost all the thorns, sharp rocks and branches that the forest had put in her way.

On top of the large, rocky mound behind the structure, Jesse found the source of her mother's scent. It was a small mesh covered exhaust vent. After ripping the bushes away from it, she pressed her ear next to it. She could hear her mother moaning. She tried to scrape away at the soil between the large boulders. It was useless. There was barely any room between them.

Jesse waited until nightfall before approaching the main structure. In the quiet night air the slightest sound she made was greatly amplified. Only the darkness of the new moon was on her side. After slowly circling the house twice, she finally decided on the best way to get inside. The steel roof was too thick and noisy to claw through and the main section of the house was too exposed. All that was left was the back of the garage.

After lining up her claws like the teeth of a saw, she repetitively scratched groves into the aluminum siding. Within twenty minutes, she had peeled off large pieces of it with hardly making a sound. Shredding through the wood beneath it was much quicker. After pulling out the insulation, the drywall crumbled in her powerful hands without any effort.

As soon as Jesse crawled between the studs, she spotted the door leading to the lab. She crept along the wall and grabbed its handle. She shook it up and down, then from side to side. At the trailer, her mother had made it appear easy. Jesse pushed and pulled at it, but nothing worked.

Frustrated, she smiled and crept towards the corner. As she turned around, her wings fanned out slightly and tripped the motion sensor. The emergency lights turned on and the alarm started wailing. Jesse quickly looked around. Seeing a trash bin in the corner with a wheelchair in front of it, she hid behind them, curled up and waited.

The large door leading into the tunnel sunk inwards, rose a little and slid into the wall behind the shelves. Using great care, Drake emerged in the doorway wearing full body armour. While looking down the barrel of his rifle, he carefully examined the garage before he entered it. He saw the hole in the wall, then the claw marks in the drywall. While retreating back into the corridor, he announced over his walkie, "She's here."

Before he could shut the door, Jesse dashed out and rammed the wheelchair into the doorway. As Drake tried to slam the door shut, one of the rims of the wheelchair became firmly entangled in the door locks. Not wanting to face Jesse alone, Drake stood back and tried to shoot the wheel apart. The bullets only mangled the metal. Holding the door with one hand, Drake released the magazine from his rifle and stuck its barrel into the track inside the wall. "That should stop you from opening it and getting in."

Jesse violently rocked the door back and forth trying to get it open. The force Jesse put on the rifle barrel was tremendous. With each bang, the rifle barrel twisted and widened the top of the metal channel that it jammed into. The rifle barrel slid upward into the newly created gap. With all her strength, Jesse forced the door open enough to peek in. After waiting a few seconds, Jesse glanced into the corridor. No one was there.

After forcing the door halfway open, went inside. She walked past several doors until her senses halted her. Concentrating on opening the door, she ignored the commotion going on down the corridor as Drake and MacNeil escorted Doctor Scott, Jane and the baby away. This time when the door handle didn't work, she twisted it until it broke off.

Claraicy could hear Jesse outside of the door and pushed on it as hard as she could. As the locking mechanism snapped, the door flung opened. With her leg still in a cast, Claraicy twirled around and crashed to the floor.

Jesse didn't recognize her. Confused, she leaped on top of her. As Jesse was about to bite her mother's neck, Claraicy screamed out, "Jesse, it's me."

Jesse stopped and smelled the soft white skin that was mostly covered the collar of Claraicy's white turtle neck sweater. Confused, Jesse ran her nose up and down every part of Claraicy's body. Standing up, she inquired, "Mother?"

"Yes Jesse, I'm your mother." Claraicy looked up at Jesse and smiled. "You have transformed nicely."

Jesse slowly recalled the way Claraicy looked before she had wings and scales. Jesse bent over, wrapped her arm around her mother's neck and helped her off the floor. With arms locked around each other, they walked out the door.

At the end of the corridor, MacNeil and Drake were escorting David and Doctor Stern to safety. The doctor saw the duo and took the pistol out of Drake's holster. With David's legs still not fully regrown, Drake had to support most of his weight. MacNeil dropped to his knee and shouldered his rifle. With the doctor standing in the middle of the corridor in front of him, he didn't have a clean shot. As the doctor began firing the pistol, MacNeil yelled out, "Get down, you idiot."

He didn't. Jesse released Claraicy. As her mother fell to the floor, she zoomed down the corridor. The bullets ricocheted off her hardened scales.

Out of bullets, the doctor froze. Jesse swung her arm and swiped the side of the doctor's face with her claws. His neck snapped to the side. Half of his cheek was peeled off.

MacNeil flipped his rifle to automatic and squeezed the trigger. At close range, the intense concentrated fire tore off some of Jesse's scales. Leaping over the doctor, she landed on MacNeil's shoulders and yanked back his head. As her claws dug under his neck guard, his blood gushed out and sprayed all over the corridor.

Drake and David were almost at the door leading into the lab when Jesse ran towards them. By the time she got within reach, they had shut the door behind them. Jesse charged and threw all her weight against the steel reinforced door, but it didn't budge.

With drool coming out of her mouth, Claraicy crawled down the corridor. A deep craving drove her past the doctor's body. After forcing MacNeil's hands away from his neck, Claraicy latched her mouth onto the gash in his neck. She drank, sucked and lapped up as much of his blood as she could. With every drop of his rich nourishing blood, Claraicy felt herself getting stronger while his body grew weaker. With her hands free, she massaged his heart and tried to extract every drop she could. Looking up from his dead body, she looked around. She wanted more, much more.

While licking the blood off the floor, she finally recognized its scent. It was the strangely simular to Duncan's. She held her bloody hand to her face and looked at it closely. It was more orange then red. As she turned her hand toward the light, she saw how it reflected off the minute golden particles embedded in the blood.

Jesse reached down and lifted her dazed mother to her feet. A ricocheting bullet had grazed Claraicy's arm. With her sweater and matching skirt covered in MacNeil's, the doctor's and her own blood, it was hard to tell how severe the wound was. Unopposed, Jesse picked her mother up and carried her out.

They had only travelled a couple kilometres before they spotted several military helicopters hovering over Doctor Scott's new complex. Jesse shielded her mother the best she could as they flew overhead. Step by step, Jesse slowly retraced her route back to the den where she had spent the winter.

While Jesse scouted ahead, with the aid of a stick, Claraicy hobbled behind her. Though the swamps and over the rougher terrain, Jesse insisted on carrying her. The lack of exercise had weakened both Claraicy's muscles and her stamina. Despite her trembling body wanting to collapse from fatigue, Claraicy was determined to keep moving.

At nightfall, one by one the helicopters had flown away. Without being harassed by them, Claraicy crawled under a tree and rested. With her mother safe, Jesse leaped into the air and stretched her wings. Each time she flew, the flights grew longer and longer.

During the following day, Jesse distracted the search parties and steered them away from her mother. Jesse deliberately appeared and disappeared out of nowhere, making the helicopter crews expand their search area.

As the search intensified, Claraicy was forced into making her own way through the forest. That night, they shared the meat from a dead porcupine. Afterwards, Jesse wrapped her wings around her shivering mother. As large snowflakes floated to the ground, she did her best to keep her warm.

The next day, they could hear the soldiers making their way through the forest trying to flush them out of hiding. Claraicy twisted her head and looked at Jesse. "What's wrong with them? Do they think we are deer?"

Claraicy's clothes were not designed for roughing it outdoors. Despite being cold, wet and covered in thorns, day by day the trek got easier. Before she woke up, Jesse was already gone. Occasionally, Claraicy found food waiting for her along the trail. A dead rabbit, a pile of edible buds off trees or sometimes a handful of enriched dirt.

After a week of trekking through the forest, Jesse surprised her mother with a fleshly killed deer. While Claraicy cleared a small area under a tree for them to sleep, Jesse ripped open the carcass to get to its vital organs. Jesse handed her mother the deer's liver, sat down beside her and ate it with her. With her stomach full, Claraicy curled up under the tree. Jesse watched as she shivered from the cold. After pulling the hide off of the carcass Jesse wrapped it around her mother. The roles were now reversed. Claraicy was the helpless one, and Jesse was now the provider.

******

While combing through the forest, Duncan heard Doctor Scott's voice over his headset. "Duncan, any luck on the search?"

Duncan stood up and looked at the small lake next to the trail he was following. "Not yet. It'll take some time, maybe even weeks, for us to get another Aurora or even some drones back. With the manhunt being old history, the top brass will have to work out another angle to justify cordoning off the park. They can't tell anyone the truth."

Doctor Scott nervously snapped back, "What do we do until then? How about dogs?"

"Too noisy." Duncan glance at the trail and smiled. "Don't worry. With Claraicy's leg in a cast, her trail should be easy to find. They won't be able to hide from us much longer."

As Doctor Scott put down the phone, Jane handed him her latest test results. After only a brief glance, he turned to Jane. "Are you sure they weren't contaminated or somehow switched?"

"Absolutely not. I even ran the sample though three times and got the same results."

"If those results are true, her knee will be completely healed in a couple more weeks."

Flustered, Jane snapped back, "That's not all. The results clearly show that the modified cells from the bats are still firmly embedded in her bone marrow. The sample we took from her knee was full of them. The porous areas that weakened her kneecap were created by newly introduced modified cells trying to kill them off. Since her brain surgery, her entire body has become a genetic battlefield."

"We need to study her now more than ever." Doctor Scott had to look away from her. With both hands on his desk, he leaned forward and bowed his head. "When we created the modified cells using bat DNA, we didn't take into consideration its inherited animalistic will to survive."

Jane approached him and softly said, "But humans share a lot of the same DNA."

Doctor Scott abruptly interrupted her. "Along with other creatures that no longer exist. Lately I've even explored the possibility that once gargoyle-like creatures actually lived. We could have accidentally unravelled their DNA and unlocked a part of evolution that was previously unknown."

"But gargoyles never existed. They are just statues that people put on their homes to scare away their enemies."

"Every legend and myth is somehow based on a grain of truth. I've had some of my European colleagues do some research for me. Most of what they had found was pure fantasy, but one obscure myth they had dug up actually backs my theory."

The doctor went into a cupboard and took out a bottle of whiskey. After taking a sip, he sat back down at his desk and stared at the bottle. "The myth was from a period before castles and medieval fortifications. As the legend goes, a Celtic king staked naked female slaves to the floor of a cave housing a colony of unusually large carnivorous bats. If the bats refused to have anything to do with her, she was deemed clean enough to become a royal servant. If the bats considered her as food, she was left there as an offering."

The doctor turned his chair around and faced Jane. "To that particular species of bats, the scent of a woman in estrus is supposed to be very similar to their own. According to the myth, if enough bats tried to impregnate her, there was a very slight chance that one of their sperms might actually succeed.

The outcome of this barbaric ritual was to obtain winged, hybrid creatures to protect the gates of his wooden palisade."

Jane looked at him in awe. "Why have I never heard of this myth before?"

The doctor smirked, "Until recently, the ancient Roman's had done an excellent job at erasing and rewriting pre Roman history, especially the Celts. They both despised and envied them. This myth only came to light after an engraved gold neckband was discovered in an illegal dig in Northern Europe."

"So this myth was very localized?"

"Yes. Unfortunately for the king, one of his enemies discovered his secret, attacked and destroyed the bat colony. According to the legend, the creatures were so ferocious that local rulers began to carve fake ones to try to scare away their enemies. To this day, you can see statues of chained gargoyles everywhere you look."

Jane smirked. "I always thought that gargoyles were just decorative spouts used to spew water away from tall roofs to protect the building from being covered in the muck from the gutters."

Doctor Scott chuckled. "As I said, the Romans did their best to destroy everything that wasn't Roman. Throughout Europe, ancient practices, religions, sciences, art and customs were all erased. They rewrote history and turned themselves into conquering heroes, instead of the brutal suppressors they really were. Only through modern archeology is the true Goth and Celtic history finally coming to light."

After a brief pause, he added, "However, it is strange that in Roman art, their demons look like gargoyles. Maybe they were other reasons they were afraid to cross the Rhine."

Jane shook her head. "That's all just a myth."

The doctor slapped his thighs. "Nevertheless, I now believe that we should've stuck to apes or monkeys, where more research was known. It would have been easier to deal with the animal activists."

The doctor extended his arms and flexed his fingers. After taking another sip of whiskey, he picked up Jane's clipboard. "Remember what happened in Ryan's body. The modified cells formed their own micro life form. If given enough time, every cluster of modified bat cells inside Claraicy's body could develop into another creature. When we cut out their only method of cooperation with each other, we may have condemned her."

Jane walked over to the baby's crib. "Like the small cluster that formed him?"

The doctor stared at her. "Exactly, but several all at once. Like parasites, they would consume her body for nourishment and maybe even each other. They would do anything to survive."

Chapter Forty-Two

Defiance

After trekking through the cold, wet forest for a gruelling two and a half weeks, Claraicy sat down on a fallen tree outside the den. Jesse went inside, pulled out the thick bear hide and wrapped it around her. It was much warmer than the deerskins that Jesse had provided for her, but too heavy for her to walk around with.

Jesse went back into the den. This time she dragged out one of Claraicy's old wings. Claraicy watched her haul it in front of the log and unrolled it. Inside of it was all the equipment and supplies that she had dug out after the explosion. Claraicy bent down and felt the wings. Tears fell from her eyes. "Why, why did they take them from me? Why did they make me weak again?"

Despite the heavy growth of trees surrounding the den, the beating thunder of helicopters made Claraicy wipe her eyes and retreat inside. Jesse climbed high in a tree. Perched like a gargoyle on a castle wall, her tight leg muscles were ready to pounce into the air after it. She watched the two helicopters whip the branches about as they slowly flew over the forest. Small dead limbs snapped off and were hurled around. Several small pieces hit Jesse, but she didn't flinch. Slowly the helicopters moved on.

******

Doctor Scott's voice came over the helicopter's radio. "Duncan, have you located them yet?"

The beating of the helicopter made it hard to hear. Almost shouting, Duncan answered, "Not yet. We keep losing their trail in a swamps. Stop worrying, they are nowhere near you. You are safe."

Doctor Scott scratched his head. "As long as they know where we are, we are not safe. If you can't trap Claraicy and that creature, at least keep them away long enough for us to salvage what we can."

"We'll do our best."

Jane looked over at the doctor as he hung up the phone. "Do you even know where we're going move everything to yet?"

"Not yet." The doctor looked up at the ceiling and added, "Just worry about backing up all the data and keep on packing. The computers and hospital equipment can be easily replaced. Leave them til last."

As she disconnected an external hard-drive, Jane asked, "Where are you going to safely store all the data?"

Scratching the back of his neck, the doctor told her, "In a bank vault. No one robs them anymore."

******

Seeing a faint line of light green leaves, Duncan told the pilot, "Let us down here."

It was over a kilometre away from where they last spotted Claraicy's distinct trail. Over soil covered earth, her cast and walking stick made her path easy to follow. The stick pushed aside small rocks and poked holes into the ground in a consistent pattern. The heel of her cast did the same. Nothing in the wild makes anything like them.

Claraicy's wide trail also left behind snapped branches and plenty of turned-over leaves and vegetation. Their lightly coloured undersides are what gave the trail away. Drake turned to DeGroot and smirked. "I wonder which swamp this path will lead us to."

Hidden amongst the branches, Jesse watched them go by. Duncan was in the lead. Drake and DeGroot followed carrying heavy backpacks containing most of their supplies. With a lighter pack, Ratlin guarded the rear.

Sitting in a tree, Jesse waited until the sun had ducked behind a cloud. Without even her shadow to warn him, she swooped down and latched onto Ratlin's pack with her feet. He was a metre off the ground before he shouted out, "Duncan!"

As the others turned around to see what was going on, they were clobbered by Ratlin's flailing feet as he struggled to get free. As they jumped up and tried to grab them, Jesse veered to the side. They grabbed their rifles as she carried him through a small gap between two tall pine trees. With barely a shot fired, the pair had vanished behind a grove of tall dense evergreens.

Ratlin pulled out his knife and cut a strap on his pack. The sudden shifting of weight twisted Jesse to the right. Ratlin dropped his knife and clung to the remaining strap with one hand. Pulling out his pistol with the other hand, Ratlin looked back and shot at Jesse's wings. The second bullet grazed the tip of one of them. Jesse reach down and seized Ratlin by the head and twisted it. The thick bones that he had formed in his neck after their last encounter worked in his favour. Facing the ground, Ratlin wrapped his pistol hand under his left armpit and fired every bullet in its magazine.

Most of the bullets ricocheted off Jesse's body armour, however two hit her armpit and managed to get lodged beneath her scales. Releasing her grip on his head, Ratlin fell forward and dangled from the remaining strap of his backpack. Jesse flew as high as she could. Then she let go of Ratlin's pack. The sudden decrease in weight bounced her further into the sky, as Ratlin plummeted towards the hard rocky ground below.

The other soldiers ran through the forest toward the site where Ratlin had fallen. By the time they finally got there, most of his body was gone. The sharp rock that his left knee had landed on had severed the lower half of his leg. That was all that was left of him.

Hearing Jesse return, Claraicy peered out of the den. She saw Jesse sitting on the fallen tree in front of it. Ratlin's body was draped over the end closest to the den. Jesse watched her stare at the body and cheerfully said, "Eat, food."

The smell of Ratlin's body drew Claraicy towards it. Her uncontrollable hunger took over. Picking a knife from the supplies that Jesse had salvaged, she cut open Ratlin's stomach and chest. The golden specks in his liver made her drool. Something inside of her snapped. As if in a dream-like fantasy, she ripped it apart with her teeth and barely chewed before swallowing it down.

Jesse watched the bloody mess with glee. She knew that there would be plenty of meat left over for her. After the feast, with fully extended bellies, they both took a nap.

******

Duncan's men pressed on as fast as they could. After seeing what the surveillance cameras had caught in the corridor, they had a good idea of what was happening to Ratlin's remains. The doctor had starved the cells in Claraicy's body. Now they were fighting back and determined to restore her body back into the barbaric creature she once was.

With Jesse leaving no trail for them to follow, they returned to Claraicy's. Gaps in the trail where Jesse had carried Claraicy over the rough terrain had slowed them down. The path they took wasn't in a straight line, making it even harder for Duncan to pick their trail up again.

If it wasn't for the remains of Ratlin's torn body scattered in front of the den, they might have walked right by it. As soon as he saw the opening, DeGroot whispered, "I remember this den. There was a big black bear inside."

Duncan glared at him and whispered back, "Set up your gun on the right side. Drake, you take the left. I want this entire area covered."

They fanned out from the den and quietly opened up their large backpacks. About twenty-five metres away from the den and twenty metres apart, they unpacked their machine guns, ammunition and camouflage gear. Any further apart, the rocky terrain and tall trees would interfere with their overlapping angle of crossfire, along with being able to cover each other's position.

Duncan carefully approached the den. As he planted two explosive charges on the sides of its mouth, he could hear Claraicy's unique low grunting snores inside. From the outside of her cell, he had heard them on several occasions. Something forced him to recheck the direction of the blasting surface. After aiming them slightly more outward, he crept back to the safety of the tree line. Getting a thumbs up from both DeGroot and Drake, he pushed the button on the remote.

The blast crumbled the rocks next to the opening and sealed the den. A cloudy plume bellowed into the air. Debris bounced off Duncan's helmet as he ducked behind the fallen tree.

A kilometre away, Jesse dropped the rabbit that she had caught and flew to the den as fast as she could. The smell of explosives was the same as before. They were trying to take her mother away from her again.

Despite the camouflaged netting laced with carbon to neutralize their scent, Jesse could smell the faint stench of gun oil and the musky aroma of the hidden men. She halted her haste. From a vantage point on top of a tree, she carefully surveyed the area around the den. The only sounds she heard were the faint moans coming from the rubble. She knew that at least her mother was still alive.

A sudden gust of wind caught hold of Jesse's left wing. As it slightly fluttered in the breeze, Duncan easily picked her out. Knowing how sensitive Jesse's ears were, Duncan didn't speak. With a few clicks over the radio, he transferred all the information his men needed to know. Three clicks to warn Drake, seven clicks to tell him that she was behind him at his seven o'clock position. Drake clicked three times to verify that he understood the transmission. Duncan turned his attention to DeGroot. Two clicks followed by four told DeGroot that Jesse was at his four o'clock. If she attacked from there, she would almost fly right over Drake. Duncan ended with a series of oddly spaced clicks to tell them that the helicopters were already on their way.

As the two shifted their machine guns slightly, Jesse became aware of the clicks and the small movements beneath what looked like strange shrubs. She climbed down the back of the tree and snuck out of sight.

The three soldiers waited for something to happen. Sweat ran down Drake's forehead. The sweat started to freeze by the time it reached his chin. He knew that if the creature had spotted them, his position was more open and would most likely be attacked first. Even if she hadn't spotted them, he knew that the creature could suddenly appear from nowhere. Either way he had to be mentally and physically ready for her.

With his position semi-protected by thorny thickets, DeGroot aimed his gun towards Drake's somewhat weaker position. Duncan crawled inside the small crevice that the explosion had created above the den. From there, he tried to get a better overview of the area.

Carrying a heavy log in the claws of both her hands and feet, Jesse fell from the sky in a blur. She soared adjacent to the ridge with all the speed she could generate. By the time Duncan spotted her, it was too late to be discreet. "DeGroot, above you!"

Both Drake and Duncan opened fire. With DeGroot's gun facing in the opposite direction, Jesse dropped the log, end first, straight down on top of him. Her beating wings along with the sudden weight loss bounced her upwards into the air. Amongst a hail of bullets she quickly flew out of sight.

Hearing the beating of helicopter blades, Drake got the courage to crawl out of his hole and run over to DeGroot. He toppled the log that was sticking into the ground and pulled off the mesh canopy. DeGroot's head was completely smashed in and his chest was embedded into the barrel of the machine gun. His legs and one remaining arm flapped around in a jerking manner. There was nothing he could do.

In total shock, he gazed at his dead friend as Duncan announced, "Drake, she's coming back."

Drake ran back towards his machine gun nest. The helicopters were right behind Jesse as she dove towards him. Her left foot latched onto his shoulder as the helicopters poured fifty caliber shells on top of them. As she tried to fly away with Drake, a section of her right wing was torn off by the massive hail of armour-piercing bullets. As she spiralled downward, the bullets indiscriminately ripped through both Jesse and Drake's bodies. Releasing him only slowed down her fall. With her wings no better than an airless parachute, Jesse plummeted into the trees.

******

Duncan climbed out of the crevice and down the pile of rubble. The pile consisted mostly of dirt, rocks and gravel. The explosion wasn't meant to cave in the den. Its goal was to confine Claraicy, not kill her. With his ear pressed against the rock, he could hear her coughing as she tried to dig her way out.

He walked over to DeGroot's body and kneeled. Parts of him were mashed into hamburger. "It's over. This time the dice weren't in our favour."

Duncan saw Drake's body hanging in a tree. His neck was broken along with both arms and a leg. The broken stump of a branch was lodged under his collar bone. The helicopter's armour-piercing shells had turned his corpse into a bloody rag. "You were always the brave one. You should have stayed at your post. I'm going to miss you. Knowing that you always had my back had been a comforting relief when we was on a mission."

Duncan looked down at where his tattoo once was. "Now, I am the last Green Dragon and I don't even have anything to show it."

Circling above him, one of the helicopter pilots told Duncan, "Sorry for your comrade. We were under strict orders. Our rules of engagement dictated that the creature was to be killed, at any cost."

With tears in his eyes, Duncan looked up. "I know. I'm the one that dictated them to your superiors." Looking down at DeGroot's remains, he added, "Have you spotted the creature's body?"

"No, not yet, but our bullets sliced her to ribbons. What's left of her could've fallen through the trees. You might have to do a ground search."

While slowly shaking his head, Duncan quietly relied, "With who? I'm the only one left."

Using a small explosive charge, Duncan felled the tree Drake was in and dragged his body into a clearing. Next to it, he dragged DeGroot's corpse and the body bag containing Ratlin's remains. After he piled as much wood as he could find on top of them, he saturated it with all the naphtha fuel he had and lit it. As the flames engulfed the pile, he snapped to attention and gave his men a final salute. No words were good enough and none were said. The air beating down from the helicopters fanned the fire and produced flames that reached above the top of the trees. Duncan stood there at attention until the flames started to die out.

As the helicopters left to retrieve the equipment and manpower needed to extract Claraicy, Duncan collected the bones of his comrades. Behind him, Duncan heard a rock roll off the pile of debris. Glancing over he saw a hand, then an arm, emerge. He walked over to the small hole and saw Claraicy's open mouth gasping for air.

Pulling down his zipper, he pissed into her gasping mouth. Claraicy scrambled away from the opening. Duncan continued to urinate over the dirt and rocks. "Taste good?"

Claraicy retreated to the back of the den. Using her hands, she fumbled through the stuff Jesse had collected. A rifle taken from a soldier was easy to identify. She aimed it at the hole and pulled the trigger.

Duncan had heard the distinctive metallic click of the bullet being inserted into the chamber and had immediately stood back. Claraicy fired another blast. The exhaust and percussion from the bullets turned the air in the confined space into a thick cloud of dust. Worse yet, the final bullet hit the rock above the hole causing more debris to cascade down and fill it in.

Duncan talked into his headset. "Get me up."

The closest helicopter turned around and landed on top of the ridge. After carefully planting two explosives above the den, Duncan climbed into the craft and told the pilot, "Fall back a hundred metres."

From behind the ridge Duncan set off the remote. The top of the ridge bounced and a quarter of it slid forward. "That'll hold her until we get back."

Flying over the area to check the extent of the damage, Duncan smiled. "As long as she doesn't run out of air, she should be all right." Turning to the pilot, he asked, "Still no word about her spawn?"

"Nothing, sir."

Tears filled Duncan's eyes as the helicopters flew off. Trying to think about his mission, Duncan pulled out a pad of paper and made a list of the equipment and manpower that he would need to extract Claraicy, along with recovering Jesse's body. Dead or alive, he had to retrieve both of them.

******

Using only one arm, Jesse pulled herself towards the den. The full metal jackets on the shells had no trouble penetrating her armour. Both of her legs and her other arm were shattered. Three shells had torn holes straight through her abdomen and two more through her left lung. Somehow she remained alive.

The fire was still smoking as Jesse made her way to where the opening of the den once was. The pile of debris was gently sloped in front of it. She sniffed the air. After a brief look around, she pulled herself up the rocky slope. She stopped at a depression three-quarter of the way up the ridge.

The small gap was made when the explosives loosened several adjoining large boulders and rocks fell into the cracks to hold them apart. Exhausted, Jesse rested face down next to it. With her ear pressed against the rock, she could hear small stones rattling down the crack. Despite having limited use of her remaining lung, she breathed in her mother's scent. Content, battered and exhausted, she slowly drifted into unconsciousness.

Jesse was awakened by the sound of her mother coughing. Weak from lack of blood, all Jesse could do was lay there. Caked in dirt, her blood soaked body was the same colour as the rocks around her. As a helicopter approached, Jesse used her body and what was left of her wings to conceal the opening and protect her mother's only source of air.

The dust clouds the returning helicopter stirred up, helped fill in the edges of Jesse's bullet-riddled body and what was left of her wings. From the air, she appeared to be just another mound of the rubble.

Despite her face being sunk into the depression, Jesse could still hear what was going on around her. Like a canyon, the loose boulders magnified and echoed every sound. Some groups of men were busy setting up camp, while others were unchaining a back hoe along with the other equipment that was being airlifted in. At dusk, a mild rain drove Jesse into a frenzy. She had neither the strength to fight or flee. All she could do was lay there. As her body temperature plummeted from the cold rain, she slowly sank into a coma.

Streams of rainwater flowed down the gap. Claraicy wrapped the bear skin over her and directed some of the water into her mouth with her hand. After getting her fill, she used her hands like a funnel and filled both canteens that Jesse had salvaged. While chewing on part of Ratlin's leg that she had pulled off his carcass, Claraicy contemplated what was going to happen to her. She had a little food, some air, water and shelter. What she didn't have was time.

The back hoe started its engine shortly after dawn. It pushed away all the dirt, gravel and smaller debris that it could, before shutting down. A loud blast barely caused any dust inside the den. The boulders seemed to stand their ground and didn't budge. The back hoe roared up and went back to work clearing away the newly formed mound of rubble.

All morning and into the afternoon the men blasted, cleared, then blasted some more. The small, well placed blasts broke apart the larger rocks and boulders without creating excessive amounts of debris for the engineers to clear away. They also tried to control the blast in such a way that the debris didn't come down on Claraicy. Duncan wanted to get her out alive.

As the side of the ridge was cleared, the pressure holding the boulders apart eroded away. Millimetre by millimetre, the small gap widened and Jesse's comatose body sank deeper inside it. Each blast shook the mammoth boulders and the smaller rocks worked their way down into the crack and helped wedge them further and further apart.

By the end of the second day, Jesse regained the strength to open her eyes. Looking into her mother's face, she extended her good arm. To her delight her mother reached up and grasped her hand.

Claraicy could feel how weak her daughter was. She couldn't even squeeze her hand. Claraicy spoke quietly as she tried to console her delirious daughter. "I'm alright."

In barely a whisper, she replied, "Jesse, not, well."

With tears in her eyes, Claraicy choked out, "I know, but I'm here."

When most of the debris was gone and the original solid rock face of the ridge was finally exposed, the workers stopped. The outline of the top of the den's opening was finally visible. The back hoe wasn't designed to excavate such small areas.

The workers' muffled voices filtered into the den. "We'll have to drill and sink a series of charges into the rock to crack it enough to move any more... We can't. ... That'll cave it in. ... It'll have to be done by hand. ... That'll just have to wait 'til tomorrow. ... A storm is coming. ... A lot of rain. ... What if the rain doesn't stop. ... It could take days."

The rumbling roar of thunder shook the rocks above Claraicy and the rain sent the men running for shelter. It continued throughout the night and most of the next day.

As the men huddled in their tents, Jesse could feel the rocks beneath her shift. The gap funnelled rain water the den. Claraicy piled rocks to stand on in order to stay dry. A large crack of lightning and roll of thunder concealed the slippery mud slide that shifted two boulders forward and opened the gap even further.

One of the engineers poked his head out of their tent. "Shit, part of the ridge gave way. Now we'll have to clear away even more debris. That'll cost us at least another day, maybe even two."

With the lower half of Claraicy's body covered in mud. She reached up and grabbed Jesse's lifeless hand. She used it to help her get free and climb into the gap. Once inside, Claraicy shifted her body and legs to help her climb out. She braced her legs against the boulders. Then she used her arms, shoulders and back to lift Jesse ahead of her as she climbed out.

With Jesse lying on the ground, Claraicy gently shook her and checked her breathing. She was barely alive. After finding a stick that she could use as a crutch, Claraicy grabbed Jesse good hand began dragging her over the ridge and down the far side.

A fast moving creek lay in front of them. She had no choice. She wrapped Jesse's arms around her and told her, "If you have any strength left, hold on."

Claraicy stuck her hand through a section of Jesse's wing that had been torn by the shells and wrapped her arm around Jesse's torso. She wrapped her other arm around Jesse's neck. After taking a deep breath, she leaned forward and dove into the swift current.

Jesse's wings flopped around and occasionally got caught up in branches and other debris. The fast current would pull them free. At times her wings acted at like a surfboard, at other times a shield against the jagged rocks and tree branches. Unfortunately in the deeper water, they also acted like a heavy blanket, holding them under fighting for air. All Claraicy could do was hang on to her daughter as the swift current pushed them along.

Suddenly the long wild ride was over. Claraicy tried to stand up but the water was too deep. Struggling to keep both of their heads above the surface, Claraicy looked around. The rushing current had swept them into a small lake.

Chapter Forty-Three

Retaliation

The water rushed away from the mouth of the swollen creek, pushing them further away from shore. Claraicy desperately fought to keep both of their heads above the water. The rain pouring down made matters worse as they both gasped for air.

The doctors had stripped away her armour, claws and wings, but not her mother's relentless drive and determination to protect her young. Her cast weighed her down. Jesse's wings acted like heavy foliage covered nets. However, the branches stuck in them helped keep the pair afloat. Swimming the half dozen metres to shore seemed impossible, but somehow they made it.

The moment Claraicy got to shore, she rolled Jesse onto her side. She couldn't do much to help her. Rocking her back and forth, she tried to get as much water out of Jesse's lungs as she could. After Jesse spewed out some water and gasped for air, Claraicy dragged her under a large fir tree and wrapped what was left of her wings around her. That was the first time she had seen the true extent of Jesse's injuries.

After collecting some yarrow, moss and clay, she tried to remember what Ryan had taught her. First the yarrow to stop the bleeding, then the moss to control it, and lastly the clay to seal and protect the wound. Looking down at Jesse, Claraicy couldn't believe that she was still alive.

Claraicy was so cold that she no longer shivered. Despite this, all that she could think about was Jesse. After finding a walking stick, she began searching the area for anything that she could use for shelter. A short way down the shore, she had found parts of a burnt tent. Looking around, it dawned on her where she was. It was where she had killed Willy and Patrick Leer. With her leg, she figured that Ryan's cabin was only a few days away.

The rain never let up and neither did Claraicy. Holding on to Jesse's good arm, she dragged her through the forest. She used up every bit of her energy she had. Like wearing a raincoat, Jesse's armour helped maintain her body's heat. One of Jesse's wings was only three quarters there and her other had been whittled down to a third. Still, they acted like a sled and partial shelter as Claraicy pulled her along.

The rain on Jesse's face hampered her breathing. Each time she breathed more water got into her good lung. Every fifteen minutes, Claraicy would stop, roll Jesse over and try to get out as much water out of her lung as she could.

Taking the time to redress Jesse's wounds, Claraicy discovered that the bullet holes had completely stopped bleeding. Not wanting to take any chances, she placed large pieces of bark over her to help protect the wounds from the rain. Afterward she tied a piece of birch bark to Jesse's forehead in an effort to try to keep the rain off her face.

Exhausted, Claraicy placed Jesse under a large overhanging rock and curled up next to her. With their bodies pressed together, she could feel how badly Jesse's temperature had plummeted. She knew that they needed to get to the cabin as soon as possible. Her fragile exhausted body had the final say in the matter as she fell into a deep sleep.

She dreamt about was the time that she had sat in the freezing rain wanting to die. She remembered how she couldn't. Feeling her large belly, she smiled. She knew that if she couldn't, neither should Jesse. With that revelation, Claraicy woke.

She could no longer feel Jesse's heart beat or detect her breath. Claraicy stood up and shrieked, "You can't be dead. If I can't die, neither can you."

It had been raining for days with no signs of stopping. Claraicy used her stick to help her to her feet. She grabbed Jesse's arm and started walking. At noon of the following day, they finally reached the cabin. Claraicy wasted no time in lighting the wood stove and putting some water into the bottom of a small pot to boil.

The cabin had been almost picked clean. A can of tuna had rolled behind several cans of green beans, corn and peas. That was the only source of meat left. While sipping on the hot water, Claraicy rummaged through the cupboards and drawers for an opener. A butcher knife was the best she could find. After pushing it into the top of the can, she worked the blade around the lid until she could bend it enough to empty it's contents into a pot. After opening the other cans, she filled the pot and placed it onto the stove.

After eating and sipping on some hot water, Claraicy lay on the bed next to Jesse and felt a faint heartbeat. With Jesse's stomach wounds, she felt that she couldn't force her to eat anything. The hot cabin dried up the scales that the continuous rain had started to soften. On the badly damaged wing that Claraicy was dragging her on, some of Jesse's scales were over half worn away. Others had been ripped off.

As Claraicy tried to relax, painful muscles cramps began to spread over her body. Unable to move, she fell asleep with her arms wrapped around Jesse.

The rain stopped overnight, and with the sun Claraicy knew that the men would soon discover her disappearance. Too sore to move, Claraicy quietly lay in the bed next to Jesse. Covered in blankets, even without a fire they were nice and warm. It was almost noon before she tried to get out of bed.

Startled by the movement of the bed, Jesse woke up spewing water out of her mouth. Jesse's sudden and violent reaction made Claraicy's stiff muscles reel with pain as she tried to quickly twist around.

******

The rain had kept everyone back at the den inside. As one of the men looked out of his tent, he saw nothing. The dark dreary sky had masked the last bit of smoke coming from the cabin. "Come on, lets get back to work."

Duncan surveyed the area and saw the gap. Using a camera attached to a long stick, he examined the abandoned den. He went to his bunk and put on his headset. "Doc, bad news. Claraicy is no longer under the rock. We found all her stuff, but she somehow escaped."

A few seconds went by before he got a response. "In that case, to be safe, we'll have to relocate the lab."

Duncan tried to console the doctor. "I wouldn't worry too much. It took her over two weeks to get here, and that was with help."

The doctor snapped back, "I'm not worried about her. What about her spawn? You still haven't found its body."

"We have found enough evidence to tell us that her spawn is probably dead. We have recovered huge sections of her wings and are still searching for her body."

"What if she isn't?"

"Even if she had survived the attack, it would take months before she could heal enough to cause us any concern. I don't think you have anything to worry about. She can't fly or walk and you had rendered her crippled mother almost totally defenceless."

******

Claraicy looked out the window and saw helicopters flying around in the distance. "All that rain had to have washed away our tracks. We should be safe for a while."

Afraid of going outside and leaving visible evidence that someone was there, Claraicy studied her surroundings through the windows. The more she moved around, the less her muscles hurt. Mounted on a rack beside the cabin were two canoes. From the side window, Claraicy could examine the hull of the canoe on the top rack. It appeared to be in good shape. Gazing at Jesse, she knew what she had to do, and where she had to go. She went back to bed and rested. It was going to be a long cold night.

******

There weren't many clues for Duncan to follow. All he could do was surmise what he would have done. On the far side of the ridge he spotted a piece of Jesse's wing wrapped around a jagged stump. "The spawn has still got some life left in her."

Standing on top of the ridge, Duncan studied the terrain. Near the bottom of the ridge was a muddy, meandering trail that was created by all of the rainwater that had flowed away from the ridge. The branches on both sides of the small muddy trench indicated the height the water rose and the furious speed it was travelling. "It must have swept them away. In their condition, neither one of them could've crossed it."

Getting into a small two-person helicopter, he oversaw two teams of soldiers as they scoured the forest below him. With one team on both sides of the muddy trench, they followed it all the way to the lake. It was getting dark and Duncan ordered the pilot to land.

As the men poured into the campsite where Duncan had found his dead brother, they found him sitting on a rock with a tear in his eye. "Set up camp. We'll stay here tonight and continue the search in the morning."

That night, Duncan walked around the campsite with clenched fists. Even with all the rain they had, some of his brother's blood still stained the rocks along the side of the campsite.

The rut that Claraicy created by dragging Jesse behind her marked a path straight to the cabin. The rain had actually worked against her by softening the ground. As she pulled Jesse behind her, she not only created a trench into the ground, but also displaced a lot of the vegetation.

Inside the cabin, Duncan saw the remains of Claraicy's cast piled next to the door. Outside, the trail the canoe made as Claraicy dragged it down to the lake was impossible to miss. Studying Claraicy's footprints in the mud, he found that they were strong and steady. They showed no sign of her knee injury.

"It was her cast that was slowing them down. They could be anywhere by now." Infuriated, Duncan gave out a loud, screaming roar as he grabbed his rifle and blasted its entire magazine into the water in front of the cabin.

******

Duncan immediately order a helicopter to take him to the cavern. The trailer had already been extracted and only the wooden patio remained. Duncan and another soldier slowly emerged from the dark water into the cavern with their rifles pressed against their shoulders. It was the same as they had left it when they had removed the cameras. Footprints from army boots still littered the floor. Claraicy hadn't been there.

******

The gossip that Claraicy had overheard between the doctors about David's ordeal was useful. Finding the small cave that he hid in was easier then she thought it would be. Dressed in a shirt and a pair of pants that she found in the cabin, she looked into the tunnel at the back of the cave. Radiating from it were distorted, unrecognizable echoes from the two men in the cavern.

Claraicy smelled the sharp, tangy aroma from the mixture of minerals and gold in the dirt below her. She looked back at Jesse. Covered in the thick material off Ryan's mattress, she appeared peaceful.

Claraicy's nose lead her down into the same narrow tunnel that David had been chased through by the bats. She stopped. There was no need to continue. Even in the pitch black she could sense a large cash of gold-laced soil in the wall of the tunnel. With her fingers she began to wiggle and remove some stones and pebbles out of walls.

Claraicy smelled everything she touched, and sometimes licked it. She rejected a large amount of debris and simply rolled it down the tunnel. In the soft decaying guano, the rolling rocks barely made a sound. A couple hours had gone by without her knowing it. Feeling extremely parched, she snapped out of her gold frenzy.

With her pockets full of gold-laced earth, Claraicy began crawling out of the tunnel backwards. In a wider section of the tunnel, she turned around. When she got back to Jesse, she found her barely conscious. Taking the richest pebbles and grains from her shirt pocket, she placed them inside Jesse's mouth, massaged her throat and forced her to swallow.

Over the following few days, Claraicy watched Jesse's wounds slowly heal over. However, without being able to eat anything, her strength was slowly withering away.

Over the following weeks, Claraicy's skin, claws and senses developed much quicker than before. It was as if her body was like a desert flower waiting for rain. Everything she ate seemed to help rejuvenate her body. The planes, helicopters and drones were easy to spot and avoid as they scoured the entire park and surrounding area.

Between snaring rabbits and stocking prey with Ryan's butcher knife, she had enough to eat. Using upper skull of a rabbit as a spoon, Claraicy poured her preys' rich blood into Jesse's mouth. Though Jesse's mind grew clearer, her body continued to deteriorate.

Everything Claraicy did for her seemed to only prolong her life. One night, as Jesse slept, she sank into a coma and wouldn't wake up.

Desperate, Claraicy tucked the blanket around Jesse and blocked the entrance with branches before getting into the canoe. She only knew of only one person that was capable of helping her daughter. Travelling by night, she ditched the canoe after four days and completed the journey by foot.

The hole Jesse had made in the garage wall had been repaired. Claraicy needed to find another way inside. She knew that if she was captured, Doctor Scott would have no reason to help her dying daughter. She needed some kind of leverage. Ten metres from the garage door, she crouched down and waited patiently behind a bush while trying to come up with a plan.

Shortly after daybreak, Claraicy saw Jane arrive. After placing her face in front of a small screen, she pushed a six digit code into the pad below it. Concentrating on her task, Jane never saw Claraicy sneak up along the side of the house. When the door opened, Jane stepped inside. The door was set to automatically close and lock behind her.

Not this time. Claraicy gently tossed a stick against the inside of the doorframe. To Jane, the sound of the stick hitting the frame was simular to the door shutting. Walking straight to the basement laboratory's door, she proceeded to unlock it.

Claraicy stealthily scooted around the inside perimeter of the garage. As the basement door opened, Claraicy grabbed Jane by the throat with one hand. "You have always been good to me. I don't want to kill you."

After wedging an empty paint can into the doorframe with her free hand, Claraicy looked into Jane's eyes. They were fiery red. Her eyes told Claraicy that Jane wasn't yet ready to die. Side by side, the pair walked down the steps. Claraicy could see the cameras sticking out of every corner of the ceiling. As one moved, she knew she was being watched. Over a speaker came, "Release her and stand aside with your hands clearly visible."

Claraicy never budged. Instead, she squeezed Jane's neck until she started to choke. Over the speaker came another warning, "Release her or we will be forced to gas the room. Either way, you cannot escape."

Claraicy looked around. "If you gas this place, she will die. My body can withstand a lot more than hers."

Marq drove into the driveway and got out of his truck carrying Jane's purse and a paper bag containing her lunch. He felt that she had left them on his kitchen table, just for him to have a reason to visit her.

Seeing the stick wedged into the doorframe, Marq returned to his truck. He pulled the gun case out from behind his seat. He opened it and took out his .270 caliber semi-automatic Browning hunting rifle. After removing the trigger lock, he slapped in a full magazine. He loaded a shell into the barrel, took out the magazine and replaced the missing shell. That would give him five shots. With two spare clips in his pocket, he cautiously walked towards to the wedged open door.

Claraicy had never been in the lab before. She tried to look around as she watched the handle on the metal door leading to the main corridor. As she led Jane into the centre of the lab, the room echoed, "What do you want?"

Claraicy looked towards the speakers and replied, "Help, my daughter needs your help."

"You'll have to bring her here."

Infuriated, Claraicy screamed, "Not as a prisoner. My daughter will never become one of your test animals."

As the door handle started to turn, Claraicy eased her hold on Jane's throat. Marq peeked in and saw Jane gasping for air. With all of Claraicy's attention focussed on the door handle, she didn't notice Marq shouldering his rifle.

The moment the hall door started to open, a bullet tore through her ear and ricocheted off the side of her head. Claraicy turned around and flung Jane over the counter.

Landing at the foot of the stairs, Jane wrapped her arms around Marq's legs and threw off his aim. Both his second and third bullets missed their mark. Claraicy picked up a metal stool and threw it against the electrical panel on the wall. Sparks zapped through the air as the lights went out.

Marq grabbed Jane's arm and dragged her out of the door while firing his last two shells in the direction he had last seen Claraicy. Using the light coming in through the open garage door, Marq ejected the spent clip and slapped a full one into his rifle. While gasping for air, Jane got to her feet and ran out of the garage. Marq walked backwards blasting four more shells into the dark doorway.

Once outside, he ran to his truck. Jane was already in the driver's seat with the engine running. Before Marq could shut his door, Jane stepped on the gas pedal. The truck's oversized tires threw a wall of dirt and stones after them as they tore apart the gravel driveway. Before getting onto the main road, Jane stopped and looked at Marq. "What about Adam? He is just a helpless child."

Marq shook his head. "Just go. There is no way she can penetrate that fortress."

With her hands glued to the steering wheel, Jane froze. Overcome by emotion, she started to sob. Marq got out and ran around the truck and opened the driver's door. "Move over, you are in no condition to drive."

Jane grabbed his arm, and bellowed, "We have to go back."

Marq pointed to the helicopters racing towards the lab. "How? The army isn't about to allow anyone near that place."

******

Claraicy watched as the door opened revealing a bright tunnel. Standing tall and authoritarian, Doctor Scott appeared in the doorway in his white lab coat. "Claraicy, come into the light."

Something inside of her compelled her to step forward. "Can you save my daughter?"

He stepped into the lab and shook his head. "Not without placing her entirely in my care. The helicopter that shot her had a camera aboard it. From the amount of damage she received, the cells that are keeping her body alive may not think it's worth saving. I would have to perform drastic surgery on her. Even then, I can't guarantee she will survive."

In the dim light he could only make out Claraicy's outline. Stretching his arms towards her, he added, "There is still plenty of time to save you. Come and let me help you."

David appeared behind the doctor and stepped forward shouldering a rifle. In the dark room he didn't have much to aim at, but he sprayed the lab with bullets anyways. A shell glanced off Claraicy's shoulder. Something inside of Claraicy snapped. As David reloaded his rifle, she jumped on the counter and leaped on top of him. With her claws not fully regrown, it took a half dozen lightning quick slashes to rip open his throat.

Seeing all the blood spraying out, Claraicy bellowed out a glass shattering roar. Doctor Scott slowly stepped backwards into the hallway as Claraicy started to suck the potent enriched blood out of David's body.

By the time Claraicy's blood rush was over, Doctor Scott had locked the door to the main corridor behind him. On her hands and knees, she looked at the locked door and yelled out, "If I bring Jesse to you, will you help her? If you save her, I would even be willing to surrender myself to you."

Claraicy listened for a reply, but got none. "I would rather have her alive and healthy than be free with no one to love."

With his back resting against the door, Doctor Scott heard every word. Shaking his head, he didn't know what to do. Smashing the door with his fist, he replied, "She is much too dangerous to be ever set free."

Bewildered, Claraicy stood up and walked up the steps to the garage. The sun shone directly into the garage's doorway. As she was about to step out, she only got a glimpse of the helicopter before it opened fire. A large shell tore through her thigh and knocked her backwards. Even inside the dark garage she wasn't safe. The armour piercing shells riddled the garage doors and the wall behind her. They sliced two long gashes into the side of the large oil tank used to run the boilers that heated the facility. The oil ran down into the basement and under the doorway leading into the large corridor.

Claraicy hid behind the doctor's Landrover until she smelt gas. A fuel line in the engine had been hit. After spotting a group of bullet holes in one section of the back wall, she rammed it with all of her might. It wasn't good enough and she bounced off. On her second attempt, she broke through as another burst of shells ripped through the garage. Before she could stand up, a bullet sliced a battery cable on the Landrover and the spark ignited the gas fumes. Within a millisecond the entire garage exploded.

The blast exiting the hole picked Claraicy off the ground and almost tossed her into the woods. In rapid procession, the cylinders in a locked storage cage exploded. The first one shot the landrover through the wall. First it flipped back over front and then side over side. Claraicy barely had time to jump out of its way as it rolled passed her.

The percussion from the blasts spun the helicopters almost out of control. As the scattered debris from the steel roof rained down from the sky, they quickly retreated as fast as they could.

Doctor Scott opened the door to Adam's room. It looked like any normal two-year-old's room. The doctor found him huddled in the corner behind the dresser. He walked over, gently picked up and hugged the frightened child. Adam was the prize result of all his experiments and research, combined with all the love and nurturing in which Jane had given him. He thought of him as a son.

As the smoke filled the corridor, the water sprinklers activated. The water helped the oil to spread even faster. With the floor covered in oil, it was hard to even stay upright. The doctor slowly worked his way to the door. Between the explosion and water, the lock had been shorted out and the door wouldn't open.

Doctor Scott looked towards his private lab at the other end of the tunnel. Looking down at Adam's face, he said, "Don't worry, there is another way out."

The lights started to flicker as he turned and slipped. While trying to get back up, oily water splashed over both of them. The doctor held Adam tight as an electrical spark from a backup emergency light ignited the fumes of a ruptured gas line into a raging fireball. The blast's combustion ignited the oil.

******

As the flames died down, Duncan entered the ruins and began searching through the rubble. He knew that neither door leading into the tunnel was accessible without electricity. However, the emergency escape exit was fashioned after a combination bank vault.

Duncan ran outside and skirted along the edge of the rocky mound. Protected by brush, finding it wasn't easy. He noticed that the texture of what looked like a large boulder was different from the rest. Using the butt of his rifle, Duncan cracked and smashed chunks of plaster off the exit.

After yanking and ripping off the chicken wire that held the plaster in place, parts of the stainless steel door became visible. Wasting no time, Duncan planted a series of small charges next to where the pins were hidden inside the walls, ceiling and floor.

The blast twisted the frame of the hot door inward. Using his shoulder, Duncan rammed into the door several times. Finally it was open wide enough for him to enter.

The once white cement block walls were darkened by the fire. There had been very little flammable material inside. The only smoke that Duncan could see was from some filing cabinets, melted electronic equipment and the furniture in Adam's room. The doctor's corpse was still clinging to Adam as if he was still trying to protect him from the fire. Duncan looked around and then down at them. Shaking his head he whispered, "To stop them like this, a fireball must've burned the lungs."

Duncan looked around for David. He wasn't in the tunnels.

At the end of the tunnel, a closed door caught Duncan's eye. Duncan opened the explosion proof door and went inside. He had sat inside of the small office before, but never behind the desk. Doctor Scott had left so quickly that he never locked his filing cabinets or desk.

As he covered everything in magnesium powder, Duncan found himself flipping through the doctor's notes. Out of the first drawer he pulled several files and placed them on top of the desk. Claraicy's file was huge. She had her own cabinet. In the top draw, Duncan grabbed what looked like a presentation package and opened it. It contained sleeves with over a dozen memory cards along with a bound copy of text that was almost the size of a university text book. Without a second thought, he shoved it under his shirt.

As small explosions shook the structure, Duncan stuffed as much as he could into his pockets, boots, sleeves and under his jacket. With the fire still burning and various canisters of compressed gas in almost every room, he decided that it was time to leave. After placing an incendiary device in the middle of room, he set the timer for thirty minutes.

Grabbing Doctor Scott's and Adam's bodies, Duncan dragged them out of the tunnel. After looking at his watch, he thought for a moment. "He must be in the lab."

Duncan glanced at his watch a second time before running to the lab. Within seconds, his flashlight shone on David's corpse. Duncan threw him onto his shoulder and rushed out of the building.

Duncan placed them all in the centre of the burnt garage. After sprinkling powered magnesium over them, he said goodbye. "May you find your way to heaven despite the damnation that was forced upon you."

Glancing at his watch, Duncan turned and walked away. From a safe distance, he stood at attention and threw a salute as the timer went off and another fireball engulfed the building.

Chapter Forty-Four

Revelation

As Duncan searched around the surrounding area for any sign of Claraicy or Jesse, more helicopters could be seen in the distance. She wasn't there. Something inside of him felt empty. With all the sensitive material he had on him, he didn't want to be there when the helicopters arrived.

After quickly packing the files he had taken from Doctor Scott's office into his backpack, Duncan followed Claraicy's trail. As Colonel Conway's men tried to follow them, he wiped out the trail behind him. To him it was personal and he wanted to keep it just between the two of them.

Duncan wasn't surprised as he came to the end of the trail. He felt that he could've been airlifted there and waited for her to show up. As a cold rain started to pour down, he stood back and watched as Claraicy wept over her daughter's lifeless body. Duncan aimed his rifle at the back of her head. It's clip was full of armour piercing bullets. He knew that one well place bullet might end the nightmare that he had been going though, but he couldn't pull the trigger.

Claraicy turned, saw him and leaped to her feet. As she bolted towards him, Duncan flung his rifle into the bushes and braced himself for her attack. Her reflexes were much faster than his. As she slashed at his face and chest, he somehow managed to grab a hold of her arms.

At the top of her lungs, Claraicy screamed out, "You murderer! You killed her! You killed my daughter."

Duncan held on to her arms as she struggled to get free. "I am all you have left. You are all I have left. The rest are all dead, even the purebreds. You killed every last one of them."

Shocked, Claraicy looked at him. "What are you talking about?" For the first time, she noticed that her claws didn't penetrate past his outer skin. A thin layer of it simply folded down his cheek. His shredded shirt and slashed skin, revealed the layer of scaly armour beneath it. "How? How could you be one of us and still want to kill us?"

"I was the very first. My body didn't start to change until you threatened it. The war that you waged did this to me."

Duncan slightly loosened his grip and slid his hands down to her wrists. Looking into her wild, confused eyes, he added, "At first, all Dr. Scott wanted to do was monitor what the cells were doing to your body. When the doctor found out the extent of your changes, he started working on a way to extract the cells and make you human again. Why do you think we gave you that trailer and took those blood samples? We never wanted to hurt you."

Duncan tightly held on to Claraicy's wrists as she screamed back, "You lie. You killed Jesse because you could. You are just like all men. You'll say and do whatever you want to anybody you want, just because you can."

"I'm not like the others. I'm barely human."

"So why didn't the doctor use you as a guinea pig?"

"He did. He once called me his masterpiece. However, the cells he introduced into my body were primitive and flawed. They took over. Without any way to extract them, my body is useless to him. My men were third generation. You, you were an unexpect surprise. You blew the doctor's mind."

As Claraicy roared and raged as loudly as she could, Duncan held on to her. Over an hour had passed. Exhausted, they finally both sat down. Claraicy looked at Duncan. "Now what?"

Duncan looked at Claraicy. Her big ears and huge round eyes seemed more attractive to him. "We find a way to survive."

Claraicy smelled Duncan's scent. There was still something about it she found intoxicating. This time she knew that it was more than just the cells inside of him. Wrapping her arms around him, she divulged, "You and me are a lot alike. Fighting to survive is all we know. Are we like a pair of wild animals?"

Duncan stood up and offered Claraicy his hand. "We have to leave. Colonel Conway's men will soon find us and I think you know what their orders are. It'll be all right. I know a bush pilot that owes me one last favour."

Claraicy looked at Jesse's body and told him, "I can't let them find her."

Duncan smiled at her. "They won't."

******

Marq pulled his plane as close as he could to the shore. Jane was strapped to the co-pilot seat. Marq smiled as Duncan carried a body bag aboard. "You finally got her? Why didn't you just get a helicopter?"

"To many questions. I met up with them on the ridge. Her daughter was already dead, so I disposed of her daughter's body." Duncan looked at Jane and added, "I'm a little surprised to see you. Marq doesn't normally have any passengers."

As Marq taxied the plane to the middle of the lake for takeoff, Jane answered, "Marq thought that a plane ride would help calm me down." Pointing to the body bag on the floor, she added, "He didn't tell me that you would be bringing her along for the ride."

As the plane got airborne, a strange sensation came over Claraicy. She felt whole again. After slicing a hole in the bag with her claw, she smiled at Duncan. Looking down a warm sensation came over him and he smiled back.

Without looking back, Marq asked, "Where to? You didn't tell me your destination when you called."

After giving out a sigh of relief, Duncan casually said, "To the middle of nowhere, or at least as far away from here as possible."

Marq looked back at him. The bandage that had held the ripped patch of skin to Duncan's cheek had fallen off. Beneath it his dark scales were clearly visible. "What's going on?"

As Jane turned around, Claraicy sat up and smiled at her. "You!" With her claws extended, she took a swipe at her exposed arm.

Duncan grabbed her wrist in the mid-air. "Remember, it's over. When a war is over, it's over. Always remember, past enemies can quickly become future allies."

Claraicy bowed her head and apologized. "I'm sorry but I can't promise that it won't happen again." Grinning for ear to ear, she added, "I'm not used to following orders. Not anymore."

******

As the plane flew towards an abandoned mine, a cat-like face peered out. Sarah's large ears heard the plane approach. As it came in sight, a young gargoyle-like creature wrapped his arms around her waist and began to growl at the craft. A dozen metres away, a large, winged, lion-like creature put down a freshly killed deer and backed up into the trees. Running behind him were two more smaller winged creatures.

As the bright red, twin engine plane got closer, Sarah recognized the wide yellow stripes along its wings and down the length of its body. "This isn't good. Wherever that plane goes, trouble always follows."

******

Mother Nature watched the plane as it flew in the clear morning sky. Looking around at the devastation man had done over the past few centuries, she added, "The last time, you controlled them. This time, I think it is my turn."

A sudden strong gust of wind blew the newly cut brush away from the mouth of the cave. Inside it, Jesse's body was no longer motionless. Her stomach started to turn and move around. Slowly, claws poked through the thick armoured skin. Next, a scaly head with huge eyes and big pointed ears peered out of the cut in Jesse's stomach. As it swiped away the film covering its face, it cried out a high pitched squeal. The ape-like creature was barely the size of a rat. It stuck its head back inside and bit off a hunk of loose flesh. Crawling on top of Jesse's head, the newly born creature looked around at its new domain as it chewed its mother's flesh.

As more young creatures sliced their way out, Mother Nature smiled. "You are my children now. To me, you are as pure as if I made you myself."

The End

~

For Now